WITHOUT LIMITS
BOOK TWO

Skyla Raines

The lies we BELIEVE

The Lies We Believe

Copyright © Skyla Raines, 2024

Without limiting the rights under copyright reserved above, no part of this publication may be reproduced, stored in or introduced into a retrieval system, or transmitted in any form or by any means (electronic, mechanical, photocopying, recording, or otherwise) without the prior written permission of the copyright owner. This is a work of fiction. Names, characters, places, and incidents are either the product of the author's imagination or are used fictitiously, and any resemblance to actual persons, living or dead, business establishments, events, or locales is entirely coincidental.

Cover Design: Design by Kage
Interior Design: Design by Kage
Formatting: Michaella Dieter

BEFORE YOU READ

Please note this book has dark elements and contains themes which some may find difficult to read. Your mental health is important, so if you need a more detailed content list, please go to page 438.

For my readers who have been dragged through
blazing fire and crawled out of it, coated in ash.
No matter how many times you crumble,
you piece yourself back together again,
because the will to fight is
etched into your soul.

PROLOGUE

Dreams were just that—a fallacy, an illusion. Something pretty that helped get you through your darkest moments. But they would never become real; they were just the lies we believed.

Don't give up, my heart begged.

It's too late, my brain said.

My bones ached, and my soul was tired. I just want to sleep...

I've got you, the world whispered as the wind ghosted over my skin. *Be patient. Your time is coming.* The darkest night is the one before the brightest dawn, and when the sun breaks, it will chase all your shadows away.

"Come back to me."

CHAPTER ONE
River

Today could fuck off.

I'd taken four loads in my ass already, and I just wanted to shut the world out. I was raw, bruised, and bleeding, and I knew it was just the beginning of a long weekend. Cum seeped from my abused hole and trickled down my thighs, making my threadbare jeans stick to me. I was nothing but a toy to be used for the enjoyment of others.

It was a fate I accepted long ago, because I was powerless to change it.

I'd become a favorite with clients who frequented Black Dahlia's services. I might have been twenty-five, but I looked eighteen, and nothing sold better than a youthful face that fed into an old man's fantasy. There were some sick fucks in this world. It didn't hurt that I never spoke either, so my clients were free to maintain whatever illusion they'd created in their fucked-up minds.

It wasn't that I couldn't speak, but that I chose not to. What was the point of having a voice if no one listened? It only led to pain and rejection. The only person I'd ever willingly spoken to was Bane, but after he left, I didn't see the point anymore. I didn't trust anyone enough to open myself up to them.

I'd taught myself to handle physical pain by shutting my mind off and drifting away to that special place where dreams came true and I lived another life—one where I was happy, wanted, and needed. I hoped for love too, but I wasn't sure what that felt like. Was that even possible when I was this broken? The fantasy came crashing down the second I opened my eyes, and the real world came back with a vengeance.

I swore to myself fifteen years ago that I'd never allow myself to feel emotions. A broken heart was impossible to heal. The muscle still beat in my chest, but I prayed to a god I didn't believe in that it would give out before I had to endure another year of this existence I called life.

I shook my head and ran my hand through my hair as if that would clear those dangerous thoughts from my mind. I was a mass of contradictions. I dreamed about a life I'd never live, hating the one I'd been forced into but was too afraid to run away from. The irony wasn't lost on me; running away from my last foster home was what landed me here. I left because I was afraid I'd get raped or beaten to death without Bane there to protect me. Where I ended up turned out to be even worse. It happened daily. If I tried to run, I'd get shot down like Hen did two years ago.

My ears picked up at the sound of the shower shutting off. I couldn't wait for my turn. Not that I'd be clean for very long—it was Friday after all, and weekends meant we didn't get a break. I loathed the feeling of the denim pulling against my skin almost as much as I hated being covered in another man's cum.

"It's all yours, Riv," Dale called and shuffled out of the tiny bathroom we all shared. "Do you need anything?"

I shook my head and winced at the pain lancing down my neck from the sharp movement. The rope burns around my throat were red and pulsing, my collar irritating them. I took a step toward the bathroom instead of saying anything. Dale sighed and grabbed my notebook and pen, forcefully shoving them in my hand. I stared at them, not really here, my mind wandering. The light that had been in his eyes faded, just like my silent words.

"You being honest with me, Riv?" I blinked up at him and gnawed on my bottom lip. Dale looked at me as if he could peel back the layers to find the truth in my soul and puffed out a weighted breath when he couldn't. It grated on me like sandpaper across my skin. "Who was your last client?"

I rolled my bottom lip between my teeth, pulling off the cracked skin, and the metallic tang of blood coated my tongue. I shrugged instead of answering. My eyes dropped to my tattered old Vans with split soles. The right one leaked when it rained, and a prayer and peeling duct tape were the only things holding the left heel together.

Dale's heavy gaze was suffocating. Tension thickened the air. He stepped closer to me, heat radiating off his body. The grip on my notebook tightened with every passing second. My knuckles bleached white as the skin pulled tightly around the prominent bones.

"Riv, talk to me," he said softly, worry coating his words. "I can't do much to help you, especially if you don't talk." His eyes tightened in exasperation.

My shoulders touched my ears as I retreated into myself.

I didn't want to tell him who I'd spent the day with. The johns that had booked me were feared more than any other client we serviced, and I bore their marks like a brand on my skin.

I sighed and scribbled down two words that invoked terror in all of us.

The Mitchells

That's what we knew them as. They were regulars who often booked a few of us, but on the days they were feeling particularly cruel, they booked one of us and used our bodies until all we could taste was blood. The world faded away, and blackness became all we knew.

"Fuck!" His hands flew to his head, running them through his hair and pulling at the dark strands, drowning in helplessness. "Go get showered and get some rest. Fuck knows you're going to need it." The ominous tone of his last words should have piqued my interest, but it was already background noise.

The light flickered in the makeshift bathroom as I shut the door behind me and collapsed against it. The space was tiny, stunk of sewage, and had black mold climbing the walls. It had just enough room to fit a shower, a toilet, and a sink, and had barely enough room to hold a person. The floor was constantly under a film of filthy water, and someone had shattered the mirror over the sink with their fist long ago. If you looked close enough, you could see the rusty stain of old blood dripping down the wall behind it.

Pain seared my lungs as I inhaled. Gritting my teeth, I climbed onto the toilet and carefully stripped off my stained clothes. I couldn't just leave them in a soggy heap on the floor—I'd have to wash them in the shower with me and hope they'd dry in time for when I needed them.

Time passed in a blur once the icy drops had numbed my skin and eased the ever-present pounding in my head. By the time I blinked back to the world, I was curled up on the old mattress I shared with Dale, teeth chattering a mile a minute. The rough fibers of the threadbare blanket covering me did little to retain heat.

"It's okay, Riv. I've got you." Dale slid his arm around me and pulled me into his body. His larger frame wrapped around my back, the heat from his skin slowly seeping into mine. "You can sleep now."

My body took him at his word, and everything went dark as unconsciousness claimed me.

"Do you want a hit? You're gonna need it to get through tonight."

I glanced up at Gabe through my lashes as he poured the baggie of coke onto the cleared surface of the one dresser we had in our shared room. There were six of us in here, with three queen-sized mattresses between us. It was squalor at its finest.

We didn't get nice clothes unless they were required for an appointment. We didn't get to leave the room either, but as disgusting as these walls were, at least we were safe in here.

"He's not wrong, you know," Dale added, taking the straw from Max, who'd just taken a hit.

I knew that, but I hated drugs and the feeling of losing control of my body. It scared me that a john could do anything to me and it wouldn't register. In a life where I had no control over the autonomy of my body, I clung to the tiny scraps I had.

"Come on, Riv." Gabe held out his hand, hauled me up, and put the straw in my hand. "Let it take the edge off. I'll give you another bump before we get there." Dahlia had built tonight up to be something incredible for her business, which meant we needed to take whatever was forced upon us without question or there'd be serious repercussions. It was the fear her words invoked in me that made me accept Gabe's hand.

My shaky fingers wrapped around the straw as I held it over the innocent-looking white powder and inhaled. It burned, probably due to being cut with shit that would kill us—if a john didn't first—but I welcomed it. It let me know I was alive for a moment. A minute. A second.

The next thing I knew, we were being let in the back entrance of a swanky hotel. The sounds of a busy kitchen echoed down the corridor as they herded us like sheep into a service elevator. Black Dahlia had sent me, Dale, Gabe, and Max, with her compliments for the night.

Our handler, Sean, leered over his phone at me before going back to his Candy Crush game. The ride was smooth, but it did nothing to eradicate the dread sinking into my bones. Something was off, and it wasn't just from the coke flooding through my veins. It was in the air, making the tiny hairs on my body stand on end, alerting me of danger. I couldn't grasp on to it long enough before a wave of euphoria washed it away.

The elevator walls rippled around us like we were in a scene from *The Matrix*. Maybe it was the drugs, after all. I blinked, and pristine white walls replaced the steel ones, so bright and clean they made my eyes burn. Sean knocked on the door in front of us. The penthouse, according to the brass plaque.

It opened, revealing a man in a white shirt and black tie. He looked like a waiter. He ushered us inside and whispered into Sean's ear. The oaf nodded and shut the door behind him. It was almost like he was never with us to begin with.

"Follow me," Black Tie Guy said and led us into a laundry room. Turning, he looked down his nose at us. "Strip and put your clothes here." He pointed to the empty counter. We followed his orders without question, the urge to fight long beaten out of us.

Shame regarding nakedness didn't exist. Whether it was one-on-one, or in a room full of people, it didn't matter. I didn't care. I'd never had the chance to be a prude growing up the way I did. It just was what it was.

"Tonight is gonna be a shitshow," Dale breathed, leaning over me to put his clothes next to mine in a neatly folded pile.

"Once you're done, line up here," Black Tie barked and pointed to the area by a stainless-steel sink. One by one, we stepped up, and the asshole snapped on a pair of latex gloves.

He shoved Max into the counter and pushed against his shoulder blades until his chest pinned against the cool granite. "You're not allowed entry until I've searched you."

It didn't register what he meant at first, and my mind struggled to hold on to his words long enough to make them make sense. But I would never forget the sight of him ramming his hand up Max's ass to do a full cavity search.

"Oh shit!" Gabe gagged.

"Silence!" Black Tie's words were whip sharp.

I flinched, hunched my shoulders, and wrapped my arms around my chest. *Retreat.* Years of abusive words went off in my head like fireworks. The once visceral blows to my flesh echoed across my broken soul.

"Someone is on a power trip." Dale pulled my hand from my face. "It's going to be okay, Riv." He squeezed my shoulder and took Max's place.

Gabe took advantage of my distraction and shoved a pill down my throat, mouthing "swallow" before slipping around me to go next.

Once Black Tie searched all of us, he ushered us through the solid oak door into the penthouse. The lights were a low, deep red that colored the walls, making it seem like we'd just stepped into the second circle of hell. A low beat pulsed through the air, already saturated with the heady scent of sex and drugs.

Whatever Gabe had given me was taking effect, and a mellow buzz drowned out the rising hysteria clawing at my insides. A tall guy, face covered by a black mask, grabbed my arm and dragged me behind him to a table fitted with straps and surrounded by seven others.

"Heads or tails?" The man who'd dragged me over asked, laughing at his own joke. I tried to focus on their voices, but they were fading, just like the room around me.

My back landed on something hard and unforgiving as they pulled my arms and legs in opposite directions away from my body. I was slipping, and the world flickered and faded into blackness.

When I next opened my eyes, I couldn't breathe. The world rocked like I was at sea in a storm, moving back and forth, back and forth. I tried to move my heavy limbs, but the straps held me down. My heart pounded in my chest, fighting to be free, while tears dripped down my face into my hair.

Screams filled the air. The music cut out and a bright light blinded me. I squeezed my eyes shut, and bile coated my tongue as I finally sucked in a breath. Intense relief flooded my body for a second as sweet, sweet air filled my lungs.

"Fuck! Run!"

Pain exploded in the back of my head as it hit something sharp, and blackness engulfed me once again.

"How is he looking?"

"He'll come around soon. Should be ready for questioning in a few hours. Start with the others and see where you get."

"Alright. Get him dressed when he's with us and leave him in room five. I'll get to him if I have time. If not, Ba—" A door closed, cutting off their conversation with a resounding click.

Sensation slowly came back to my body, but it was like moving through quicksand, and I hated it. My brain was trying to burst out of my skull, with every little movement only intensifying the pain. I tried to peel open my eyes, but the light made my gut churn until I lost the battle and vomit prised my lips apart, covering me and splattering on the floor.

"Oh, for god's sake. Fucking junkies." The door banged against a wall, and heavy footsteps moved into the room as another wave purged itself from my body. "Get this on me, and it'll be the last thing you do, whore." Rough hands grabbed my wrists and wrenched me up so hard, blackness claimed me again.

The cold metal felt good against my flushed skin and held my head up when I couldn't. Didn't have the strength anymore. My eyes pulsed with their own heartbeat, and the sound of blood whooshed in my ears. They had chained me to this table for what felt like days, but it was probably only hours. My mouth tasted like ass, like someone had stubbed a cigarette out on it. Wouldn't be the first time.

I cracked an eye open and stared at the two-way mirror opposite me. I knew they were watching me, discussing me. They thought I was some fucked-up junkie, but I wasn't, even though it might seem that way. Especially if they'd run a drug test on me after the hotel. But I didn't really remember anything past being in that laundry room.

Alone and in itchy, ill-fitting scrubs, there wasn't anything I could do but wait. Three different men had been in here to talk to me but lost their shit when I didn't answer.

Didn't.

Wouldn't.

Couldn't.

It didn't matter to them; they thought I was purposely standing in the way of their investigation into trafficking and Black Dahlia. I wasn't, not intentionally. I just couldn't communicate with them on their level, and they despised me for it.

My throat was raw after throwing up so much. All I wanted was a drink of water to wash the acidic taste away, but that never came. I didn't know if the other guys were here or if it was just me. I didn't know if they were going to charge me or not.

I didn't know anything.

I hated my life.

Footsteps echoed outside my door, then paused as the handle turned with an ear-piercing whine. Did they leave it like that on purpose to make people uncomfortable? It fucking worked. My skin crawled at the sound, and bright light burst behind my closed eyelids. A wave of nausea rolled through my empty stomach, the muscles clenching hard around nothing, making tears burn at the back of my eyes.

The air moved as the door swung open, warmth invading the room. The fresh scent of sunshine and salty waves washed over me, and my heart skipped a beat. A phantom memory tickled the edges of my mind, but I shoved that back into its box and buried it.

"Right, then, shall we get started?"

I'd heard the same words a dozen times already, but awareness prickled across me. The chains grated against the table as I pushed myself up. The room wavered in front of me, but my mind latched on to one sky-blue eye and another the color of the deep, dark woods.

He was a dream. A vision. A ghost.

He was everything I'd ever wanted, and that scared me more than death itself.

Folders crashed to the floor, creating a cacophony of sound that vibrated through me. I clenched my jaw as he fell to his knees with a resounding thud, a giant redwood on the forest floor.

"R-River?"

My dead heart leapt at the sound of his voice. Any resilience I thought I'd had to the delusions my mind created shattered, and tears flowed down my cheeks. "B-Bane?" I rasped, my unused voice dragging across broken glass as it clawed its way out of me, wrenching each sound from my shattered soul.

CHAPTER TWO
River

As I stared at the ghost from my past I thought I'd never see again, a mountain of memories crashed over me like a suffocating avalanche.

"Take him! I don't want that thing in my home a moment longer."

"Mrs. Jenkins, if you could just sit down a minute and explain to me what happened?" Elise said calmly as she took my hand and pulled me onto the grubby couch next to her.

"Explain?! I don't have to explain anything. Just get that thing—"

"Please calm down, Jean. River is just a child."

"That ain't no darn child. That's...that's a monster. An abomination! And I don't want it in my house. Get it gone."

Elise sighed and looked at me. "River, can you go sit in my car for a minute, please? I'll be right on out." I looked at her, trying *not to show how scared I was, because I didn't want to move again. I didn't want...I didn't want...*

I shook my head as the first tear fell.

Mama Jean scoffed. "Cut that out now, you little heathen." Her eyes turned black like they did at night when she came into my room and hit me. But last night, I'd had enough and bit her when she smacked me across the face for something Jackson did.

All it did was make her worse. She'd wailed like I'd broken her arm or something. The other boys in the room hid under their blankets, pretending to be asleep.

They didn't help me. No one ever did.

Mama Jean grabbed my hair and dragged me downstairs before kicking me out the back door. She made me sleep on the dog's bed outside on the back porch in the pitch black. I hated the dark. Bad things happened in it.

The heat hit me as I stood on the crumbling concrete steps as the screen door banged in its frame behind me. It was too hot to sit in the car, so I sat on the stairs instead. The other kids played in the street. Some were on bikes, while others kicked a ball around. Mama Jean didn't allow us to play in the backyard. That was her space and wasn't for us kids.

I wiped away my tears with the back of my hand and watched a line of ants as they walked around the tufts of grass growing through the cracks and waited.

And waited.

"Come on, River." Elise patted my head, and I followed her to her old Toyota. "Get in." She held the back door open for me, and as I climbed in, she raised her head to the sky and sighed before shutting the door.

"Are you going to tell me what happened?" She asked as she slipped into her seat. Her light blue eyes found me in the mirror as she reversed out onto the street. I shook my head. "I can't help you if you don't talk, River."

I shrugged and picked at the thread on my jeans.

"You can stay at my house tonight while I find you another foster family. If any will take you. This will be your third home since I've taken over your case."

I said nothing. What was the point? Adults didn't listen to me, anyway. I'd learned that quickly. It was better to stay quiet.

At the time, Mama Jean seemed like the biggest monster I'd ever known, but I soon came to realize she wasn't all that bad. Within months of leaving her care, I came to crave her brand of cruelty.

"Get out, ya little thief." Darren's boot swung for me again, so I ran faster. He was old and slow. He couldn't run due to his size and having bad knees. Luckily, I was small and quick. "Don't come back!"

I made the mistake of thinking I was safe once I was out the door and away from his one-story shack of a house, but I forgot he had friends. Friends that were like brothers to him. Friends that sat around the yard on lawn chairs drinking and smoking weed all day like they were kings. Friends who would come when he called, claiming I'd stolen fifty bucks from his stash.

I hadn't; it was his nasty son Derek that had done it so he could get his own weed rather than risk a beating from his dad for stealing his. Weed and beer were the only things Darren seemed to care about, other than the check he got for fostering me.

Instead, Derek blamed me, and Darren searched my room, trashing it in his rage until he found what he wanted. Hidden under my pillow was ten dollars I'd earned by helping Mrs. Winslow next door take out her garbage, but Darren thought it was his money and punched me before I could run. And run I did, straight into the arms of his friends.

"We've got you now, you little shit."

That was my first trip to the emergency room, but only one of many. I had a broken arm and a concussion. Elise arrived when my cast was being set. Darren claimed I'd fallen out of a tree, but as I sucked the lollipop the kind nurse gave me, I heard her talking with Elise.

"You need to remove him from that home. This isn't the first time something has happened to him." She glared at Elise. *"Unless he's very accident prone. But the facts speak for themselves. There is systemic bruising on his body, centered around his torso, which is easily hidden. Placement on the body like that is not accidental or caused by falling from a tree."*

"He is a very troubled little boy. It's hard finding placements that will accept him." Elise sighed. She looked tired, and dark circles ringed her pale-blue eyes. She didn't look like the lady I'd met months ago; she looked old.

"That's not been my experience with River. Other than only communicating with a head nod or shake, he's been very brave. He just needs a home that's going to give him the right support to come out of his shell."

"That's easier said than done with his record. Shit! Ignore me, Kesha." Elise waved her hands around and caught my eye. I glanced away and watched the other nurses buzzing around their busy station.

Just after I turned seven, Elise moved me to another town with the Wilkinson's. There had been so many places, each one merged into the next, but this one was different.

There was something special about this latest home.

Mrs. Wilkinson had pale blonde hair streaked with gray that she wore in a bun at her nape. Her gray eyes were warm, and she gave the best hugs. I couldn't remember the last time someone hugged me.

Elise ushered me out of her car and knocked on the door of the white house with blue shutters, door, and trim. A funny feeling bounced in my tummy.

"Hello, Elise. It's so nice to see you again. Is this the newest member of our family?"

"Yes, this is River."

I held out my hand as Elise had taught me to do, and Mrs. Wilkinson chuckled. It sounded like musical bells. She crouched down in front of me, ignoring my hand, and pulled me into a hug. "Welcome to my home, River," she said softly and brushed the hair I hid behind off my face. "Would you like to come in?"

My lips twitched as I tried to smile. She had asked me, not Elise. Me. She spoke to me in a way no one else had for as long as I could remember. I nodded. Mrs. Wilkinson took my hand and led me through a clean house into the kitchen.

"Have a seat." She pulled out a chair for me at the table in the middle of the room, and once I'd sat down, she gave me a chocolate chip cookie. "Elise? Coffee?"

"That sounds perfect. Then we can discuss everything we need to."

Mrs. Wilkinson hummed. "Of course." She looked at me over her shoulder as she filled the kettle. "When you're finished, River, if you head through that door, the rest of the boys are out in the yard playing with cars in the sandbox."

I smiled for real this time and shoved the rest of the cookie into my mouth. Mrs. Wilkinson laughed and held the door open for me before turning back to Elise. I covered my eyes when I stepped out onto the small deck and saw four boys laughing and messing around. They weren't silent like the kids had been in the other homes I'd stayed in. They smiled.

It was there I met a boy who became the center of my world. Jacob arrived after I'd been there a few months. He was as tall as Mrs. Wilkinson at only twelve and had shoulders like a pro wrestler. Some of the other boys were afraid of him because he towered over everyone else, but I could see how sad he was. I felt his pain like it was my own.

He spent most of his time sitting under the large willow at the edge of the yard, crying. It was strange to see someone so big crying like that. He looked like a grownup, and they didn't cry, did they? That's not what men did. At least, that was what Darren said the first time I cried when he hit me until blood coated my teeth.

I quickly became Jacob's shadow, following him everywhere he went unless he was at school. I felt safe around him. The other boys didn't like me because I didn't talk and they feared Jacob. It was like we were outcasts together.

One sunny Sunday morning, I was lying in the grass close to Jacob's tree, watching the clouds, when he laid down next to me.

"What are you looking at?" I pointed to the clouds in the sky that were blowing over the vast expanse of blue. "Don't talk much, do you?"

I shook my head, and he sighed, tucking his hands behind his head. I copied him, and his deep laugh was so loud it made me jump, which only made him laugh harder.

He turned and looked at me. "I'm Jacob, but you can call me Bane." A small smile lifted the corner of his lips, but his eyes were still red rimmed and swollen. "What's your name?"

I looked at his eyes, one the color of the sky, the other a brown so dark it was like being lost in the woods. I didn't blink for a long time as I studied them, noticing all the little flecks of colors hidden in their depths. He differed from me in so many ways but lost too, just like me.

"R-River." My voice squeaked and sounded rough, like I needed to cough and clear my throat. It was the first word I'd spoken in years.

"That's a cool name. Who gave it to you, your mom?" I shrugged and turned back to the clouds. I didn't know where my name came from or who chose it, it just was. A bit like I didn't know who my mom was. All my memories were of being shipped from home to home but never having one of my own.

A shudder worked its way through me, coiling in my aching gut. I gasped and retched as the already strained muscles burned like they were dipped in acid. Black spots covered my vision as I blinked heavy lids, trying to clear the fresh wave of tears from my eyes. I clenched my jaw to keep the whimper of pain locked away, sinking my teeth into my tongue. Blood filled my mouth, making my stomach roll again.

I flushed hot and cold as fear and anger warred inside me. He shouldn't be here. I didn't want him to see me like this. To see what I had become. How low I'd gone, what I had to do to survive. Shame. That was what I was feeling; it sunk into my feet like lead boulders that refused to let me move. Trapped. Chained. I couldn't go anywhere. Despair licked at my skin until my fingers and toes went numb. Tears streamed down my cheeks, but I was too tired to wipe them away. I couldn't... I just couldn't handle it anymore. Please make it stop!

A pained cry pulled my eyes back to him, where he was kneeling on the floor. Shoulders hunched, head hanging low, mournful sounds breaching his trembling lips. He looked up at me, his blue and brown eyes swimming in an endless sea of pain. For him? For me? I couldn't tell, but it radiated off him.

Bane was a monolith of a man, now fully grown, but he seemed so small right now. My heart stopped beating as he shook his head and collected the folders off the floor. He clutched them like a lifeline as he got to his feet, looking at me like he wanted to say something before running through the door like he was escaping a fire.

Bane left! He left me here to rot in a cell for a crime I had no choice but to commit to keep breathing.

Why do they always leave me?

What did I do that was so wrong to end up with a life like this?

CHAPTER THREE
Bane

What fresh hell had I walked into today?

The world as I knew it was now changed forever. Irrevocably.

River had already been broken when I met him at the tender age of seven, but the man I saw before me was nothing but ash and smoldering ruins.

I couldn't be in this room a moment longer without breaking completely. It was impossible to look like I was holding myself together as I fractured to the bone. Sucking in a deep inhale, I grabbed the scattered folders that lay strewn across the floor and hauled my ass out of that interview room, collapsing against the wall as my legs crumbled beneath me.

"What in the ever-loving fuck happened to him?" The folders slipped from my grasp, falling to the floor as I ran my hand over my black hair. I'd walked in there blind, and that was my first mistake. My second was walking away from him again.

Tears burned my eyes like molten lava, eating at the peace I'd spent the last eighteen years trying to make with my life and the events that conspired to take my whole family from me. Even the hours of therapy I'd sat through could never have prepared me for this—for him and the devastation he'd undoubtedly wreak.

River had come back into my life like a wrecking ball that shook the foundations of everything I believed. I'd convinced myself that he was fine and now realized that was a dangerous lie to believe. The world clearly hadn't finished trying to tear me apart, one brick at a time.

"Oh, sweet Jesus. What's wrong, Benson?" I'd been so lost inside my head I hadn't heard Montoya walk down the corridor. I looked up at her through watery eyes and the look of concern that washed over her face as she crouched down in front of me somehow made everything more real. "You want to talk about it?"

I shook my head and bit the inside of my lip, trying to corral the storm raging inside me into a box so I could breathe. I screwed my eyes shut and rubbed them with my fists until colors burst in the darkness. Releasing a shaky breath, I uttered the words that threatened to destroy me all over again. "I can't do this. I-I know him."

She tipped her head to the side and assessed me. "You know him?" Confusion laced her tone.

"Yeah," I rasped. "W-we were in foster care together for a couple of years before the Hendrix family adopted me." A fresh swell of tears pooled on my lash line, and I fought to blink them away before they fell.

"Ah, that makes this extremely difficult for you, then." I nodded numbly. "But..."

"No." I shook my head, my hand latching onto her shoulder, knowing what she was going to say.

"We could use him to help build this case. We could finally catch this ring and take them down for good. Come out with a win."

Logically, I knew she was right. River could be our in and provide insight we didn't normally get. In cases like these, the workers rarely talked or gave us anything useful, but Montoya was proposing I leveraged our history to get what we'd need to finally nail this ring.

"I..." Pain and guilt threaded through me like a poison, infecting one cell at a time. I knew I should do this. This could end up being the bust that makes our careers, but I didn't know if I could.

Do I want to, though? The answer was a resounding no. I didn't want to use my former friendship with someone for the sake of a case, someone I'd only ever wanted to protect. All my instincts screamed at me to get him out of here and somewhere safe so he could heal, not leverage him for information.

On the other hand, the trained officer in me knew I couldn't waste this opportunity. If I could glean some vital information from River, then I could save others from living the life he had. That was worth it, right? The needs of the many outweigh the few and all that?

I was supposed to serve and protect, but if I did this, how would I be protecting River?

"Come on up, ya big softie." Montoya grabbed my large hands with her delicate ones and hauled me to my feet. "Let's go talk to Bower." What the hell could I say to that? Nothing. That was what. I had a duty to do, even if my conscience hated me for it. I heaved a sigh, picked up my files, and followed her like a little lapdog.

Montoya and I met at the academy and struck up a fast

friendship. Over the years, she became like a sister to me. I was the annoying, overbearing big brother, and she was the larger-than-life little sister who got up to mischief. She acted like she hated it, but deep down, I knew she loved me for it. She was a once-in-a-lifetime kind of friend, one I knew I'd do anything for.

"I'm still not sure this is the right thing to do, or even ethical, considering our history," I said as we neared Bower's office. Tension coiled around my body, making each step harder than the one before. For all her confidence, Montoya hadn't considered that we weren't really part of this case; we were just extra bodies they pulled in for the extra manpower, hence why we weren't part of the raid last night.

For all I knew, we could propose this and Bower would either turn us away or use one of his guys who was actually a part of the task force to take it on and just pull me in to emotionally manipulate River. And fuck, I hoped against all hope that wouldn't be the case. I'm not sure I could live with myself if that was what he decided.

"Go on then." Montoya knocked on his door. The brass name plate glinted in the bright office lights, with his name, Jack Bower, standing in stark relief. I shook my head, my fingers white-knuckling the files I held on to like a lifeline.

"Enter." Bower's voice boomed over the hive of activity buzzing around the office. Whiteboards with suspect profiles skirted the room, and my eyes caught on a new one that had Riv on it, along with the other guys they brought in overnight.

"You've got this." Montoya gave me a thumbs up just before she shoved me over the threshold and shut the door behind me. *Bitch.*

Bower glanced up at me over his laptop, his desk littered with stacks of files that seemed to hold no semblance of order, and made my fingers itch. "What can I do for you, Benson? I thought you were in interview room five, trying to get the kid to talk?" Accusation hung in the air as his stare hardened.

"Ah, yes. I was, sir," I stammered out. "That's what I wanted to talk to you about."

He arched a thick, dark brow. Even though it was threaded with gray, it still made me quake in my boots. "Well? Time is of the essence here, as you well know. We need to make use of these leads before they go cold."

I pulled out the chair in front of his desk and collapsed into it. My shoulders rose as I sucked in a deep breath, trying to tamper down my racing heart. "Alright, I'll level with you. I know the guy in room five. We were in foster care together." Bowers eyes gleamed, formulating ideas on how this would help his case. If he could crack this, doors would open and he'd no longer be a small-time detective. "I was thinking our relationship would be beneficial to the case. That I might get information from him that no one else could."

Bower braced his arms on the only clear space on his desk and steepled his hands under his chin. "You think you're up to it?" I nodded, because I knew I wouldn't be able to say it without my voice cracking and betraying me. "He hasn't spoken to anyone since we brought him in."

"He won't, either."

"What makes you say that? Other than you knew him eighteen years ago?"

My gut sank like a lead weight, and it took every ounce of strength for me to not fall apart at the fact he knew my history so well. "He's mute."

"Well, that explains a few things, doesn't it? I assumed it was because of the concussion, but Dr. D'Souza cleared him for questioning." My teeth sunk into my bottom lip as I processed his words. Concussion? Why wasn't I told about that before they sent me in?

Davis, that little shit. He hated me. I'd long suspected it was because of the color of my skin. The snide remarks and how he kept trying to make me look incompetent, but this? This just confirmed he was out to get me.

"No one informed me of that before I went in. That information should have been shared," I ground out and scrubbed my hand over my face. "So?" I let the unspoken question thicken the air between us as Bower sat back in his chair and rested his right ankle over his knee.

"Are you sure you're up to this? It won't be easy, especially if there is an emotional connection." His steel-gray eyes bored into me. It felt like he was sifting through my memories to find the history River and I shared.

"I think so. We were just kids back then, and while I looked out for him—"

"Good, that's good." Bower picked up one of the case files littering his desk. "Get Montoya to dig up as much information about the kid as possible while you go back in and see if you can get him to talk." He glanced at me. "Take a pen and paper with you. I'm assuming he doesn't know how to sign?"

"No. From the time I spent with him, I believe it's a case of selective mutism that's more trauma based than anything else."

"Alright, get started with that, and then we'll get a plan in place." The room fell silent for a moment. "Will you be okay keeping him in protective custody with you? He's going to be a key component of this case, and I fear if we let him go, he'll be dragged right back into that shitshow, or worse, killed."

My heart fell through the floor at his words. Bower wasn't heartless—he was married with three kids—but he was a straight shooter and didn't mince his words. That made him an effective leader, but he often came across as brash and inconsiderate.

I hadn't even thought about how River ended up in his current situation. He seemed somewhat settled at Mrs. Wilkinson's while I'd been there, but I didn't know what had happened after. I called Mrs. Wilkinson to check on him once I'd got settled with the Hendrix's, but she hadn't been able to give me much information as River had moved on about six months after I did. Turned out the sweet old lady had a stroke and never fully regained the use of her left side, so she couldn't continue her passion as a foster carer. She had a soft spot for River, said he was such a bright kid and had a great future ahead of him. She just prayed the system didn't ruin him before he'd gotten the chance to live. And here we were, eighteen years later, and it seemed her prayers went unanswered.

I cleared my throat. "That's not a problem at all."

Bower nodded. "Good. You can go now."

My chin touched my chest, and I let everything we'd just discussed sink into me, knowing my life was about to change in ways I'd never expected. The door shut with a snick behind me, the weight of expectation resting on my shoulders. I grabbed a couple of large coffees, then headed over to where my and Montoya's desks were.

"Well?" She spun around in her chair, her thick black braid almost whacking her in the face.

I cracked a smile and hid my laugh behind my coffee cup. "Here you go." She smiled that too-sweet smile up at me as she clutched her cup to her chest. I parked myself on the edge of her desk, toying with the lid on mine. "He said yes."

"Hell yes!" She fist bumped the air, and heads swiveled in her direction, the rest of the guys looking at her like she'd gone crazy. Maybe she had. I knew how much this job meant to her and what her parents did to support her to get to where she was today. "So what's the deal, then?"

My tongue hit the roof of my mouth, and I grabbed the chair from my desk behind hers and sat down, taking the weight off my feet for a minute. "Bower is on board but doesn't know exactly for how long or to what end. Right now, he wants you to find out everything you can about River, while I try to get him to tell me as much as he can about last night."

"The guys say the kid hasn't spoken the whole time he's been here." Concern etches her features, and I nod. "D'Souza said he had a concussion, lacerations to his arms and legs—"

I held up my hands. "I don't think I can take knowing any more about what they did to him, if I'm honest. Although I can usually detach myself from cases, this one is personal, and..."

"And he's someone to you, isn't he?" Her hand gave mine a brief squeeze. "This case is going to take its toll on you, Benson, and I'd suggest hooking yourself up with an appointment or two with your therapist. I know you'll get seen by the station shrink to check if you're fit for work and all, but I think you need someone you can trust to go through the deeper repercussions of it all."

"I know. You're right." I scuffed my boot against the shitty carpet covering the floor. "He was just a kid when I knew him. Now he's a man with a whole life I know nothing about. It was such a shock seeing his eyes looking back at me. Eyes I remember in the round face of a kid, but now..." But now he wasn't.

The River that was waiting in interview room five was not the River I knew, and that was damn hard to get my head around. I hated to even think about the hell his life had been, but I guessed that dark mystery would unravel in the upcoming days.

"Do you know his full name? I checked his prints against the system, but there were no hits, so he's never been arrested. That's good, right?" Montoya's dark eyes burned with hope, and all I could do was shrug.

I didn't know—that seemed to be my saying of the day. Just because he hadn't been brought in, didn't mean he hadn't lived in the gutter. It didn't mean he hadn't had to fight to survive every day. There was no telling what he'd been through. I just had to be brave enough to ask, and I wasn't sure I was.

"Pull yourself together, Benson." The sharp edge to her voice pulled me out of my head. "While he's in the station, you need to be the professional I know you are."

"But what about after?" The back of my eyes burned as my mind churned through a million possibilities I didn't want to be true, a million lives he could have led. Fuck.

"Then you break if you need to. Let it out like a purge and make that therapist appointment. Name?"

"Sure."

Montoya turned to her computer screen and waited, but when I didn't speak for over a minute, she glared at me. "His name, Benson."

"River Lane."

"Parents?"

I shook my head. "As far as I'm aware, he's been in the system his entire life."

"Huh, that sucks." That sucks, she says. My eyes rolled back in my head so hard, all I saw was bleak darkness. "School?"

"I don't know. He was only seven when we met, and I was at middle school while he was in elementary." I shrugged. "So I don't know. I don't know if he stayed in that home long enough to make it to Rayleigh High like I did."

"No problem. At least you gave me something to go on." I tried to force a small smile, but judging by the look on her face, I failed. "You take a walk, grab some air, then head back in and see what he's willing to say."

I pushed up, stretched the stiff muscles in my neck and shoulders, and kicked my chair back to my desk. "Thanks for having my back."

"I'm your partner and your friend, idiot." Her smile beamed across her face. "Is there anything you need when you get back?"

"Just an extra notepad and pen." I walked away before she could ask anything else and tugged on my collar. The stiff material felt like it was slicing into my neck, and I couldn't breathe.

I loosened my tie as I stepped outside, exhaling like a weight had been lifted off my shoulders. How damn selfish was that thought? It wasn't like I'd endured whatever River had. I'd lived through my share of shit too, but his was on a whole other level.

The early afternoon sun mocked me as it shone in a cloudless blue sky while a hurricane of emotions brewed inside me. My hand absentmindedly tapped my pocket, making sure my wallet was there as I ambled down the road in a daze to the local coffee shop. The crap back at the station hadn't cut it, and I needed to see that there was something good in the world before I dove back into the hell that was waiting for me in interview room five.

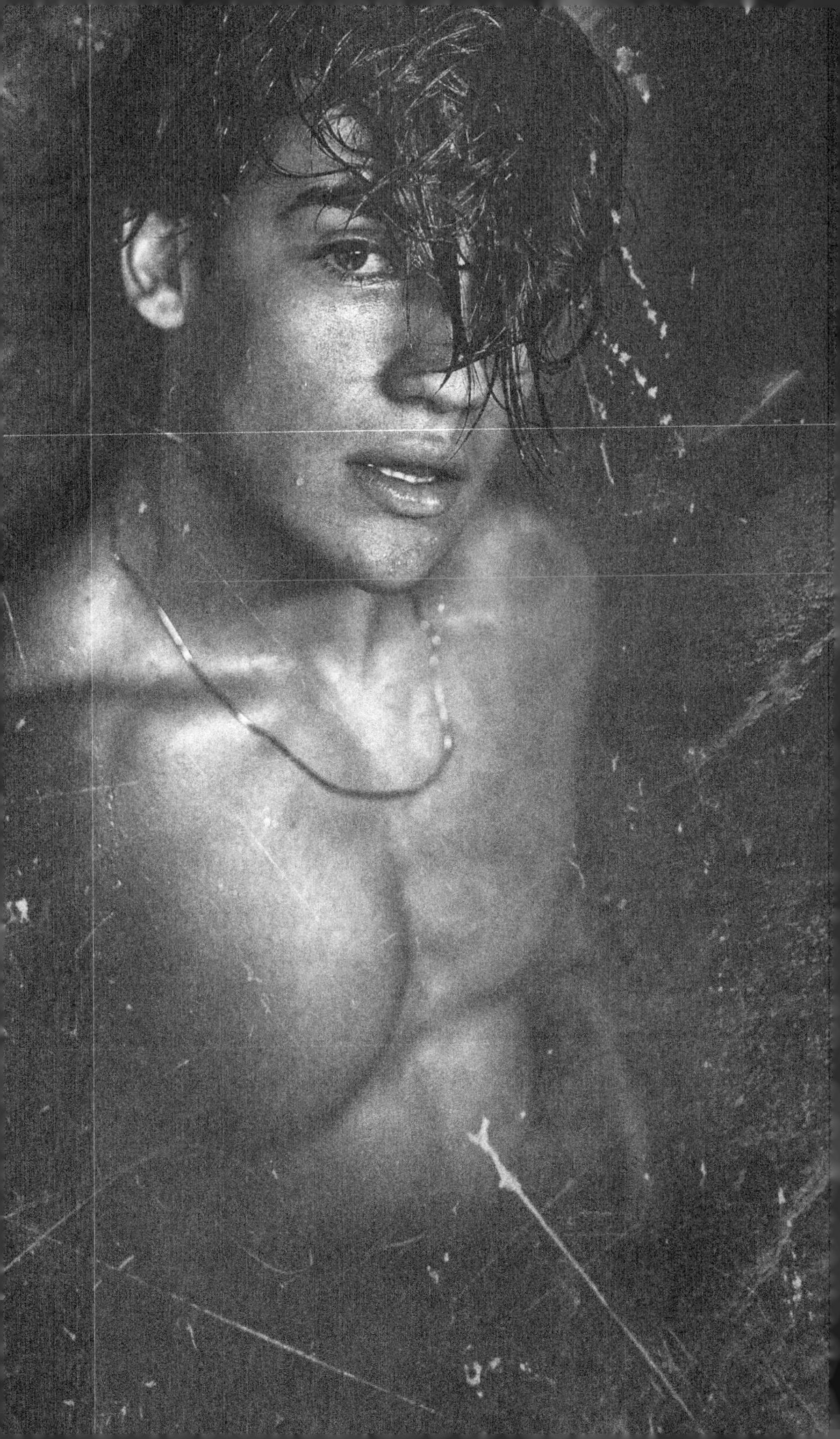

CHAPTER FOUR
River

The silence left in his wake was suffocating. It had been oppressive before, but now it was crushing with its intensity. The walls were closing in around me, caging me in, just like they had one way or another throughout my life. Just because you couldn't always see the bars, didn't mean you weren't trapped. It was a lie to believe cages were only physical; the mental ones were far more dangerous and could be effectively manipulated to control you.

Bane had burst back into my life only to leave it once again, taking the last fractured pieces of hope that I'd clung to with him. He might have only been in this godforsaken room with me for a few seconds, a minute at most, but he had saturated every part of it.

It was hard to think with a pickaxe chipping away at my skull, but I tried. I needed to know how Dale, Gabe, and

Max were. They were the closest thing to a family I had, even if it was only our shitty circumstances that united us. I prayed they weren't stuck in a room like I was, being drilled for information by some hardass who thought he was on the side of the righteous, fighting the good fight.

How could they believe that, when it was people like me that got charged with prostitution, and the ones who bought and sold our bodies walked away free? I'd bet everything I had that whoever booked us that night didn't spend more than an hour in a cell—if they even made it that far. There would be no criminal record of them on the system because money paid. Guys like the ones from the hotel always had deep pockets and could lawyer up in seconds.

People like me, lost in this twisted world, trying to survive as best we could, were the ones that suffered. With no education or money to start out with, I had to do whatever it took to make it from one day to the next. After living on the streets, anything was better than that—even selling myself for nothing more than a roof over my head.

My clammy cheek rested on the cool metal table as my eyes shuttered closed, darkness becoming my solace. It was better than the dots of color that had been dancing in front of my eyes as I stared fixated on the door, wondering if he would return.

"Have you had a drink recently?" Bane's deep voice rumbled in my ear. I jolted upright, the two-way mirror in front of me rippling as my stomach coiled tight. Blinking slowly, taking steady deep breaths, I pushed through the vicious waves of nausea that rose within me.

Once the world stopped turning itself inside out, I turned to face him. Even crouched down next to me, Bane still towered over me. His black uniform shirt hugged his well-defined broad shoulders, the sleeves coming down to the thickest part of his bulging biceps. Tattoos decorated his dark skin. He always said he wanted them when he was younger. I guess at least someone's dreams came true. My eyes traced the geometric fine lines flowing down his corded forearms and onto the back of his enormous hands and thick fingers. Everything about Bane should intimidate—his size, power, the presence he filled the room with. But me? I felt nothing but safe.

"Riv?" I dragged my eyes away from the intricate artwork on his skin and looked into eyes that made my soul ache. "Have you had anything to drink since you've been in this room?" He spoke softly, like he was afraid of scaring me.

A smile flickered at the corner of my mouth that I tried to hide by rolling my bottom lip between my teeth. He was so damn sweet. His brown and blue eyes fixed on me, a furrow forming between his brows as he patiently waited for my answer.

I wanted to fall headfirst into his arms and never look at the outside world again. My heart stumbled over itself in my chest, and I shook my head.

A look of defeat washed over Bane's features that bled into anger that tightened the corners of his eyes. "Nothing?" His tone thickened, darkened, and his fingers clenched into a fist before releasing. "You've been in here nearly four hours and not had a drink?"

I shrugged and sat back in my seat before I could bury my face in his neck and inhale him like I used to. Cedarwood and leather consumed me. It was a scent he'd possessed even as a child, one I'd clung to the nights after he left when I cried myself to sleep, my nose buried in a T-shirt he'd left behind.

Bane smelled like *home.*

With an exasperated huff, Bane pushed up, wrenching his gaze from me, and headed for the door. Hand wrapped around the handle, he paused and glanced over his shoulder. "Have you eaten, Riv?" I stayed silent and watched his shoulders rise and fall with each inhale and exhale. "I'll take that as a no." He pulled the door open and slipped out, leaving his foot to catch the door before it shut, almost like he didn't want to be separated from me. What a fucking stupid idea to have in my head. I could hear the low rumble of his voice as he spoke to someone on the other side.

My stomach grumbled, preceding a painful cramp that had me folding in half. I tried to remember when I'd last eaten, but it escaped me. I'm sure I had a sandwich or something over the past week, but I hadn't had a proper meal in years. Must have been sometime near the beginning of the week, and today was...

"Here you go." The scent of fresh toast and thick creamy butter made my mouth water. Christ, that smelled amazing. "I also got you a bottle of water. Drink it slowly, okay?"

I rolled my eyes. Tentatively, I reached out with a shaky hand and undid the cap, which took far more effort than I'd be willing to admit. The cool water trickling down my throat felt like heaven, and the back of my eyes burned, thanks to Bane's tiny act of kindness. It was the first one I'd received since I'd woken up, puking my guts out and being called a fucking junkie. I recoiled as the memory slammed into me, the nearly full bottle of water slipping from my fingers and crashing to the ground. It was like everything happened in slow motion, and my eyes darted between the bottle and Bane as he pushed out of the chair he'd taken opposite me.

No matter how fast he tried to move, it wasn't enough, and water spilled from the bottle. Bane jumped around the table, and I flinched when his hand crashed down on the surface. Bane froze, shock written all over his face as I curled into myself, pulled my knees up, and tucked my head against my chest, rocking side to side, waiting for the inevitable pain to bloom across my body.

"Shit! Shit!" A muttered curse, a grunt, and a pained exhale had me screwing my eyes shut. "Riv? It's okay. No one's going to hurt you."

I felt him move closer to me. I always could. *He's safe. He's safe. Bane would never hurt me.* The air became magnetized, crackling across my skin. The hairs on my arms and the back of my neck stood on end as the surrounding energy built, increasing in voltage. *Safe. Safe. Safe.*

"River, I'm going to touch you, okay?" Warmth filled his whispered words, a tenderness I craved but knew I didn't deserve. "I'm not going to hurt you, okay?" Each word sounded like it cut him open, and that pain echoed in my chest.

Why did I always hurt those around me?

"I'm going to touch your shoulder to make sure you're okay, alright?"

Sharp, shallow breaths breached my lips. My fingers sank into my legs, ripping the fabric of the scrubs I wore. When was the last time someone asked if they could touch me?

Thick fingers carded through my hair, down my neck, and settled on my shoulder. I trembled as his tender touch sank deep beneath my frozen skin. Goosebumps prickled across my body, making me ache for something different, but knowing I was not worthy. I needed to build my walls back up before I became too weak to survive this cruel world because the one I was in now wasn't real. It was just a dream.

Pressure under my chin forced my head up. "There you are." His exotic sky blue and dark wood brown eyes shimmered, emotions swirling in them I didn't understand. "It's okay, Riv. You did nothing wrong." I sucked in a stuttering breath, my lungs squeezing tight. "You did nothing wrong," he repeated.

My teeth sunk into my bottom lip and chewed the dry skin until the metallic taste of blood filled my mouth. Tears welled in my eyes. I tried to blink them away, but when I shook my head, fighting against his muted words, they fell, staining me. *Worthless.*

"Shh. I've got you now."

Bane wrapped his arms around my shoulders, pulling me into him. I collapsed into his embrace. The fight drained out of me as my head found its home against his neck. I sighed, inhaling his scent. Cedarwood and leather encased me as he held me in the safety of his strong arms. He should feel disgusted by me. I wasn't the broken boy he once knew. I was an amalgamation of nightmares and relentless demons.

"It's okay. You're safe. I've got you, and I won't let go." He chanted the words over and over into my ear like he could make me believe them if he repeated them enough. God, how I wanted to, but people like me didn't deserve the grace of his kindness.

I didn't know how long we stayed like that, but by the time he pulled away, I was warm. Not the type of warmth you got from a sweatshirt or a good coat, but the type that was like an ember burning inside you. Bane pulled back until he was looking me right in the eyes. Thick thumbs brushed away the tear tracks running down my flushed cheeks.

A shudder rolled through me that had nothing to do with his touch, but everything to do with my body shutting down. I clenched my jaw, a muscle ticing in my cheek as I tried to hide the fact my teeth were chattering. I needed to get out of here before I hurt him. Bane was good to the core, and I was every dark creature hiding in the shadows.

"How about I get you another one and try to find you some proper clothes?" Bane tilted his head as he spoke, his eyes roaming over my dirty scrubs, lips pressed into a grim line. He picked up the bottle off the floor, cast his gaze over the room, and huffed. "I'll be back, just going to get something to dry that up. Won't be long."

The two-way mirror in front of me taunted me with my reflection. A man stared back at me I didn't recognize. How did he, after all these years? Exhaustion flowed through me. Every limb felt impossibly heavy. The sweet scent of salted butter was the only thing keeping me from closing my eyes. Flavor burst across my tongue as I chewed the lightly toasted malt bread, a groan slipping from my lips as one small bite turned into me ramming as much as I could in my mouth in case someone came in here and took it from me.

Buttery goodness dripped down my fingers, glowing golden in the harsh white light of the sterile room. I focused on sucking each drop off my fingers rather than thinking about what would happen next. The clank of the chains attached to the cuffs around my wrists refused to let me forget nobody really wanted me here, no matter how caring Bane seemed. He was just doing his job.

I was his job. Nothing more, but always infinitely less.

That thought drove home how stupid I was, thinking there was more to his actions than there was. Tears leaked from my tired eyes, and my throat grew tight and scratchy. I was still just that stupid little boy who dreamed of having a home. Of being wanted. Of love.

How could someone love me, when I didn't even know what it was?

"Here." Bane entered the room, a bright smile plastered on his face, arms full of items he set on the table. "I got you another bottle of water." Passing it to me, he continued, "Montoya, my partner, got hold of some clean sneakers and pants for you. She wasn't able to find a shirt, but you can have my hoodie until we get you something better."

The bottle froze halfway to my mouth, my eyes widening as his words filtered through my foggy brain. *Until we get you something better?* I tilted my head to the side, assessing him as he shuffled from foot to foot. If I didn't know better, I'd swear there was a slight flush to his rich dark cheeks. After all, I was just a job.

"Don't look at me like that, Riv. We're friends." I shrugged, because yeah, we kind of were once. But now? "We are, aren't we?" Vulnerability flashed across his face as he wrung his hands in his lap.

A weak smile flickered on my mouth, and I took the coward's way out and hid behind my bottle. My throat was drier than a desert after swallowing down that toast like I was in an eating competition. Bane seemed to understand that I needed some time to process everything fully and sat silently as I looked over everything he brought.

Shamelessly, I brought his massive hoodie to my face and inhaled his intoxicating scent, making Bane chuckle. When I glanced up at him, his eyes darted to the ceiling, his smile morphing into something contagious as he tried to pretend he was coughing.

"Once you're changed and comfortable, I hope we can have a little chat. That okay?" Just as elation had sparked inside me, it died. *See? You're just a job.*

I nodded, locking down any sign of emotion, and held my chained hands up to him.

Bane pinched his nose, and his shoulders slumped. "I've got you." He stood up and pulled a set of keys from his pocket. Leaning over the table, he unlocked the cuffs, a heavy sigh breaching his lips. Warm fingers wrapped around my wrists, the thumbs making soothing circles over my inflamed skin. "I'm so, so, sorry, River."

I sucked in a stuttering breath and screwed my eyes shut as they burned. My heartbeat whooshed in my ears as a wave of dizziness washed over me. I counted to ten and back again, bile thick on my tongue. I knew what was happening —a panic attack was creeping up on me. It had been a long time coming, like waves lapping at the shore, growing stronger before calming and left me balancing on a knife edge.

Bane's mismatched eyes bored into mine, adding layers of weight to his words. "I mean it, Riv. I'm so sorry for everything that's happened to you. Let me help you. Help me make them pay."

Hope fluttered in my heart, small and fragile, an exposed flame in the eye of a storm. Withdrawing from his touch took everything in me. I pointed at the clothes, then looked around the room.

Bane studied me for a minute. "Here." He tapped a pen on a small pad and handed it to me. "Tell me." I picked up the pen and started writing while he continued talking. "I hope one day you'll feel comfortable enough to talk to me again. It's been years since I heard your voice."

I snorted. *Me too.* I turned the pad toward him.

Where can I change?

Wincing, Bane looked at me apologetically, arms out to his side. "Here." I slumped back in my chair and bit the inside of my cheek while bundling the clothes in my arms. Turning away from the mirror, I picked the corner under the camera to give myself some semblance of privacy. I'd never been ashamed of my body; the johns who used me didn't care what I looked like as I was just a hole to use to them.

But now I felt different. I didn't want Bane to see how visible my ribs were or where my hips protruded. I didn't want him to see the scars, cuts, and bruises that decorated my skin in a litany of my suffering.

You're disgusting.
Worthless.

I ripped off the wet top and hauled on Bane's massive hoodie. It swamped me, falling halfway down my thighs, and making me feel like a kid playing dress up. I kicked the sliders off my feet, followed by my wet pants, and pulled on the jogging bottoms, rolling them up at the waist to stop them from falling down, and slipped my feet into nearly new sneakers. Even without socks, they were the comfiest things my feet had felt in as long as I could remember.

"Done?" Bane asked where he stood facing the door. I coughed instead of answering, and the smile that lit up his face when he turned to look at me made all of this worth it.

Even if it wasn't forever. Even if it was just for one moment.

I'd made him smile, and that meant more to me than anything ever had.

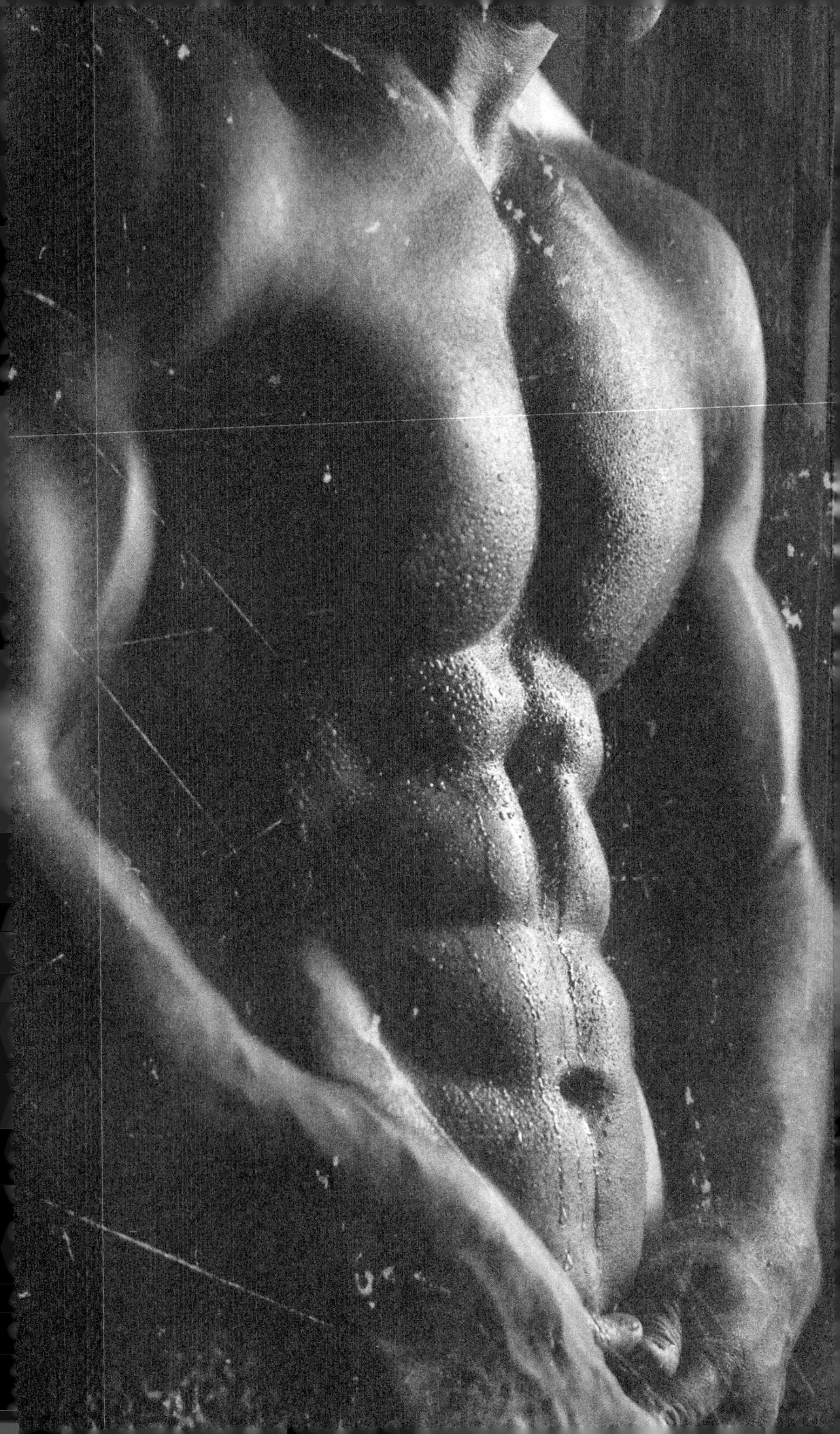

CHAPTER FIVE
Bane

The sight of him in my hoodie was like a sucker punch to the chest. He still didn't look like the River from my memories, but he looked human at least. The smile that pulled at my lips was instantaneous. All I wanted to do was wrap my arms around him and get him away from here, from his old life, to somewhere safe where I could look after him.

I puffed out a breath, trying to calm myself down. I was getting way ahead of where things needed to be right now. When it came to River, I had to take baby steps. He was emotionally volatile. Vulnerable. Broken. He'd been systemically beaten down and ground into dust. He needed time and patience, and if there was one thing I never ran out of, it was patience.

He needed love. A home. Family.

This was going to hurt me as much as it would him, but I

couldn't let my emotional state affect him or any information he could provide in relation to this case. Once I had something I could take to Bower, I was going to take River home and help him heal and rebuild himself. It was the least I could do for him, considering all he'd done for me when I was at the Wilkinson's. He might not have spoken even then, but his constant, unwavering presence brought me a level of comfort no one had ever been able to compete with.

"Have a seat, River. I'll make this as quick and painless for you as I can. We want to make sure what you've experienced doesn't happen to anyone else, so any information you can give us will be a step in the right direction. Then, well, then we'll see what comes after, alright?"

The light that had flickered in his eyes making them glow like emeralds extinguished the more I spoke. I wanted to kick myself in the ass for snuffing it out, but I hoped over time I could make sure they burned brighter and never went out.

River stumbled back into his seat and collapsed against the table. I didn't know exactly what he'd endured over the last twenty-four hours, but it had drained him of every ounce of strength he had. Exhaustion carved itself into the flawless skin on his face, and dark circles surrounded his hollow eyes.

I wetted my lips, ready to begin, when River shoved the pad I'd given him across the table. He pulled his legs up so his knees were against his chest, wrapped his arms around them, and chewed on his puffy bottom lip. All the while, he watched me like a hawk. It was an automatic response, likely to monitor the most dangerous person in the room. It made me feel like I'd failed him already.

I picked up the pad and read his messy writing.

Where are Dale, Gabe, and Max?

"Were they with you at the hotel?" He winced and nodded. "Have you known them long?" I pushed the pad back across to him and kept talking. "I'll find out for you once we're done here." It was my turn to wince at how heartless my words sounded, but if I came away empty-handed, I doubted Bower would let me take River home and look after him, no matter how important he might be for the case.

A whimpering whine tore its way from his chest as he glared at me. His fist crashed into the table, knocking over the bottles of water. We sat there watching them as they rolled to the floor, animosity building in the tense air.

"I—" River cut me off as he banged on the table again, frustration staining his pale cheeks. I held my hands up in surrender. "If I find out about them, will you talk to me?" A tear trickled down his right cheek as he released a pained breath. I held mine, waiting to see if my compromise would work. The ticking of the minute hand on the clock grew louder and louder as time stretched between us. Eventually, he gave one succinct nod. I was up, out of my seat, and out the door before I'd even blinked.

"Everything alright, Benson?" Montoya asked as I tapped her on the shoulder.

Scrubbing my hand over my face, I slumped into my chair and tucked my hands under my legs to hide how much they shook. "Uh, yeah. Do we have an update on the guys that were brought in with River?"

"Sure, I'll see what we've got on them." Her fingers clacked away on the keys as she searched the system. The rest of the floor had cleared out, bar a couple of rookies who were practically rocking in the corner, a haunted look in their eyes.

"Nixon on the warpath?"

Montoya snorted. "The guy's an ass, and when he gets fired up, even the photocopier wants to run and hide. Poor kids."

"Can't believe he's still here. The old guy does nothing but shout at people."

"True, but I believe he has friends in high places, so he gets away with more than anyone."

"Makes me sick. I joined to help people, not deal with that," I muttered.

"I know, Benson." She sighed and tightened her messy bun. "Right. Here we go. So, I have Dale Underwood, Gabriel Drake, and Max Woolf. All have priors—"

"I don't care about their pasts. I just want to know if they're okay and what's happening with them."

She turned and smiled up at me, and for once, it wasn't a mocking one. "You can tell your boy they're all out. Officers took them to a local hostel, as they refused to give any information. Wait, no."

"What?"

"They said a woman named Dahlia held them..." Her voice trailed off, her breath hitching. My eyes widened as she kept talking. "Shit. Black Dahlia? I knew that bitch was in deeper than just a strip club. Fuck!"

"If she's who we're looking for, we'll take her down," I reassured her. Montoya nodded, even though she didn't look convinced.

Black Dahila had a well-known reputation for operating a seedy as fuck chain of strip clubs in the surrounding towns. There were rumors that the girls and guys that worked there went missing from time to time, but nothing we could prove. Police had raided the establishments once or twice because undercover agents suspected the dancers were kids, but that woman was as slippery as fuck, and every raid turned up nothing but air.

This investigation was now personal to not only me, but Montoya as well. A couple of years back, twins went missing from the neighborhood that she grew up in, and where her parents still lived. They vanished one day from their front yard. Their mom had gone inside to grab their drinks, and when she came out, they were gone. Eight months later, hikers found their bodies dumped at a rest stop close to Little Rock. The perpetrators had assaulted them in every way imaginable, and the trauma their bodies had endured would have been enough to kill them without the heavy presence of drugs in their systems. The thing that stuck out —that has haunted me—was the flower found tattooed on the inside of their thighs. A black dahlia. It was a calling card, a sign of ownership, and one I couldn't scour from my mind.

"Thanks." I squeezed her shoulder. "We won't let them get away with it again, no matter what it takes."

"These operations are like a damn hydra, though. Take one of the bad guys out and four more pop up to take their place. It's a war we can't win, Benson. And I hate that." She stared back at me, desolation leaching the normal healthy glow from her face. She wasn't wrong; we were fighting an unwinnable war, but it was one I'd never give up on.

"You and me both. But if taking out one of them saves a child's innocence, then we've done some good. Maybe not enough, but one day...." She hummed in agreement and turned back to her screen, but I didn't miss the way she dabbed at her eyes.

THE NEWS ABOUT HIS FRIENDS TEMPERED RIVER'S GRIM MOOD, at least for now. It was like his walls cracked, and I got a glimpse of what he'd been trying to hide. He cared deeply about those around him, especially if they were unjustly hurt. It irked me how he didn't seem to hold his own safety to such a high standard, but I would make sure he learned to value himself and what he had to offer to the world.

The afternoon was an eye opener and would remain ingrained in my memory for as long as I breathed. His messy scrawl filled almost half of the notebook by the time we wrapped up. Each word of his suffering and torment was branded on my soul, even though it was just the tip of the iceberg. They flayed me open with a thousand cuts that felt like they would never heal, but I knew no matter how much it hurt me to read them, it was nothing but a dreary shadow of what he'd experienced.

Guilt ate away at me the more he divulged. My life might have had its own share of heartache and pain, but his continued suffering was incomprehensible. Tears burned my eyes as they spilled down my cheeks, and raw emotion grated through every part of me. I wanted to scream for the injustice he'd endured, to wrap him up in a heated blanket and hide him away from the world like a dragon hoarding treasure.

River was a treasure. He might not see it, but I did, and I'd do whatever it took to make him see how worthy he was of living. Of love.

Thanks to the information River provided, I'd been able to petition Bower into allowing him to be in protective custody with me, rather than with a random uniformed officer at a safe house. I just hoped I could make him feel safe enough to allow me to breach his walls and help him heal.

The urge to take care of him should have scared me with the intensity it flowed through me, but it didn't. Instead, it settled a part of me that had always been searching for something, like it had needed a purpose and now it finally had one.

As we stepped out of the station, vibrant pinks and oranges filled the sky. The sun was a molten ball, slowly descending below the horizon of building roof tops. Cool wind tickled across my cheeks and rustled the leaves on the trees that lined the street.

River shivered beside me and wrapped his arms around himself, creating a barrier between him and the world. He hid his hands in the long sleeves of my hoodie, the sight making my heart squeeze. He looked like a younger, more innocent version of himself.

"Here." I placed my jacket around his shoulders as we made our way to my work car. Usually, I rode my bike, but today I'd felt like taking the old sedan I'd recently fixed up. I guess I knew why now. Some might even call it fate.

Eyes squinted against the glare from the sun, he peeked up at me through thick dark lashes and offered me a small smile.

"Here we are," I said, stepping up to the car and opening the passenger door for him. Stupefied, River blinked at me in confusion. "You're coming home with me."

Head tilted to the side, he stared at me for a beat. His lips parted like he was going to say something, but he shook his head instead. I protected the top of his head as he slipped in and collapsed back into the leather seat. I clipped his seat belt in place and gave his shoulder a gentle squeeze before I hopped over the hood and got in the driver's seat.

As the engine rumbled to life, my eyes were automatically drawn to River like he'd disappear if they weren't constantly on him. One thing I'd noticed was River was perpetually cold. He didn't seem to notice his teeth chattering away, as if he was accustomed to it. Not under my watch.

I turned up the heating as I backed out of my parking space and hit Main Street. "It'll warm up soon, I promise," I said lightly. His forest-green eyes flicked to me before sliding away and focusing out of the window. Trying not to be perturbed, I kept talking. "I thought it would be a good idea to hit up Walmart and get you some things of your own. You know, so you feel comfortable."

River shrugged in the periphery of my vision as I kept my eyes on the road, allowing a comfortable silence to settle between us. I didn't want to push him or make him feel uncomfortable by being too in his face. The after-work rush caused congestion on the roads, and heavy foot traffic filled the sidewalk as people filed out of offices and into bars and restaurants. I enjoyed city life, but nothing beat the open road with the wind in my hair and nowhere to go. I wondered what River would think of going out on my Buell Hammerhead.

By the time we reached the limits of Echoes Hollow, I was boiling. Sweat dripped down the back of my neck, and my shirt clung to my shoulders. Dusk had finally settled, the sky a blanket of darkness swallowing the last embers of color from the sun. The street lights flickered on as I pulled into a spot right at the front of Walmart. River was curled up into a little ball on the seat next to me, sleeping restlessly. I didn't know whether to let him sleep or wake him up. He startled awake as I debated what to do, solving the problem for me.

"We're here," I stated the obvious and rolled my eyes at myself, nerves skittering across my skin. River blinked the sleep away from his blood-shot eyes, unfolded himself slowly and looked around us, taking everything in before the weight of his gaze landed on me. "You ready?"

River's teeth scraped over the cracked skin on his bottom lip, chewing it as he seemed to think about his response. I rolled my keys in my hand and looked out the windshield while I waited for him to decide if he was up for this. I knew from what he'd told me that Dahlia hadn't allowed him out of the room she kept him in, other than when he saw clients. And even then, they led him down dark corridors and into an underground parking lot before placing him in a van he couldn't see out of.

So having the freedom to walk into a store would undoubtedly be a nerve-racking experience, but one I hoped he'd take on. I had spent my walk back from Bower's office wondering if this was the right thing to do. We didn't know if anyone was looking for River or the guys he came in with, but as the three of them were still at the hostel, I decided it was a calculated risk.

The sound of the handle being pulled back yanked me out of my thoughts just as the passenger door cracked open. A smile lifted the corner of my lips as I got out to meet him on the sidewalk. Shoulders hunched halfway up his head, River looked like he was reinforcing the walls he surrounded himself with as he fell into step beside me. I tried not to take it personally, because this was a lot for him, and I knew that. I just had to remind myself of that fact more times than I had expected.

"Do you want to push the cart?" I asked as the doors opened with a whoosh and the blinding lights of the store bore down on us as we meandered inside. The hum of the air conditioning whirled, and the chatter of other shoppers seemed louder than it ever had as I led us toward the homeware section.

River shuffled closer to me, using me as a shield as we passed couples and families with boisterous children. He seemed skittish and uncomfortable as a little boy ran right toward him like he couldn't even see River. Luckily, his mother grabbed the back of his shirt before he crashed right into River, but the damage was done.

"I'm so sorry." She chuckled and hefted the unruly little boy onto her hip. "He's on a sugar high. His grandma filled him with so much candy, I don't think he'll sleep tonight."

"No problem," I said softly as River tried to melt into my side. My arm automatically wrapped around his shoulders. "Hope he lets you get some sleep, ma'am." She smiled at me but eyed River cautiously before shaking her head and walking back to who I could only assume was her husband and daughter.

"How about you pick out some towels and bed sheets you like? Maybe a blanket or two as well," I said as I moved us along down onto a quieter aisle as a violent shudder rolled through River. "Hey." I turned him in my arms so I could cup his face in my hands. The stark contrast of his pale skin against my large dark hands was a stark reminder of the abyss that stretched between us. It made me ache for the healthy golden glow it had when I met him. "Are you okay? Do you want to leave?"

Wide green eyes looked at me through steel shutters. Soft pants punched through his dry lips as his fingers sunk into my forearms to the point of pain, like he needed the contact between us to stop from shattering completely, and reminding him we were here and it was real. A single tear slipped down his cheek, and his beautiful eyes closed before his head crashed into my chest.

Protected and encircled in my arms, River broke. I tightened my hold around him as his shoulders shook. Full body tremors rolled through him with enough force to make my knees weak. Tears soaked through my shirt over my thudding heart, slicking my skin with his pain. I didn't know how long we stood there as I tried to fight back the demons that stalked him, but without knowing his full truth, all I could do was be a bystander to his torment.

Pulling back from my chest, River looked up at me through water-logged lashes, the whites of his eyes spider-webbed with burst blood vessels. A stuttered gasp wrenched out of him, and his bloodied lips quivered. I didn't need to hear his voice to hear his plea.

His knees buckled just as I tucked my arm under them and hauled him to my chest. Abandoning the cart in the middle of the aisle, I marched out of the store like I'd set it on fire and headed for the car. River was nearly catatonic by the time the first drop of rain fell.

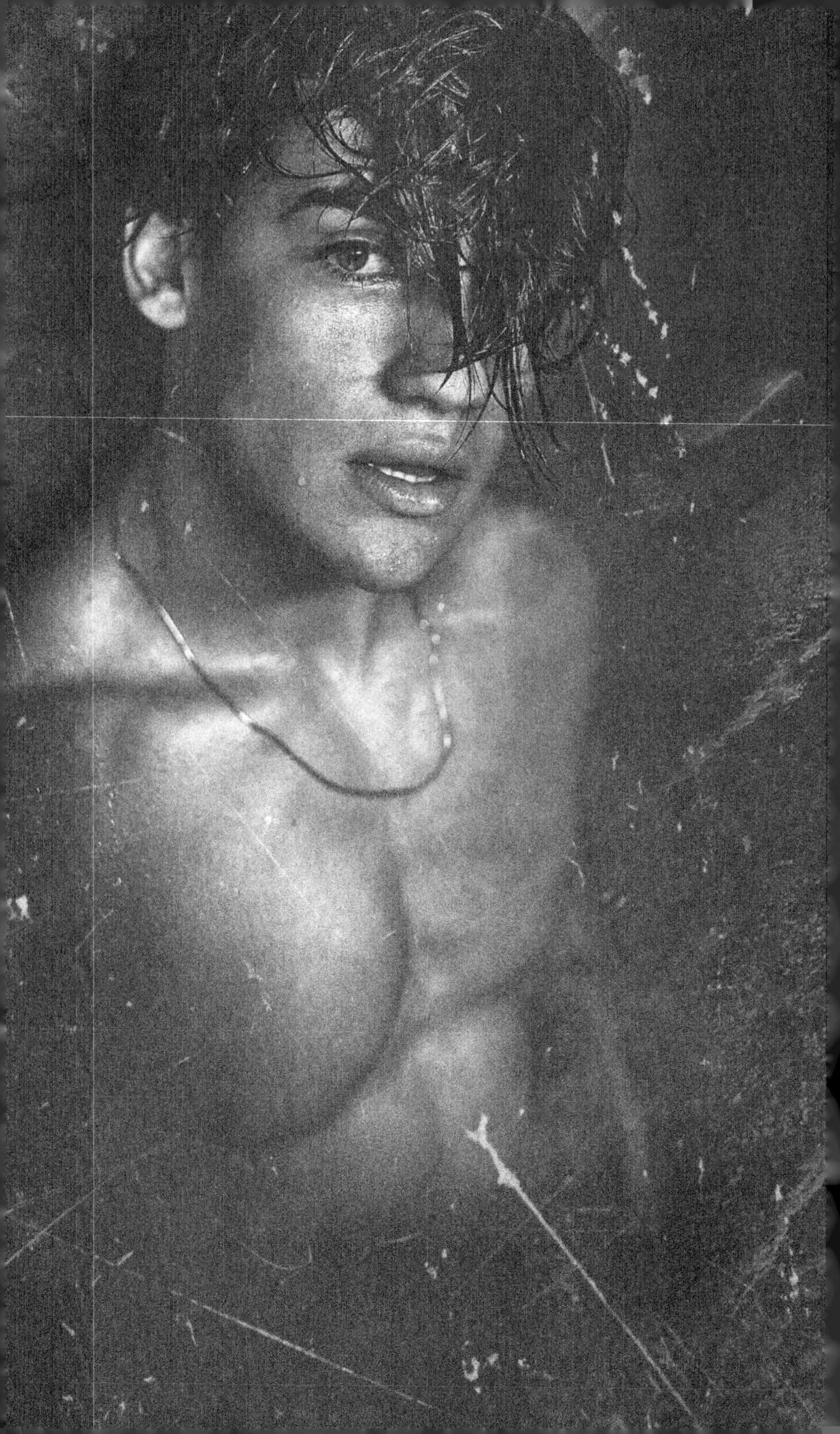

CHAPTER SIX
River

I could feel myself splintering under the store's bright lights. Oh god, the oppressive noise. The children. The air conditioning. The sound of the voice over the tannoy speaker. It was too much. Too loud. Too busy. Too everything.

For years, I'd longed to escape the walls of my cage, but now I craved them. Even contained and restrained as I was, I knew who I was. But now, I was lost in the open waters and sinking fast. I needed darkness and isolation. Silence. I could handle pain—I'd endured it for years. But life? That was too much.

Cold air pricked my skin as I sunk into the darkness as I slowly shut down, cutting off the world that was paralyzing me. My heart hammered so hard that it was permanently etched into my bones. Tears carved their way down my cheeks as inhales and exhales sawed their way out of my lungs.

"It's okay, angel. I've got you."

A whimper caught in the back of my throat, choking me as his soft words whispered in my ear. Was I flying or sinking? I couldn't tell. But I was moving, and moving fast, until the slam of the car door granted me blessed silence.

"I'm sorry. I'm so fucking sorry, River. It was a stupid idea." I wanted to reach out to him. To reassure him it wasn't his fault, it was mine. I was the broken one, the one who couldn't act like a normal person no matter how much I tried. I'd been conditioned into a being that wasn't human.

I DIDN'T REMEMBER IF I FELL ASLEEP OR PASSED OUT AS MY mind spiraled out of control, but as I came to and peeled my heavy lids open and the world came into focus, I realized I was somewhere new. Cocooned in soft blankets that made me feel safe, the thick scent of cedarwood and leather invaded my senses and eased the tightness that had gripped my lungs. My fingers curled around the fluffy blanket covering my mouth and pulled it down from my face, freeing my shoulders. I lifted my head from the soft cushion and shuffled from my prone position until I was sitting up and took in the room I was in.

A TV on the wall opposite flickered with a show I'd never seen, the characters moving around silently above a wooden fireplace littered with ornaments and small photo frames. An electric fire glowed below it, the red and blue flames dancing calmly as they phased in and out, illuminating the room as my eyes adjusted to the muted light.

A low level coffee table beside me contained a glass of

water covered in condensation sitting on a coaster with two tablets next to it. My dry throat ached, but I was too warm in my blanket cocoon to move to ease the pain. Soft snores drifted through the otherwise silent room, pulling my eyes to Bane, where he sat rather awkwardly in an armchair, fast asleep with his head tipped back, exposing his Adam's apple that rolled every so often in his throat. The tip of his pink tongue teased across his full bottom lip before he startled awake because his feet fell off the edge of the coffee table.

"Wh-what the who?" The shock on Bane's face was priceless. It brought on a tentative smile that tore the fresh scab on my lip bottom as it twitched. I snickered a rasping laugh that morphed into a heaving cough that made my eyes water.

"Here," Bane said softly, holding the glass of water in front of me as I sucked in a gasping inhale while my lungs were fighting to push the air out. "Have a sip, slowly. It'll help." My shaky hand wrapped around the slick glass that instantly started to slide through my fingers. Thankfully, Bane helped guide it to my mouth. The cool liquid felt like the first drops of rain following a drought as it flowed down my throat.

When I'd finished, he took the glass from me, placed it back on the table, and ran his hand through my hair. The soft rhythmical scrape of his blunt nails over my scalp soothed the ragged edges of the panic attack that still clung to me. I sighed, sinking back into my blanket cocoon. My eyes felt heavy again. Sleep called me, but I didn't want them to close and erase the tender look on Bane's face, and the way his mismatched eyes glinted in the dancing light from the fire.

When was the last time someone looked at me like that?

PALE MORNING LIGHT FILTERED THROUGH THE BLINDS covering the sliding doors leading to a deck overlooking a large backyard. I rubbed away the sleep from my eyes with the heel of my hands and stretched out my aching muscles. A shiver rolled through me when I realized I was alone. It felt wrong being in Bane's house unsupervised. It's not like I was going to rob him, but I could run. Run where? It's not like I had anywhere to go, but being here didn't feel right. It felt like I was taking advantage of him, no matter why he said I was here.

"Here you go." His large hand appeared in my line of sight, and a steaming mug of coffee taunted me. It smelled strong and rich, and had me salivating for just a taste. "Be careful, it's hot."

My eyes narrowed at him, letting them speak for me. *I'm not a child.* Bane snorted and held up his hands as mine wrapped around the cup of liquid gold. I inhaled its delicious scent and shuffled until my back rested on the armrest so I could stretch my legs out, and blew at the soft swirls of steam.

"I didn't know how you took it, so I only added a little milk to take the edge off. But there are creamers and stuff in the fridge in the kitchen if you want, or you can have mine if you prefer it without milk," he rambled as he sat on the couch by my feet, automatically pulling them into his lap. He froze as I eyed him over my cup. "Is this okay?" he asked.

I nodded, feeling heat rise in my cheeks as my stomach gave an almighty rumble, making me wince from the painful pang.

"Hungry?"

I shrugged instead of acknowledging his question and continued to blow on my coffee. I knew he wanted me to give them information to help their case, but there wasn't much more I could give him, other than all the gruesome details of what the johns who had bought and used my body subjected me to. Bane was good people, and I didn't want him to know the details of what I'd experienced. That led to only one logical conclusion—I had to leave before I broke or tainted him. I had to go.

Bane, ever the optimist, refused to let the silence stretch between us any longer. "Since our trip to Walmart didn't go to plan last night, I thought we could do some online shopping. Get you some new clothes that fit, and all the bits you'll need to make your room upstairs, well, yours."

My room? I'd assumed he'd keep me here on the sofa. It wasn't like this arrangement was permanent. Once I'd lived out my usefulness, he'd kick me to the curb, right?

"Don't look at me like that, River." I blanched at the hard edges of his tone. "I told you last night we'd get you some bedding." He sighed and scrubbed his hands down his face, shoulders dropping in defeat.

Bane lifted my feet so he could turn to face me, tucking one of his thick thighs up on the couch before he kneaded my soles with his thumbs. Fuck, that felt amazing. "River, I know I said we want you to help with the case." I nodded along like a bobble head. "But I care about you." I blinked in confusion, and a sad smile flickered on his striking face. "I know you don't believe me, but you made a massive impact on my life. Those two years... they left footprints on my soul. I've thought about you often over the years since the Hendrix's adopted me. I tried to get them to adopt you too, but they refused." His sadness at that fact was palpable. I raised my eyes and pinched my lips together as if to say, *what can you do?* "I'm sorry I couldn't,

Riv." He squeezed my foot to emphasize the depth of his words.

My head fell back on my shoulders, hiding the emotions burning my eyes. I couldn't get attached again. That only led to a pain I didn't know how to cope with, so I did what I had taught myself to do. I shut it down and locked it away in that box in my mind and added a hazard sticker to it for good measure.

Bane continued, either unaware of my internal struggle, or graciously ignoring it. "They said they adopted me because I reminded them of their son that died from leukemia on his seventeenth birthday." I choked on a mouthful of coffee. What the fuck?! That was wrong on so many damn levels. Bane deserved to be chosen because of who he was, not because he was an imitation of a memory or a lost loved one. I wanted to reach out and comfort him, but I didn't know how to. My throat grew tight as he blinked away the glassiness coating his eyes.

"Anyway," he went on, "They removed me from foster care and into what appeared to be the perfect home. They had—have—money, a large house, a pool." He cracked a smile at whatever look was on my face. "But they didn't give me a family, not even a facsimile of the one I lost. I was their stand-in. It was like they were made of cardboard, moving like shadow puppets through life. They had everything at their disposal, and Rosalie spent all of her time down at the country club while William had a mistress and his job. I never saw either of them other than Sundays for lunch at the country club, where I had to dress in the clothes Annalise—the housekeeper—laid out for me. It wasn't a life or the family they promised me."

An indignant snort ripped through the tense air. What I wouldn't have given to have had that life, the one he was describing. Even with parents that had checked out mentally, it would have been better than running away at twelve and living on the streets. Raiding bins for scraps of food, hiding under bags of trash for warmth, hearing the rats scrabble around me. And when begging provided no money, working out that I could turn tricks in the back allies of bars. A quick blowjob here and there on a Friday night could give me enough cash to get a hot meal or a coat to sleep in.

Bane pinned me with those mysterious mismatched eyes of his and watched as I traced my bottom lip with my tongue. Clearing his throat, he blinked himself out of a daze. "I know it's nothing like you've lived through, but I'd like to know, to understand, Riv." He leaned forward, placing his too hot hand on my now bent knee. "I want to help you re-acclimate to the world. To find your feet. Heal." His words sounded wonderful, but that's all they were. Words. Empty promises. He'd soon see that I was so far beyond help. This—me—was a waste of his time and energy.

"How about we start with something simple? Clothes and a few things for your room, including a toothbrush and soap. I'm sure you'd love a shower or a bath?" Fuck me, that sounded amazing. I wanted to ask if he had hot water, since it'd been years since I had a hot shower, but I swallowed down the urge.

"Move." Bane pushed my feet and gestured for me to sit up as he leaned over the side of the sofa and pulled a laptop onto his lap. "Grab me the cushion behind you, please."

After setting my empty cup on the table, I passed it to him. My heart thumped as he shuffled closer to me, close enough that his thigh pressed against mine, and started tapping away on the keys. The bright screen was so different from the one I occasionally caught sight of in the apartment Dahlia kept me in. It was sleek, slimline, clearly new, and obviously expensive. I wanted to touch it as much as I was terrified to.

Caught looking at the thing like it might bite me, Bane chuckled. "Do you want to have a look? I need to get my card." My lips parted, and my throat tightened as he placed the cushion and laptop on my lap. "Add whatever you want to the basket. You remember how to use one?" I winced. He wasn't being malicious, but it made me feel lesser, and my hackles rose. "I didn't mean it like that." Bane puffed out a frustrated breath. "I wasn't saying you couldn't, okay? I'm just assuming it's been a while since you were on a computer?" Bingo. I'd only had a few lessons on one in elementary school, and that felt like a lifetime ago.

"It's nothing to be ashamed of." A large hand wrapped around my knee and squeezed, reassuring me. I still couldn't unpick how it felt safe, natural even when Bane touched me, but when others did, it made me want to burn my skin off with acid. "I suck with them. Montoya—my partner—is always fixing my mess ups." Warmth infused his eyes as I tried out the keypad and looked at the screen. "Have a look through and pick what you want and add it to the basket. I'm going to grab my wallet and get us something to eat. Bacon, eggs, and toast sound good?"

Before I realized it, Bane left me alone as I scrolled through the site, trying to work out what I needed. Maybe I should start at what size I was? I had no idea. I didn't care if the stuff I picked was too big. Just to have something that was mine, and new, and clean, would be more than I'd ever really had. My hand shook as I scrolled through pages. Boxers or briefs? Pants or joggers? Hoodies or shirts? As for bedding, what did you need? What did a normal person have? I'd lived on a bare mattress with a threadbare blanket for so long, all this choice was too much. Scary.

What if I picked wrong and Bane didn't like it? *Don't be*

stupid. He wants you to be happy and comfortable. What was happy and comfortable? My life was about surviving each day while simultaneously praying it was my last. So being thrust into a situation where I could have whatever I wanted within reason scared the shit out of me.

The salty smell of bacon saturated the air that I was trying to breathe to remain calm. Calm? What was that? I shook my hands out, like that would stop them from shaking as adrenaline spiked through me. Sweat beaded along my hairline and dripped down the back of my neck. The bright screen flashed like it was mocking me, like it knew I didn't know what I was doing. My fingers trembled as I scrolled through the listings, and my palms grew slick. Pants, jeans, joggers, slacks, khakis. Sneakers, boots, high tops, chucks. Socks—black, white, sports, striped, dots, colored, plain. Hoodies—zipped or pull on, sweaters, cardigans, jackets. Tees, henleys, wife beaters, shirts.

So much choice, and that didn't even include the bedding options—sheets, blankets, throws, cushions. Why did people need so much stuff? With my heart pounding and blood whooshing in my ears, I clicked on a few things, the basket filling up at an alarming rate. All I could see was dollar signs spotting my vision, while guilt and fear coiled inside me. Would Bane be upset that I'd selected so much? Had I picked the wrong things?

Being under Dahlia's control was easy. Simple. She provided us with what we needed. If we had to dress a certain way, the clothes appeared for the appointment before disappearing again after. We were only permitted two changes of clothes that were our own. Most of it was hand-me-downs or leftovers from previous boys that had left. Even though we all knew "leaving" stood for something completely different.

Once I'd chosen clothing and bedding, I moved onto

shower stuff. Razors, antiperspirant, cologne, soap, shower gel, loofahs, shampoos, and skincare. What scent did I like? Sweet, woodsy, manly, strong and lasting, or light and fragrant? It hit me then that I didn't know who I was or what I liked. I'd never had the chance or opportunity to become my own person. I was molded into who people wanted me to be. Beaten down and shoved into a box. Controlled and forced to do things that no one would want to do willingly. I had to remember what I was. I couldn't let Bane's current kindness blind me to the truth. I was a hole. A body to be used.

I was nothing.

Forcing in a deep breath, I filtered through a barrage of memories of my childhood; the good, the bad, and the ugly, trying to prise out moments of happiness or scents I'd clung to that brought a modicum of warmth to the wasteland that was my soul to find out what I liked. The trouble with my line of work was that most scents made me want to bleach my nostrils and have my head examined. Every one was associated with despicable acts some john performed on me, or by the guards Dahlia employed who thought it was a great idea to sample the goods they protected. A hysterical laugh breached my lips as my brain latched on to that thought. Protect. They weren't keeping us safe; they were controlling and cruel, selfish and self serving. If they had a bad day, they kicked and fucked the shit out of us, whether or not we were willing.

They preferred it when we weren't.

Consent was a word people bandied around like it was a right. Since the day I was born, I'd had no rights or autonomy over my wellbeing or body. Others used me for their gain. First, it was foster carers looking for a quick buck to line their pockets and an innocent child to sink into. Then it was the drunks, the men in denial who drank themselves stupid at bars and couldn't bear to fuck their wives because they wanted "a sweet young piece of ass to ruin."

Later, at my lowest moment, starving and freezing in a back alley, came Dahlia. I'd been on the street for close to eighteen months by then and was on my last legs as the first frosts of winter coated the damp doorway I huddled in. I hadn't slept more than a couple of hours a night for months, thanks to fearing for my life, and hadn't eaten in nearly a week.

"Hello there, little guy." I blinked through the haziness in my vision to see an elegant lady looking down at me. Her dark hair was pulled back from her face, but a few soft strands framed her dark brown eyes. Blood-red lips curved in a soft smile as she lowered herself to my level. "Are you cold?" she asked softly, slowly extending her gloved hand towards me. Her thick fur coat shimmered as the icy wind whipped between the buildings. I could only imagine how warm she felt wrapped up in its softness while I sat there in stained wet jeans and a moldy jacket I'd pulled out of the dumpster outside the department store a few streets over.

I sneered at her as she patted my head like I was a lost puppy, hating the world and loathing her for showing me an ounce of empathy. I was freezing, my lips were numb, and my teeth chattered, but I clenched my jaw and refused to answer her.

"How about you come with me, hmm? I'll get you some clean, dry clothes and something to eat. I just want to help you out." Her minty breath fogged the air around us.

My eyes narrowed. No one ever did anything for nothing. But I couldn't find my voice, so instead, I wrapped my arms around me tighter and shrunk against the cold steel door behind me. Maybe if I ignored her, she'd go away. Even the volunteers that helped the homeless and vagrants on the street didn't stay this long. They dropped off food parcels and boxes of clothes, then left before the fights and bloodbaths ensued.

"Come now." Her gloved hand latched on to my arm and pulled. "Come on. Come with me. Let's get a hot meal in you and find you somewhere to sleep. I've got a pot roast on with mashed potatoes, and I might even have some chocolate cake left..." Her words filled my head with heavenly images, making my empty stomach ache. It had been so long. So, so long.

Tears pricked the backs of my eyes, and I sniffed back the snot running down my nose. I shouldn't do this. I didn't know her, but I was so desperate for food and warmth that the lessons I'd learned during my time on the streets vanished, leaving me vulnerable and exposed. My better judgment abandoned me, and I could feel myself caving, craving everything she'd said.

"What do you say?" She gave me a forceful tug and pulled me to my feet, my sneakers squelching in the puddle. "Here, let me look at you." She cupped my face, turning my head from side to side before lifting my chin and stroking my neck. "You're a pretty boy, aren't you? Half starved and frozen to the bone, but those eyes—they're my meal ticket. So, shall we go get you something to eat? Who knows, I might even find you a job so you can earn your keep."

I wish I knew then what I did now. I'd have screamed and kicked, spit and slapped and bitten her to get away. Dahlia was the devil, disguised as an angel, and she knew exactly how to manipulate me to get what she wanted. She did exactly what she said—fed me, cleaned me up, and gave me somewhere warm to sleep. She gave me a new beginning, and before I knew it, I owed her for everything she'd done for me.

"It'll only be this one time, River. My friend Jason is all alone and needs a little comfort." Her red lips lifted as she smiled, her voice saccharine and sweet. "You'll look after him, won't you? Keep him company while I go out, yes? I'll take it off the bill you've racked up over the last couple of months living here, eating my food and using my water and electricity."

That was the beginning of the end. She caught me in her web, and I had no way out. Jason wasn't a friend—he was a john, and my first. He turned into a regular until I got too big for his tastes, as he preferred them little, when they couldn't fight back. Fragile. Broken. Sweet. Innocent. I was his kryptonite, and he was the monster I could never escape.

"River? Are you done?"

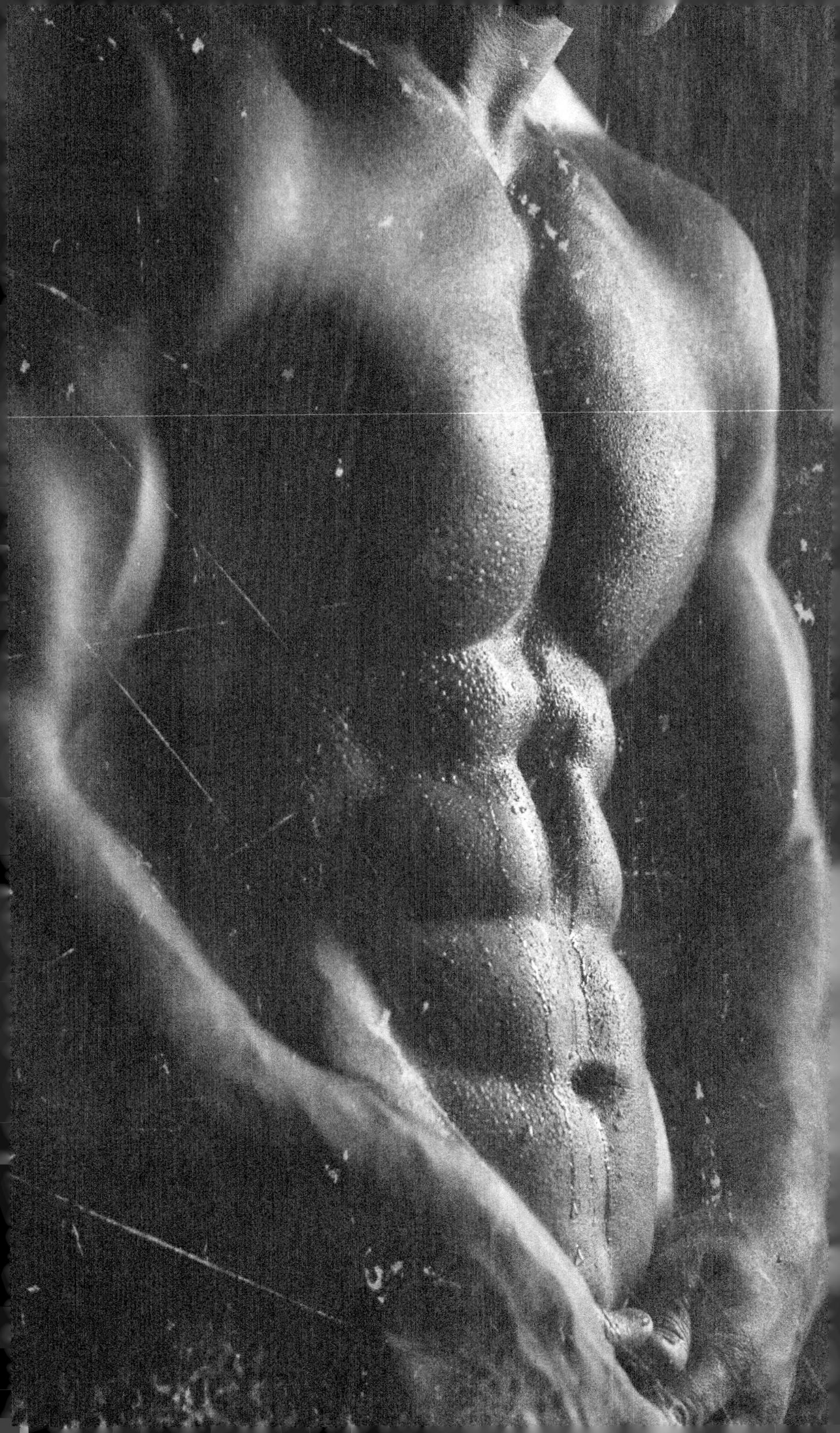

CHAPTER SEVEN
Bane

I finished plating up the eggs and bacon, stuck a couple of slices of buttered toast on the plates, and refilled the coffee cups. River seemed to like it on the stronger side. At least, I thought he did. He'd drunk the last one I made, and I was sure, with time, I'd be able to figure out what he actually liked. At the moment, he was compliant and going with the flow. He might have looked tough with his narrowed eyes and pinched lips, but he couldn't hide just how scared he was. I caught a moment when he thought I wasn't watching, and I saw the tremors that ran through him. How he flinched at every sound and hunched his shoulders up. He had a habit of picking the broken skin around his left thumb, an automatic gesture he probably wasn't aware of. How his ruined bottom lip scabbed and bled almost constantly.

In my line of work, you saw everything. Nothing

surprised me these days. Horrified, yes. I was exposed to the darkest, most depraved parts of humanity the average person could ignore and pretend didn't exist. But I saw it day in and day out. The training we'd received at the academy had been invaluable. We learned to show empathy but to never get invested. But everything with River was different. It might have been years since I'd last seen him, but I knew him, had spent time with him, had a relationship with him, even if we were just kids.

Being emotionally involved with a case of this nature was dangerous, but even Bower couldn't pry River from my cold, dead hands. He had ingrained himself in my memories. I felt his presence, his every breath. I didn't know if I'd survive this, but there was a part of me that knew I had to take care of him, to protect him from the horrors he'd lived through, the ones that had broken and molded him into the shell he was today. Whatever it took to help him, I would do.

With everything placed neatly on a tray, I headed through to the living room. I thought about eating at the breakfast bar or at the table, but River seemed to enjoy being wrapped up in the blankets I'd put on him last night. I wanted him to feel safe and comfortable, so we could just eat on the couch. Anything to help make it easier for him to acclimate to what his life would be like now. I knew I'd have questions to answer from Bower, although since agreeing to me having River here, I could see the cogs turning in his mind. My exposure was too great. He knew I was emotionally invested in him, and that was a weakness for both the case and the team, but the two of us were the best shot we had of cracking this case wide open.

"River, are you done?" I asked as I set the tray on the table and put his plate and cup out for him. "River?" The soft taps of the keys and the click of the mouse had stopped by the time I was plating up.

The hair on my arms stood on end as his breathing hitched. My heart froze, and my gut clenched as a wave of icy fear washed over me. When I glanced over my shoulder, River sat frozen, tears tracking down his pale cheeks, his eyes unfocused as if lost in memories. I grabbed the laptop off his lap, shoved it under the table, and kneeled at his feet, placing my hands on his knees.

"River? Can you hear me?" I gently increased the pressure on his knees, hoping it would snap him out of whatever he was trapped in, but nothing. "River?" I waved my hand in front of his eyes, hoping to trigger a response, a reflex, anything, but it was as if he was gone.

My heart sank. This was the second time in less than twenty-four hours that I'd lost him. I inhaled and exhaled in a steady rhythm, trying to calm myself down so I didn't startle or accidentally hurt him. I was stronger than most. Montoya liked to joke that I didn't know my own strength, especially in a heightened emotional state. That edge of fear was enough to grant me the clarity I needed.

River was like a statue carved from ice. Frozen perfection. My hands coasted up his arms that were still in my jacket that hung off his smaller frame. He vibrated under my touch like high voltage electricity flowed through his veins. The tendons in his neck strained as he fought a battle I couldn't see.

My large hands cupped the cool skin of his cheeks, and I wiped away his tears with my thumbs as they fell. "River," I exhaled. "You're okay. You're here with me. Nothing can hurt you here." I whispered words of encouragement and platitudes until my knees burned and turned numb. Until the strength it took to hold my arms still, pushed my limits. Slowly but surely, I felt the layers of ice thaw, and his body became pliant under my touch. My heart skipped a beat when he leaned into me, his shallow breaths evening out and his jaw unclenching.

Deep evergreen eyes fluttered, narrowed, and eventually focused on me. River licked his wet lips, tasting his salty tears and shuddered. His lips parted and formed shapes like he wanted to say something, but nothing would come. But the whole time he leaned into me like I was the guide rope leading him out of the darkness and back into the light.

The tip of his tongue touched his top lip, the light pink a contrast to the darker red of his lips. I swallowed, watching intently, hypnotized as it wet the stretched, chapped skin. My breath caught in the back of my throat when he mouthed *thank you*.

Emotion burned the back of my eyes, and goosebumps littered my skin. I cleared my throat and the ball of emotion that was lodged in it. "I'll do anything for you." My voice was strained and thick, but I meant every word. It was a promise. A vow. One I'd hold on to until my last breath.

River's breath faltered, and if I wasn't in such proximity to him, I would have missed the way his eyes dropped to my mouth. The intensity of his gaze made the world freeze for a second. My heart stammered and thoughts I had no right to think assaulted my mind. What would it be like to pull him into me? To tease and taste his full lips? To give in to this connection there was between us? It was more than traumas and shared past.

It could be so much more. If only...but no, I couldn't. There was a major imbalance in the power dynamic between us. River trusted me to care for and protect him, and I refused to take advantage of his fragile situation. If things were different when we'd reconnected, then maybe. But as it stood now, it would only hurt him more, and I'd never forgive myself if I hurt him. I had to protect him from everyone that wanted to hurt him—even myself.

Shaking my head, I dropped my hands like touching him had burned me. Pain lanced across his face, and the walls that he'd dropped quickly rebuilt, strengthened with adamantium as I pulled away and stood. Turning to face the table, I squeezed my hands into fists to hide the fact they were shaking with fear, with want. With the need to touch him and pull him back into my arms.

"Why don't you go freshen up," I croaked, feeling raw as I tried to lock down these inappropriate thoughts and feelings. "The bathroom is just down the hall, third door on the right." River pushed up from the sofa, blankets pooling at his feet. The thud they made when they hit the floor felt like a nail in the coffin of what could have been. "I'll get you a clean change of clothes and stick it on the counter in there."

I didn't hear him leave. He moved like a ghost on light feet, probably trained to not be seen or heard. But I felt him go, like he'd taken half of me with him.

"Fuck!" I grunted and ground the heels of my hands into my burning eyes. "Get your shit together, Bane. This isn't you. It can't be." I coached myself through the turmoil and grabbed the plates, sticking them in the oven to keep warm. I'm sure if I was thinking rationally, I'd have realized it would have been better to toss the cold food and start again after he had a shower, but fuck if my mind was working right now.

By the time I reached the hallway, I could hear the shower running. Compartmentalize. Control. Care. The words ran through my head as I took the stairs three at a time up to my room and threw the door open. I grabbed a tee and another pair of boxers and sweats for River, not sparing a glance at the door of what would become his room just across the hall from mine. Was it tempting fate? Maybe, but I was strong. Strong enough to ignore the way his shattered green orbs called to me.

I could do this. I could. I had to. There was no other option, because I refused to hand River's care or safety over to anyone else. I hadn't told him the full story when we left the station yesterday, which was maybe for the best because Montoya confirmed my worst fears when she updated me while frying the bacon. River's friends were gone, taken from the hostel we'd placed them in during the night.

Around one a.m., firefighters evacuated the building after a fire broke out. Preliminary reports hinted at arson, as they found an accelerant in the external electrical box where the fire originated. After a final headcount, it was determined that Dale, Max, and Gabe were gone. CCTV was no help, as it had mysteriously malfunctioned in the surrounding blocks.

You didn't need to be a genius to work out there was a lot more going on than a simple fire. River now had a target on his back, one bigger than the one he already had when we took him into custody. I needed to speak with Bower to arrange for someone to watch the house and check over my security system.

After leaving the clothes on the counter as promised, I put a load of wash on, adding my uniform to it before slipping on the jeans and hoodie I'd left in the dryer the day before. Back in the kitchen, I busied myself with tossing out the rubbery eggs and started on a fresh batch. The butter sizzled in the pan as I cracked and stirred the eggs in. Focusing on small, simple tasks helped me regain control over my wandering thoughts so I could approach everything logically. That's what I needed to do right now—take it one logical step at a time.

The sound of a chair scraping on the tiled floor clued me in to River's arrival, along with the cloud of steam that followed him in. I glanced over my shoulder, loving the sight of him in my clothes far more than I should. He sat with his head in his hands, drops of water sliding down the still damp dark strands of hair covering his face as he stared at the countertop.

"Here." I slid a fresh plate across the counter, only turning to look at him fully when I asked, "Coffee or orange juice?" I held both in my hands as I waited for him to look up at me, and when he did, my heart swooped in my chest.

River tilted his head to the side and chewed on his bottom lip, indecision written all over his face. I huffed a laugh and set the coffee down next to his plate. "How about both?" A smile transformed his features before he dropped his head to look intently at his steaming plate of food.

After plating my breakfast and grabbing cutlery, we ate in near silence. River inhaled his in the time it took me to eat a slice of toast. I chuckled when he pushed his plate away and rubbed his stomach. Without thinking, I pushed my plate across to him and nodded when he glanced up at me through his thick lashes.

"Have at it. I'm good." I swallowed the last mouthful of coffee, rinsed my cup, and set it in the sink. "Are you finished adding stuff to the basket?" River hummed around a forkful of bacon, refusing to meet my eyes. But nothing he did could hide the blush staining his cheeks. "Cool. I'll get it ordered now."

River nodded, focusing on his food as I headed to the living room, the sound of cutlery against porcelain the only sound in my home. I hoped one day it would be filled with the sound of River's voice, his laugh, his dreams. Today was not that day, but I was a patient man. I settled on the couch and opened the laptop, intrigued by what he'd selected, and quietly hoping it would give me insight into who he was and what he liked.

That excitement died when I saw what he had added to the basket. It was all black, and consisted only of the bare necessities. One pair of sneakers and boots. Two pairs of jeans and sweats. A couple of tees, a henley, and a hoodie. A black biker jacket that made me wonder once again if he'd like going out on my bike, but now wasn't the time to approach anything like that. River needed to trust me, to feel safe with me before I took him out on my Hammerhead. The more I worked through his basket, the tighter my chest felt. Surely he needed more than two of everything. One set to wear, and one to wash?

"He can always get more," I muttered as I filled in the payment details and selected the option to pick it up in store. While that was processing, I grabbed my phone and chuckled when I saw a text from Montoya.

MONTOYA

I can't believe you get to have a week away from this shit!!!

ME

It's only to help River acclimate and make sure he's safe here, especially after the other guys from the raid are now MIA.

ME

The target on his back just got bigger.

MONTOYA

I know! I'll be taking one of the first stake out shifts tonight. Don't panic, we'll keep your boy safe.

ME

That's good to know, but I need a favor.

MONTOYA

Dare I ask?

I snickered as I pictured her rolling her eyes at me. I grinned down at my phone as I typed.

> ME
>
> I need you to pick up an order for me from Walmart. I got River to order some clothes and bits considering he has nothing and my stuff drowns him.

> MONTOYA
>
> I can only imagine! You're a giant among men 😂

> MONTOYA
>
> Sure, no probs. Let me know the deets and I'll drop it all off later.

> ME
>
> Thanks, M

> MONTOYA
>
> Fuck off 😂 you know I've got your back.

I did. She was the best partner I could have asked for, but she was more than that—she was my friend. We confided in each other about so much, and most days, it felt like it was us against the world when we walked into the station. But I wasn't sure I could tell her about these feelings I'd been having. I didn't want to see disapproval in her eyes, because I wanted her support, always. She was a part of my life, and I didn't want to jeopardize our working relationship or friendship.

My eyes flicked up to the screen, confirming the payment had gone through. I quickly confirmed the collection time with Montoya, then slipped my phone into my pocket and headed back into the kitchen to load the dishwasher.

River was clutching his coffee mug, looking out the window to the backyard beyond it. "You can sit out there if you want for a bit, or I could show you where everything is in your room? Montoya is going to pick up your order and drop it over later so you can make it into your space." River tilted his head to the side to show he was listening, but seemed thoroughly consumed with the outside world. "Whatever you want, really."

Not knowing what else to say, I rinsed the empty plates and loaded the dishwasher before searching my junk drawer for a notepad and pen. "Here." I placed them on the counter for him. "Did you want another coffee? Juice? Water?"

Shaking his head, River got up, rounded the counter, and rinsed his cup and glass before sticking them in the dishwasher while I wrung my hands, unsure what to do next. I wanted to hug him, but this wasn't about me. As if River could read my mind or my sheer lack of direction, he scribbled on the notepad.

Can I see my room?

"Oh sure, follow me." He did, following me into the living room, where I grabbed the blankets and headed upstairs. It was unnerving how silently he moved around. The stairs that creaked under my weight stayed silent under his. I cleared my throat. "This one is mine," I said, pointing at the door to the right. "And this one is yours. There are two more at the other end, but they're empty." I shrugged when River's eyes widened. "It's not like I have anyone else to visit me, no family or anything."

River scribbled on his notepad.

Partner?

"Montoya is my partner. You met her at the station."
Exhaling heavily, River started writing again.

Girlfriend?

A deep laugh punched its way out of me. "Good god, no. She's a friend. More like the little sister I lost, and the closest thing to family I have. I have..." I licked my lips, feeling seriously confused by his line of questioning. "I'm not in a relationship." My shoulders slumped. "I've never really..." I spread my hands wide. "Never really had any long-term relationships or anything."

A look flashed across his face that I couldn't decipher before he nodded, accepting my response. Opening his door, I gestured for him to go in first and shuffled in behind him, plopping the blankets down on the bed.

"The sheets on the bed are clean, but as you can see, it's not much." I opened the door to the bathroom and explained what was in there, and pointed out the closet and how to work the TV. "I know it's not much. You deserve so much more." My words caught in my throat, emotion threatening to drown me as the memory of him explaining how he'd been living came forward. Here was me saying a room of his own with a queen bed and hot running water wasn't much when it was a million miles away from what he'd had.

My eyes flew open when River's cool fingers wrapped around my wrist, a watery smile on his face, and his deep green forest eyes glassy. Releasing my arm, he passed me the notepad.

This means more than I can even say.

"It's the least I could do, Riv." I wanted to say so much more—about how I wanted to take care of him and show him how much he deserved to be happy, but a yawn split his face. "Do you want to come back downstairs while I make some calls, or do you want to watch TV and chill?"

Rivers' eyes ping-ponged all over the room before settling on the bed. He ran his hand over the fitted cotton sheet and pulled the pillow into his chest, squeezing it. A vise tightened around my chest at the small childlike gesture. He climbed onto the bed, piled up the pillows in the middle, and pulled the blankets up to his chest.

"Here." That seemed to be my favorite word at the moment. I passed him the remote, sitting on the edge of the bed as I walked him through how to work the old TV. After explaining Netflix and Prime, I closed the blind and ran downstairs to grab him a bottle of water.

"I'll be downstairs if you need anything." River regarded me with heavy-lidded eyes and nodded. The TV drew his attention away from me as he surfed through the offerings on Netflix, slowly sinking deeper under his pile of blankets. I slipped from the room unnoticed.

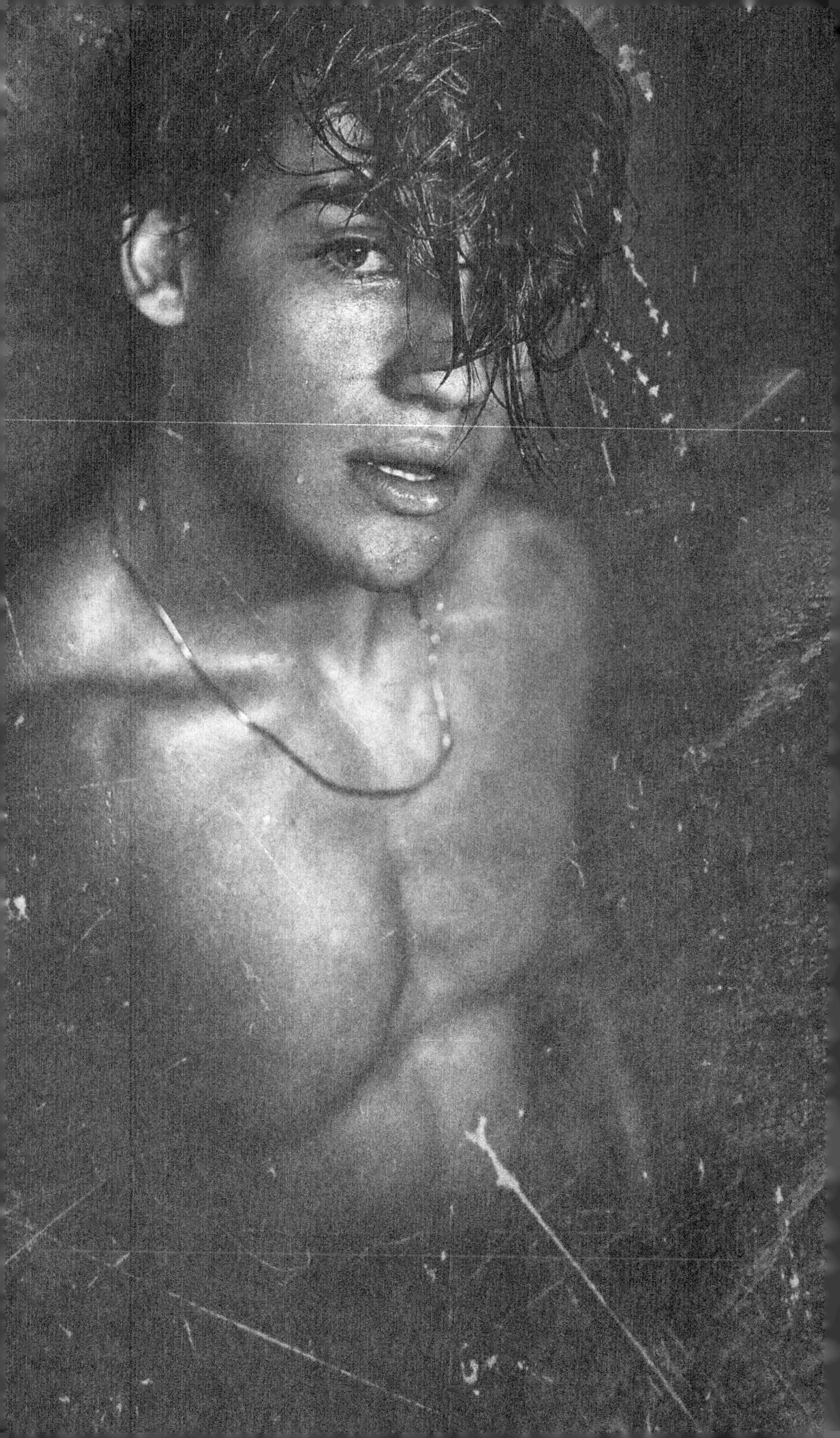

CHAPTER EIGHT
River

I jolted awake to the sound of a husky feminine laugh echoing through the quiet house. I pushed the lingering effects of sleep away, scrubbing a hand down my face. The door to my room was closed, not open like I remembered. The floor was now littered with several bags and packages. Stretching out the tight muscles in my back, I rolled my shoulders and cracked out the kink in my neck.

Cool stale air of what was now my room hit me as I kicked off the blankets, making me shudder. The chilly wooden floor was a shock to the system as I shuffled my way across to the bags someone had left while I was sleeping. The TV was playing something I have no recollection of selecting. The actor with dark messy hair was hot, but his icy blue eyes made me think of other more perfect blue-brown orbs that called to a part of me I'd locked away in fantasies.

The sheer amount of bags and boxes took my breath away. I didn't remember ordering this much stuff. But as I carried them over to the bed, I realized I hadn't. One small parcel caught my eye. It was the size of a small book, wrapped in black paper with a rainbow-colored bow. I set it aside for later, even though I was itching to know what was inside. Rifling through the bags, I pulled out the pants and tops I'd ordered, along with the bedding and scent-free toiletries, but that still left a number of bags that must have been brought up here by mistake.

My jaw clenched tight enough to crack my teeth when that husky laugh reached my ears again. I wanted to slam the door shut and hide away, overwhelmed by the feelings that surged inside of me. I wanted to storm down there and lay my claim on the only person who'd ever made me feel anything other than apathy for myself.

He was mine, goddamn it. *Mine.*

But he wasn't, not really. Nothing ever was. Shaking my head, I pushed those possessive thoughts away because what right did I have to them when all Bane had shown me was kindness? And platonic kindness at that.

I tried on the clothes I'd ordered to make sure they fit, which they did, even if they were a little loose. But they were clean and new and mine. It was strange having more than two outfits and somewhere to put them that was bigger than a single moldy drawer. I didn't really know what to put where, so I settled on pants and underwear in the drawers below the TV and shirts in the closet.

The bathroom was as intimidating as it was gorgeous. Clean marble tiles sparkled in the bright light, while a large vanity set under an unbroken mirror dominated one wall. I stuffed the towel and toiletries I didn't immediately need into one of its drawers. The tub wasn't cracked or lined with mold and was actually big enough for me to soak in. I'd never learned to swim, but I wondered what it would be like to float in it, my body completely suspended. It was like a dream, or maybe I was in an episode of The Twilight Zone —I couldn't decide which. But it made that empty cavity inside me feel less hollow, and that was a dangerous, dangerous thing, because it made me ache for things that could never be real.

This isn't permanent. You're not wanted here, I reminded myself, hating reality as much as I clung to it. I was here because I was useful, not because Bane wanted or cared for me. I was helping with the case. That's why he needed me, why he was keeping me close. Once they had what they wanted, knew everything I knew—which, to be honest, wasn't a lot—they'd send me on my way without a backward glance. There was no point in allowing any of these delusional thoughts or feelings running rampant through me to take root.

The shiny tap turned with ease, no pipes clanking or groaning, just clear fresh water spilling from the faucet. I splashed my face with cold water, washing away the beads of sweat that had covered my skin and breathed deeply, clutching the edges of the counter until my knuckles turned white. "You've got this," I mouthed. My reflection looked back at me, one I tried to ignore for years because I didn't know the person who stared back at me.

My skin was pale, and dark shadows bloomed under my empty flat eyes. I was skinny, gaunt, and underdeveloped for my age. I might have looked like a tired eighteen-year-old, but my eyes whispered secrets of the horrors I'd endured like they were etched into the flecks of green. My dark black hair was a matted riot, with wayward strands stuck across my forehead. I ran my fingers through the wilderness on my head and slicked it back before pulling the hood of my top over my head, feeling the white walls closing in around me. I needed to get out of this perfect space that was the opposite of everything I was before I tainted it.

My feet slipped into the black boots I'd found. The distressed leather comforted me, reminding me that even new things weren't perfect. I grabbed the bags that didn't belong to me, ignoring the box wrapped in black paper on the bed, and headed downstairs. My senses were heightened after a lifetime of waiting for someone to jump me any second.

"How's it going?" The husky voice was low, but I heard it clearly. "It can't be easy on you or him." My teeth clenched, biting down on my tongue until I tasted blood.

"It'll take time for him to trust me, Montoya." Bane sighed. I slipped down the hallway on silent feet and flattened my back against the wall. She perched on a stool and leaned across the counter, her hand resting on his forearm. It was a tender gesture, intimate in a way I hated. "It's not like I can make him tell me anything." Bane winced and dug the heel of his hand into his eyes. "Or that one night's sleep will change everything he's been through."

My heart panged as his voice broke and pain tightened his eyes. I'd told Bane the bare minimum back at the station. I'd answered his question, yes, but in the simplest way. If he had an inkling of what I had been through, it would kill him. And I never wanted him to hurt because of me. He was too good, too damn pure for someone like me.

"I know. Trust me, I know, but what he knows could crack this wide open." Montoya leaned forward, ass rising from the stool as she pushed into his personal space. Bane's breath caught in his throat, Adam's apple bobbing in his throat. My hands clenched involuntarily, the paper bags crunching loudly as emotions raged inside me, making it feel like I was splintering to pieces.

"That's... he's not. Not just... Fuck! I know, but..."

I couldn't listen to this anymore, to be reminded no one really wanted me here. I stormed into the kitchen and dumped the bags on the counter next to the Latina beauty with her thick, glossy black hair in a messy bun on the top of her pretty little head.

"Hey there, cutie." Montoya smiled softly at me and sat back in her seat. I met her deep amber eyes with a glare and turned to Bane, pointing at the bags.

He looked slightly dazed as he leaned across the counter, his eyes running over my body in my new—thanks to him—clothes. A small smile flickered at the corners of his mouth. "They look good. Sleep well?"

I rolled my eyes, crossed my arms over my chest, and huffed, nodding at the bags with agitation eating away at my insides. They looked at the bags, then at each other, like they were having a silent conversation, then back at me.

Bane cleared his throat and peered into the bags, confusion marring his beautiful features. "They're for you," he said, so simply my heart skipped a beat.

My arms fell to my sides, hands clenched into tight fists while my eyes darted around, looking for a pen. I chewed my cracked bottom lip but couldn't see anything past the beauty sitting at the counter making freaking heart eyes at Bane.

"Here." Montoya passed me a pen from her pocket and pulled out a small flip pad. She watched me intently, like she could chip away at my walls and see every thought that ran through my head. Nervous energy flooded me, making me jittery. The pen slipped through my sweat-slicked fingers.

I didn't order them.

Releasing a heavy exhale, Bane's shoulder slumped. "I know, but you...I..." He shook his head. "I thought you might like some more stuff. You barely selected anything. I wanted you to have more options, to feel at home here. I want you to make this your home. Y-you deserve it."

I scoffed.

No!

"But..." Bane's voice pleaded with me. The behemoth of a man looked crestfallen, his eyes dropping to the mug he twisted between his fingers rather than continue looking at me. I didn't know how to explain to him I felt so goddamn guilty about uprooting his life like this, relying on him for everything when I had nothing to give him back.

No! I can't pay for what I've got. So no, keep your money.

I slapped the pad down on the counter, stomped past the pair of them, and opened the sliding door onto the back deck. Tears pricked the back of my eyes as I flushed hot and cold. Emotions I didn't understand pulsed beneath my skin. I wanted to throw myself into Bane's big thick arms, to scream at him for giving me stuff I couldn't pay for. I wanted to cry because I knew everything came with a price, and the clock was ticking.

I wanted to be worthy of his kindness. Of his love, time, and attention. But I wasn't. I was like a cancer, slowly infecting him until I took over his life and drained him of everything that made him so perfectly perfect. I broke everything I touched, and I couldn't stand to ruin him.

The door slammed shut behind me as a gust of wind whipped across the deck, cold and biting, but not as ferocious as my heart. The backyard was large and laid mainly to lawn beyond the deck. I headed down the steps as a light misting rain fell. The pale gray clouds churned above my head, pulling in darker shades that gave the afternoon an ominous feeling. I trudged through the knee-length grass, heading as far away from the perfection of the house and the intimate scene in the kitchen that I just couldn't process.

The weight of Bane's gaze seared into my back with every step I took, but I ignored every spark it lit in me. The fence at the far end of the lawn was a simple post and rail, not like the tight featheredge one that ran along the sides, offering a sense of seclusion and privacy. There was a small gate in the middle of it, leading to a wooded area, but it was what lay farther back that piqued my interest. A tall weeping willow towered over the shrubby trees that surrounded it, its long tresses swaying in the building wind. Twigs and dead leaves crunched under my boots like brittle bones as I headed toward it. The gate caught on a nasty gust of wind and latched itself closed behind me. Absentmindedly, I picked at the broken skin around my left thumbnail as I settled into the hollow bow and pulled my knees up to my chest. I finally felt like I could breathe.

I'd never experienced such intense emotions as I had since I'd woken up. It had been my mission to keep everything locked down for so long that people had accused me of being ice cold. But really, it was just self preservation at its finest. Everything was beyond overwhelming, and I didn't know how to process it all. It had been almost as long since I'd been around nature and able to enjoy it.

Was this what heaven felt like? The icy wind whipped

against my cheeks, and water misted the air. The woods smelled of damp earth and life. Freedom. Not four walls and a cage. It was like free-falling with no end in sight. It was exhausting and exhilarating. I tipped my head back and allowed my eyes to fall closed, praying it would quiet the noise in my head.

Something cold and wet nudged my hand as it hung over my knee, making me snort awake. I blinked rapidly just as something warm and rough ran up my finger, making me flinch. A soft yip and a solid weight butting into my leg made my lips twitch. I looked down at my accosted finger and battered leg to see a golden puppy chewing on the digit. Its little tail flicked from side to side at warp speed, and its big dark eyes looked like pools of happiness.

"Hey there, little one," I whispered, each word grating as my muscles struggled to form them. The little pup tilted its head to the side like it was listening intently to me, something I doubted very much. I stretched my legs out in front of me, and the pup took it as an invitation to sit on my lap and shuffle around.

"Cooper?" The voice carried on the wind, making my little friend's ears prick and his head dart in that direction before knocking on my hand, demanding scratches.

I chuckled. "You're trouble." I swear the little monster winked at me. His tongue hung out the side of his mouth as he grinned.

"For fuck's sake, Cooper, where are you?"

"Someone's looking for you." Cooper tilted his head again, then lurched up so his paws were on my shoulders and licked my face. "Oh my god!" I choked on a laugh as his tongue invaded my mouth. "Yuck." I wiped off his slobber with the back of my hand.

"Cooper, come on, bud. Please?"

Cooper yipped right next to my ear in answer to his

owner, but refused to move and nuzzled his head against mine. I should have been freaking out that an unknown person was coming toward me. I could feel my hackles rising, the air thickening around me, but this little obnoxious bundle in my lap kept it at bay.

"Cooper?" He yipped again, his tail nothing but a blur. "Cooper! What have I told you about—" A young guy appeared around the tree and fell to his knees at my feet. His bright blue eyes crinkled as a smile lit up his concerned face. "Oh my god, I'm so sorry about him," the guy started and slipped a collar and leash onto Cooper as I held his wriggling body still.

I nodded along as he kept talking, telling me that Cooper was a Houdini-level escape artist, and nothing he did to his backyard could keep him in. It turned out Colton fostered pets when the local shelter was overcrowded. He currently had Cooper, a six-month-old lab; Terry, the chihuahua; and Talulah and Daphne, French bulldog sisters. It sounded manic, but his enthusiasm was as infectious as Cooper's licks.

"You should come over and meet them. Cooper loves you, and I bet the others will too. Hey, maybe you could adopt one of them?"

"What the hell is going on here?" Bane growled, and I shuddered at the low, menacing tone of his voice. My heart thundered in my chest, but I couldn't work out if it was fear or something else. My fingers sunk into Cooper's coat as I clung to him. Bane bent over, chest heaving, hands braced on his knees. "Oh shit. Hey, Colton."

"Hey, Bane. You okay there, big guy?" Colton's eyes lit with hunger, and it was my turn to growl—although rather pathetically. I made no sound, only choked on the spit in my mouth as my chest rumbled and ended up hacking up a lung.

Colton and Bane moved together, both lunging towards me, bodies towering over me like night and day. In a split second of fear, I shoved Cooper off my lap, threw myself on the ground, and curled into the fetal position. Hot tears tracked down my cheeks, dripping onto the damp ground. I squeezed my eyes shut like I did when I was a child. If I couldn't see the thing that scared me, it wasn't there. It wasn't real. It couldn't hurt me.

"Oh fuck. Shit! Did I? Was it me?" Colton's frantic voice sounded like it came from the other end of a really long, echoey tunnel. I tried to breathe, but there was a weight on my chest that made it impossible.

"No. No, just step back slowly, okay? Give him some space." Bane sounded calm and controlled, but still so far away. I wanted to reach out for him and anchor myself to him, but I couldn't move. "Hey, Riv? It's just me, okay? Colton's gone. I'm going to bring you back to the house where it's safe. Where you're safe. I'm sorry I didn't come out sooner," he whispered against the shell of my ear as his arms scooped me up and pulled me into his chest.

His heart beat frantically like an echo of mine as he held me tightly against him like I was something precious. Twigs and leaves crunched under his feet, but that soon gave way to the squelch of the lawn as we headed back to the house. "Can you pull your hood over your face? The rain has picked up since you've been out here, and I don't want you to drown." He snorted at what he said. "I mean, I won't let you drown, but I don't have a jacket on or anything to cover you with, and I don't want you to be uncomfortable."

I nodded stiffly against his muscled chest and pulled my hood down as I buried my face into his well-developed pectorals. His usual cedarwood and leather scent entwined with fresh rain and damp wood. It reminded me of the past, of hiding in the trees when we played hide and seek. Unlike the other kids at Mrs. Wilkinson's, Bane and I didn't need to talk. He accepted me as I was and didn't try to change me or call me names because I preferred not to talk. It took over a year before I started talking to him back then. Little did I know he'd give me the most amazing year of my life.

The sliding door slammed shut behind us. Bane had somehow opened and closed it without dropping me. The man had muscles carved from adamantium; his hold on me unwavering. His shoes smacked into the wall as he kicked them off before carrying me back to the room he claimed was mine.

"Stay here," he muttered as he set me down on the edge of the bed. The warmth of the house caused a violent shiver to roll through me as the cold fabric of my hoodie clung to me. I sat there, teeth chattering, as he headed into the en suite. Bane hummed softly as he turned on the taps for the tub. "I got you some bath salts and stuff to help you relax." I dipped my head like he could see me and wrapped my arms around myself.

My eyes caught on the black wrapped box with the rainbow bow. It was the most colorful thing in this room and seemed to glitter under the glow of the lamplight. My fingers itched to touch it. I'd always been inquisitive, but I wasn't that naïve child anymore. I'd learned long ago not to touch things that didn't belong to me.

"Open it." I jumped when Bane's voice came from beside me. My gaze shot to his, but it was his body that stole my breath. Water droplets slid down his temples, looking like diamond fractals as they caught on the thick five o'clock shadow on his jaw. I licked my lips as my eyes dropped lower to where the wet fabric of his tee clung to the defined muscles of his shoulders and pecs. His nipples were hard buds, fighting against the fabric suctioned to them. I could count each and every one of his eight abs, the ridges and grooves in high definition. I wanted to touch him in a way I'd never wanted to touch another person.

It was a mindfuck to want someone with the latent raw power to destroy me. Bane was dangerous in more ways than one. Physically, he could overpower me with one hand, but emotionally, he could devastate me. I'd never survive him. The air thickened, and the temperature seemed to rise until it felt almost impossible to breathe as we remained focused on each other, not saying a word. His chest rose and fell with heavy labored inhales that matched the ones I forced in and out of my nose. His scent was heavy, enticing, and I could taste it on my tongue.

"River." Bane's gravelly voice was like a physical caress that started at my toes and flushed me with heat all the way to my fingertips. My tongue darted out and wet my lip, his hypnotizing eyes tracking the movement. Bane moved forward, completely unaware of his body's actions until he was crouched down right in front of me. He raised my chin with two fingers. "River." I shuddered and my eyes fluttered closed as his minty breath ghosted over mine. "Open your gift."

When he stepped back, it felt like I'd been thrown in a vat of ice. Goosebumps prickled across my skin. Bane cleared his throat, pulled my hand out so it was facing palm up, and placed the black present on it.

"Open it while I check on your bath."

I weighed it, trying to work out what it was. It took me a second to realize my hand was shaking, and my heart was working its way up my throat. I swallowed it down, steeling myself as I pulled on the shimmering rainbow bow and carefully pulled the tape off. I was left staring at a white box that said iPhone 16 on it.

"Do you like it?" Bane asked softly as he knelt in front of me once again and carefully took the box from my hand and opened it. He pulled out a beautiful teal phone and flipped it over in his grasp so I could see the front and back. "I've added my number and desk direct line to it." I blinked up at him through water logged eyes. "I thought it would be easier for you than writing all the time. It also means you can reach me when I have to head back to the station."

There you go. What more proof did you need? He's going to leave you. Just like everyone does.

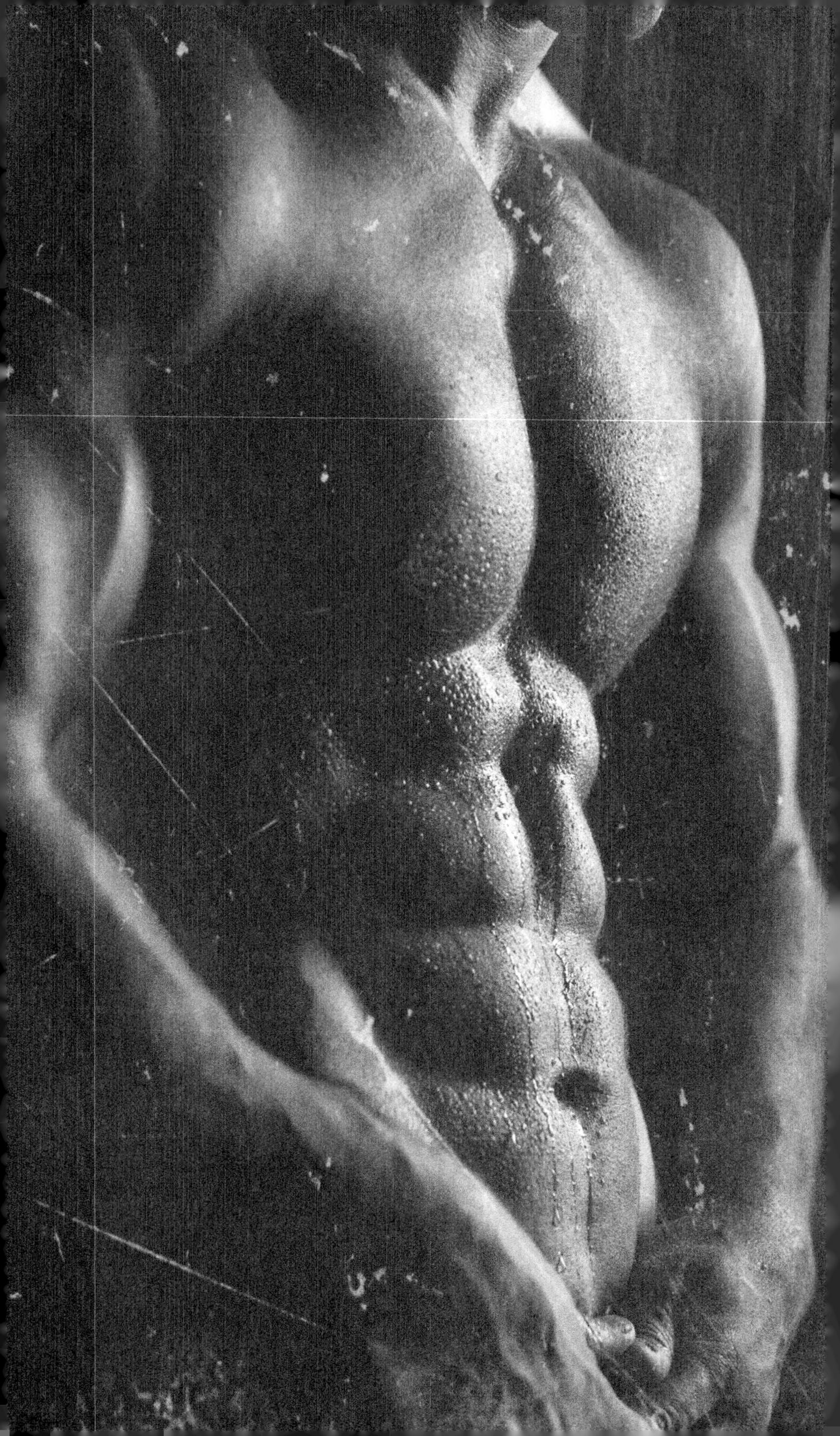

CHAPTER NINE
Bane

I'd always been conscious of my size. Being six foot five, broad shouldered, and covered in tattoos, I cut a rather intimidating form that saw more than one person cross the street on a dark night. Not to mention the color of my skin or the fact I had one blue eye and one nearly almost black—all things that made me uniquely me also cemented me as something different from what people conventionally accepted as normal. I'd always made it a priority to not take up too much room, to not be too outspoken, and to keep my temper under control at all times.

It'd been two days since I'd run into the yard in a blind panic because a storm was drawing in, and River had disappeared into the woods my house backed onto and hadn't returned after two hours. I couldn't help but feel like my carefully crafted control was slipping through my fingers. I was slowly unraveling, stuck pacing my living room, held captive by the boy who refused to leave his room.

Every inch of my house sparkled. It was never messy; everything was always in its place, but every surface that could shine did. I'd even given my bike a spit and polish. The stylish black and chrome bodywork gleamed more than it did the day I bought it.

My shoes squeaked on the floor as I paced in front of the fireplace, trying to work out how to bridge the crater that separated River and me. I had thought that even though we'd just found each other again, that our shared past was enough to build from. That it was enough of a foundation for River to trust me and allow me to help him, but it seemed things were more tenuous than I thought.

God, all I wanted to do was help him heal. Help him realize he was so much more than he thought, than what he'd been conditioned to believe. To prove to him I cared for him beyond the boundaries of the case he was helping with and to show him he mattered to me. But how could I do any of that when he wouldn't unlock his door or reply to my messages? I felt like a fool for giving him the key to his room, even if it was under the advice of my therapist.

Joelle had been there to support me since I'd given in to Martha Hendrix's demands just before I started college. She'd preached at me the virtues of therapy since they'd adopted me, telling me I had to work through my past and that I couldn't keep running from it, allowing it to control me. And as the child they'd adopted to replace the son they lost, I'd been drowning in survivor's guilt. Not just for living when my family died, but because I was living the life their son should have been.

I'd never chosen to fight, but life had thrown me in the pit and dared me to survive. So that's what I did. I got up every day and fought. My life might not have been pretty, but I was still here. I just didn't know if I could manage another twenty-four hours of silence from River. That fight, that need to survive, had shifted its focus from my life onto his, and as hard as it was to accept, I knew I couldn't control another person.

Instead of allowing everything in my mind to run riot and dredge up issues with myself that I'd spent years dealing with, I did the only thing that seemed logical and picked up my phone to speak with the woman who had been a constant source of support.

"Hello, Jacob. How are you today?"

"Hi, Joelle. Do you have a few minutes to talk?"

"For you, Jacob, always." Her voice was smooth like molasses, and it immediately calmed me enough so I wasn't climbing the walls. "What's going on that made you reach out to me before our appointment next week?"

I sighed and collapsed onto the couch. "I... um... did what you said and gave River the key to his room after I spoke to you."

"I see," she said softly. "And how is that going?"

"Well." I huffed out an exasperated breath. "The last time I saw or spoke to him was the night I gave him the key."

"And how does that make you feel?"

"Like I'm going crazy, if I'm honest."

"That's understandable. Tell me why."

I cleared my throat as I tried to think of a way to bring order to the feelings that were running rampant inside me without sounding like I was as close to the edge as I was. "He's locked himself in that room since the moment I closed the door."

"Go on."

"I'm really worried about him and how he's coping with everything. It must be a complete mindfuck going from the life he was living to being here. I'm concerned he's not eating or drinking, but if I spend another night sleeping on the floor outside his room, I'm afraid my body will hate me more than it already does. Who knew wooden floors were so unforgiving?" I chuckled uneasily and ran my hand over my face, feeling the coarse stubble that was closer to resembling a full beard.

"Who knew, indeed?" Joelle hummed under her breath. I could hear the tapping of keys before she came back to me. "Do you understand what you've given River?"

"Uh, no?"

"You've given him something he has probably never had before in his life—control. He was in foster care since he was a baby, correct?"

"Yes."

"Then he ran away when he was twelve?" I made an affirmative noise in the back of my throat. "So it's safe to assume that he's never had autonomy over his body or a space that is his and his alone."

"Sure. He alluded to that much. When we were at Mrs. Wilkinson's, we roomed with three or four other boys. But he's shutting me out, and all I want to do is help him."

"Try not to look at it as River shutting you out, because that's as far from the truth as you can get. You've pulled him from the only life he's ever known and thrust him into a completely new space with someone he doesn't know—"

"He knows me, though." My fingers dug into my thigh as I became more agitated.

"No, Jacob. He knew you. He doesn't know you now. Yes, you have history, but he doesn't know the man you have become. He probably feels like the only reason he is there is to help with the case, but once he's served that purpose, he'll be on his own again. To be frank, he's likely scared and uncertain about everything that's going on, not considering the trauma he's dealing with."

"What?! No! That's so far from the truth."

"Does he know that's how you feel though?"

"I mean. Well, yes? I think?"

"Jacob, unless you have told him that staying with you isn't a conditional offer, then he will assume it is. So while it might frustrate you that he has, as you put it, 'locked himself away,' that's not how he sees it. River is merely setting boundaries in place to protect himself. He's also probably never felt safer than he does behind that locked door. You have no idea what he has endured."

"But I've—"

"You might have seen reports from the doctor who treated him for a concussion, but you don't know, not really. The sooner you accept that, the better. River is safe in that room. His body is his own for quite possibly the first time in his life. He's able to decide when and if he wants to eat and drink. It's highly likely from what you've said that his abusers managed his intake or used it as a form of punishment and control."

"Yeah, I guess."

"All you can do right now is be there to support him however he needs. But hovering outside his door or constantly knocking on it won't help anyone and will only drive a wedge between you." I gasped and winced. "Mmmm, I thought as much." Joelle chuckled.

"I just want to help him more than anything."

"More than the case?"

"I, umm..." I sighed and shook my head. I hadn't really thought about putting one above the other. Not consciously, anyway.

"You're in a tough position here, Jacob, stuck between your responsibility and the guilt you feel toward River for living a life he could only dream of."

"I...yeah. How did you know?"

"I've known you a long time, Jacob. You take everything to heart. Misplaced guilt is a big thing you've spent years trying to come to terms with. It's not your fault what happened to him. You were just a child. It was out of your control—just like with what happened to your family or the Hendrix's son. None of it was your fault. Nothing you could do or say would change the outcome of what happened."

I tipped my head back on the couch and sighed as it sunk into the soft cushion, allowing my eyes to fall shut. My head pounded like my skull was too small for the maelstrom that was brewing inside it. I pinched the pressure point on my nose, trying to alleviate the pulsing ache. "So what can I do? How can I help him?"

"Be there for him. Respect his boundaries and give him time."

"That's it? But what about the case? I'm getting pressure from my boss because I haven't been able to provide any new leads or intel to him."

"What's more important right now?"

I wanted to say River. I couldn't handle seeing the desolation that churned in his eyes, or the ghosts that seemed to pass across them like shadows. Joelle was right. I didn't know what he'd been through, not really. I could assume so many things, but without him feeling comfortable enough to tell me, pushing him might do more harm than good. And the last thing I wanted to do was cause him more pain or make him feel like he was an obligation.

"I should say my job."

"The work you do is very important, even if it can feel like a thankless task most days."

I snorted. She wasn't wrong there. "But there's something about River. There always has been something that filled me with this irrational need to take care of him. To protect him, and..." My words died on my tongue when I realized what I was about to say. Love him.

"You are an amazing individual, Jacob. You're led by your heart and want to fix everything for everyone, but you can't. Just be there. Be open and calm when he's ready to let you in."

"Okay, that... that I can do. I think."

"I know you can, Jacob. He's lucky to have you in his corner." I could hear the smile in her voice. "That's all I've got time for now, as my next client is about to arrive."

"Thank you, Joelle."

"It's my pleasure, Jacob. Just remember what I've said, okay? If you push him, he will react. Every action has an equal and opposite reaction. If you push him too hard, too fast, he will either shut you out completely, or run."

"I don't want to lose him." I coughed, attempting to hide the way my voice broke. "I mean, I don't want him to lose this chance at a new life."

"I know what you meant, Jacob. Take care."

Joelle ended the call, and the silence felt even more suffocating than it had before. I had to find a way to reach River before he closed himself off from me and I lost my chance to help him or the case. I pulled up the one-sided message thread I had going with River. He'd read each one, but hadn't responded to any of them.

> If you have any questions about the phone or TV, let me know. I thought this would be easier than writing on scraps of paper for you.

> Did you sleep okay?

> Did you like the extra things I got you?

> Just making some breakfast. Did you want anything?

> Fancy anything for lunch?
>
> Riv, talk to me? I just want to be here for you, but I can't if you don't reply.
>
> Would you like takeout?
>
> What desserts do you like?
>
> Or candy?
>
> I'm just watching a movie called The Old Guard. Do you want to watch it with me?
>
> River?
>
> Let me know you're okay.
>
> River, I keep knocking, but you won't come to the door.
>
> You can't stay in there forever! Talk to me.
>
> I'm sorry, that was rude.
>
> I just want to help you.

Jesus, I was a mess, hounding him like that. "Fuck!" I groaned. Talking to Joelle had helped a bit. She knew what she was talking about, but it didn't change the fact that this situation was frustrating. I hated feeling helpless, like I was letting him down.

> I'm making coffee. Want one?

Three dots appeared and disappeared so many times I was on the edge of my seat until they disappeared completely. "Fuck it." Jaw clenched, I headed into the kitchen to make a pot of coffee. If he didn't want to talk, then fine. I'd make him a drink and leave it by his door like I had all the others before going to work on old Mrs. Burrows's car. It needed an oil change and a new battery fitted. Plus, I needed to check in with Montoya and find out when someone was going to check over my security system.

It wasn't like I couldn't do it myself, but Bower had wanted something more advanced than I could pick up from the local hardware store, so that meant Davis being involved, which set me on edge. The old timer didn't like me because I challenged the "status quo." More like it was a case of making him look bad, because I cared about my job and helping others.

The kettle boiled, and I filled up the carafe, added the beans, and depressed the plunger. It felt like the type of day that called for proper coffee. I needed something with a sharp kick if I was to focus on anything other than the boy in my guest room. While it was percolating, I sent Montoya a message, asking her if she had any updates on how things were progressing in the outside world.

River hadn't touched the last lot of food I'd left him, so I made him a sandwich while I was at it. Although I didn't know his preferences, I remembered him enjoying ham and cheese melts back at Mrs. Wilkinson's, so quickly put one together and added it to the tray along with a bag of Doritos. When I reached his room, I rapped on his door softly.

"Riv? Here's your coffee. I also, umm, made you a sandwich." I licked my lips as I set the tray down in front of his door and listened. His room was silent, but he must have had the blinds open, because his shadow moved underneath the door. My phone buzzed in my pocket, and a squeak pushed past my lips when I saw a message from him.

RIVER
Thank you, Bane.

ME
It's nothing. Enjoy.

I wanted to fist pump the air, to jump up and down, to push the door open and wrap my arms around him and never let go. But I couldn't. *Respect his boundaries,* I mentally scolded myself as I headed for the stairs. I only made it down the first couple when I heard the door creak open, and I caught sight of River. My breath caught in my throat, my heart freezing mid-beat as I took him in.

He looked paler than before—if that was even possible—his shoulders hunched and curled around himself. The dark smudges under his eyes had spread like a fresh purple-black bruise that was in stark relief to his skin. The hoodie he wore was down to his knees and swamped his frame. His choosing to wear my clothes made my stomach fall to my feet. His hands shook as he picked up the tray and grunted with the effort it took not to drop it. Fuck, how I wanted to run up there and help him. My teeth sunk into my lip hard enough to split the delicate skin, but my eyes remained riveted on him.

When the door snicked shut and the click of the lock engaged, I deflated, expelling a deep breath. I spun my phone in my hand on my way back to the kitchen, where I grabbed my coffee before heading to the garage to work on Mrs. Burrows' car. My feet slipped into my worn work boots as I shouldered open the door. I had just enough time to put my mug down on the workbench when my phone rang, the quick succession of vibrations the only way I could differentiate between a text and a call.

"Hello?" I said, wedging the device between my ear and shoulder as I hunted for the tools I needed.

"Hey, Benson." Montoya's voice was chipper but had an edge of unease to it.

"What's up?"

"Davis is bringing his lackey out tonight or tomorrow morning to look over your security system."

"Alright, I'll be here."

Her sharp intake of breath was all I needed to know that something was up. "Ah, yeah, about that..." She cleared her throat in that way she did when she steeled her spine and looked at you with the full force of her penetrating gaze.

"Tell me," I demanded.

"Bower wants you to come in tomorrow." The sound of a door closing cut off the normal buzz of the war room. "He wants an update and feels like you're purposely being evasive."

"Seriously?" I growled and scrubbed my hand down my face. "I had a week. That's what he said, before he'd..." I shook my head and slumped against my workbench.

"I know. I know, but something has him spooked—"

"What?"

Montoya sighed. "I've got no idea. I haven't been in the office as much since I've been staking out your place."

"Did he say when?"

"First thing. Tell him to make sure he's here, and that he doesn't weasel out of it. He has a job to do," Montoya said, mimicking Bower's low authoritative tone.

"Got it. You coming in too?"

"Yup. He's calling us in for a meeting at ten."

"Okay. I'm gonna focus on Mrs. Burrows' oil change, and I'll see you in the morning."

"You know it, Benson."

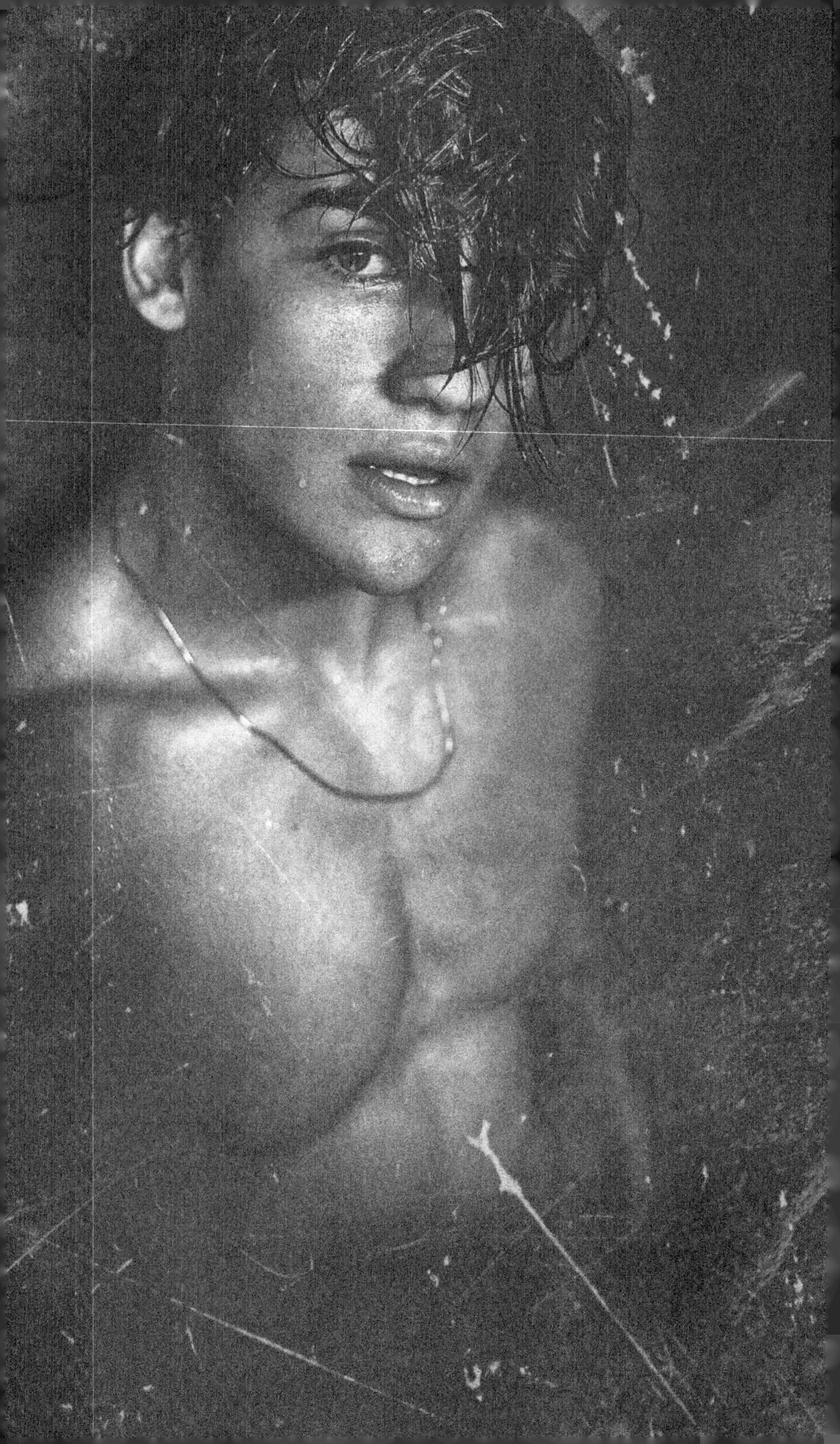

CHAPTER TEN
River

I didn't expect to be woken up by my phone vibrating like mad on the nightstand, but here I was, rubbing the sleep from my eyes and trying to focus on the ultra bright screen. There had to be a way to make it less bright, so it didn't feel like it was burning my retinas.

> **BANE**
>
> I've been called in for a meeting. I won't be long.
>
> One of the team is bringing someone over this morning to update the security system, but I'll hopefully be back by then. If I'm not, you'll have to let them in. Make sure they show you their badge. It should look like this.
>
> *photo*

I let the phone fall beside me before interlinking my fingers and stretching them over my head, rolling my neck to ease the stiffness. I'd never felt as exhausted as I did right now, even though I'd slept more than I had in years. It didn't make sense. I was waiting for the day when I'd wake up feeling refreshed and full of energy.

Bane was under the assumption I had locked myself away in my room for the last few days. While accurate as far as he was concerned, his assumption wasn't correct. I had left my room, but only when he was out cold, leaning against the wall opposite my door with a snore rumbling in his chest.

I wasn't sure he'd understand how overwhelmed I felt right now. The only way I felt like I had any control was to lock myself away in a cage of my own making. It wasn't about setting boundaries; it was about trying to replicate how I'd existed for so long that the possibility of being free, no matter how fleeting, was absolutely terrifying. Even if it was everything I'd ever dreamed of.

The phone fell to the floor when I kicked the blankets off and landed with a thump. I cringed, hoping I hadn't damaged it, because I had no way of paying Bane back. There was only one thing I was good at—getting on my knees and taking whatever they forced on me. My fingers trembled as I scooped the phone up and headed to the bathroom. I needed a shower. My—Bane's—hoodie was stuck to my body. My skin felt tight, and I stank of stale sweat.

After a quick piss, I turned the shower on and brushed my teeth while I waited for the water to heat. After years of ice-cold showers, hot water was a luxury I never wanted to live without. Steam filled the room as I stripped off and kicked the clothes into the corner. Remembering I hadn't replied to Bane, I fired off a quick message.

K

Feeling refreshed and a bit more awake after my shower, I scooped up my dirty clothes, stripped the bed, and unlocked my door. I paused, listening to make sure there was no one else here. When the only thing I could hear were the muted voices from my TV, I breathed a sigh of relief and ambled downstairs, trying not to trip on the way down.

It had taken me nearly an hour of YouTube videos to figure out how to work the washing machine. Bane was right when he said I didn't have a lot of clothes, but it meant I could take as much as possible with me when he kicked me out.

While the wash was on, I poured a coffee from the pot on the counter. Wrapping my fingers around my mug, I inhaled the delicious aroma and sipped the warm nectar down like it was my lifeline.

"Hello?" I almost dropped my mug at the voice shouting through the mail slot. "Hellooooo?" A loud knocking came from the front door. I placed the mug on the counter and checked my phone to see if there were any new messages from Bane, but there weren't. Great! Radio silence. I chewed on my bottom lip, my heart racing as indecision had me rocking in the middle of the kitchen, my eyes darting between the guy looking through the windows and my escape route back to my room, where I'd be safe behind a locked door.

"Benson said there'd be someone here to let me in to check over the security system." Gripping the cuffs on my hoodie, I walked toward the door. I could still see the guy standing in front of the window, so I quickly typed a message and held it up to the glass.

> Show me your badge.

The guy chuckled. "Alright, kid. Let me get him." His silhouette moved away, the sound of his footsteps fading.

My knees buckled, and I slid down the wall while I waited for him to return. I gripped my phone to my chest as tears pricked the backs of my eyes. God, I wished Bane was here. He'd know what to do. He'd be calm and take control. His heart wouldn't be fighting its way out of his chest. Tears wouldn't be leaking down his cheeks.

"Hey, kid." I jumped at the sound of the guy's voice and pushed up onto my knees so I could pull the blind back enough to see what he held against the window. "This is my business card and the guy's who brought me down. I'm James Stevenson. I work in security, and Detective Davis is here escorting me."

I looked down at the image Bane had sent of his badge, then googled James Stevenson and High Bar security to make sure he was legitimate. All the details on his card checked out against those listed on the company website.

> Okay, I'll unlock the door.

I held my phone up to the window and heard his low chuckle again.

"Alright kid, thank you. Unlock the door, then knock twice to let me know you're done, okay? Then go keep yourself occupied while I work. I'll lock the door and put the key back through the mail slot when I'm done."

I nodded even though he couldn't see me and crawled from the front window to the door. My hands shook so hard it took me three tries to get the door unlocked. After pushing myself up, I knocked twice before tripping over my feet as I turned toward the stairs. Sweat drenched my skin, making my tee cling to my back like a second skin underneath my hoodie. I'd only made it to the bottom step when I heard the door open and two distinct sets of footsteps walked in. One was light, almost bouncy, and matched the guy who had spoken to me. The other was heavy and dragged slightly, like the guy had a bad knee or hip.

"I'll get right on it now. Shouldn't take me more than an hour. I've got all new cameras, sensors, and an updated control panel to install."

The heavy footsteps rang out against the hardwood floors and continued deeper into the house. I tracked the sound into the living room where the unused armchair squeaked. "That's good, James. I'm just going to sit back and take a nap."

Every muscle in my body tightened at the thready sound of that voice, freezing me in place. My breaths shallowed and punched in and out of my chest. Darkness clouded the edges of my vision. Shit. Shit. Shit. I knew that voice. I'd heard it many times before.

"Ha. You do that, man." The lighter voice chuckled, followed by a heavy metallic clunk, like he'd dropped a tool bag on the floor.

My hands slipped on the wooden steps as I dragged myself up them, knowing I had to get away from that voice and the barrage of memories that flowed through my mind on an endless loop. I'd never seen his face, but I knew his voice and what it felt like when he struck my body with his hand, his shoes, and his favorite wooden cane. I knew what it felt like when he pulled my hands behind my back and pinned me down, and how he loved to kick my feet wide apart and fuck into me like I was a blow-up doll, like I didn't have any feelings. I knew how he sounded when he laughed and crowed because he made me scream, what he sounded like when he came. I could remember the bitter taste when he spilled in my mouth and over my face. I remembered how I had to swallow down the vomit that rose in the back of my throat.

I remembered them all. Millions of hands on my body. Fingers digging into my flesh, sometimes hard enough to draw blood, while others left scars. I could feel every cane and whip that struck my skin and split my flesh. I remembered every word of hate, ownership, and degradation. Every slut, every worthless hole, and every whore that was whispered in my ears as tears streamed down my face. I remembered choking on the taste of my blood as it filled my mouth when my nose got broken from being slammed into the nightstand, a table, the floor.

Every moment was accounted for, no matter how hard I tried to forget. It was like my brain had hard-wired them into its deepest dark recesses just to taunt me as soon as I had the opportunity to escape.

I screamed silently when arms wrapped around me and lifted me off the floor as I hyperventilated. I shook my head from side to side, silently trying to free myself. My arms and legs pushed and punched and kicked. Deep grunts punctuated the static that drowned out every other sound until all I could hear were my whimpering cries. My pleas. My prayers.

"Shhhhh."

Steel bands held me in place like an immovable force, trapping me against a hard body. Why wouldn't they let me go? I needed to run. Please, please, don't hurt me. *Please.*

"It's okay, River. It's okay." I threw my head, smashing it against the body that caged me in. "You're safe. You're safe."

I'm not! I'll never be safe as long as I'm breathing! I'll never be safe. My memories will always be there. "I...I'll...n-ne... ver...be...f-f-f-free." The words wrenched their way out of my soul unbidden and coated my tongue with ash.

"Oh, River." A pained whimper rocked through me. I couldn't tell if it was me or him or both of us. "Please, please don't say that. I'm here. I'll always keep you safe, no matter what. I promise you. I won't let them hurt you. I promise. I promise. I *promise*..."

Every inhale burned like I was inhaling poison, making my lungs melt. My throat ached like I'd swallowed shards of glass. I could hear someone calling my name far, far away.

Warm hands cupped my cheeks, and soft pants of air brushed over my lips. "It's okay. You're okay. You're not alone, River. I'm here. I'm here." His deep melodic voice repeated the words over and over until it became a metronome for every beat of my heart. His inhales became mine as he breathed against me, filling my lungs, forcing the panic that had ravaged me to retreat. "That's it, good boy. Again." His lips brushed against mine, warm and soft. His hand cupped my face, his thumb brushing away the torrent of tears that still streamed down my cheeks.

A whimper pushed its way up my throat, and I shuddered under his tender attention. His hypnotic eyes bored into me as my vision slowly cleared, the darkness receding. The depth of emotion that glistened in them made my heart rate spike once again. I clutched at his navy henley. I didn't know if I was trying to pull him closer, push him away, or imbed myself into him so he could never leave me.

Every thought and memory in my mind was a chaotic mess. I was drowning in a raging storm, and he was the lifeline that had been thrown my way. I hated feeling like this, so lost and out of control. Being around Bane made me weak, and that was something I couldn't afford to be. The armor I'd encased myself in for years had been stripped away, leaving me vulnerable and exposed. He was my kryptonite, my damnation, and my salvation. No matter how much I wanted him, wanted to be saved by him, I couldn't be. I knew that. His life was his own. He was strong and practically perfect in every way, and I would be nothing more than a stain on everything he'd achieved, everything he could be.

I needed to dig deep and bury every feeling that had started to bloom inside me. They could only be shadows of what could have been, for they will never see the light of day. With my mind made up, I pushed Bane back. His intoxicating cedarwood and leather scent threatened to dissolve the resolve I'd forced upon myself. A look of hurt flashed across his face as I pushed against his shoulders again. It hurt more than I wanted to admit. Every time he hurt, it was like hammering a rusty nail into my heart. But this was the right thing to do. It was the only choice.

Bane drew back and sat against the headboard of my bed, and wiped away the dampness from his face with a shaky hand. "Are you okay?"

I licked my lips, tasting the salt of my tears, and nodded. "Yess," I hissed, my inner turmoil granting me the power to use my voice.

Bane didn't look convinced as the furrow between his brows deepened. "That's the second time today you've spoken to me." A light flickered in his eyes, almost like he was proud of me. He couldn't be—I wouldn't allow it. "What happened?"

His deep voice was soothing, a gentle wave lapping at the icy fire that licked through my veins. I shrugged and hauled myself up, so I mirrored him. With my back against the headboard, I pulled my knees up to my chest, wrapping my arms around them and creating a barrier between us. The bedding between us became a no-man's-land, a barren wasteland of everything that could have been, of every thought and feeling neither of us wanted to admit. A death before life had ever taken hold, the place where all good intentions went to die.

Out of words, I pulled my phone from my back pocket and typed a message.

> I had a flashback. It felt like I was back there with...

Bane's phone vibrated in his hand and a look flitted across his features that I couldn't name as he read my message.

"Do you want to talk about it?"

I shook my head and chewed the inside of my cheek.

"If you don't want to talk to me, I can recommend someone else. Joelle is very good, and she's helped me a lot over the years. She could help you process everything you've been through."

> No!

"River, please." Bane looked at me, using the full force of the magnetism that surrounded him like some kind of manipulative mind control.

> I SAID NO!

He held up his hands in surrender. "I won't force you to do anything, okay?" I nodded but couldn't meet his eyes. *Please, please force me. Don't let me go.* "I'm here for you, however you need me to be. Always."

I scoffed and shook my head. He didn't know what he was promising. As beautiful as it sounded and as much as I wanted to, it could never come to fruition. I wouldn't allow it.

> I know.

"James should be nearly finished. Would you like a coffee?" I blinked up at him once. "Or what about a hot cocoa with marshmallows? Then we can chill and watch a movie or something downstairs?"

A shout from downstairs saved me from answering. "Uh, Mr. Benson, I think I'm all done here. I just need to make sure everything is all linked to your phone."

Bane looked at me and sighed, scrubbing his hand over his face. "I'll see to this, then you can join me downstairs when they're gone. There's something I need you to look at as part of the case." With that, Bane pushed up off the bed and closed the door behind him, not sparing me a second glance.

He wanted to talk to me about the case. Now that, I could do. It would be the perfect distraction and give me time to remember who I was before Bane came back into my life, so leaving wouldn't be so hard. Hurting him would be a fatal wound I'd never be able to heal from.

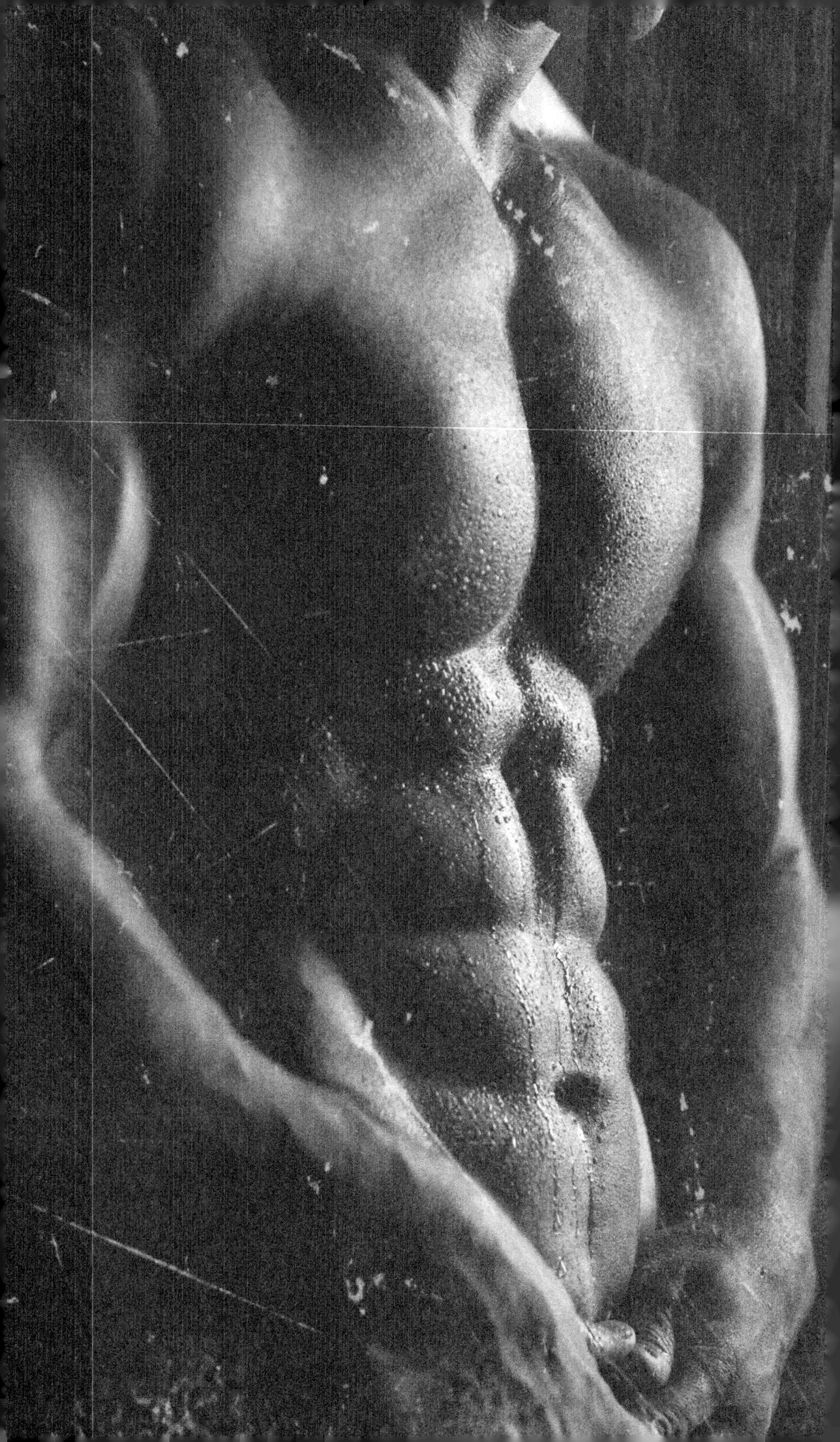

CHAPTER ELEVEN
Bane

"Ah, Mr. Benson?"

I couldn't contain my snort even if I wanted to. "James, it's just Benson," I said as I shook his hand. "How'd it go?" I gestured for him to follow me outside so we could discuss the details without River overhearing. I didn't want to spook him any more than his encounter with James and Davis had already. That's the only thing I could assume had triggered his earlier episode, and I didn't want him to feel unsafe in my house.

"Great, mister, umm, Benson," James stammered as he followed me out the front door that snicked shut behind us. "I've installed new cameras to replace the old ones and fitted a new motherboard to the control panel." He opened the back doors of his van and sat down on the bed, patting the space next to him.

I looked at it and cringed. "Not sure we'll both fit," I said as diplomatically as I could.

James looked up at me over the laptop he'd pulled out of somewhere, then up and up a bit more. "Ah, you might be right." He chuckled nervously. "You're, um, quite the big guy, aren't you?"

"Sure." I braced myself against the side of the van so I could see the screen James angled toward me and observed him as he ran a diagnostics program.

"Phone, please." He held out his hand without even looking at me. When I didn't move, he lifted his gaze to mine. "I won't do anything besides make sure the software has mapped across properly, so you'll be able to operate the system remotely. You'll also have individual control over each camera and sensor I've installed around the perimeter."

I held my phone up, making him frown. "This is my personal cell. I want to make sure it's the only one that will have access to the system unless I decide to add another to it. Do you understand me?"

James's lashes fluttered as he processed what I said, and he shrank back into himself. "I...yes, sir. Totally. My system isn't, or should I say won't be, connected to it once I've uploaded everything to your phone. And if you want to add another, then call me and I'll make sure there are no issues." He pulled a business card out of a silver tin and flourished it in front of me.

"Good." I placed my phone in his hand, having already pulled up the app for my previous installation. He shook his head, a rueful smile lifting his lips.

"You won't b-be needing that anymore. It's a completely new operating system, one I've been working on for a while, so you're kind of like a test dummy." His nervous chuckle set me on edge, making my lip curl back.

"You mean to say—"

"Maybe I didn't choose my words correctly. It's a system I designed myself that will go into production next year. I just meant you're the first person who gets to use it."

I dug the heel of my palm into my dry eyes and eventually nodded in agreement. I guess I should have felt lucky to get a brand new system, but something's felt off today. It had started since I left the house this morning. I had that feeling in my gut that I knew I shouldn't ignore, but I just couldn't pinpoint what had triggered it. River's panic attack, while disturbing in its ferocity, wasn't that surprising given the nightmares he'd been having on top of the upheaval and the complete one-eighty his life had taken. But that just felt like the tip of the iceberg heading straight toward me.

I loosed a breath and shook out my hands before folding my arms over my chest as I watched him connect my phone to his laptop. He uninstalled the old app and installed the new one that linked to the cameras, sensors, and video doorbell system he had just installed.

My front door opened and closed, and uneven footsteps headed in our direction. A raspy cough heralded Davis's arrival, the stench of cigarette smoke as putrid as the man himself. His beady dark eyes looked up at me, and a sneer curled his lips. "Is everything done? I've got far more important things to be doing today."

"Almost, Mr. Davis, sir. I'm just—"

"I don't really care, James," Davis said flatly. "I need to get back to the station. Just send me a full report when you're done here."

"I...um. Yes, sir."

"See you later, Benson." If he could have spat the words in my face with a glob of mucus, I'm sure Davis would have. He needed to learn a few lessons in civility. His passive aggressiveness did not hide his thinly veiled hate.

"Yup. See ya." I waved him off, my eyes tracking him as he headed down the road to his car. I was just about to take my eyes off him when he pulled his phone out and started talking to someone, gesticulating wildly while leaning against his car and looking right at me. Or, more accurately, my house. I continued to watch him out of the corner of my eye as I asked James, "How long have you known Davis?"

"Huh? Oh, he's f-friends with my uncle. H-he puts a lot of work my way. He's always said I'm the best at what I do."

"Mmmm, I see. Does that mean the force gets a discounted rate for these jobs?" I didn't know why I asked, but his nervous disposition indicated he was unraveling. Sweat beaded in his hairline, and his expert hands moved with a slight but unmistakable tremor.

"I...ugh, suppose so?"

The guy seemed to get more and more flustered under the weight of my scrutiny. As the seconds ticked past, Davis didn't move from his car. His cigarette was long gone, but his gaze remained fixated on my home. I just couldn't work out if it was me he had more issue with, or with whom was staying with me.

As far as I knew, Davis had never been involved in a case like this. He hadn't done a stake-out since his rookie years, nor accompanied a witness into protective custody. At the station, he pretended to work while keeping his ear to the ground and his finger on the pulse. Making underlings' lives hell was his favorite sport, and god help you if he found you lacking. He'd tried to bully me when I first joined the force. His racism was apparent from the get-go, but he failed to intimidate on so many levels. He was pathetic and so physically out of shape that I had nothing to fear from him. I just wished it was the same for Montoya. She got it two-fold from him for being Latina and female. He'd say things like "your place is taking care of the children at home" or "you need a good man to take care of you. You won't be that pretty forever, now will you?"

I'd wanted to punch him in the face that day and had barely restrained my anger from bleeding out and spilling his blood. Montoya was my balance; she made me see reason even as he spewed vitriolic hate at her. I couldn't wait for the day he retired. It was pointless putting in a complaint about him and his tyrannical tirades, because he was well-connected and therefore untouchable. Everything got brushed under the carpet. All you succeeded in doing was making a rod for your own back by becoming persona non grata. I was in no doubt he'd do something one day that even his friends couldn't protect him from, but until then, I had to act as amenable as possible around him.

"Here," James said with a cough. "It's all done. Want me to walk you through it?" He stood up, placing his laptop down, and looked up at me expectantly.

"Yeah, sure. You can tell me about all the upgrades you've made and anything you think I might need to watch out for that could be improved."

James's smile beamed. "It's so refreshing to get someone who understands the importance of progress," he muttered and took my phone from me, opening up the secureX app he'd installed. He walked me through every camera, its range of motion, and the areas they covered. He even suggested a couple of blind spots when it might be pertinent to add extra if I so wanted, but as it was a residential property, that choice was mine and mine alone. His depth of knowledge was amazing and he could be a real asset to our team back at the station.

Once I waved him off, I cast one last glance up and down the street, noting that Davis had also vanished. My heart sank when I realized Bower had recalled the car that should have been watching the house. He'd made a semi compelling argument at my debrief this morning, stating that River's friends had been spotted around town the past couple of nights. Since there was no imminent threat to him or the case, the new security system and six-foot fence I was going to install in the backyard should be enough.

I hadn't bought it for a second. It felt like a line the powers from above told him to spin. But without irrefutable evidence that River was in danger—or even a flight risk—I had no leverage to demand a patrol car. Bower had been extremely disappointed that I hadn't gleaned any new intel from River. Even as I tried to explain the complexity of the situation, which he assured me he was well aware of, he refused to accept that the case wasn't moving forward.

Bower reminded me I had a job to do and that maybe he'd been wrong in giving me this opportunity to prove myself, stating that my emotional investment in River was causing me to be an ineffective agent. It'd taken every ounce of willpower to not scoff at him and storm out of his office. As a parting gift, he gave me a file containing surveillance images of everyone we knew to be associated with the Black Dahlia ring. He wanted me to get River to verify if he knew them, who they were, and under what capacity they operated within the ring.

I strolled over to my driveway, where my sedan sat baking under the heat of the midday sun. Old Mrs. Burrows waved to me as she pulled into her drive. As she walked up to her porch, she paused long enough to call over another thank you, even though she'd already thanked me profusely for the work I'd done on her car when I returned her keys to her earlier this morning.

I opened the car door and reached into the passenger footwell, retrieving my bag and the file sitting on the seat. After locking up, I hurried back into the house, pleasantly surprised to find River curled up under a pile of blankets on the sofa with It's Not Cake playing on the TV.

"Would you still like a hot cocoa?" I called out as I dropped my keys in the pot on the accent table and hung my bag up on the peg. My phone buzzed in my pocket, but I ignored it and headed into the kitchen, flicked the kettle on, and pulled out the marshmallows, milk, and cocoa.

A smile lit up my face when I looked at my messages to see a GIF of a steaming cup of cocoa and a thumbs up emoji. River's sweet cinnamon and orange scent saturated the kitchen and sent a thrill through me. I felt comfortable and whole in a way I'd never experienced with another person in my space, even Montoya.

I'd had a few relationships in my life but nothing I would ever class as serious or long term. Hookup culture wasn't for me. No strings sex just wasn't my thing, nor was sex on a first date. It took time for me to be confident enough to open myself up and be vulnerable with someone. I needed something more, something deeper and meaningful, but every relationship left me feeling like I was missing a piece of myself, something vital that provided a foundation for the relationship to grow. I'd never been able to pinpoint what it was or why I was this way. Joelle had several theories about it, some related to the loss of my family and the impact that had on me. But she believed I could be demisexual, meaning I needed that deeper connection with someone prior to intimacy. But I wasn't sure. My hand provided me with enough relief. I didn't feel like I needed more than that, especially with a job like mine.

The kettle boiled, pulling me from my meandering thoughts, ones that had no place being thought of right now. I had a job to do, someone special to guard and look after. My own wants and needs were secondary to River's. I couldn't afford to make him uncomfortable; he was too fragile, mentally and physically. I had to look after him while he wasn't capable.

After making up the drinks, I carried them into the living room. "Here you go," I murmured, making River blink blearily up at me through heavy-lidded eyes. "Sit up and take this while I grab some snacks."

A small smile flickered around his mouth, and his full lips formed the words thank you. My heart skipped a beat, and heat flushed my cheeks all the way to the tips of my ears. He shuffled into a sitting position and reached for the cup, wrapping his hands around it and holding it possessively to his chest, gently blowing the steam as the marshmallows melted.

After setting my coffee down, I went back to the kitchen to grab a couple of bowls, filling them with chips and popcorn before placing them in front of River. I settled on the other end of the couch, clutching the file to my chest. All I wanted to do was pull River into my body, to feel how his body would mold into mine, but now wasn't the time for such thoughts. I had to figure out a way of broaching the subject of the images in my hands.

We settled into a comfortable silence, sipping our drinks while River watched the judges on TV try to figure out which Mona Lisa painting was actually a cake. "Which one do you think it is?" River held up four fingers and fist pumped when the judge confirmed it by sinking his knife into the beautiful artwork. "Good one."

River glanced up at me. He looked at peace, settled in a way he hadn't since he'd come to my home. It was like all the stress and anxiety that surrounded him was gone. I could fool myself into thinking he was happier here than he'd been anywhere else, but the more logical answer was that he'd burned it all up earlier and was simply exhausted.

We sat there till the bright blue sky turned into a beautiful watercolor of oranges, pinks, and lavenders. The light streamed in through the sliding doors, filling the room with a natural warmth that nothing manmade could replicate. It made me appreciate the little things. It made me thankful for what I had and the time he granted me in his company.

When the next episode started, I flicked my gaze over to where River sat curled up in his blanket nest and sighed. I didn't want to ruin the peace we'd found, but this couldn't wait any longer. I cleared my throat and sat up straighter. Riv looked up at me through his dark lashes, his thick brows furrowed like he knew the status quo was about to change. Tension lined his jaw, and the tendons in his neck became taught.

"Riv, when I went in for a debrief this morning, Bower asked me to go through some surveillance photos with you." He sucked in a sharp breath, and pain swirled in his deep green eyes. "We were hoping you could look through them and confirm who people are and what they do. If you know, that is."

I left the ball in his court as I wouldn't force him to do it, to revisit the people who had controlled and used him like property. I held my breath, steeling myself as he went through a silent battle I wanted to protect him from. Eventually, after nearly an episode had played, he picked up his phone and started typing.

Ok

The tension in my shoulders eased but didn't disappear. I pulled out the file from where I'd stuffed it down the side of the sofa and motioned for him to come closer to me. He didn't have to, as I'd respect his boundaries, but I wanted to hold him, support him, as he did this. I didn't know if it was right or wrong, but I felt compelled to do it.

As River moved closer to me, I kept talking to keep him calm and make this as painless as possible for him. "We can do this in a few ways," I said, ticking them off against my fingers as I went. "You can look at them and text me. I could grab a pen so you can write on the images directly, or you can talk to me, whichever you're most comfortable with."

He regarded me for a beat, then held out his hand for the file, inadvertently moving closer to me. He sat cross-legged, his knee brushing against my thigh. It felt like a brand on my skin, even through my jeans and his blankets. River's spine was rigid, every muscle tight with tension as he went through the photos one by one. His lips pinched, eyes narrowed he passed a photo over to me and tapped it.

> Who is this?

I choked on a laugh. "That's Dahlia," I said self-assuredly. "She's the one who runs all the clubs."

River gaped back at me, completely dumbfounded. He picked up his phone and started typing.

> That's not Dahlia.

I looked at his message, looked at him and back at the screen on my phone. "What do you mean?"

> Why do you think that's Dahlia?

I huffed out a breath and rubbed my damp palms on my thighs. "That's who the Black Dahlia clubs are registered under. We have a file on her; driver's license, social security number, everything that identifies her as Dahlia. We've verified and cross-referenced everything. Where she was born, parents, relatives, the whole lot."

River shook his head, a resigned look on his face as he stared at his screen.

> She might be a Dahlia but she isn't *the* Dahlia.

"What do you mean?"

> For a start, she's too young. The Dahlia that picked me off the street is in her late fifties. This woman is too young. Her hair and eye color are wrong too. She even wears the wrong type of clothes.

"Seriously? Shit!" I lurched over and wrapped my arms around River's shoulders, pulling him into my chest. He let out a little squeak as I held him to me and buried my nose in his hair and inhaled his delicious scent. I pulled back, my fingers gently massaging the taut muscles in his shoulders, and felt my face split in half. I was vibrating, this... this was the kind of break we were looking for. "River, I could kiss you right now." He blushed, his thick lashes kissing his cheeks as his eyes fell closed. "This could change everything for us."

River nodded, his tongue tracing his full bottom lip. My eyes tracked the movement involuntarily. It was only when he sucked in a deep inhale that I realized I'd closed the distance between us. My hand gently cupped his soft face, my thumb skimming over his sharp cheekbone, my lips a hair's breadth from his. I could feel each stuttered exhale like a physical caress.

I sat there frozen, mesmerized by his proximity, the heat radiating off him, his scent. The flush of color that rose up his neck that made him look edible. Time seemed to stretch, seconds became minutes as our eyes remained locked on each other. The air became electrically charged. One spark, and we'd burn down the world. My heartbeat echoed in my ears. My whole body was aware of River, affected by him in a way I'd never experienced with another.

Heavy-lidded eyes at half mast, the deep green of his irises darkened with lust that licked across my skin. River moved forward slowly, his eyes flicking between my mouth and my eyes until he closed the distance between us and brushed his lips against mine. Every cell in my body lit up, and my nerves felt like they were hit with lightning. How could the slightest touch be so profound it altered every atom that made me?

When River moved back to give us space to breathe, it took my mind a few minutes to come back online. He sat on the opposite side of the couch once again, eyes glassy and unfocused as he looked at me. "That is not the Dahlia you're looking for." His raspy voice was like a gift from the gods. He swallowed reflexively and winced like it pained him to talk.

I bolted over the back of the couch to the kitchen, grabbed a bottle of iced water, and handed it to him. "Drink this, it'll help. I need to make a call and see if Daniel can come over. He's a forensic artist. Could you describe the Dahlia you know to him?" River nodded as his guarded blank look walled off his emotions. "Thank you, angel." I leaned down and pressed a kiss to his forehead, then stepped out into the yard, my phone clutched to my chest, hoping this would be the breakthrough we needed.

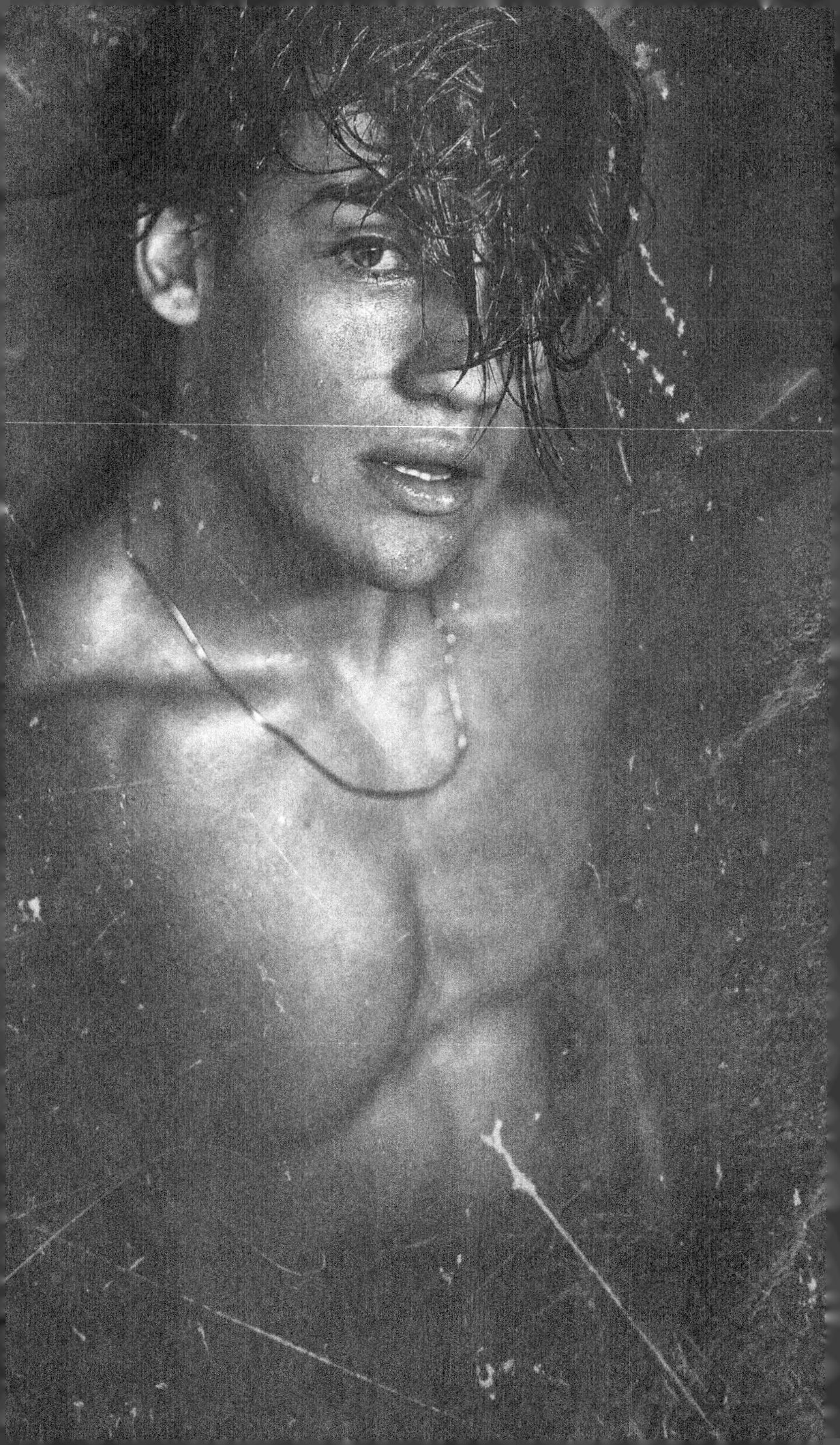

CHAPTER TWELVE
River

When Bane said he'd call Daniel, the forensic artist, I didn't know exactly what I'd been expecting, but it was not the young man who sat opposite me at the table. My mind had conjured some balding old man with white hair and round glasses. That was about as far from the truth as it could get. Well, apart from the glasses. Daniel looked like a cross between your typical nerd and a prince. He'd coiffed his light blond hair and hidden his bright blue eyes behind a pair of thick black-rimmed glasses, while a permanent smirk played on his lips.

For someone so small, he was extremely intimidating.

"I want you to give me as many details as you can. The more insight you can offer, the more accurate my impression of Dahlia will be."

I nodded along as I listened to him explain that while hair and eye color were sometimes the most obvious characteristics people noticed, it was the little things like moles, scars, and imperfections that really helped in cases like this.

Bane set down three mugs of coffee and took the seat next to me. His hand dropped to my thigh and squeezed in that reassuring casual way normal people touched. I jolted, nearly knocking my mug over as I tried to pick it up. I narrowed my eyes at Bane, who gave me an unrepentant grin and a firmer squeeze.

"Daniel's right, Riv. It's the little distinguishing features that people remember, like crooked teeth or a scar. It's weird what sticks in people's minds, and it can make all the difference when we run her through facial recognition."

Daniel pointed at the surveillance photo that started all of this off. "You said this isn't the Dahlia you know. Can you talk me through the main differences?"

I glanced at Bane, begging him to help me out, because I didn't like it when people judged me for not being able to vocalize my thoughts. He cleared his throat and shot me a small smile before turning to Daniel. He mirrored Daniel's pose and clasped his hands in front of him, resting them on the tabletop. "River is nonverbal. I can give you my phone—"

"Oh, that's not a problem. I've got a text speech app on my tablet. So if you message me the details, it'll talk me through everything, and I can make any necessary adjustments." He turned to look at me with a note of understanding in his eyes. "I've worked with lots of individuals who have been through extremely traumatic events, survivors just like you. Take your time. I have nothing else to do today."

"Great. That's just great, isn't it, Riv?" Bane ground out through his clenched jaw, the muscles in his cheeks rippling.

I nodded and pulled out my phone, but Bane snatched it

before I could hand it to Daniel, looking like he wanted to smash it. I snorted at his antics and shook my head before taking a much needed sip of coffee. It was almost like Bane wanted me to have the least amount of contact with Daniel as possible.

As if he could read between the lines, Daniel shot me a smirk and an eye roll over his cup as Bane connected my phone with the app on Daniel's tablet.

"This is going to be interesting," Daniel muttered under his breath as he clicked a few things on his tablet. Amusement danced in his eyes as he glanced between Bane and me. "Whenever you're ready, River."

Over the next hour, we went through every aspect of Dahlia's appearance in fine detail. From the more obvious things like hair and eye color, to her age and preferred clothing and makeup choices. By the time we were finished and Daniel handed me his tablet, my stomach was filled with lead and my chest was trapped in a vise.

> That's her, right down to the dead, heartless eyes. It's like I'm looking at a photograph of her.

I didn't think I'd ever get used to the automated voice on his tablet, but I felt compelled to tell him.

"That really isn't the Dahlia we've been looking into," Bane said. "We'll get to work on that right away once you send it through. You've got my email, right?"

"I do, yes." Daniel began packing up under Bane's watchful eye just as a call came through and Bane left to take it. We both watched him walk away, the silence stretching between us. "I know today wasn't easy for you, River," Daniel said. "But I want to thank you for being so thorough. I'm so sorry for everything you've been through. I can't even imagine how you've survived, but I'm glad you did." He got up and tucked his chair under the table. "You're good for him, you know."

I tilted my head in confusion and picked up my phone.

How so?

Daniel smiled. "For once, he has something far more important than work to think about."

I don't understand.

"You're as bad as each other." He rolled his eyes and rested his arms on the back of the chair. "You'll see. Just be patient with him. He's been completely focused on work for as long as I've known him. It's his life." I blanched at his words like I'd been physically struck. Every word out of his mouth just confirmed my thoughts. "Oh god, no. No, River." Daniel's shoulders slumped. "I wasn't referring to you as a job. Quite the opposite, in fact. Take care of him. I wish you both happiness."

I sat there in confusion as Daniel shut the front door behind him. "Has he gone already? That's a shame," Bane called from the kitchen. The sound of cupboards banging and the happy humming sound he was making made me realize he really wasn't as upset as his tone implied. Annoyed that he'd left without saying goodbye maybe, but that wasn't what had gotten him all riled up while Daniel was here, or what now made him so happy he had left. Maybe there was an issue at work that made their relationship tenuous?

"How about we have some lunch?" My stomach rumbled as if on cue, loud enough for Bane to hear all the way in the kitchen. He barked a laugh and asked me what I thought about soup and a grilled cheese sandwich. The last time I'd had that was at Mrs. Wilkinson's. The memory of her kindness made my throat feel tight and my eyes burn from emotions I had no place feeling.

AFTER LUNCH, I CRASHED ON THE COUCH WITH ANOTHER episode of *Those About To Die* queued up. There was something about the scheming and backstabbing that I could relate to, along with the amount of sex slaves that were used, bought, and sold. I didn't know what it said about me, but I had a morbid fascination trying to work out who was going to be the next one to die.

Sometimes, I wondered what would have happened to me if Dahlia hadn't kept me as part of her Holme Oaks operation. I wasn't naïve enough—any more—to think she kept me because she liked me. It was more that I fit the clientele she had, although I didn't know whether it was because of my age or looks. All I knew was that I made her money, and it kept me off the streets with a somewhat questionable roof over my head.

"What's this then?" Bane said as he sat at the other end of the gray couch. I hit the info button so he could see a synopsis of the show. The warmth on his face cooled as he read it. His lips thinned, but he said nothing as he pulled his phone out and started typing.

Ignoring him, I hit play and lost myself in the twisted world of the Roman Empire. I was so engrossed in the threesome happening on Domintiaus's bed that a loud knocking at the door made me freeze and drop the remote onto the wooden floor.

"Who the hell..." Bane yanked the door open. "Oh, hey, Colton. What brings you around?"

I glanced over the back of the couch, straining to hear the muttered conversation taking place, but it was pointless, so I restarted the episode. Just as Tanax lost everything, Bane's voice rose. "You can't be serious?!" he said. "I'm working right now." His words landed like a sucker punch to my gut.

"It doesn't look that way," Colton challenged. The scraping of claws against the wood floor, accompanied by soft yips, had me slowly unclenching. "Oh shi—shoot!"

A small black bundle charged across the house and threw itself onto my lap. A little black puppy bounced on my legs and worked its way up my chest until it was licking my face with abandon. My hands smoothed down its wriggly back of fine curled fur as its cold wet nose sniffed my neck. "That tickles," I rasped at the little intruder.

"Oh. My. God. I'm so sorry, River," Colton said as he knelt at my feet, trying to pull the little pup off my lap. But it had other ideas and dug its way under my blankets. "Umm." Colton looked at me with wide eyes and a smile. "I think he likes you," he whispered conspiratorially.

"No, Colton. No way."

"Aww, but Shadow seems so at home snuggled up with River."

Bane stomped over to us, shoulders tense, agitation radiating off him. "I told you..." he bit out, but the strain on his face melted away when he looked at me and Shadow. The ice thawed in his eyes the longer he stared at us, and something I couldn't name flitted across his features.

"It's only while I take Cooper and Lady to the vet. It'll be like two hours max." Colton waved his hand from side to side as if to say thereabouts. I could see Bane's refusal on the tip of his tongue as he inhaled deeply and screwed his eyes shut.

"I-it's...f-fine," I rasped, stroking Shadow as he slept against my chest.

"It is?" Colton's eyebrows hit his hairline and a cunning smile curved his lips. "Of course it is. I won't be long." He patted Bane's heaving chest, turned on his heel, and whistled his way out of the house.

"I can't believe you," Bane grouched, shaking his head as he toed the floorboards. He shoved his hands in the back pockets of his pants and peeked up at me. "What did you want to do with it?"

"Shadow?" I whispered, holding the little pup against me and feeling some of the ice that had lanced my veins thaw at Bane's question.

Bane nodded. "He's clearly here for you, not me." I scoffed. "So we can stay in and watch TV, or we could go out and get you some fresh air and take the little guy for a walk. The choice is yours."

My teeth sunk into my bottom lip, thrown by the question and the choices. I'd spent so much of the last few years scared shitless and following orders that it was strange to be given a choice. I didn't think I was allowed to go outside after the first time I'd met Colton. Bane had made it seem like an impossibility for my safety, but now? Now, it was an option, and I didn't exactly know what to make of that. I mulled over the merits of watching the rest of the episode or getting outside for a bit. The chance of fresh air and the wind on my face was something I'd missed so much being caged in that rotten room. The sky was overcast, a dove gray with wild clouds rolling in that made it look like it was going to rain.

"I've always wanted to dance in the rain." I smiled a wobbly smile, wincing at the pain that seared my throat as my breath stuttered.

Bane tipped his head to the side like I was a puzzle he was trying to piece together. "Dancing in the rain, huh?"

Heat filled my cheeks, and I hid behind the blankets. "Yeah." My vocal cords ached so much, tears pricked my eyes.

"Here."

Bane handed me an uncapped chilled bottle of water, which I gratefully took, swallowing down a few mouthfuls. The cool liquid soothed the raw lining of my throat, numbing the pain for a while. I smiled in thanks and handed it back to him. Bane chuckled with amusement as he leaned over me and whipped a bead of water off my lips with a gentle swipe of his thumb. I froze, mesmerized, as he then brought that thumb to his mouth and sucked off the single bead of moisture.

"O-oh," I gasped. Warmth flushed through me, every part of me magnetized, drawn to the beautiful monolith of a man standing in front of me. I wanted to merge myself with him so we could never be parted, so he would never forget me. Our time was fleeting, and I hated that more than anything. Right person, wrong time and place. Maybe in my next life, I'd be a person worthy of his love.

Bane cleared his throat, effectively breaking the moment. "I'm, uh, just going to go take a piss." How pleasant. I rolled my eyes and sunk my fingers into Shadow's soft fur to stop the aching burn building in the back of my eyes. "And grab a jacket before we head out. I, um…" He licked his lips and shifted foot to foot. "I suggest you do the same."

"Well, that was interesting, huh?" I whispered, as I looked into Shadow's dark eyes and shrugged. "Don't look at me like that, please. I know exactly what you're thinking, but I can't. He's too good for me. In what world do we work, huh?"

I pulled Shadow tightly against my chest and carried

him up to my room. Once the door closed behind us, the vise around my chest loosened, and I sucked in a deep breath as the little pup settled onto my bed, scooting around until he found a comfy spot to curl up in.

My mind was in turmoil. Being here was more dangerous than I could have anticipated. I wanted things I shouldn't, couldn't, want. *Don't make me fall for you, Bane, because there will be no one there to catch me if I do.*

I wiped the stray tear from my cheek when I caught sight of it in the bathroom mirror. The man staring back at me had changed. The richer tone to my complexion looked more natural, and my cheeks were flushed with life. The dark bruises beneath my eyes had softened, and the glimmer in my eyes looked a lot like hope. Warning bells sounded in my head. *Abort. Abort. Abort.*

Every wall I rebuilt, Bane effortlessly destroyed. He crushed them under his feet like a barbarian coming after my soul. The part that hurt the most was he didn't even realize he was leaving me defenseless in a world that wanted to swallow me whole and spit me out in the gutter.

Just one more night, I promised myself. Just one more chance to look at him. One last opportunity to taste him. One last time to see him smile, that special one belonging only to me.

Tomorrow, I would set him free.

With my jacket and scarf on and Shadow in my arms, I raced down the stairs, ready to savor every last second I had with him.

Bane looked up at me, his heart-stopping smile spread across his face. "You ready to go?" I nodded. Shadow wriggled in my arms and jumped down to the floor, pawing at the door.

"C-can we keep him?"

Bane laughed. The deep rumbling boom was one I'd

never forget. It was tattooed in my memory. He gave me an indulgent look, a small smile tilting his lips, and wrapped his arm around my shoulders, holding me close, the movement as natural as breathing, and guided us out of the house. "We'll see. Now come with me. There's somewhere I'd like to show you."

My heart lurched in my chest. *I'd follow you anywhere, in this world and the next, if only I could.* "Sure."

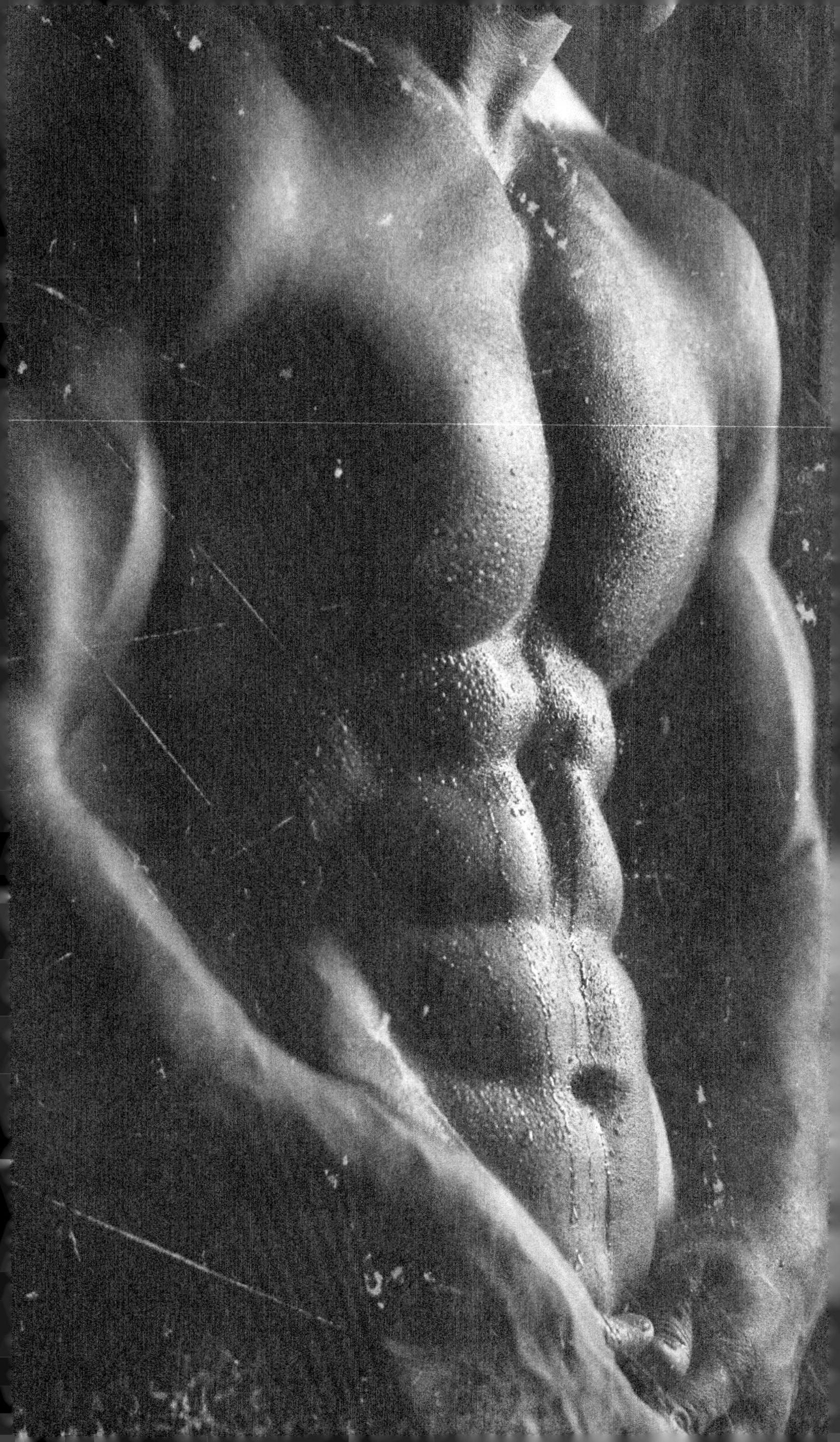

CHAPTER THIRTEEN
Bane

As broken as River seemed, he had this undeniable strength to him that captivated me. I craved his presence. Even if we didn't speak, just breathing the same air as him filled me with a strength I didn't know I possessed. He was a mystery I wanted to unravel. There were layers and layers to him I couldn't wait to peel back, but fear of what I might discover held me back.

Every time I thought I breached his walls, another one came up stronger than the one before. The push and pull was infuriating, but it breathed life into me and gave me hope. Every little morsel I learned about him had me on my knees, begging for more. I wasn't naïve enough to think he'd given me anything more than the Cliffs Notes version of his life. He'd done what he agreed to and given us vital information that related to the case and had made the next set of raids that we were planning possible. Without him, we would still be sitting there with our dicks in our hands, going around in circles.

I hadn't slept on the floor outside his locked door for some time, but that didn't mean I didn't lie in bed listening to his haunted screams. The visceral agony from each sound that was wrenched from him flayed the flesh from my bones before it ground them to dust. I was trapped in an impossible position, and I didn't have the mental capacity to work out what was the right thing to do.

My heart made me believe I'd follow River into a burning building because every thought I had was consumed with him. Only him. My brain was filled with logical, if somewhat cynical, thoughts. It urged me to err on the side of caution and not lose myself to overt romantic notions. Something that had never been an issue before in my few fleeting relationships, but this wasn't one. It couldn't be.

River was a sex worker, whether I wanted to face that truth or not. They had abused, used, and beaten him in every conceivable way. It had caused irrevocable damage he might never heal from. I had to be a realist, but being around him made me want things I knew I couldn't. He had severe PTSD and flinched at the slightest sound, cowering on the floor or underneath the nearest surface. He had no sense of self or self worth. It was clear every hour that passed that his mental state was declining. The psychological trauma was consuming him. Every day, another piece of him flaked off and died. His body was recovering, but his mind was failing him.

The amount of guilt I felt for feeling peace in his presence made me wonder if I was making him worse without realizing it. I wanted to hold him. Love him. Keep him safe with me always. But what if letting him go was the best way

I could help him? What if I had to set him free so he could learn to fly on his own?

I hated the thoughts that perpetually churned in my mind, but I couldn't see the light for the trees. Joelle always said I struggled to separate myself from other people's circumstances when my emotions were involved, and River was a prime example. But even with her words ringing in my head, I couldn't convince myself to walk away. I needed him as much as he needed me, maybe more.

River had yet to come down this morning, so I thought I'd take his breakfast upstairs to him. It had been particularly bad last night. At one point, I tried his door handle, but he'd locked it—as usual. I'd ended up sitting with my back to the locked door, crying as I listened to him howling in agony, hating myself for being unable to help him. I stayed there until the shower turned on and then passed out in my bed in a fitful sleep.

Nothing beat the smell of freshly cooked bacon in the morning. My stomach agreed as it grumbled and tightened, but I could see to myself later. I added eggs, toast, and coffee to River's tray before topping up Shadow's water bowl and adding a bit of kibble for his breakfast. It baffled me how looking after the pup for one afternoon meant he'd assimilated himself into my home, but he had, and he thankfully brought River some solace. Otherwise, I'd have sent him back home. Watching the way River's dull eyes sparked like embers when Shadow licked his face was enough for me to hold my tongue on the subject.

I knocked heavily on River's door. It opened from the force, and without thinking, I stepped inside and froze. My body flushed with incendiary heat, and fire licked through my veins. My eyes zeroed in on River's tight ass as he bent over and pulled black boxers up his toned legs. The tip of my tongue wet my bottom lip as images of my hands sliding up his thighs, feeling the dark hairs against my palms, swam through my mind, dissolving every rational thought that should have been in my head. How I'd spin him around and bury my face in the apex of his thighs, in the crease between his legs and his groin. How my mouth would water as I inhaled his intoxicating cinnamon and orange scent. My nose would charter a course across the soft cotton until it ran the length of his hard shaft. Would he smell sweeter, or have a deeper, muskier note that would make my dick fill and tighten my pants?

River made a sound that snapped me back to reality, and I hastily locked those thoughts in a cement box, wrapped it in lead chains, and threw it into the deep dark abyss in the back of my mind.

The cutlery clattered on the tray as my hands shook. River's shoulders tensed before he slowly straightened to his full height. My breath caught in my throat as the light streaming from my open bedroom door illuminated his back, revealing angry red welts and still-healing cuts that seeped blood. I edged forward cautiously, as if approaching a wild animal. My eyes traced the tapestry of silvered scars etched across his skin, silent witnesses to the suffering he had endured.

"R-River..."

"No," he rasped and pulled on one of my missing hoodies.

"Who hurt you?"

River shook his head and crawled onto the far side of his bed, pulling his legs up to his chest and making himself as small as possible. He pulled his hood up and rested his head on his knees, hiding himself from me. Fear and guilt rioted inside me, making me sick to my back teeth. The taste of acid burned the back of my tongue as a million scenarios from previous cases were plucked from my memories and laid out before me. I didn't want to contemplate him experiencing any of them, but the truth spoke for itself, plain as day. The tray clattered on the nightstand as I rounded his bed and sat down in front of him.

"Go away, Bane." His broken voice felt like sandpaper on my skin, abrading and rough. I shook my head and reached a tentative hand toward him.

"Who hurt you?" Each word an apology. Each word a plea. I couldn't rewrite his past and undo what had been done to him, but I could change his future. I could rewrite his stars and give him a future he deserved, no matter the cost.

River jerked when my hand started stroking smoothing circles on his back, and an agonized whimper punched its way out of him. I felt every muscle tighten like a tightly coiled spring. He was vibrating, edging away from me, but I couldn't let him go. I needed to know who had done this to him so I could tear them limb from limb and watch the light drain from their eyes. Taking a life wasn't something I ever thought I'd willingly do, but for him, I would. I would raze the world to dust if it meant he'd be safe.

"Please, River, talk to me." My voice trembled as I edged closer, drawn by a fierce, inexplicable need to protect him. I didn't even know how, but the urge burned through me. The only threat in this moment was the one inside his own mind —or maybe, somehow, it was me, because I would fight him for the truth. I would drag it from him before I let him crumble in silence any longer.

"No." His voice was hoarse, brittle, like shattered glass. "It doesn't matter. I-I'm not worth it." The words were barely audible, cracking as they slipped from his lips, but a sob caught in his throat, choking him, made it impossible to ignore. He was breaking in front of me. I could feel it. His resolve was collapsing under the weight of everything he refused to say.

"It wasn't your fault, River," I said, my voice soft but firm, each word deliberate, as if I could cut through the iron walls he'd built around himself. He shook his head violently, refusing to meet my gaze. His breath came in uneven gasps, chest heaving like he was drowning right in front of me. "It wasn't your fault," I repeated, desperate now, hoping against hope that he'd hear me, that he'd let me in before he slipped too far. But it felt like I was losing him, inch by inch. He was falling through my fingers, no matter how hard I tried to hold on.

We sat there, trapped in a silence so thick it felt alive, pressing down on us. His breath hitched in shallow bursts, while my lungs seized, like the very air had grown too heavy to breathe. Tension swirled between us, suffocating, his anxiety filling the room like a riptide dragging us both under.

"It wasn't your fault, River," I whispered, my voice barely more than a breath. "Look at me."

He lifted his head slowly, his movements stiff, like every part of him fought against it. But when his eyes finally met mine, everything else faded away. The world around us dissolved, leaving just the two of us—two broken boys, stranded on a fragile bridge. One wrong move and it would break, and all the progress I was trying to make would be lost. He would be lost to me forever, and I refused to let that happen.

"It wasn't your fault."

His eyes, rimmed red with unshed tears, locked onto mine, and something shifted in the air. There was a vulnerability there, raw and unguarded, that cut deeper than any of the words I'd tried to offer him. River was a walking contradiction—an innocent child buried inside a man's body, yet weighed down with the scars of someone who'd seen too much, suffered too long. Where there should have been laughter and light, there was only pain, a quagmire of suffering that threatened to swallow him whole.

He licked his cracked lips, a shuddering breath rippling through him as if he was fighting just to stay present. "I know," he whispered, the words so faint, so broken, I almost missed them entirely.

I nudged his head up with my knuckles, needing to feel his skin under mine. He said the words I wanted to hear, but they held no weight, no truth. I shook my head, refusing to let the moment slip away. "It wasn't your fault, River." My voice was firmer now, each word etched with urgency. "It wasn't."

His face flushed with shame, eyes dropping to his hands as he picked at the broken skin around his thumb until it bled. The first of his tears finally broke free, slipping down his cheeks in heavy, silent trails.

"It wasn't your fault," I repeated, pouring everything I had into those four words. I needed him to hear me, to really hear me—not just parrot the words back like a meaningless echo, but to let them sink in. To believe them. To feel them. To understand that his shame was misplaced, that the weight he carried wasn't his to bear.

River trembled beneath my hands, his whole body shaking like a fragile dam about to burst. I cupped his face in my hands, my thumbs brushing over his high cheekbones. I wanted to haul him into me, to merge his pain with mine and take it from him. To set him free. Desperate for him to stay with me, to not disappear into the void he was teetering over. "River, it wasn't your fault," I ground out, my jaw clenched so hard it sent a sharp pain through my teeth.

His bottomless green gaze finally lifted, his tear-clumped lashes trembling as he looked up at me, eyes filled with a depth of pain that left me breathless. We stayed locked like that for what felt like forever, the world shrinking down to just the space between us. His tears fell freely now, each one a stain on my soul. Each one carrying the weight of years of silent suffering.

"I should've... I could've stopped it..." His voice wavered, breaking apart mid-sentence, as if the mere thought of what he believed to be his failure was too much to bear.

"No," I said, shaking my head more forcefully. "There was nothing you could've done. None of it was your fault, River. None of it." My voice was almost harsh now, desperate to make him see the truth.

He opened his mouth to speak but stopped, his lips trembling. The guilt was still there, lurking behind his eyes, clinging to him like a dark shadow. But for the first time, I saw something else—a flicker of doubt, a small crack in the armor he had worn for so long. A flicker of hope sparked in the emptiness.

He collapsed into my arms as that dam finally broke and carried him down the river of his pain. His fingers curled around my henley, clutching himself to me. I felt every sob and gasping breath as he relinquished his hold on the trauma he kept locked inside his head.

I was beaten black and blue, charred to the bone, as his words burned right through me. I held him tighter as each story of humiliation spilled from his lips. As he described how johns wrapped wires around his throat so he couldn't breathe and laughed as he cried until he passed out.

How some tied his arms above his head and whipped him with riding crops, chains, and broken chair legs until his skin broke and bones shattered. Until his legs buckled and he passed out on the floor while they violated his unconscious body before discarding him without a second thought.

He'd been pissed on, defecated on, and forced to eat vomit. He'd been gang raped at gunpoint and had every inconceivable inanimate object thrust inside him, injuring him so badly they dumped him on the steps of the local hospital because they thought he was about to die.

They'd forced River to scream until all he could taste was blood. And when he'd tried to leave, they'd threatened him with death and starved him for a week.

He told me how they'd made him and the other boys watch as they executed an escapee with a bullet to the brain before being locked in the room with his body until they disposed of it, so they would understand the consequences of their actions.

I held him through every whimpered word, through every soul-crushing cry. I held him as he screamed in my arms, and the fight drained from him. Until the gut-churning sounds cracked and broke into nothing more than sawing breaths that echoed in the stagnant silence of his room.

When unconsciousness took him, I finally allowed myself to break and cried silently for the boy I'd known and for the man I was starting to understand. I cried for the injustice of the world and the horror humanity wrought on its own kind. I didn't understand how another soul could do that to another human being without care or remorse.

I shuffled us around until my back rested against the headboard and arranged River so he sprawled across my chest, protected in my arms as he slept. Exhaustion lined his face. The dark pits under his closed eyes were back, where his wet lashes kissed his tear-streaked skin. His full lips were bleached of color and pressed into a thin line. Even unconsciousness didn't allow him a reprieve from everything locked away in his head.

With nothing to distract my mind, it wandered to River's

explanation about how he shut down whenever they touched him. How he'd drift off into another place, a life he wished he'd lived but knew was never possible. Today proved his memories were like Pandora's box. Once he opened that seal, everything came spewing out, visceral and scathing, leaving nothing but rubble in its wake.

River broke me beyond comprehension today. I couldn't fathom how he managed to smile, let alone had the strength to get up every day and keep going. It wasn't that I lacked empathy; I just didn't know how to traverse the hell he was trapped in and bring him back to a world where the sunrise was a positive thing. I didn't know how to show him I'd give my last breath to see him live.

I held my broken heart in my arms as the pale early morning sun passed and painted the room with golden hues of late afternoon. I held on to him like I would never let him go. And after today's revelations, they would have to pry him from my cold, dead fingers before I relinquished my hold on him.

BY THE TIME MY LEGS WERE NUMB, AN IDEA STRUCK THAT I hoped was a stroke of brilliance. I had to get River out of here, away from the morning that had drained both of us and every depressing thought he'd associate with it. I wanted to show him what it felt like to be free. How amazing it was to fly without wings and blow the cobwebs away and start the day afresh.

My fingers trailed through his matted damp hair with one hand while the other rested protectively on his back, subconsciously checking his breathing was soft and even. God knew he needed a lifetime of sleep, but he'd have to wait a bit longer. My heart rate picked up as my resolve solidified, and my plan came together. A bolt of nervous energy struck my heart at the thought he might not want to do this with me.

I ran my knuckles down his cheek, brushing back the black strands that obscured his beautiful face. "River, angel?" I breathed him in as he stirred on my chest. I felt the moment he awoke as tension snaked through him, and his breathing stopped for a second as his eyes fluttered open.

River pushed back on my chest, re-situating himself so his chin rested on his hands as he looked up at me. A wavering smile flickered across his lips before the tip of his tongue toyed with a fresh scab. "H-hi," he said shyly, a delicate blush staining his cheeks.

"Hey angel," I murmured, running my fingers through his hair. My heart grew three times too big when he leaned into my touch, even after everything we'd been through this morning. "I thought we could go out? I want to show you something. How does that sound?"

He made a strangled sound in the back of his throat, and a wariness crept into his eyes, shutting off his emotions. River scooted back and knelt at my feet. It took everything within me not to chase after him and pull him back into the safety of my arms. He needed time to decompress and piece himself together. Time to decide if he was going to remain open with me, or if he was going to close himself off and shore up his walls that had fallen spectacularly.

Not wanting to tempt fate or push him any further, I got up and walked to the door. With my hand wrapped around the handle, I looked at him over my shoulder. "Why don't you have a shower, put on something sturdy, and I'll meet you downstairs."

River blinked at me. A wild animal stalked through his eyes, testing the bars of his cage like he didn't know whether he wanted to run or kill me. I stood patiently, waiting for any kind of signal as to where his mind was at. I might have looked calm, but I felt like a duck treading water, on the verge of sinking, because I didn't know how to swim.

After what seemed like hours, his top teeth sunk into that abused bottom lip, and he nodded once before getting up and locking the bathroom door behind him. I remained there at his door, stuck in stasis, waiting to hear the shower turn on, but everything remained deathly silent. I sent up a prayer to any god that would listen that River would come downstairs to meet me and left.

While I waited on tenterhooks, I quickly threw together a small picnic, grabbing chips, snacks, and making a couple of subs before packing it all in my bag and pulling a couple of bottles of water from the fridge. I left a glass of water and some Tylenol on the counter, along with a note to meet me out front. I let Shadow out into the yard to do his doggy business before shutting him in his crate. "Sorry, buddy, but you can't come with us," I soothed and poked his favorite treat through to him.

I headed into the garage, locking up behind me, and gave my all-black Hammerhead 1190 a quick once over to make sure it was in tiptop condition to transport my precious cargo. I wouldn't allow anything to go amiss this afternoon. River's safety was my top priority. It was a burden I'd chosen to bear, and I'd do so to the best of my ability. I should have realized the turn my thoughts had taken, but I was too focused on my tasks as I waited for the garage door to open. Bright sunlight blinded me, and fresh air filled my lungs as I took a long, deep inhale and pushed my bike out on the driveway to wait for River. Excitement thrummed through me. I'd never allowed someone else on my bike with me, and I couldn't think of anyone more worthy to break my rules for than River.

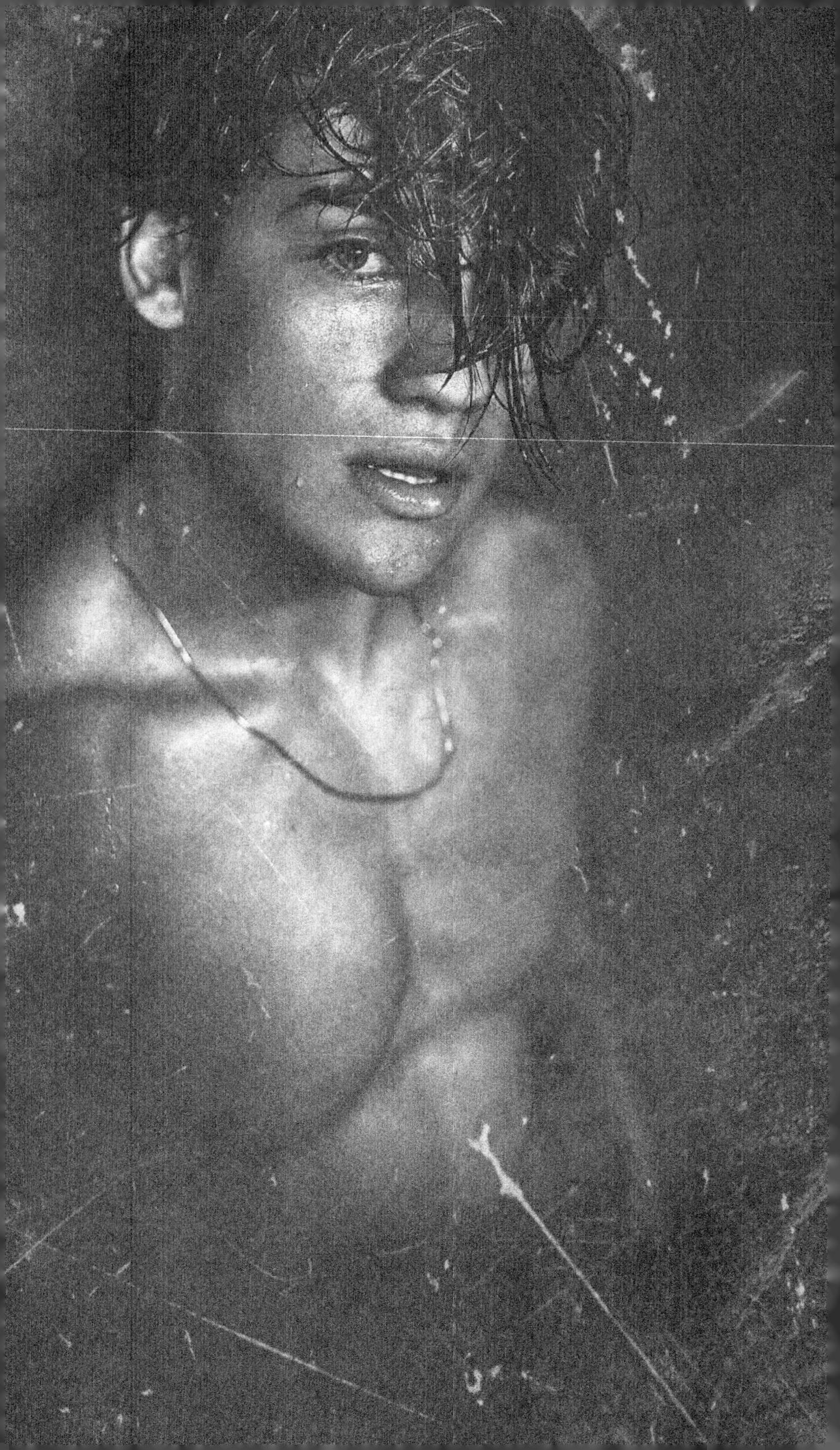

CHAPTER FOURTEEN
River

How Bane could still look at me so tenderly threw me for a fucked up loop after I'd spilled every dark facet that was locked away in my mind. The images, sights, and sounds I'd tried to bury in a place where the sun would never shine had been released from their cage. Something about the earnest look in his mismatched eyes brought them back to life in a kaleidoscope of suffering that was now stuck on repeat. Every time I closed my eyes, a different memory assaulted me, dragging its claws through me until I was nothing but ruined ribbons of red. I felt flayed wide open and vulnerable to my core. When I glanced down at the tiles beneath my feet, I expected to find them running red with a river of blood. Instead, the white tiles gleamed back at me, almost in mockery of my pain.

I hadn't been totally truthful with Bane—there was still one secret I'd kept from him, and I would take it to the grave. The brothers promised me that their faces would be the last I ever saw. It wasn't an idle threat; I'd seen the bloodlust and insatiable need in their eyes. They had taunted me about how good it would be to fuck me as I took my last breath, and then tortured me with all the things they'd do to the body I left behind.

I couldn't bring that to Bane's door. I refused to. It would break him in ways I couldn't even contemplate. I just needed to find the path of least resistance to break away. My bag was packed and stuffed in the back of my closet. I'd been squirreling away items of food and a few bottles of water, so I had something to get by with when I ran. I just needed to work out where to go or how to get as far away from here as possible. Holme Oaks was a large town, but it wasn't big enough for me to become invisible in, like a sprawling city metropolis would be. Dahlia had a wide reach and was well connected. She'd followed in her father's and grandfather's footsteps, and her business spanned most of the USA, South America, and beyond. One night, I'd overheard her laughing about the raids on her clubs and how pathetic the local law enforcement were. Dahlia thought she was untouchable, and I wanted to prove her wrong as much as I wanted to do right by Bane.

An idea grew like a seed in my mind, pushing back the faces of men that infected it like a poison. I knew what I had to do to pay penance to Bane for upending his life. I just hoped he would forgive me, because everything I was about to do would be for him.

By the time the hot water had run out, I had settled on a plan. It was simple but dangerous, and would probably cost me my life. But what kind of future did a fuck-up like me really have? None. So I might as well go out with a bang and doing it all for the only person who had ever cared about me seemed to be the best way.

Steam filled the bathroom, and I reached blindly for a towel and quickly dried off. New purpose filled me like a deadly venom, but I didn't regret it. The towel landed somewhere near the hamper as I discarded it and turned to the mirror, covered with condensation. With a trembling finger, I wrote a message through the tiny water droplets.

Thank you for everything, Bane.
This is for you.

Tears flowed through the gullies in my skin as I leaned forward and kissed the mirror, transferring all my pain into it. I might not like what I saw in the mirror, but as of right now, I couldn't hate it either. I didn't know if my actions were selfless or not, but at my core, I believed they were and convinced myself this was best for everyone.

My emotions were a mess, consuming me as I slipped on a pair of jeans, a black tee, and another one of Bane's hoodies. His scent saturated it, and each inhale of the cedarwood and leather smell made me feel like his arms were wrapped around me, and he'd always be with me. While yanking on a pair of boots he had gotten me, a new item in my closet caught my eye. A sweet-as-fuck leather jacket that hadn't been in there before. It fit like a glove. The distressed leather was supple and strong, and I loved it.

The downstairs was deserted by the time I got down there, and Shadow was snoozing in his crate, looking at home in a way I never would. On the counter was some water and a couple of tablets. Without thinking, I knocked them back and downed the water, welcoming the cool liquid into my raw throat. It was only after I set the glass down that I saw the note Bane left me to meet him out front. Swallowing down the nervous energy flowing through me, I headed to the front door.

The golden afternoon sun hung low in the sky, blinding me as I stepped out of the dark house. With my hand covering my eyes, I blinked, trying to clear my vision as fireworks burst across it. Bane came into focus and holy shit, I would remember this moment forever. When the time came to take my last breaths and the final montage of the time we'd spent together flashed before my eyes, this scene would be the last one. The one I'd keep forever with me in hell.

Bane was the embodiment of every fantasy I'd ever had. His six-foot-five frame leaned effortlessly against a black bike, sleek and hot as hell, its chrome exhaust gleaming in the light like it was studded with diamonds. The sight scrambled my thoughts and made my mouth water, desperate for just one taste as I struggled to take it all in. His dark-washed jeans clung to thick, powerful thighs, while biker boots hugged his calves, one foot casually crossed over the other. My gaze slowly traveled up his long legs to where his white shirt rode up just a few inches, revealing rich dark skin, a glimpse of deeply carved abs, and the top of an Adonis belt that made my knees weak.

I had never wanted anyone this intensely. Touch had always left me feeling violated and repelled, but with Bane, it was different. It was easy, as natural as breathing. It felt right. He felt like home.

A throat cleared, making me jump. I looked up through my lashes to see humor dancing in his hypnotic mismatched orbs. "My eyes are up here." He chuckled, pointing at his eyes with his fingers while a delectable smile lit up his face. I swallowed and licked my lips in case there was any drool on them, because the man was perfection.

"Do you like my baby, angel?" His gravelly voice wrapped around me like a physical caress, pulling me toward him.

Did he realize he kept calling me angel? Did it mean something more than just a slip of his tongue? "Mmmm." The sound resonated in my chest as I nodded, and his smile spread to his eyes, making my heart flip-flop in my chest. Fuck me, leaving was going to hurt even more than I imagined. It's for the best.

I'm nothing. A no one.

Unloveable.

"Would you like a ride?" He stepped up to me and unfolded his arms. "Let's get you zipped up and a helmet on, okay?"

I blinked, frozen by the tattoos revealing themselves as he stretched his arm out toward me. How had I not noticed the small intricacies of his tattoos after all this time? Hidden in the trees that made up the sleeve on his arm was a little boy lost in their depths. That little boy reminded me of me. Had he always kept a part of me with him? I flushed hot and cold as he stepped closer and zipped up my leather jacket. My breath started coming in short sharp pants as brushed his knuckles over my cheek, but my eyes focused on the way his teeth sunk into his full bottom lip. When he pushed a ridiculously large helmet over my head, my heartbeat echoed in my ears. Bane kicked his leg over his bike and straddled it, moving like he had no bones in his body.

Bane held his hand out to me, palm up, and without a thought, mine slid into his. The rough calluses sent waves of electricity across my smooth skin. He wrapped his fingers around my wrist and yanked me closer until I was flush with his side, and a wicked chuckle seeped past his lips. "Come, Riv, hop on. Put your feet on the kickstand, then wrap your arms around me. Simple."

Simple? Was he insane? Like a marionette on a string, I

followed his instructions, and soon I was nestled up close and personal with the solid slab of muscle that was his back, trying to mold my body to his as the bike snarled to life beneath us. Deep vibrations rolled through me as I clutched the sides of his jacket, unable to wrap my arms around his broad chest.

Bane laughed when I squeaked and glanced at me over his shoulder. With the visor up, I could see the joy sparkling in his eyes. The deepening lines around them pulled at the frayed strings of my heart as he smiled. "You good?"

Relinquishing my hold on him, I pulled my arm back and gave him a shaky thumbs up. He snorted, shook his head and pulled on some gloves before saying, "Good. Hold on."

He pulled my arms tighter around his chest, gave them a quick squeeze, then leaned forward and revved the engine. "I want to take you to my favorite places." With that, he pushed his visor down, twisted the throttle, and the bike lurched forward, wheels spinning on his driveway in his quiet, sleepy suburb.

Within seconds, we were flying across the blacktop, leaving the sprawling neighborhood behind. I'd been in Holme Oaks a few years but had never really seen any of it other than the inside of a blacked out van or a room. The less I focused on that, the better. So this experience really was a once in a lifetime one for me. A bucket list moment where I'd discover what it was like to fly without ever leaving the ground.

Things changed pretty quickly. Quaint two stories with neatly trimmed front yards morphed into oak-lined streets and yards so big you couldn't see the houses behind them. I noticed the cars also changed from sedans and trucks to town cars and sleek sports cars. When the houses became mansions, it felt like I'd been transported to another world.

Walls rose around the properties and electric gates at the entrances came with their own guard booths.

Jealousy burned through me like a solar flare. While I suffered, wishing for death, people lived in gilded cages that my dreams couldn't even comprehend. It made me sick to my back teeth. Not wanting to see any more, I screwed my eyes shut and buried my head against Bane's back, shutting the world out. It felt like he was rubbing everything I could never have in my face. Emotion clogged my throat as tears pricked the back of my eyes. How could this be what he wanted to show me?

"Riber, ook." Bane's muffled voice startled me. I could tell we were still moving, but the brutal sound of the wind rushing past had faded. "Ook." My eyes opened reluctantly and followed the direction his arm was pointing.

"Holy fuck!" I muttered in awe as my eyes swept across the breath-stealing views before me. We were halfway up a large hill, looking out over the whole of Holme Oaks. But the town spanning out in front of us wasn't what captivated me. My arms tightened around Bane as rays of golden light skittered into a kaleidoscope of colored fractals that danced across the water of the biggest lake I had ever seen. The far side seemed to meld with the horizon in a haze that made it look almost ethereal. Banked by a dark forest, it felt kind of symbolic, reminding me of the man my arms were wrapped around.

We continued along the road for about a mile before we turned off and headed down a well-worn track. I'd expected Bane to pull over on his bike as the terrain became seriously uneven, but he skillfully navigated our way down to a parking area by the bluffs before we rolled to a stop. He kicked out the kickstand and turned the engine off.

In a move that seemed to defy physics, Bane pulled me around him, so I sat in front of him, my back to his chest and overlooking the lake lapping at the shore. He tapped my helmet, unclipping it for me before doing the same with his and stowing them on the back of the bike. I tipped my head back against his shoulder as a gentle breeze coasted over my heated cheeks and smiled up at him before my eyes returned to the view.

Never had I ever felt peace like this before. I didn't know if the stunning vista, being in nature, or being wrapped in the arms of the only person who had ever made me truly feel safe in my life. Or if it was a combination of all of them. I should have been exhausted after I bared my soul to him this morning, and I was, emotionally, but I also felt rejuvenated, like right now was a fresh start.

But it couldn't be, no matter how much I wished it could. We were too different. Our lives were on completely different trajectories. Bane deserved the best of everything, and I deserved nothing. I would treasure these last few moments with him. I'd use the memories to keep me warm when I let the darkness back in. When I switched off my emotions and gave over control of my life to the devil.

"This is one of my favorite places to come to think," Bane said, the low resonance vibrating through me. "I love being surrounded by nature, leaving all the shit that comes with my job behind, and just feeling like I can breathe for once."

I slid my hands over his where they rested on my thighs and squeezed them, letting him know I'm here, as if it was something I did every day. Bane might be intimidating with his tall, broad, and dark form and strength enough to crush bone, but he was the sweetest, most caring person I'd ever met. He was a bleeding heart, open and honest to anyone who would give him the time of day. I was so glad his job hadn't made him closed off and jaded. He needed someone to protect him, who would nurture this side of him, who would cultivate it and allow it to grow. Bane deserved to be loved wholly, truly, with every beat of someone's heart, and that person could never be me.

The tip of my tongue wet my lips. "I-it's...peaceful." Every letter burned as I forced it out, but I did it for him.

Bane hummed in acknowledgement. He spread his fingers so mine slipped between them and held on tight, like I might float away if he stopped touching me. His heart hammered against me, mirroring the chaotic beat of my own. A small smile flickered around my mouth as tears pooled in my eyes and the beautiful view before us wavered. I swallowed down my emotions and blinked away my tears before they fell.

This felt like goodbye. A dream that I would wake up from. *Please, please let me never wake up.*

The longer we sat, the less meaning time held. The rest of the world slipped away and became nothing but a shadow. Clouds passed over the lake as reality shifted and we created our own. Wrapped in his arms, I relaxed into him, listening to stories from the years we were apart. How even though the Hendrix's were perfect on paper, they were nothing compared to the parents he lost, because they were searching for something in him they would never find. He wasn't the son they lost. The more he told me, the more my heart hurt for him, and I couldn't allow myself to fall deeper in l—

"I thought about you often, you know," he said earnestly. "I wondered where you were, who you had become. When I turned eighteen and had left the Hendrix's to start my training, I called Mrs. Wilkinson, but she said she hadn't seen you in years. That she'd tried to keep tabs on you, but after Elise left, no one would tell her anything."

I shrugged, because what could I say to that? *Oh, by that time I was on the streets, dumpster diving and turning tricks to get the occasional hot meal? That I was that close to giving up, that I prayed I'd die in my sleep and have done so every night since then?* No, I couldn't. He already knew enough to haunt him for a lifetime.

After we shared a small picnic, we sat with our legs overhanging the bluffs like kids, creating memories we wished we could have when we were younger. When the wind picked up, whipping up the waves on the lake, we packed up and headed back to the bike.

This time, when Bane sat on the bike, he pulled me on so I was facing him, my legs draping over his thighs. My breath hitched as his large hands cupped my face, pushing back the strands of hair covering my eyes.

"Thank you for today, River."

I looked up at him in confusion and arched my brow. Thank you? Had he hit his head on a rock? Nerves niggled in my gut, and I picked at the scab on my thumb as tension licked my shoulders.

"I know it wasn't easy." He licked his lips with the tip of his tongue, my eyes following it like disciples. "Thank you for trusting me, for opening up to me." I sniffed, my throat feeling tight. "Thank you for trusting me to be there to take care of you."

I shook my head, breaking free of his intoxicating hold. I couldn't think straight when he was touching me. His magic fingers short wired my brain. My arms formed a wall between us as they crossed over my chest, while that alarm blared in my head. *Run. Run. Run, before he gets too attached.* It was becoming difficult to breathe. I couldn't feel the icy wind howling through the trees. My fingers sunk into the soft leather, desperate for something to hold on to. Darkness drifted like smoke across my eyes as thunder rumbled above us in the clouds.

"River." Bane's hands sunk into my hair and pulled tight,

anchoring me to him. "Fight it," he growled. "Don't let your mind win. Stay with me. Fight. Please fight."

Static rang in my ears as he started to be swallowed by the smoke. Inhales and exhales sawed in and out of my lungs. The tenderness in his eyes was too much, his sweet, gentle touch suffocating. The emotions flowing across his face made this all too real, and it could never be more than this.

It could never be real.

"You're worth fighting for, River."

No. I shook my head and sunk my teeth into my bottom lip to hold back the whimper building in my chest. *No, I'm not. Why can't you see?*

"You are, River. You deserve to be happy."

No! That's a lie! A thick teardrop slipped from my eye, searing my skin. Bane sucked in a stuttering breath and caught it on his thumb, brought it to his lips, and kissed it like he could breathe life back into me. My heart did a backflip in my chest, and my resolve crumbled like a house of cards built on quicksand. My hand shot up to my throat, fingers digging into flesh, pulling at the invisible rope that was wrapped around it as I gasped, lungs starved for oxygen.

"I will prove to you that you are." Bane closed the distance between us, his thumb gently stroking my cheek bone.

It was heaven and hell. I was trapped in purgatory with everything I wanted right in front of me, everything I could never have. I was like an addict being offered a hit of crack.

When his lips met mine, I whited out. His tongue traced the shape of my mouth, making me gasp. Waves of electricity flowed through me as his tongue wrapped around mine, tasting, teasing, owning me. He kissed like I was the first drop of rain after a drought. He kissed me like he'd been made to worship me. I felt every minute movement of his fingers as they flexed in my hair, positioning me so he could deepen the kiss.

I was drowning in him. His cedarwood and leather scent saturated me as his mouth stole the air from my lungs, pushing me to the brink before kissing life back into me. His touch tried to reform me as I broke and shattered under his ministrations. Tears poured down my cheeks as I felt cherished. Wanted. Needed.

I felt like I was dying, because nothing real was ever this good.

Bane kissed me as the wind whipped around us, and every thought left my mind. Tension eased in my muscles, and I melted into him as he tried to fuse our bodies together like he wanted to get under my skin and hold my heart in the palm of his hands.

My arms wrapped around his neck, my legs wrapped around his hips, our chests touching as we shared oxygen with each stroke of our tongues. Bane's hands coasted down my back to my ass, his fingers sinking into the globes, kneading the needy flesh trapped in my pants. I bit his lip, making him groan as he rocked me against him. His thick length was like steel against me with every upward thrust. I needed to stop this before he regretted it, regretted me.

But I was drowning in him, and I found it hard to care. Thick drops of rain fell from the sky, heightening every touch, every taste, every sensation he elicited from me. I'd never been kissed like this. I'd never been kissed by another man. Fuck! Thunder cracked above us, booming like a shockwave, making the bike shake beneath us. Bane pulled back from me, wild and frantic, his lustful eyes nearly black as they darted all around us.

"Shit. Fuck," he gritted out and clenched his jaw, scrubbing his hand over his face like he needed to wipe me off him before I tainted him with my venom.

I shrank back at his rejection, and an ache formed in my chest. How stupid was I to think he actually cared about me? His words were just pretty lies painted in promises that were dipped in poison. Beautiful, but deadly. I was a hole, a body to be used for another's pleasure, not my own. Never my own.

Another clap of thunder rendered the air, temporarily deafening me, leaving a ringing in my ears. Bane's lips moved, but I couldn't hear anything he said. My heart beat so hard I thought it would shatter my ribs.

The rain was so heavy now I could barely see the lake through the steel curtains falling from the sky. Lightning illuminated the tumultuous clouds that churned above our heads.

Bane shoved me back and got off the bike. Ice slithered through my veins, my fingers and toes turning numb as he walked away. I closed my eyes, letting my head fall back against my shoulder, surrendering to the pain that fell as relentlessly as the rain from the sky.

Bane shoved a helmet over my head, and before I could react, he bodily moved me onto the bike, pulling me into him. But it was too late. His arms wrapped around me, but they no longer brought comfort. Not after he'd shown his true colors.

Every thunderstorm was a church without walls—and we were the eye—because we were all sinners, and we needed to repent. No one was perfect, not even Bane.

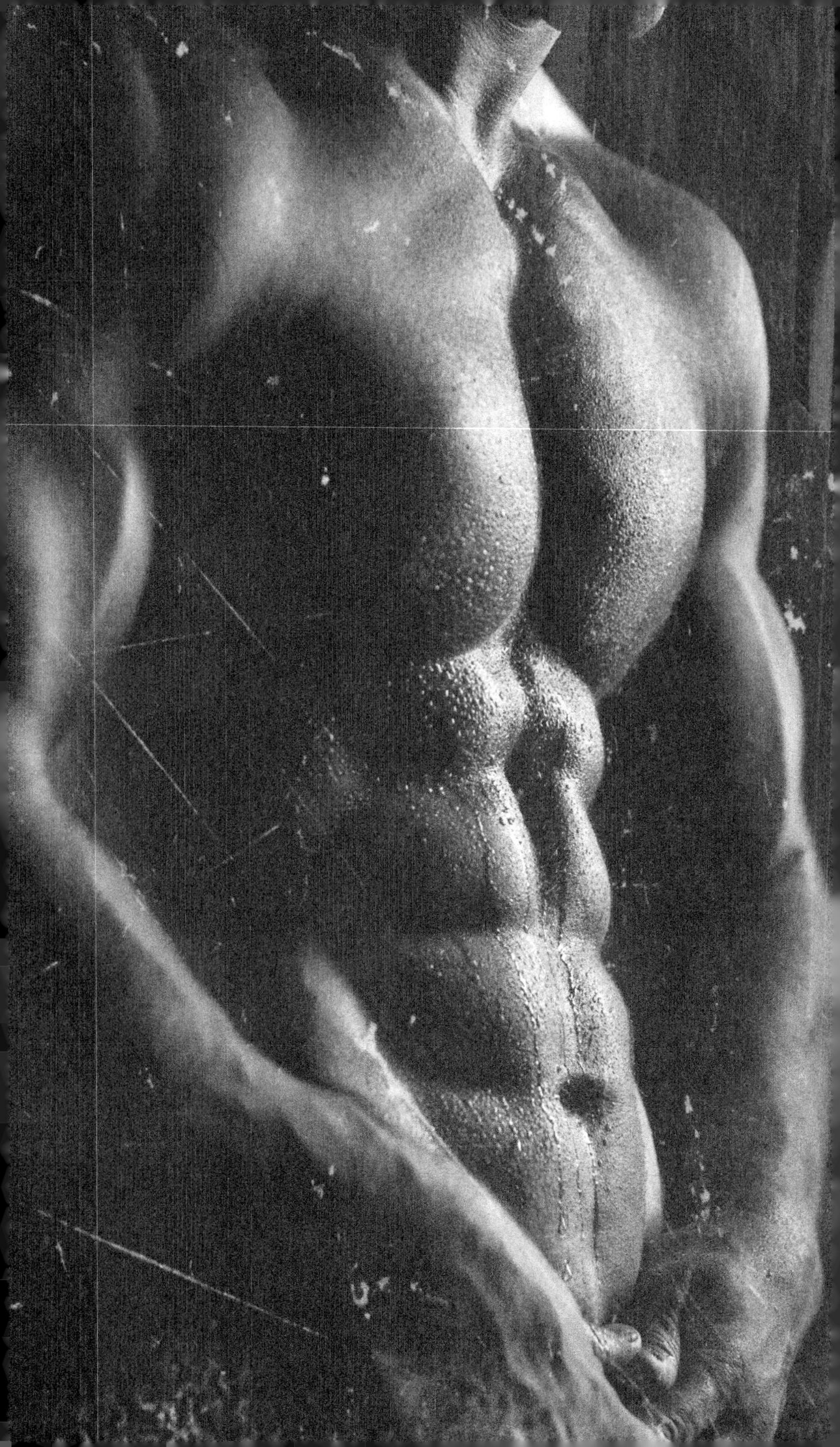

CHAPTER FIFTEEN
Bane

We'd barely made it through the connecting door from the garage before I was tearing at the jacket suctioned to his body. He was a vision. A dream. He was fucking everything. I couldn't get enough of his plush lips. Tasting him felt like a sin, but it was one I'd burn in the eternal fires of hell for without a second thought. I backed him up until his back slammed into the door and pushed my knee between his legs, needing to be closer to him, to feel his slick skin against mine. I'd never craved another person the way I did River.

Even if all I ever got was to feast on his mouth, it would be enough. Liar. I growled against his lips as his jacket bunched and caught around his wrists. He looked up at me through water logged lashes, cheeks flushed, those deep green eyes burning with lust. He was a siren's song, and I was bewitched.

I buried my head in the crook of his neck, gritted my teeth, and yanked at his jacket again while raining down kisses along *his fluttering pulse. My cock throbbed in my jeans, pushing against my zipper, trying to break free. My hips rolled, dragging my length against his. River was hard and hot, even through layers of sodden material. He tilted his head to the side, baring the column of his throat to me, and whimpered when I nibbled along the straining tendons.*

"Oh god, Bane."

I groaned against his cool skin, tracing the goosebumps spreading along it with the tip of my tongue. His jacket finally fell to the floor with a resounding wet thud, and he flinched at the sound. "Shh, angel, I've got you. I won't let anyone hurt you," I soothed, stroking his sides. He shuddered under my ministrations like a shot of adrenaline to the heart.

My lips trailed open-mouthed kisses up his neck to that sensitive spot just below his ear, then sucked on it hard. I wanted him to have a reminder of our time together. If this was the only time he allowed me to touch him, I wanted my marks on his skin. So in the coming days, he'd remember this moment as he touched and traced it with his fingertips. He'd remember us and everything we could be.

River's hands fell to my hips and pulled me into him as if he was trying to meld us into one. I wanted to bury myself under his skin. I wanted everything he was willing to give. I wanted him to choose me and never leave, but I couldn't ask that of him. Not yet, maybe never, but I had to hope. It was all I had.

"More," he whispered as my lips brushed the shell of his ear. "I want...I..." His fingers dug into my ass, holding me still as he thrust against me, his words dissolving into heavy, heated pants. Trepidation radiated off him, every touch tentative, scared, like he didn't know what pleasure was. That broke my heart. I knew what he'd endured and suffered through. It was wrong that he'd only been used, never worshiped like he should have, every second of every day. I would change that. I would willingly get on my knees for him every day until he understood passion.

Obsession. Until he knew how it felt to be the center of someone's world.

I nipped and sucked my way across his jaw, his hot gasping groans flushing against my face until my lips stole the air from his lungs as they locked back onto his. His hands wrangled my jacket off, then traced the planes of muscles across my back before slowly working the damp fabric of my shirt up my back. It took every ounce of strength to break contact with him—to stop touching—as he pulled it over my head.

"I need to taste you. I want to give you pleasure you've never felt before. I want you to cry my name when you come. I want you to wake up dazed, feeling like liquid gold. I want to give you everything you've never had before. Please?" I breathed against his mouth, my lips brushing his, painting every word into his skin.

His thick eyelashes fluttered at my words, and he rolled his lips inwards. A broken sound caught in his throat as he screwed his eyes shut. Emotions warred across his features from pain to elation, as if he couldn't believe the words he was hearing. Words I doubted he'd ever heard. River didn't answer, just dipped his chin to his chest and stroked the hairs on my nape. It was the only way he felt comfortable communicating. A fissure opened across my heart that was bleeding out for this perfect broken boy in my arms.

Without giving him time to think, I dropped to my knees and pulled off his boots. His fingers curled into the thick strands of my hair, nails scraping across my scalp. My cock throbbed in time with my thundering heartbeat. Stepping into him, I pulled his arms around my neck, bent my knees, and hauled his smaller frame up against my body. He wrapped his legs around my waist, hips rocking against me, his tantalizing length seeking friction against my abs. I cursed the layers that kept us separated.

The house blurred around us as I moved, my lips finding his like they were the only things that would keep me alive. Each *brush of their chapped skin sent pulses of electricity across me, lighting me up everywhere we touched. I took the stairs three at a time and stumbled on the top step, because I only had eyes for him. My bedroom door slammed into the wall as I kicked it open. River peppered my neck with white-hot kisses, and the tip of his tongue teased my ear as he panted against it, making a full-body shudder roll through me.*

Starving, I pinned him against the wall and lapped at his mouth, blindly reaching for the door to close it. I wanted him cocooned in the safety only I could offer him, like this moment would evaporate before my eyes if I didn't. River opened for me, and I growled into his mouth as his tongue tasted mine. Hot, wet, and sloppy, he consumed me, devoured me, a starving man finally tasting food.

Blindly, I crossed my room until my legs hit the edge of my bed, and we tumbled down onto the soft surface entwined. Hearts beating as one. Pulling back, I looked into his burning eyes, the exotic green consumed by his lust-blown pupils. I cupped his cheeks, brushing my thumbs across his flushed skin. I kissed him once, twice, before sucking his lip into my mouth. A promise of what was to come.

My fingertips trailed down his chest, my palm resting over his heart. I could feel it punching its way out of his body, and the air around us thickened. He'd never voluntarily bared his body in front of me. I knew his back was ravaged with scars, and I prayed that was the only part he had lasting signs of the abuse he'd suffered. But I wasn't a fool. I knew that was an errant dream, but I wanted him to be comfortable with me in every way.

"You're beautiful, River." *He scoffed, his eyes shuttering as I pulled his hoodie up, slowly revealing his stomach. He had filled out some since he'd been in my care, but it was still a stark reminder to see his hip bones straining against his skin. A delicious trail of black hair led from his naval down to the top of his black boxer briefs. The cool air made goosebumps prickle his damp skin. I soothed them away with my tongue, licking and tasting every inch of flesh I uncovered while inhaling his deliciously sweet cinnamon and orange scent. My mouth watered, my need growing with each passing second.*

River pushed up onto his elbows. The heady weight of his gaze tracked me as I worked my way up to his chest. His hoodie was bunched up to his chin as I toyed with the hard nubs of his nipples before sucking one into my mouth and circling the other with my thumb. The deep groan that rumbled in his chest had me leaking furiously into my boxers. No one had ever had this effect on me. I'd had sex before, but I always had to force myself to remain present and in the moment with my partners. I'd never been able to let go and be completely absorbed like I was now.

River was everything I'd ever dreamed of. One look, and I was under a compulsion only he could wield. I was done fighting myself. I was done fighting him. I would fight for us and make him see the truth that he was too broken to see, too scared to give credence to. I had enough strength and faith for the both of us to guide us into the light, one he could never refute.

"Up." My voice was low, gravelly. River's dick flexed under me, and I smiled against his chest before rising onto my knees and pulling his hoodie and tee off in one go.

My breath punched out of my chest as I took him in. His ribs and collarbone stood out in stark relief against his taut skin. He was littered with silvered scars that sliced into me. How could someone so perfect have suffered so much? Tears pricked my eyes as I traced them with my fingers and mouth. I worshiped every one, replacing pain with adoration.

His head fell back onto the twisted sheets, fingers twisting into them, holding himself back. Insecurity flickered across his face like he didn't know if he wanted to push me off or pull me closer.

"It's ok baby, I've got you," I whispered against his neck, inhaling him. Lust burned through me, reshaping me into some-

thing that was worthy of him. "I want to see you, all of you." I could beg and plead, instinctively knowing he'd give me anything I asked for because that was what he was conditioned to do. Be a fuck toy, a hole to use. But I wanted him whole. I needed him to choose this. Me.

"I..." He licked his lips and gasped for breath. I pushed up onto my elbows, giving him some breathing room and notching down my intensity. It was the hardest thing I'd had to do. "I-I want... t-to see you too."

My breath whooshed past my lips, and I nodded. Bracing on my right arm, I flicked the button of my pants open with my left and pulled the zipper down. With trembling hands, River released his hold on the sheets to wrap his fingers around my jeans and slowly pushed them down my thighs until I could kick them off.

"Wow, Bane." His words were pained. I couldn't tell if it was from desire or fear. His Adam's apple bobbed in his throat, then his eyes flicked up to mine. Shadows swirled in their depths, coiling around us, suffocating me.

With my arm wrapped around him, I repositioned us until we were lying on our sides, resting against the pillows. I cupped his face, brushing my thumb over his cheekbone. The heat radiating off him made my fingers tingle. "We don't have to do anything you don't want to. I..." My teeth sunk into my bottom lip as I rolled over words in my head. "I want you." His lips twitched, but his eyes still looked haunted. "I want to give you everything." I brushed a kiss against his parted lips. "You need to be comfortable, to feel safe."

River cut my words off, placing his finger on my lips before pushing against my chest until I was on my back. My fingers latched onto his hair, pulling him into me like our lips were drawn together by a magnetic connection that even fate couldn't stop. He licked into my mouth, savoring each time our tongues wrapped around each other. My free hands stroked over the rigid scars along the lean planes of his back, wishing I could map them out with my lips and suck the memory of other men's touch off his skin.

Breaking the kiss, River nuzzled into the crook of my neck and took a deep inhale before setting me alight. His touch superheated the blood pulsing through my veins. The feel of his sweat-slicked skin against mine made my body a molten ball of sensation. He teased and tortured his way down my chest to my abs, tracing each muscle with the tip of his tongue while incoherent sounds poured from my mouth.

"River..."

He sunk his fingers into the top of my thighs. The bite of pain made my cock jerk and slap against my abdomen, leaving a thick trail of precum across my skin. My eyes rolled back in my head as he lapped up the slick trail. He groaned as my taste spread across his tongue and flicked his eyes up to mine. Fire and ice warred in them. He was fighting his demons to bring me pleasure. I was his only focus. It was a heady feeling, but my stomach dropped as a darkness stole the light from him. Before I could say anything, he wrapped his hands around my shaft, giving it a slow pump.

River lowered his body to the bed between my spread legs. I bent my knees up, making room for his shoulders as he sank down and licked my balls before sucking one into his mouth. Tortured moans spilled from my mouth as he continued to work my length in his loose grip, alternating attention from one ball to the other.

I was a writhing mess, my body nothing but nerve endings. One hand buried itself in the damp strands of his hair, guiding him to my aching dick, while the other gripped the pillow by my head like I'd be swallowed into the vortex of the storm building between us if I let go. I was coming apart at the seams, drowning in sensation, and he hadn't even wrapped his lips around my cock yet.

A filthy chuckle vibrated against my inner thigh. River's talented mouth carved pleasure into my skin with lips and teeth, mapping out every erogenous zone I had, driving me to the brink of insanity. It had never leaked so much in my life. Precum flowed from my slit, lubricating the slide of his palm against the sensitive skin.

I blinked heavy lids when the tip of his tongue dipped into my slit. "Ooh, fuck." He smiled around my tip as I forced my eyes to focus on the image I'd only ever dared dream was possible. And fuck, my imagination sucked, because it didn't hold a candle to the vision before me.

River's full lips stretched around the glans as his eyes bored into mine. A connection formed between us that could never break. I felt it take root in my soul; something precious I would spend the entirety of my life cultivating.

"Shit." I gasped as he teased the frenulum with short feather-light licks before sucking on the tip and moaning as a bead of precum burst out of me. "So, so good, angel."

He blinked up at me almost innocently, hollowing his cheeks and swallowing down my thick length. I nudged the back of his throat until his esophagus constricted around me. Tears filled his eyes, but it was like he didn't need to breathe as he continued to swallow me down until his nose brushed my groin.

"Fuck. R-River..."

My head thrashed from side to side as he set a punishing pace, working up and down my length. Loud salacious noises filled the air, mixing with my labored inhales. Every thought in my brain scattered to the far reaches of the cosmos. Fireworks burst behind my eyelids as his drugging lips dragged me into a euphoria I'd never contemplated could exist. I was liquid, molded by his touch.

He looked exquisite kneeling before me, and if my brain worked, I'd have told him to stop. That it was me who was supposed to give him this level of pleasure, but every word died before it had a chance to form, and I succumbed to the spell he wove.

"I...fuck...I'm...c-c..."

River pressed two fingers on my taint, just below my prostate. A bolt of electricity shot straight to my balls, drawing them up tight against the base of my shaft as liquid fire flowed through my veins. My teeth sunk into my bottom lip so hard the copper tang of blood coated my tongue as my orgasm rolled through my body. It wasn't a smooth build up; it was a ferocious storm. Lightning and thunder exploded through me as I thickened in his mouth, shaft pulsing, my balls impossibly tight. I fought to hold on for a second longer, fearing I'd never get to see this again.

"Oh, fuck! Ohmygod. Shitdamnit. Angel!!"

With a final gasping breath, River pulled off before swallowing me down even stronger than before. My hips arched off the bed, and I buried myself deeper inside him than was truly possible. White light blinded me and spread through me, my toes curling up as my orgasm detonated.

Wet heat surrounded me. So warm, so fucking real, I could smell my arousal thick in the air. My eyes flew open, and my heart caught in my throat as my erotic fantasy and reality collided. River's lips stretched around my pulsing cock as I spilled thick ropes of cum down his throat, flooding him. He wasn't able to swallow it all, and it seeped from the corners of his lips.

"Oh my fucking god," I cried, leaving my body. I floated among the stars, drowning under a sea of sensation so immense I couldn't draw air into my lungs. My fingers wrapped in his hair, holding him to me, making sure he took every last drop before I released him.

Gasping breaths punctuated the silence filling my room. I forced my eyes open again to realize it wasn't a dream. River knelt between my legs, chest heaving, my cum dripping down his chin. Tears streamed down his cheeks as he fought to get air into his lungs.

"Fuck! This...You. Oh my god." Tears pricked my eyes as

I doused the euphoric glow in ice water and jumped off my bed. River blinked, his eyes tracking my movements as I paced across my bedroom floor, back and forth like a wild animal caged and starved.

Shame and guilt blistered through me. Fuck! I'd thought I was dreaming. Even though it had seemed so real, it was a dream, a fantasy. But it wasn't. It was real. Guilt seared my lungs as I struggled to catch my breath. I'd used him, just like everyone else. I was a piece of shit who didn't deserve to breathe the same air as him. How could he ever trust me after this? Acid burned the back of my mouth as I swallowed a mouthful of vomit back down into my tumultuous stomach.

"This was a mistake—" I shook my head, words failing me. I was being swept out to sea for the crimes I'd committed against him. He trusted me, and I violated it just like everyone else had done. I'd used him. "This was a—"

"If you say mistake again..." River rasped, barely able to form words from the abuse I'd inflicted on his throat. He clutched one hand around his neck, stroking it absentmindedly with his thumb while the other knuckled over his heart.

"It was a mistake, River. I should—" My phone rang, cutting me off. That was Montoya's tone. I knew I needed to answer it, but I needed to fix this more. My hands clawed through my thick hair, as I agonized over what to do. Shit! Each inhale burned, flooding my lungs with venom until I was frozen with indecision. I had a job to do, and I'd never hated it more than at this moment. I was at a crossroads, and my choice now would send ripples across my life that I might not survive.

River knelt on my bed, his arms wrapped around his chest like it was the only thing holding him together, looking like he was about to break. The tension between us was suffocating and insufferable. The ringing stopped only to start again, and my eyes darted between his fracturing form and the phone on my nightstand.

"Wait there," I barked harshly and winced as River flinched like I'd struck him, making himself as small as possible, like he wished he was invisible. Fuck! I keep fucking everything up. Why was I such a shitty person? The boy who owned me heart and soul was suffering because of me, and I was choosing my job over mending what I'd broken. Selfish. Shaking my head, I sucked in a ragged breath and grabbed my phone. "Yes."

"Well, shit, that's one way to answer the phone," Montoya snarked back at me to hide the hurt lacing her tone. *Might as well keep on digging now.*

My head tipped back on my shoulders, and I pinched the bridge of my nose. My head pulsed, and it felt like my eyes were about to explode. "Sorry," I grunted through gritted teeth. I was fraying, unraveling each moment I couldn't right this wrong with River. The feeling of River under my touch was fading as inhales sawed in and out of my dry mouth. Montoya's voice became background noise as I spun on my heel to find him gone. The snick of the lock engaging on his door filled me with dread.

"Benson! Are you listening?!"

"Huh?"

"Jesus," she muttered. I fell to my knees, staring at the locked door across the hallway. All I wanted to do was crawl on my hands and knees and beg him to forgive me. To give me a chance to explain. It was as obtainable as stopping water from slipping through my fingers. "You need to get down to the station. Now. We've got a body—"

"Shit! Be there in fifteen." I hung up and threw my phone on the bed as images of River assaulted my addled mind and jumped into the shower. Ice-cold water burned my skin, freezing me to my core. My heart stuttered in its prison and shattered. The tiles were unforgiving as my head crashed into them, tears seeping from my closed eyes before being washed away like they never existed. It felt like I was grieving, even though I knew he was breathing just a few feet away from me.

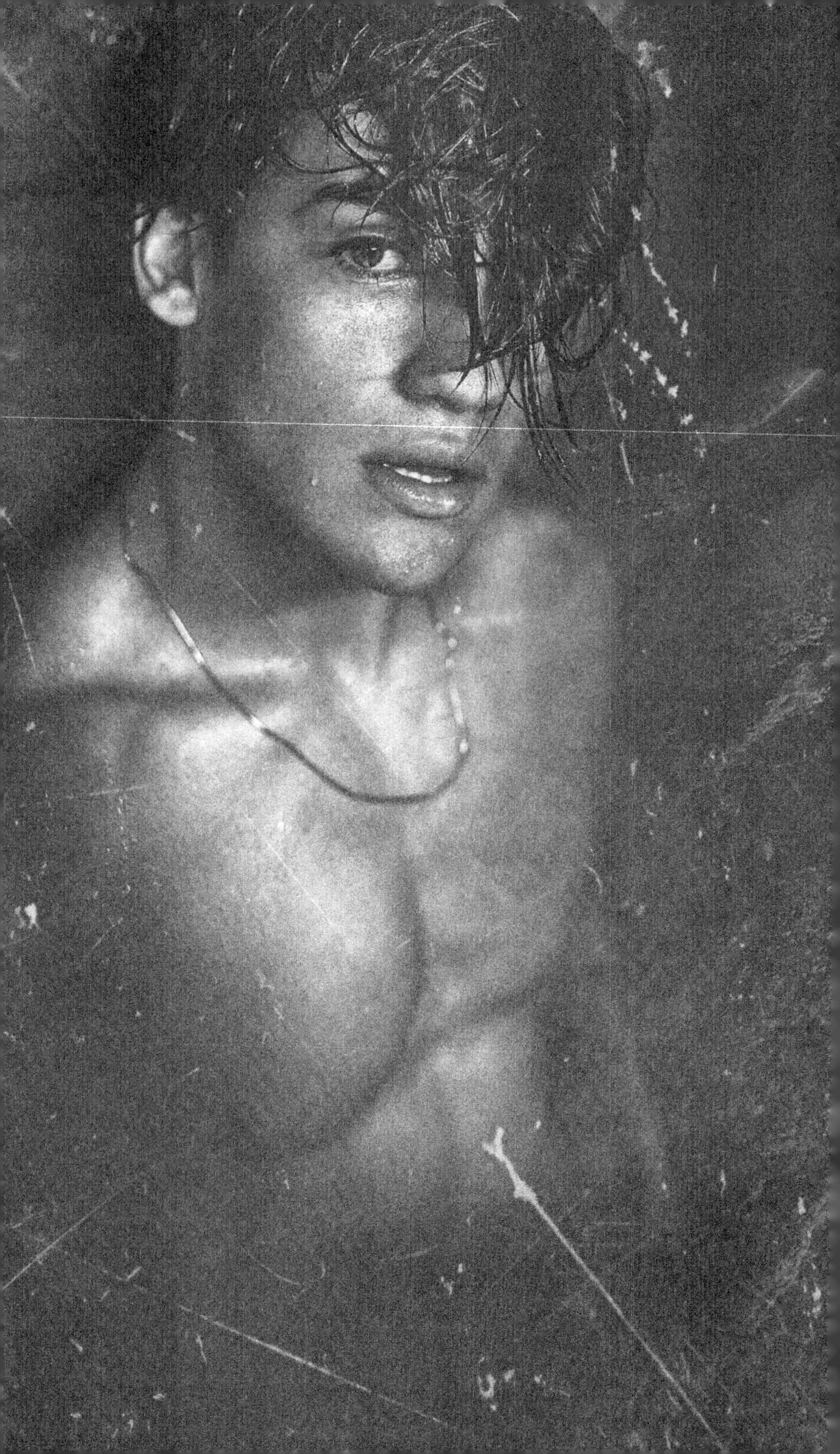

CHAPTER SIXTEEN
River

I stumbled from his room, choking on my breaths as my lungs revolted when I sucked air in through my clenched teeth. Tears burned down my cheeks, carving agony into my bones. This is what happened when you gave your heart to someone and trusted them. I gave him the power to destroy me, and he did it with four little heartless words. *This was a mistake* played on repeat in my head like a scratched record, drilling my pain into me until I was consumed by it. I tripped over my feet as I fell into my door and ended up sprawled on the cold floorboards.

The desire to move was long gone. If he didn't care about me, who was left? I'd rather be six feet under. I was more alone in the world than I'd ever been, flying high one second, only to crash back into the ground, smashed to smithereens.

His muffled voice sounds distorted, like he was trapped

on the other side of a landslide. I wanted to call out to him, beg him to keep me, but what was the point? What happened today was my fault. I fucked everything up.

I was worthless.

Broken.

Disgusting.

I gave him the only thing I had to give that really meant anything—my body. He loved it until he didn't. They always love the illusion over reality. I should have known better than to let myself dream. No one tells you that nightmares were also dreams. The look of disgust and loathing that distorted his beautiful features would be etched into my memories for as long as I breathed.

The shower turned on, drowning out the last time I'd ever hear his voice. This was my swan song. My last goodbye. I tried to convince myself that this was okay, that this made everything easier. If only I could turn those pesky, manipulative emotions off. On my hands and knees, unable to find the strength to stand, I pushed the door closed and locked it, then curled up on my bed. Silent tears poured from my aching eyes. Visceral agony consumed me, and I gave in to the darkness clawing at me.

I was trapped in a war between my mind and my heart. My brain knew the truth, but my heart refused to accept it. I wanted him to want me the way he said he did. I craved it, fucking needed it like I needed air to breathe. My body was scarred from the abuse of a million faceless men, but the wound Bane left on my heart was the one that made me pray for it all to just end.

Time passed unchecked, but the pain inside me didn't abate; it only grew in its intensity. His heavy footsteps stormed out of his room, halting by my door. His labored breaths sounded like a battering ram. I held my breath, praying he'd knock or kick it down, desperate to hear his voice as he begged me for forgiveness, but it never came.

A door slammed downstairs, echoing through the hollow walls. I expected to hear the throaty rumble of his bike, but all I caught was the low hum of an engine from the driveway. Tires squealed against the blacktop as he floored it away from me. He couldn't wait to be rid of me, leaving me behind like he'd done before. I should have known history would always repeat itself.

My knuckles bit into the flesh of my thigh, fire burning under the skin as I brought my fist down onto the same spot again in another bruising blow. I needed another source of pain to unlock my chest. It might sound crazy, but I could regulate physical pain. Own it. Even seek release in it. The scars on my arms were testament to that. My thigh pulsed, but it wasn't enough to override the surge I was drowning in. I could smash my fist or head into a mirror, but that would create too much mess, and I'd already stained Bane's life with my presence.

Gritting my teeth, I let the memories flow. They shredded what was left of my heart as his bright smile flickered through my mind. The taste of his lips. Soft and warm as they devoured me. The silky heavyweight of him on my tongue. His intoxicating cedarwood and leather scent. The one that permeated the entire house and my godforsaken soul.

When the only thing I could focus on was the poisonous pain spreading through my leg, I could finally breathe. This, I knew and understood. I was a master at it. Slipping off the bed, I wobbled as my feet hit the cold floor, the room spinning around me. Unable to bear weight on one side, I pushed myself to the closet and grabbed my bag. Glancing over my room one last time, my eyes snagged on the permanent marker on the nightstand, and I shoved it into my pocket before picking up a tee off the floor.

The walls moved of their own accord as I stepped into his room and shoved my shirt inside his pillow. I wanted him to have a piece of me with him, even if he didn't want me. There would always be a part of me that wanted him. From there, I walked into his bathroom. His scent hit me in a cloud of steam. My heart stuttered for a beat before it started racing. The mirror above the sink was clean and dry, thankfully. I pulled the pen from my pocket and wrote the words I'd never be able to say.

I'm sorry for ruining everything.
Forgive me.

Downstairs, I kissed Shadow goodbye. His large eyes blinked up at me as he tilted his head to the side in confusion. "I'm sorry, baby boy." He licked my face, making me swallow around the ball of emotion lodged there. "I can't stay." I sobbed, tear drops clinging to my lashes. "Look after Daddy for me." He licked me again, and I took that as a yes and gave him a treat before shutting him in his crate.

My boots were where I'd left them by the front door. I grabbed them and headed into the attached garage and slipped them on. From listening to Bane's conversations with Montoya, I knew there was a blind spot on the side of the garage where his property bordered the old lady's next door. This was my only shot at getting out undetected, leaving Bane none the wiser.

Luckily, the garage window was unlocked. I flicked the latch and pushed it open enough to drop my bag down. After one final glance around, I slipped out and closed it behind me. I slid my arms through the straps and tightened them around my shoulders. I didn't know how long it would take me to get back into town, but knowing I had some supplies was enough for me to trust the plan I had would work. It had to fucking work. I'd only get one shot.

The boundary fence was low on this side of the house, so it was easy enough to climb it and get into her yard. The drop on her side took me by surprise, but a bush broke my fall and the rest of the undergrowth gave me enough cover to get to the end of her property unseen. I could hear her talking to someone on her back deck. Guilt ate away at me as I clambered through the post and rail fence at the back of her yard by the woods. Bane had recently had a six-foot solid fence installed on his for my protection.

I scoffed at the idea. The only thing I needed protection from was him. The devil couldn't reach me, so he took the most precious thing I had out of my life. I wouldn't go willingly to my grave. I would make every second count, because even though Bane turned his back on me, I wouldn't turn mine on him. Everything I did from here on out was for him.

It wasn't long before I came to the end of the row of houses and reached the sidewalk. I paused, taking in the surrounding streets, and tried to regulate my breathing before heading in the opposite direction to the one Bane had taken me on his bike. Every step hurt. I was already raw, but it rubbed salt on my open bleeding wounds. I could suffer for him, to help bring an end to the suffering Black Dahlia brought to so many like myself.

A craving crawled under my skin that I hadn't felt since my eyes fell on Bane in that interrogation room. The scent of tobacco smoke drifted on the gentle breeze as the golden sun in a cloudless sky mocked me with its brightness. At the bus stop, a man sat in a heavy coat, with a cigarette between his lips, staring intently at his phone.

"Hey." My voice sounded like I'd swallowed glass. "Can I bum a smoke?"

The guy looked up. He was younger than I expected but had a refined air to him. His brown eyes narrowed for a second as he inhaled, the cherry burning a fiery red. "Sure." He held out the packet to me, flicked the bottom to make one pop forward, and passed me his lighter.

"Thanks," I mumbled around the tip as I placed it between my lips and lit up. Taking a deep inhale, my eyes fell closed as the thick toxic smoke filled my lungs, pushing its venom into my veins.

"No problem, kid," he said in a gruff, no nonsense voice. "You got somewhere to go?"

I grunted in response and chewed the inside of my cheek as I toed the cracked pavement, unwilling to answer his question. Why couldn't he be like everyone else, too wrapped up and consumed in their own lives to notice mine spilling around me in a pool of blood?

"I'm not some kind of stalker." He huffed a breath, smoke billowing between his lips. "You just look like you're running."

I snorted. "Story of my life." My voice cracked and broke, just like my shattered heart. I inhaled a long drag and rolled my lips inward to stop the flow of words and palpable pain that wanted to spill from me.

"Don't talk much, huh?" I shook my head. "Spent time in the foster system, I assume?" He took my silence as agreement. "Me too, kid. It might suck now, but if you want to, you can make it out and stop the cycle from repeating." He ran a hand through his shaggy dark hair. "I left at eighteen, with only the dollars they gave me to my name. Now I run shelters across the state."

I blinked up at him in his sneakers, jeans, and big thick coat. I couldn't see it if I was being honest, but he laughed like it was no skin off his back. Probably wasn't—we had to grow a thick skin early in the system or it'd chew you up and spit you out before your age ended in teen.

"Don't look at me like that." He snorted. "It wasn't easy. I worked my ass off to get where I am." He stuck his hand in his pocket and pulled out a card, passing it to me.

Better Together was embossed on the thick white card along with the name Alan Rothschild. I flipped it over a couple of times, noting the phone number scribbled on the back before shoving it in my pocket. I could feel the weight of his gaze on me, but I ignored it and took another inhale.

"Keep that with you. Never know when you might need it. My name is Alan, by the way. Stick with me, and I'll make sure you get to town. I'm assuming you don't have any money?" Without waiting for me to answer, he handed me a new packet of smokes and a lighter. My heart flipped from this random act of kindness by a total stranger. "Come on kid, let's go," he said just as the bus pulled to a stop at the curb in front of us.

Holme Oaks was bustling and vibrant, the main strip filled with hoards of shoppers and friends. But like any metropolis, behind the glittering facade, you could find the darkness that existed around every corner. Blood money flowed just below the surface. Extortion, racketeering, and every addiction under the sun walked hand in hand with glowing white smiles and million-dollar haircuts. You just had to know where to look, then follow the breadcrumbs to the places where the sun never shone as sin owned your soul.

I'd never walked around downtown, but all towns felt the same. It didn't matter where you were in America—whether in a small town or a sprawling city—it was never hard to find the places where the broken and the addicts drifted, clinging to the shadows.

For my plan to work, I had to be exposed long enough to be seen, so I stopped by a coffee shop on the way and grabbed an XL Americano before taking a side alley and leaving the world most knew behind. There were always districts that lived in the shadows, even on the brightest days, where the shop facades had barred windows, cracked glass, and the bullet holes. Sidewalks were broken and weed ridden, unattended and overused. Litter, broken bottles, and used needles hugged the curbs and built up in building entrances. The old industrial units that had yet to be repurposed were where I was heading for the night. They wouldn't take me in the cold light of day, not when they could be seen. The stench of urine and rotting food replaced clean air and the delicious scents drifting from artisan shops selling handcrafted delicacies.

A faded tarp covered a hole in a wall. I'd spent long enough on the streets to know this marked the entrance. I pulled it aside and stepped through into hell on earth, where the living prayed for death and the dead begged for life. The stench of desperation and discontent was smothering. Small fires flickered faintly in the darkness, surrounded by groups of people while others lay passed out on stained mattresses with needles still in their arms and vomit drying on their lips. The hairs on the back of my neck stood on end as a woman's screams rendered the air, but no one ran to her rescue. It was a regular occurrence in drug dens like this. If you had no money, you used whatever means you had to pay. It began with stealing, but when the monster of addiction had you firmly in its grip, you'd sell your soul for another hit. What was a beating or rape when oblivion was but a few seconds away?

What did it say about me, that I felt more at home, more at ease in this environment than I did at Bane's? He kept his clean, ordered white on white house perfectly maintained, but it made me realize the gulf standing between us. I felt like the filth on the bottom of his shoes; a pretender, an actor playing a role, expecting to be thrown back onto the streets before I could blink.

Beams of light seared my eyes as I trudged in the opposite direction of the screams, exhaustion settling into my bones. In our own way, we were all just trying to survive, to make it from one day to the next in places like this, chasing oblivion, a fleeting moment of reprieve, of happiness. But death stalked us all from the shadows, counting down the seconds until he could claim us.

"You're new," a voice snarled from the dark corner. "No one comes in here without my knowing. Pay the levy, or I'll take a payment of my choosing." A sneer curled the man's lips, revealing rotten teeth as he stepped into the muted light.

Without answering, I shoved my hand in my pocket and pulled out a fifty, holding it up so he could see it. He reached for it, but I stepped back, only to walk into a wall of muscle. Glancing up over my shoulder, I saw two men who looked like they could rip my throat out with their bare hands. The confidence I'd had in my plan evaporated, and my heart thundered up my throat. "I-I." I clutched at my throat. "Just need...t-t...l...la...low...night."

Rotten Teeth looked me over, then nodded to the guys behind me. "Take him." The bald guy behind me put his hand on my shoulder and squeezed, eyeing me like I was his favorite snack. His yellowed tongue teased his bottom lip, and I shuddered at the implication. "But first, payment." I held the bill out in front of me as Rotten Teeth reached out a gnarled hand, his black-tipped fingers snatching it from my grasp and stuffing it into his inside pocket. "This gets you one night. If you bring the feds to my door, there ain't nowhere you can hide from me."

With my arm wrenched painfully behind my back, I was forced through puddles of filthy sewage, the foul stench making my nose bleed. Each step felt heavier as my guilt weighed me down and my resolve crumbled. The farther we went, the darker and more oppressive the air became. My skin crawled, every nerve alight with disgust, and my stomach twisted in revolt. Rats darted through the heaps of rotting garbage lining the path they pushed me down, their slick bodies vanishing into shadows as our waterlogged footsteps echoed through the cavernous, crumbling warehouse. A suspicious-looking bag covered in duct tape was half buried under rubble, and I thanked the gods I was led away from it. I'd spent enough time with dead bodies to last me a lifetime. I might not have known who was in there, but I couldn't do another night with one.

"This is yours." Baldy pointed to a two-foot square dry bit of cement. A pile of cardboard boxes lay a few feet away, strewn across rubble where the wall had collapsed. "Pretty boy like you won't last an hour in a place like this." He huffed and leered at me.

Little did he know, I'd spent nearly two years on the streets. I knew exactly what I'd have to do to survive. I spun around and flicked the pocket knife I'd lifted off him open and pushed it against his gut. His eyes widened in shock, but all it did was intensify the way he looked at me.

Holding his hands up, he took a step back and licked his

lips. "I'll be seeing you later." His words hung in the air, a threat as much as a promise. I watched him walk away. I wouldn't be sleeping here tonight or any night, but with nothing else to do, I grabbed some boxes and made a makeshift bed to keep my mind occupied instead of thinking about the colossal mistake I was making and the guilt encircling my heart.

With that done, I pulled my legs up into my hoodie, grateful Bane had never taken his back from me. This one was large enough to fit my legs and bag under it, so I could keep everything safe. Blindly reaching into the bag, my eyes darting around checking for threats, I pulled out a bottle of water. The lukewarm liquid was enough to soothe the abused flesh of my throat. The damage done from Bane's dick would pass in a few days—if I lived that long. As long as I had enough time to do what I needed to help him, that was all that mattered. I couldn't care less about my life, not if it didn't include him. Without realizing it, he had been what had kept me going all these years and now, knowing the truth that we would never be anything, I had no reason left to fight.

By the time the temperature dropped, my teeth were chattering, and I struggled to keep my eyes open. I was losing my fight with staying hypervigilant. It was hard to determine how many hours had passed, but I assumed it was the early hours of the morning. I was on the edge of unconsciousness when I heard the first sloshing footsteps since I'd been abandoned in this corner. I was under no assumption that I wasn't being watched, but the streets worked in their own mysterious ways. Just because you couldn't see someone, didn't mean they couldn't see you. The walls had eyes.

The footsteps grew louder, and muttered curses carried to me, making my stomach revolt. I knew that voice, one that belonged to a face I hadn't seen until recently, even though I've heard it for years.

"Its fucking disgusting. I should be booking these fucking vermin, not collecting them like a goddamn prized pet."

Cold sweat pickled under my hood and dripped down my neck. Fear coiled around me, making it hard to breathe. I'd expected Dahlia to send Sean or Devlin, not a fucking cop. She really was untouchable if she was sending him to collect me. The sound of a gun cocking made me freeze. The way the sound echoed around the space was disorientating. I blinked a few times until a figure materialized in the darkness before me.

"Fancy seeing you here, you little whore," he spat at me. "Didn't think you'd leave Benson's house, all protected like the man in the high castle." He tilted his head to the side, something wild and unhinged glinting in his eyes as he flicked the muzzle of the gun at me. "Up. She wants to talk to you."

Gravel crunched under the tires as the car rocked down some unknown road. Unable to see anything from where I'd been stuffed into the trunk, my other senses heightened. The rough lining of the trunk cut into my cheek like it was covered in dirt and stones. The cloying stench of gasoline and mold made my stomach churn relentlessly. I had only the hum of the engine and the pounding of my heart for company as I anxiously waited to find out where Davis was taking me.

A fresh wave of bile scalded the back of my throat as we hit a pothole, the taste lingering on my tongue. Davis had tied my hands and legs with a smooth rope that felt like it was coated in wax, which allowed him to tie it even tighter, cutting off the circulation. The burning sensation had faded long ago, and now they were just numb. I couldn't even feel if my fingers were touching.

The car brakes squeaked and the groan of the engine fell silent as we jolted to an abrupt stop. I knew my time was up and what had seemed like a brilliant idea when it first solidified in my head now felt impossible. If Davis or Dahlia put a bullet through my brain before I managed to get anything that could help Bane, then what was the point? I didn't care if I lived or died—not after how he'd reacted to me—but regardless of how shit he'd made me feel, I still wanted to help him. To prove I was worth more than a hole to be filled.

Davis slammed his door shut, making the car rock from the force, and moved toward the trunk, his steps heavy with one foot dragging slightly through the gravel. The lock clicked open, and a bright beam from a flashlight shone directly in my eyes, making me blink away white stars until I could focus on his face and the ugly sneer curling his lips. He braced his arm against the trunk lid and pulled his gun out of the darkness, the black barrel glinting in the bright light. His hand was deceptively steady for a cop who had just kidnapped someone at gunpoint.

"Get out," he grunted, and when I didn't move, he cursed under his breath. Leaning forward, he yanked at the ropes, loosening them so I could sit up and move my feet enough to clamber out of the trunk. "Hands behind your back."

The nozzle of the gun pushed into the base of my skull as his free hand wrapped around my wrists. "Move."

Icy wind whipped across my face as I stumbled over my feet, with only his hold on me to act as a counterbalance. After a few minutes, the outline of a building became visible through the darkness. The pressure against my neck increased, the old metal biting into my skin as a doorway took shape in front of me. Before I could react, something hard crashed into the back of my skull, and my legs gave out underneath me. The last thing I saw before my eyes rolled back in my head was a stone step getting closer to my face.

"WHAT ARE YOU DOING HERE, RIVER?" DAHLIA'S VOICE ricocheted around my head, landing like bullets in my brain.

My eyes peeled back slowly, and colors danced across my vision until I saw her leaning against a large wooden desk in front of me. I licked my lips, tasting that distinct coppery tang of blood.

"I didn't expect you to leave the safety of the fortress he built for you." My muscles locked up tight at the knowing gleam in her eyes. "Did you think you were safe?" She laughed hollowly, and a chill skittered down my spine. "Did you think I didn't know where you were? That I couldn't get to you if I wanted to?"

I tried to move but couldn't. My heart raced as awareness of my body crept back in. A hand held down my shoulder, while another did the same to my lower legs, where something sharp dug into my skin.

"Why did you try to run from me?" Dahlia circled me before coming to an abrupt stop by my face. I blinked up at her and clenched my jaw, grinding my back teeth against the whimper trying to work its way up my tight throat. "You will never escape me. I've known where you were. Every. Single. Day." The back of her hand slammed into my cheek, the rings she wore slicing into my skin like hot knives through butter. The impact knocked my head to the side as white-hot pain flared through me. "I left you there for a reason."

My breath caught in the back of my throat, heart hammering against my ribs as her blood-flecked fingers stroked her chin and her head cocked to the side. A predatory grin cut across her face, and triumph flashed in her eyes.

"He means something to you, doesn't he?" I shook my head, but the tears falling from my eyes said everything I never would. "He's clever and handsome, I'll give you that, but what could he want with someone like you?"

My thoughts turned to Bane. Every one of his sweet smiles flashed through my mind like a highlight reel of the best moments of my life, and I felt my heart crumble.

Her fingers laced through my hair, and she wrenched my head back. "The others knew their place! They came back. But you? You thought you were better. That you deserved more." She spat, and a fat glob of saliva dripped down my face. "You are nothing. Never were. Never will be." I flinched at the vitriol in her words. "You will have to live with the knowledge that their suffering, their lives are in your hands."

Unbridled fear raced through me, turning the blood in my veins to ice. Words tried to form on my lips, but nothing would come except sharp stuttering breaths that caught in the back of my throat.

"You've always been a dreamer, River. Had your head in the clouds. Now I'm going to remind you what hell is really like." Pain seared into my back as something sliced through my back. "Now I know you have something to lose." Another strip of white-hot agony lanced down my spine. Hot liquid spilled down my cold skin and darkness shrouded my vision. "I'll spare his life and yours if you make him stop." Pressure increased on my legs, and I bit back a scream. "Otherwise, you'll watch everyone you care about die." Her nails sunk into my cheeks, prising my mouth open. "Or I'll make sure you have a front-row seat to his death." As her words echoed through my mind, darkness swallowed me.

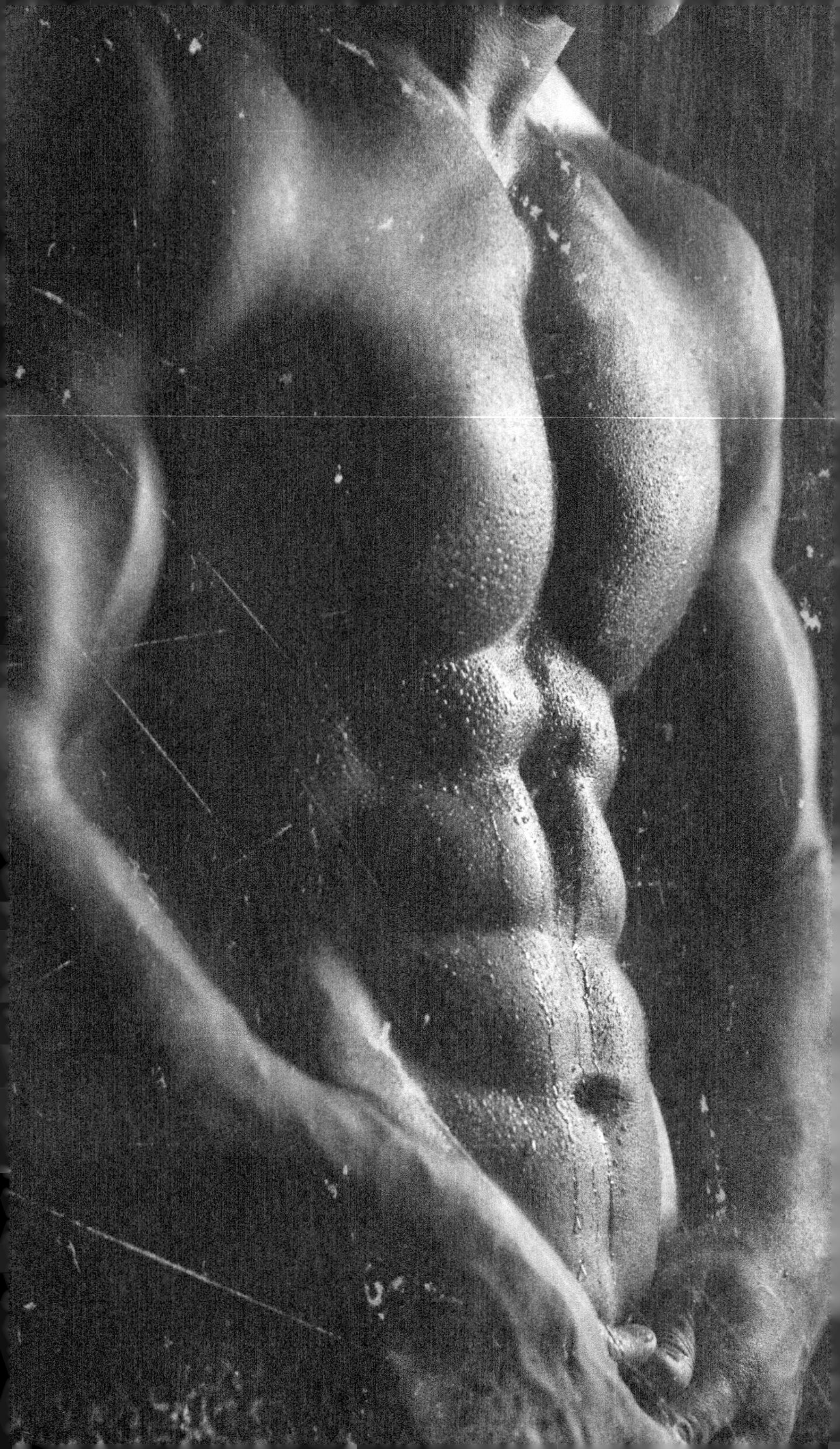

CHAPTER SEVENTEEN
Bane

My conscience warred with me the entire drive to the station, with roads, junctions and houses all passing in a blur. My head knew I was doing the right thing. I had a job to do, and a homicide possibly connected to the case was not something I could put above my own selfish needs. No matter how much I wanted to reach out to River, I didn't think a text or a call would be enough. No, this needed to be a face-to-face conversation. It was hard enough at the best of times to get a true read on River's emotions, yet I itched to let him know I was thinking about him, and that I hadn't brushed what had happened under the carpet.

The thought of him being home alone, lost in a quagmire of emotions from our interaction this morning, was gutting. The pain and rejection had been clear to see in his deep green eyes, the clearest emotions I'd ever witnessed on him, and I had been the cause. I'm not sure how he expected me to react, waking up to find his full lips wrapped around my cock as I spilled down his throat. It was heaven and hell incarnate. The best and worst moment of my life. I wanted him. The connection I felt to him was unsurpassable, but it was wrong on so many levels. He was my protectee, my goddamned job. He was vulnerable and broken in so many ways, and though I might not have initiated the act, I felt like I'd betrayed his trust. I was just another man that had used him. Fuck, how I hated myself.

A kiss was one thing, but face fucking him until I blacked out from euphoric pleasure was a whole other issue. He might have come to me for comfort during the night, and I somehow manipulated him into sucking me off. Or the more probable reason was that he thought the only way he could level the playing field between us was to offer what he thought I valued most—what men valued most— his body.

I'd single-handedly ruined all the progress we'd made over the last few weeks. He had finally let me see behind his walls and learn more about what he'd survived. River had let me see him in a way no one else got to. I knew without a shadow of a doubt that he was still holding information back from me. I had a feeling when I discovered what it was, it would annihilate me. In my line of work, you saw and experienced things no one in their right mind would wish on another, but having a firsthand account from someone you cared about wrecked you on a whole other emotional level.

I needed to book another appointment with Joelle, but I was hoping by giving it some extra time, I could convince River to meet her. Maybe he would feel comfortable enough to open up to her and get the support he needed to process his trauma. But after this morning, I felt like I'd shot myself in the foot where that idea is concerned.

The parking lot out the back of the station was eerily deserted for this time of day. That had the hairs on the back of my neck prickling with trepidation as goosebumps spread across my skin and down my arms to my cold fingers. I was in a bad enough place; I didn't need anything unexpected throwing me off. As an officer of the law, the image I portrayed was of the utmost importance, and looking like I was on the verge of a mental breakdown when I came on shift would not go over well, especially with Bower, who was close to revoking our arrangement.

The engine ticked over as it cooled, while my eyes locked on the thread of messages between me and River. I had so much to make up for and explain, but finding the right words was tough. Anything I said would be inconsequential, but I couldn't leave him alone, suffering in silence.

> I'm sorry.

I hit send, berating myself for my inadequacy. I'd never been good with words, but even I knew that wasn't enough to convey the gravity of the situation or even give him an inkling of my emotions on where I stood regarding BJgate. I pulled up the tracking app I'd hidden on his phone and checked his location, fear thrumming under my skin as I waited for it to load. There was a need to make sure he was safe, because there was a darkness looming on the horizon that grew every day this case progressed. With the team working on getting the warrants in place to search the properties of the real Dahlia, my gut told me this case was about to take a turn for the worse. The tightness in my chest eased somewhat but didn't fade altogether when it showed he was safe at home.

"Pull yourself together," I muttered, grabbed my pack, and slammed the door shut behind me. My eyes were glued to the ground, as if it could provide me all the answers I needed.

"You look shittier than you sounded on the phone." Montoya's voice crashed into me like a semi. My eyes bugged out of their sockets, and my head snapped up. "What the fuck is going on with you, big guy?"

Ignoring her where she stood leaning against the wall, arms folded across her chest, eyeing me suspiciously next to the back entrance, I wrenched the door open and headed to my locker.

"Seriously, the silent treatment? How grown up. What are you, twelve?" I rolled my eyes, grabbed my vest, and slipped it on while she huffed and puffed next to me. She hated being ignored. It brought out her fiery side. Without looking at her, I knew her hand was resting on her cocked hip.

"If you keep going like that, you'll blow the station down."

She snorted and slapped my back, finally cracking a smile. "Once you've checked your hair, we need to go. Daniel is holding the site for us."

"Sure." I glanced at the mirror on the back of my locker door, noting just how wrecked I really looked. Bloodshot eyes, puffy lids, and sweat beading in my hairline. I was a walking train wreck, but I needed to lock it down before we stepped out of here.

"Benson, Montoya? What the fuck are you still doing here? Get moving," Bower bellowed from where he leaned through the doorway to the station. "I want a full report written up on my desk by the morning."

"On it," Montoya and I replied together. Her lips quirked

as she nodded at me and went to grab the keys for the squad.

"Meet you out there," I called after her and slammed my locker shut, leaving everything that was hanging by a thread behind. I exited the station, and by the time I got to the squad, it flashed as Montoya unlocked it.

"You can drive," she called out, hurling the keys at me. I caught them in one hand and slipped into the car.

"When don't I?" I muttered as she belted in. "Where are we heading?"

"To the docks." She called through to dispatch as I maneuvered us into the busy early morning traffic. The docks were located down the south banks of Black River. It was an import hub that was also used by local fishermen who had been banned from using the marina, where those with money kept their fancy yachts because the smell of fish disturbed their peace. The sad fact was the Hendrixes had been one of the many families who had signed the petition.

"All right, read me in."

Montoya hummed before answering. "The initial call came in just after six a.m. Jenkins was first on the scene, secured it, and referred it over to us. Vic is a white male, late twenties, early thirties. Dark hair, dark eyes." Her gaze slid to me for a beat. "He was DOA, but from what Jenkins said, it's not pretty."

"Just what you want on a Monday morning. What made him pass it to us?"

"The vic has a tattoo..." Her voice trailed off. I didn't need to ask what tattoo. The one the twins had, the one that resembled the name of the ring we were investigating. It seemed all roads led back to Black Dahlia. We just had to hope the warrants came through so we could find out if Christine Hamilton really was the Dahlia we were looking for.

By the time we reached the docks, the sky had turned to pale shades of gray, and a heavy mist clung to the ground. The air was bitingly cold and filled me with a sense of foreboding. Every exhale formed a cloud that hung in the air as we left the car behind and donned our waterproofs. Gravel crunched under our boots, and containers rose out of the low level mist around us like mountains. The smell of fish and rot saturated the stagnant air until I could taste it on my tongue.

"Why do they need to stack the damn things so high?" Montoya groaned, craning her neck to take them in.

"They wouldn't seem so big if you were taller than a child." She whacked my vest with the back of her hand and glared at me. "Land is a premium commodity here—"

"Yeah, yeah." She waved me off just as rain started to fall, turning the damp ground slick under our boots. Gravel gave way to broken tarmac, where fishing debris formed a perverse graveyard. Discarded nets and broken crates slowed us down as we picked our way toward the cornered off scene where I could just about make Daniel out through the mist. His blond hair was plastered to his face, drenched strands sticking to his glasses as he blinked up at us.

"Hey, guys." Daniel carded his hand through his hair, lifting it off his face before pulling his glasses off and drying them on his sweater. After slipping them back on, he held the tape up for us. "Follow me."

"Thanks, man."

"He's a bit tricky to get to. I can't confirm exactly how he died. You'll see why—" I caught his eye as he glanced over his shoulder, his face grim. "The site is too clean for it to have been where he was murdered. Judging by the number of injuries inflicted on the body, it's clear he was tortured before being dumped."

"Great," Montoya muttered as we weaved through an

alley of stacked containers. The weak light barely penetrated their peaks as we walked through the shadows. Her eyes scoped for movement around us as her fingers tightened around her gun. It wasn't often she showed how much a crime scene affected her, but I could tell by the set of her shoulders and her whitening knuckles that today was getting to her. And we hadn't even laid eyes on the vic yet.

Clearing his throat, Daniel motioned us forward, pointing to where a container door was propped open. "I won't be able to identify the vic until I get him back to the morgue and run dentals."

"That bad?" I asked, unease coiling around me.

"Yeah, um, you'll see." Daniel chewed his lip as Montoya stepped into the container and drew her flashlight.

"Ho-lee shit." The halting tone of her voice froze my feet to the ground.

I glanced at Daniel, and he grimaced. "They were thorough..."

"I thought you said this wasn't where he was killed?" Montoya said as she stepped out of the container, hand covering her mouth, golden skin gray.

"It wasn't." Daniel shook his head, toeing the mud where we stood a few feet back. He motioned to the ground in front of the container, flashing his light to highlight two grooves in the mud. "They dumped his body here before dragging it inside. It matches the mud on his heels and lower back. But the blood splatter patterns don't match the injuries on the body. He wasn't tortured here."

"You good?" I rested a hand on Montoya's shoulder as she drew closer to me.

"I-it's...one of..." She shook her head and drew in a deep inhale, holding it for a second before slowly releasing it.

"One of who?"

"One of the guys that was brought in with River," she

said in a broken whisper. I swallowed down a surge of anger at her words.

"That's impossible. They were seen—"

"A few days ago," she finished.

I spun on my heel and looked at Daniel. "How long do you estimate he's been here?"

"A couple of days? Three at most." He shrugged. "Once I get him—" I waved him off, knowing what he was going to say.

"Here." Montoya handed me her flashlight with a nod, then squeezed my bicep and headed over to speak to Daniel. The low murmur of their voices accompanied me as I stepped over the drag marks into the container and flicked on my light.

The putrid stench of aged blood assaulted me as soon as I entered the contained space. My eyes watered from the intensity as my stomach churned. There, dumped unceremoniously, was our vic. Extensive contusions and deep lacerations covered every ounce of exposed skin. There were multiple wounds that could have been fatal on their own. To my untrained eye, it seemed like some were administered post mortem, as the residual bleeding wasn't what you'd expect from such a wound.

I took a moment to lock my humanity down so I could process the scene. The vic's dark brown hair was a matted mess of dried blood, but what chilled me to the bone was his vacant stare through lidless eyes. Those were eyes that had stared back at me through the mug shot Montoya had pulled up when River had demanded to know how his friends were when he was chained to an interview table. I couldn't help but feel like we were being played. It seemed like only yesterday that we'd checked up on the guys who were brought in with River, and we had tracked them through the CCTV in town on a night out. Naively, I'd taken it all at face value, because all my concern had been on River.

Hindsight was a fucking bitch. Whoever had killed this guy had played us. They knew we'd check up on them after they left the station, so they gave us exactly what we needed. "Fuck!" My fingers clenched around the flashlight, pulling the skin tight over my knuckles as my nails bit into the palm of my other hand.

"We've been played," I ground out as I stepped back outside. Montoya made a disconcerted noise in the back of her throat as she peered at me through a watery gaze.

"Did you see—"

"The black dahlia on his ankle?" She nodded. "Yup. It was like the killer posed him, so that would be the first thing we'd notice."

"I thought that too. Just like the twins." She shook her head, blinking back tears before they fell. I wrapped my arm around her shoulders and turned to steer her away from the scene. "Daniel," I said as an afterthought over my shoulder. "Catalog everything and let us know what you find out." He gave me a thumbs up and pulled a camera from his pack while his assistant got to work. Hopefully, by the time we got back, Jenkins would have pulled up all the relevant CCTV footage for us to trawl through.

The oppressive atmosphere did absolutely nothing to improve our somber mood as we trudged back to the squad car, lost in our thoughts. TV crews and reporters had set up at the first cordon that was manned by a couple of the guys from the station to preserve the crime scene. Eyes followed our progression as we stepped under the tape and into the cacophony of bodies that waited like sharks, ready to get the scoop.

"Can you tell us who the victim is?"

"Officer Benson, can you tell us what happened here?"

"Officer Montoya, is this victim related to an ongoing investigation?"

Questions rained down on us like bullets as cameras were aimed our way. I patted Montoya on the back, letting her know I had this. I turned to the soulless rabble that converged on me and nodded at the guys beyond the tape to stay put. With my shoulders pulled back, I cleared my throat and looked through the vultures who shoved microphones in my face and repeated the party line that was drummed into us. "We will not be answering any questions relating to today's incident. The investigation is ongoing, and no details will be released until the family has been informed."

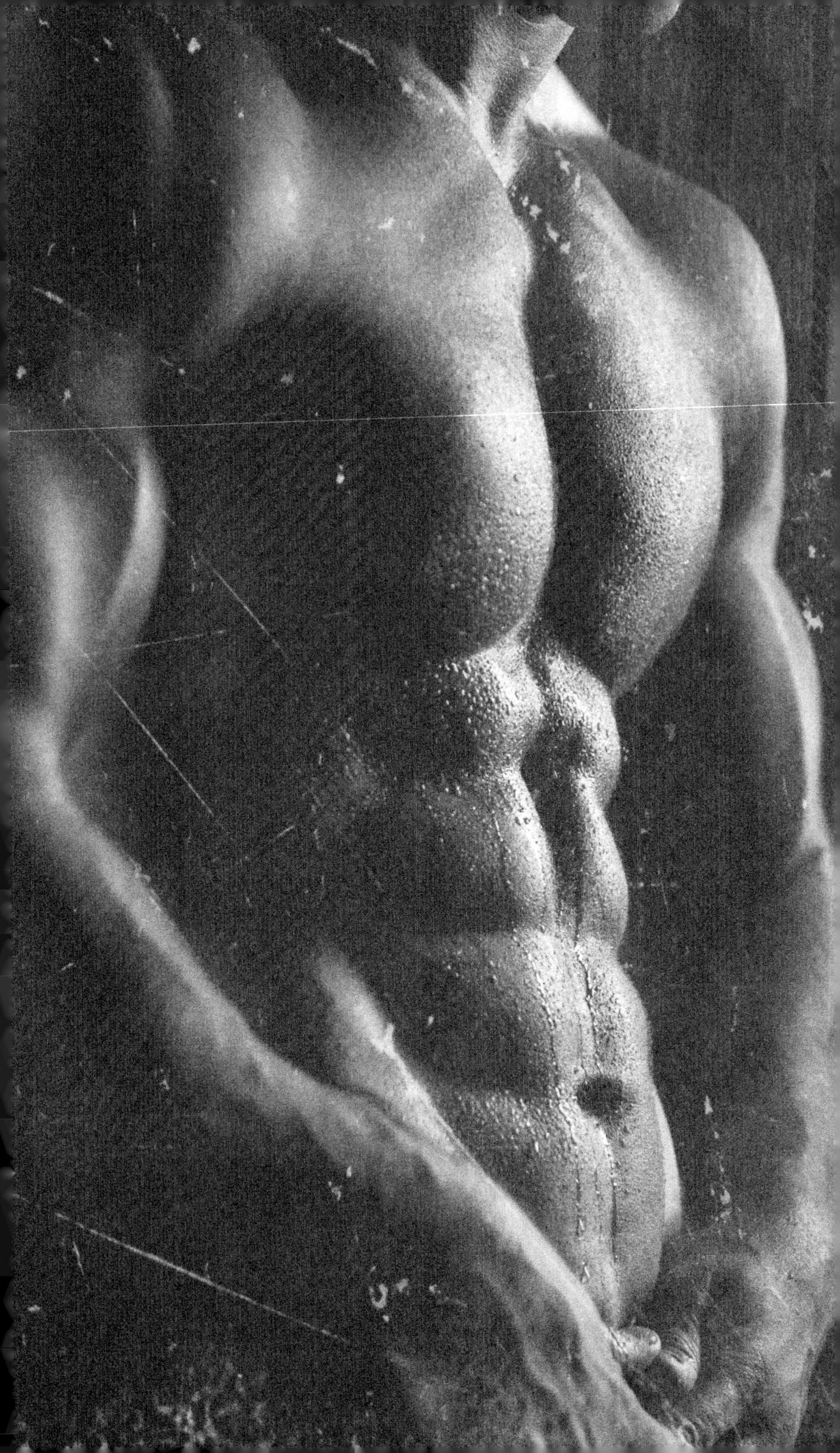

CHAPTER EIGHTEEN
Bane

Until *the family has been informed.* The sound of my voice ricocheted inside my head like a pinball machine mocking me. If I'd learned anything since those guys were brought in, it was that they had no family. There was no one waiting for them at night. No one was searching for them. They have no one, which made sense when you were running a trafficking operation. You didn't want people with attachments or dependants. Black Dahlia was smart, and this latest incident proved it beyond doubt.

"You doing okay over there?" The sound of Montoya's voice was a welcome reprieve from the thoughts spiraling in my mind.

"Yeah." I scrubbed my hand down my face before settling it onto the steering wheel. "Just...fuck. This case is turning into a shitshow."

"You said it," she muttered. "Are you going to let your boy know it was one of his friends?"

"I. Umm..."

"It's better to come from you than to hear about it on the news. Especially when you're not there to support him." Her words landed with the precision of a sniper. The smirk that lifted her lips when I glared at her in the passenger seat said everything.

I expelled a labored breath. "It's not that easy." My fingers flexed around the leather, my knuckles bleeding white.

"Sure it is. Unless..." She hummed thoughtfully, finger tapping her bottom lip in the periphery of my vision. "Unless, your bad mood this morning was because you fucked up with him?" My body tensed until the tendons in my neck were strained. "What did you do?" The weight of her accusing gaze made me feel like I was drowning.

"Now is not the time." I gritted my jaw, teeth clenched so hard they practically ground to dust. "We have to stay focused on the job—"

"Like you are?" she snarked. "You're a mess, Benson. I've never seen you in such a state in all the years I've known you." I rolled my eyes, then focused on the road as we crossed town back toward the station. "Call him when we get back, then we'll talk it through tonight when you buy me pizza."

If only everything in life could be solved by food. "Deal." Even as the word left my lips, I knew I'd be taking the coward's way out. There was no way River would answer, even if I called. I might have ruined things between us, but I wasn't a complete idiot. *Are you sure about that?*

The rest of the drive passed in strained silence, both of us lost in thought about the atrocity we'd witnessed and what repercussions it would have on the case. The death of

River's friend felt like a warning, one we couldn't ignore. But we couldn't allow it to derail everything we were working on. Bringing down this ring and saving thousands outweighed the loss of a few casualties. That wasn't to say I didn't value human life, because I did. I lived to serve and protect, but we all knew innocents were a casualty of war. They had drawn the first blood, and I just had to hope we would spill the last.

"Call him now," Montoya urged, as I turned the ignition off and pushed my head back into the headrest. My eyes shuttered closed as an ache throbbed in my temples. "Take as long as you need. I'm going to check in with Jenkinson and see where we are with the CCTV footage. I just hope Dixon is out, because I can't deal with that asshole today."

I grunted in acknowledgement as she squeezed my arm in solidarity.

"It can't be as bad as you imagine, big guy. Pull up your big boy panties and speak to him." The car door slammed shut, leaving me alone with myself, which was the worst damn place because it allowed my mind to wander and my heart to take control. I wanted to say fuck it and drive home. Kick the door down, wrap River in my arms, and take him far, far away from here. I wanted to protect him from this cruel, fucked-up world and keep him safe.

Reality was a cold bitch, because I was far too late to do any of that. Releasing a stuttering exhale, I pulled my phone out of my pocket. My thumb hovered over his number, the green phone icon taunting me, goddamned laughing at me for being too weak to risk hearing his voice. "Shit!" I smacked my head against the steering wheel, feeling so messed up and weak. Tremors ran down my arms as indecision warred within me. *Do the right thing.* Even my conscience knew what I should do.

Ignoring it, I typed out a quick message instead.

> Just checking in to make sure you're ok.

I don't know how long I sat there staring at the screen, but by the time I'd blinked back to reality, the screen was black and locked. Tapping it to bring it to life, I prayed I'd see a message icon, but there was nothing. Clicking into our chat, nothing. Not even a read receipt. *Call him!* But I couldn't. Instead, I checked the tracker app and saw he was still safely tucked away in his room. That would have to be enough for now. I needed to remain focused on my job.

My obsession with my broken angel would have to wait.

"All good?" Montoya asked as I pulled my chair from my desk and sat on it backwards next to her.

"Yup." I glanced at the grainy CCTV footage on her screen. "Are those the docks?"

"Yeah, from three days ago. I've been working backward from today and other than the guy who found our vic, there's been nothing untoward. I've crosschecked the comings and goings of everyone that's shown up against the shipping logs, and it all matches up. No one else has been near that area."

I mulled her words over as I signaled Jenkins for a coffee by holding an empty mug in the air. The guy looked wrecked, but nodded as he headed to the kitchen. "What was the guy who found the vic doing there?"

Montoya snorted. "He went for a piss." She scrolled through the footage to show him walking down there, unbuttoning his pants. "Only advantage to being a guy as I see it." I arched my brow at her in question. "The ability to piss wherever you want."

"Mmm."

"You all have an advantage on a stakeout. You can just whip it out and go in a bottle, whereas I need to get cover in, so I can go to the local store." She rolled her eyes at me. I'd never thought about it like that, the disadvantages women faced.

Brushing it off, I asked, "Has he been contacted for an interview?"

"Yeah, James Michaels will be in once his boat comes back in. Jenkins took preliminary notes from him first thing."

It struck me as odd how the guy could go about his day as if he hadn't witnessed something horrific. Maybe he hadn't gotten a good look at what was in there, or perhaps the stale scent of blood was enough to send him packing. We didn't know now, but we would. Soon.

"Alright, let's do a full background search on him to see if there's any way he could be linked to Black Dahlia. Something—"

"Smells fishy?" She grinned. "I know. It's all a little too convenient, isn't it? We finally get the identity of the real Dahlia, and then one of the guys we brought in turns up dead. Doesn't take a genius to put it all together."

The day passed slower than molasses, and every minute made the ache in my splintered heart grow larger until it was all I could think about. River was at the forefront of my every thought, no matter how hard I tried to push it down. It turned out James Michaels was a twenty-year-old who'd been working part time for his uncle while attending a university, where he was studying computer science. His mother's health insurance didn't cover the full treatment she needed for her quickly advancing multiple sclerosis, so he took on an extra job to help pay for it. The kid was badly shaken up, even though he admitted to only glancing in the container before he called us. The station kept a list of therapists for situations like these, so Montoya referred him to one. Mental health still held a lot of stigma, but Montoya and I were leading the force by providing it for witnesses.

Once we'd concluded his interview, which only served to waste an hour and a half of our time, Daniel called to officially confirm our vic was Max Woolf. My heart sank at the confirmation, even though I already knew it was one of River's friends. We then spent the rest of the day trawling through reams of CCTV footage of the docks and surrounding areas from the last ten days to see if there were any unusual patterns or individuals that cropped up, but nothing changed. The ebb and flow of people stayed the same until James stumbled into the container this morning.

My eyes felt like they were bleeding. Everything seemed to be made of little black and white blocks. No matter how many times I blinked, my vision didn't clear, and it only served to aggravate the pounding in my head. "Have you submitted that report to Bower?" I asked Montoya as I leaned back in my chair and stretched my arms over my head, trying to alleviate some of the tension in my shoulders.

"Yup, all done. I could use a stiff drink after today," she said, signing out of her computer and spinning around to look over my shoulder. "I thought doctors were meant to have the worst handwriting?"

I snorted as I stared at the dockmaster's shipping logs. "Whoever they are clearly haven't met fishermen."

"Come on, up."

"Ow! What the hell?" I rubbed the back of my head where she'd slapped me. "What was that for?"

"You owe me a drink and pizza." She pushed up from her chair and kicked it under her desk with a bang.

I pointed at my screen. "Got too much to do, Montoya. Raincheck?"

"Hell no, big guy. You can't get out of this. Don't promise a girl food, then take it away. That's when you get the teeth. Meet you out back in ten."

"Fine. Fine." I sighed and rolled my neck as she stomped off with our dirty mugs. The tightness building in my muscles all day hadn't abated. If anything, it had only increased with every hour that had passed that I hadn't heard from River. I picked up my phone and swallowed my pride to call him, but the damn thing went straight to voicemail.

A LITTLE HOLE IN THE WALL ON THE WEST SIDE SERVED THE best pizza in Holme Oaks, run by a small Italian family that had been here for three generations. They also made the cheesiest Alfredo pizza, and Montoya was a slave to her taste buds. Apparently, as her pseudo big brother, it was my responsibility to feed her. I was working on the assumption that as long as her mouth was full of the cheesy goodness, she couldn't fire questions at me.

"So..." My stomach dropped at the weight of that one word. "What happened this morning?" She pinned me with her dark eyes and crossed her arms over her chest. The don't fuck with me attitude radiating off her even had the servers taking a different route to get to customers.

I tipped my head back and swallowed down a few mouthfuls of beer, trying to come up with anything but the truth. Unfortunately for me, my mind was blank. "I fucked up," I said simply.

"Well, duh! But how?"

"That's not a simple question." I spun the now empty bottle between my fingers.

"Jacob Benson." I jolted at being full named, my back ramrod straight as I sat to attention. "You can't stew like this." She waved her hand at me. "Whatever happened is eating you up inside, and it's going to affect your ability to do your job. If it isn't already." She muttered the last part around another oozing slice. "If we were paper pushers, I'd leave you to figure it out by yourself, but we're not. Our job is life or death. One wrong decision…one wrong call…" She dragged her finger over her neck.

"I know, I know." I huffed a breath and shook out my hands, not knowing what to do with them as my palms slickened. I rubbed them against my thighs and chewed on my lip as my heart thundered in my ears.

"Hey." Montoya flagged down a server. "Can we grab a couple more bottles, please?" She flashed the young guy a beatific smile, and he all but melted under her gaze before scurrying away to get our drinks.

"You're evil," I joked.

Her lips curved in a smirk. "I know." She waved me off. "Stop trying to distract me. Talk!"

"I crossed a line…" When my voice trailed off as images of my dream/reality flitted through my mind, she cleared her throat and rolled her hand to get me to continue. "We kissed—"

"Oh, fuck me." Montoya slammed her hand down on the table and belted a laugh. "Is that all? I thought you were going to say you fucked him."

I sat there silently and felt the color drain from my face. Her eyes widened as my expression registered with her.

"You didn't fuck him, did you?" Her voice dropped to a fractured whisper. "Benson, what the hell?!" Disbelief washed over her features.

"No. No, I didn't. I…it's…" The heels of my hands dug into my eyes. "It's complicated."

"Well, uncomplicate it for me, because I'm struggling to understand how it's anything other than black and white here. You know right and wrong? You have a vulnerable adult who's suffered abuse for years and you... fucked him?"

"No. I didn't."

"But you said!"

"No." I shook my head vehemently. "I said I crossed a line. He did... he was the one... God, why is this so damn hard?" I threw up my hands as frustration riddled through me.

"Let's simplify it, yeah? Start at the beginning."

I mulled over her words but didn't break eye contact with her as hers bored into my soul. I was just lost, trapped between right and wrong. My life was quickly becoming a car crash, drawn to the one guy I really shouldn't be, but felt this irrefutable connection to. It was tenuous at best. It thickened the air between us and made it alive with electricity that covered my skin and sunk its claws into me.

River was an amalgamation of every one of my deepest fantasies plucked right out of my head. Maybe they'd been molded by the time we spent together when we were younger and I was discovering my sexuality. Dark hair, deep hypnotic green eyes, and the face of an angel. Even though he'd survived atrocities that had stripped him of his humanity, he still shone brighter than the sun.

My fingers itched with the need to feel his soft skin under mine. To map out every scar that he wore like a warrior. I'd never known someone as strong as River. His suffering was an intrinsic part of him, but I would lavish him with my love for the rest of his life if it meant he granted me a second of his time. A moment in his life.

I cleared my throat and sat back in my chair, splaying my legs under the table. Montoya raised her brow at me, eyes dipping down to her watch, then back to me. "I knew him when I was younger, as you know." She nodded. "The two years I spent with him in foster care were not great because I was reeling from the loss of my family and being an orphan. But River became the foundation that held me up. He became my home, I guess you could say. He was nonverbal when I arrived, but he shadowed me, kind of like he was seeking shelter being around me because I was big enough to protect him when no one else would. And from there, we formed a bond that has stayed with me all these years."

"I see, but that doesn't explain… this."

Cool beer slipped down my throat, washing away the tightness I felt as my words started to flow. "When I saw him in the interview room, it was like I'd been struck with a wrecking ball. Every memory from that time came flooding back until I felt like I was drowning. I couldn't understand how the broken boy I'd known was sitting before me like a ruin. The spark I'd nurtured in him over those two years was extinguished. And do you know what my first instinct was?"

Montoya blinked at me through her lashes. "No?"

I shook my head, a rueful smile curling my lips. "I wanted to run to him and wrap him in my arms. I wanted to kill anyone who had dared to hurt him. I wanted to burn the world down and remake it into one worthy of him." I sucked in a shuddering breath, tears pricked the back of my eyes like razor blades. "I felt like a failure, and it made me hate myself. Do you know why I signed up to the academy?"

"Because you wanted to make the world a better place? You've always been an idealist."

"Yeah, I guess that's it, in a sense. I wanted to get justice for people who were killed like my family, but I also wanted to make sure innocent children like River were not subjected to the type of life he'd led—"

"And when you saw him, you took it as a personal failure?" She reached forward and took my hand in hers. "But you didn't know, big guy," Montoya said softly.

"You're right, I didn't. But I could have found him. I could have tried harder after I'd spoken to Mrs. Wilkinson, the lady who fostered us, but I didn't. My arrogance left me secure enough to believe a system I knew failed kids every day was enough for him."

"That wasn't your fault. Neither is it that you guys kissed. There's history between you, and you're a caretaker, a bleeding heart. Whatever happened can't have been that bad."

Unfairly comforted by her words, I continued, "You know how I've only had a few relationships in all the time we've known each other?" Montoya made a noise of affirmation in the back of her throat. "After doing some research, I discovered I was demi. They never worked out, because I didn't have a connection with them."

"Right, that I can totally understand. You could have told me, you know. I wouldn't have pressured you into letting off steam and hooking up like I have."

"I didn't say that to make you feel bad." I rolled my bottom lip between my teeth. "I just wanted to help you understand that being around River has been like nothing I've ever felt. Initially, I thought it was our childhood friendship reestablishing itself into something stronger. But over the weeks, it's like he's become my sun, and I'm orbiting around him, drawn to him on a cellular level but never able to get close enough. To be honest, it's been a total mindfuck, because I know he's vulnerable physically and emotionally. That he's been taken advantage of and used like a disposable toy."

Tears built along my lash line, and I blinked furiously to keep them at bay, but it was a losing battle.

"The need to protect and care for him has become a necessity. A need. He is the air I need to function. Over time, he's started to let me in, allowing me to see behind his walls. With each glimpse, I feel like I've become Icarus. I don't care if I get burned; I want him." I licked my dry lips, tasting the salt of my tears, and swiping them away with the back of my hand as my emotions poured out of me. "I took him for a ride on my bike, because I could see it in his eyes that the walls were closing in on him and his mind was splintering. I told him he was free, but I was keeping him caged under lock and key. He needed to breathe, to feel alive and...and that's when we kissed. I'm not sure who initiated it, but I freaked out after that. It was like the barriers in my mind were crushed under every pass of his tips. His taste lives rent free on my tongue, and it's ignited insatiable dreams—"

"Oh, no." Montoya hid her face behind her hands. "I think I can guess where this is going."

"Last night, I dreamed we came back from the lake. His clothes were drenched, and I pushed him against the garage door and stripped him—"

"Ahh. La la la la. I don't need all the details." She peeked through her fingers. "Even though I kind of do."

I smirked. "The dream felt so real. The silkiness of his hair, the intensity of his mouth." I cleared my throat, my eyes darting around to make sure no one was paying us any attention. "It was unlike anything I'd ever experienced. The goddamn intensity of it... I could feel my orgasm barreling through me, and then I opened my eyes, and fuck." My fist crashed onto the table, making our empty bottles topple over. "And there he was, working me over. Before I could say anything, I shot my load down his throat."

"Oh shit. Then what did you do?" It was like she was sitting there eating popcorn, listening to the best story of her life.

"You're enjoying this, aren't you?"

Montoya nodded readily, her lips lifted in a taunting

smile. "It's nice to watch Mr. Perfect fall off his saintly pedestal."

"When I came too, I freaked out. I told him it was a fucking mistake, and then you called. He was kneeling on my b-bed with tears staining his face, and I couldn't look at him. I felt like a monster. I was abhorred with myself. It still feels like I somehow manipulated him into doing it." I shrugged and buried my face in my hands as shame and guilt washed over me. A chair scraped loudly against the floor nearby, and I jolted when a hand landed on the back of my neck, Montoya's coffee caramel scent washing over me. She squeezed until her nails bit into my skin, and I raised my head to look at her, feeling like I was in the burning tundras of hell.

Sorrow lined her face, deep lines at the corners of her eyes. "I can't say why he was there, but if he felt safe with you, Benson, your words and actions would have cut him deeply. You can't take back what you did, even though I'm certain you wish you could."

"I do." The whispered words were wrenched from the depths of my soul. "I never meant to hurt him."

"Shh. I know. I know." Her soft words were a comfort I didn't deserve. "But you have to make this right. When you get home, explain it all to him. That you weren't disgusted with him, but yourself. That you felt like you took advantage of him even if you didn't initiate anything."

"What if he won't open his door to me?" I asked brokenly.

"Then you write him a letter, not a text. You tell him everything." I blinked at her through hazy eyes. "Don't just explain your actions, but tell him how you feel, like you did with me. If he's the guy you think he is, he'll listen, even if it takes time."

"Should I tell Bower?" My heart stuttered in my chest,

constricted by fear that I might lose River before I even got a chance to make things right. "Honestly, as your partner, I would say yes."

My head thunked on the table as reality smacked into me. "But as my friend?"

Montoya snorted. "I'd tell you to go get your guy. But just know that a real relationship between you might not be possible. That boy is psychologically damaged, so you need to be very careful. If, and this is a big if... anything happened between you, he has to be the one to initiate it. He has to want it. Understand?"

"Yeah," I breathed. "I understand. I-I just want to show him how special he really is. I... I think I..." *Love him.* I didn't need to say the words, my feelings were etched into every line of my face.

"Yeah, big guy, I think you do."

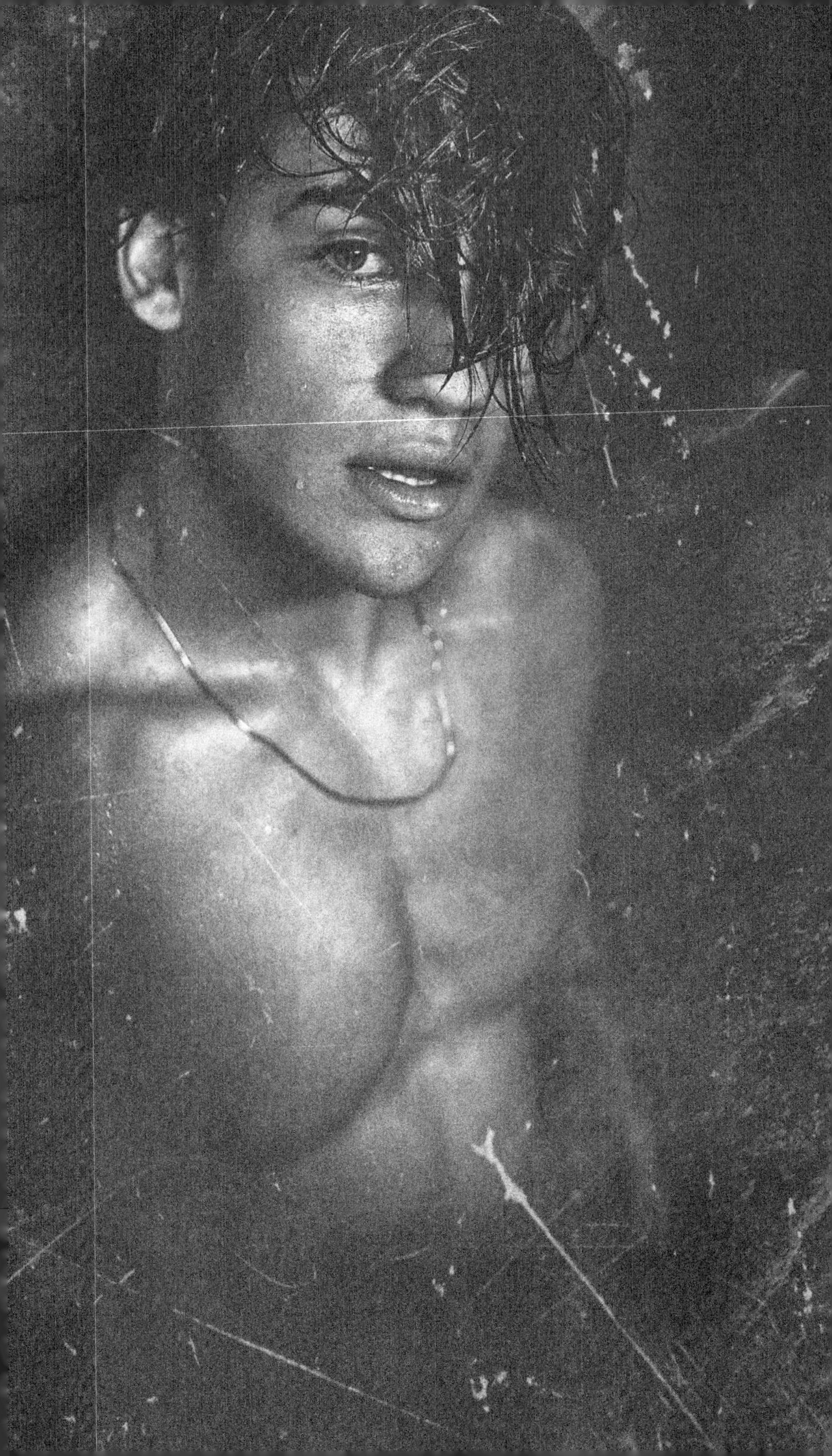

CHAPTER NINETEEN
River

Ice-cold dread slithered through my veins as consciousness slowly crept over me. I didn't want to open my eyes and find myself lost in the dark, even with my eyes open like the lingering memories from only hours ago. The stinging burn of glass sinking into my shins was at the forefront of my mind, even though it felt like I was lying down. Maybe my mind had finally reneged on me and this was what death felt like. I didn't know, and I wasn't sure if I wanted to know the truth, either.

After working up the courage, I finally opened my eyes, squinting against the bright light. A pained groan rumbled in the back of my throat, and I screwed my eyes shut as an aching agony sparked through every nerve in my body.

"Welcome back, handsome," a gentle voice said. I turned toward the sound, but my eyes refused to open again. "Here, you're probably thirsty."

Before my mind could work out what the feminine voice was saying, I felt a plastic straw push between my lips. I gratefully swallowed down some lukewarm water, the liquid reviving my parched, aching throat.

"I've rung for the doctor to come and check on you now you're more awake. He'll be here shortly. Can you tell me your name?"

My head rocked slightly from side to side, as much as the growing pain in my neck would allow. It felt like my chest was being crushed under an almighty weight. My fingers clawed at the sheets, something sharp catching on the back of my hand.

"Hush, hush, now. Don't hurt yourself, okay? Just listen to me and take a slow breath for me." A warm hand wrapped around my wrist, grounding me. "That's it. Breathe in one... two... three. There you are, your heart rate is slowing. Keep it up for me. One... two... three... four. Good boy."

Her grasp loosened, and a whimper slithered through my parted lips at the loss. The sound of something being dragged was so loud, my ears felt like they were about to burst.

"I'm not going anywhere. I was just getting a chair, as my old legs don't hold me up as long as they used to. I'm Marianne, by the way, not sure you remember from when you first opened your eyes."

Marianne chattered away, trying to calm me down. Slowly, the high-pitched beeping receded. I assumed I was in a hospital, although I had no recollection of how I got here, and I didn't feel comfortable enough to ask.

"Do you think you can open your eyes now?"

I must have drifted off as my racing heart finally steadied. When I opened my eyes, the hazy world around me sharpened. The once-blinding light overhead had softened, and the blinds were drawn, blocking out most of the daylight, though a faint glow seeped around the edges. The sharp scent of antiseptic and bleach burned my nose, anchoring me to the sterile space. Slowly, Marianne's figure solidified in front of me. Her brown hair, streaked with gray, framed softly aged features, but her golden eyes gleamed with a surprising vitality that seemed almost out of place in this washed-out room.

A cool cloth dabbed my flushed face before she brushed my hair back from where it clung to my forehead. "You're back again." She chuckled. "Do you think you can tell me your name?"

My eyes darted from side to side, and a wave of nausea rushed over me. I pitched forward automatically, my free hand going to my stomach as it churned. Black dots spotted my vision as the pain increased.

"Stay still. You've been hurt quite badly, young man. We had to give you a sedative so the doctor could treat you and clean you up." Alarm must have shone in my eyes, and my lips pinched into a tight line. "You weren't bad enough to need surgery, but your legs needed a lot of attention. It took a couple of hours to get all the glass out and dress them. You were very lucky. There should be very little scarring."

Her words triggered a flashback of me kneeling on shattered glass as a figure loomed over me.

"Do you think I don't know where you've been? Hmmm?" Booted feet stood on my legs, forcing me down into the glass. "I've known your every move, River." Fingers sunk into my hair and wrenched my head backward. "I'll let you live to serve as a warning." Fists crashed into my chest. "Others won't be as lucky, but I think your life hanging in the balance will be enough of a warning." A heavily ringed hand backhanded my face, the metal clasps peeling off my skin. "Tell Benson this is his only chance." Her hot breath ghosted over my face, and it took everything in me not to throw up. "If he keeps coming for me..." Her sinister smile shone

in the darkness. "I'll tell the brothers where you are and let them enact their fantasy." She pinched my cheek, making blood spill from the wounds. "It's only been my word keeping them from fulfilling it. I know they told you what they wanted to do. I'll let them if he doesn't stop coming for me. Then I'll tell them to end him, too."

"Dr. Morris is on his way. I'll wake you when he gets here. Just rest for now." I'm not sure if I dipped my head to my chest or not before I was floating again.

When I next opened my eyes, the golden light surrounding the window had deepened to an orange hue that made me think of sunsets and lakes, the wind on my face, and muscular tattooed arms wrapped around me. Of harsh kisses that melted my bones and bruised my lips. Of safety and desire.

The sound of a softly murmured discussion reached my ears, but I couldn't turn my head enough to see where the sound was coming from. I vaguely recognized one of the voices, but I was too spaced out to work out where from. The voices grew louder, footsteps on the hard linoleum floor echoing in the silence of my room. A sharp inhale made me freeze like a statue as Montoya's face appeared in front of me, her lips pinched in a tight line, her brows furrowed.

"You have got to be fucking kidding me. He's going to be pissed when he sees you, kid. They gave you one hell of a beating, huh?"

What the hell was she doing here? I had no idea what was going on, and I couldn't even ask, since my voice was trapped in my head again. Inside, I was screaming, clawing at my skull, but nothing but a wobbly breathy exhale left my lips as words died on my tongue.

"He's going to lose it when he sees the state you're in. Fuck." Her eyes ran over every exposed inch of me, cataloging a multitude of injuries I couldn't feel right now. It transported me back to a night I was paraded around naked and plugged, while men touched, slapped, and groped me. I was just a toy for them to play with.

Hearing Montoya's voice in the background as the images played in my mind fucked with my heart. I sucked in a shuddering inhale, pain seeping through my veins like mercury. I blinked up at her through a glassy haze as a loud sound threw me back into the room. She sighed heavily and plopped down on the chair next to me, staying in my field of vision. Her elegant hand ran across her mouth like she was thinking about what to say as resignation swam in her weighted gaze.

"I know you don't like me, River, but please listen to me. I know Benson well..."

The fond familiarity in her voice was like a blunt knife to my humiliated heart. A tear slipped from the corner of my eye and down my cheek at the mention of his name. My chest squeezed tight as memories of the last time I saw him assaulted me. She looked at me with sympathy in her dark brown eyes, like there was some kind of kinship between us. I hated her for every minute she had gotten to spend in his presence that I hadn't over the years. I'd rather gouge her eyes out with a rusty fork than willingly listen to her, but I was trapped in the bed, unable to move or breathe.

"I know he fucked up."

Not where I was expecting her to go with this. She smirked at me. The look on my face must have given me away.

"Yeah, I bet you thought I was going to tell you to stay the fuck away from him, right?" She shook her head. "He's like a brother, always looking out for me. He told me everything." My eyes widened in alarm, and she waved me off. "Well, not every-everything, but enough. He knows he fucked up. Benson doesn't always think before he speaks, especially where his heart is concerned." She chuckled. "He's a good guy, and what happened between you two messed him up, big time. But not in the way you're thinking."

My breaths shallowed, coming in short, sharp pants. She reached over, taking my hand in one of hers before wrapping the other one around it, cocooning me in her hold. I wanted to hate it on principle, but I felt her sincerity in the gesture.

"Stop whatever you're thinking."

I screwed my eyes shut, pushing more tears down my cheeks. My lips trembled. I wanted her to beg him to come back to me and not throw me away. I'd been discarded like trash too many times and was terrified the only person who had ever felt safe—like home—wanted nothing to do with me.

"River, stop," she ordered. "He's not angry or disgusted with you. He feels like he fucked up. Like he used you, just like every other guy has in your life. It's eating away at him. He's had a shit forty-eight hours. This, coupled with the case we're working on." She shook her head, her thumb rubbing soothing circles across the back of my hand. "He's sorry, alright? Just hear him out, kid. Please."

I chewed on my bottom lip as her words rolled around in my head. Bane felt guilty? Like he'd used me? It just didn't make sense. What did he have to feel guilty for? All I was good at was giving pleasure to others; it was all I had to offer. I'd only wanted to make him feel good, like he did for me, but I didn't know how else to show him.

All I was good for was being a hole, so that's what I did.

I'd heard him groaning and calling out my name while I laid in my bed, and it was like an unconscious tether pulled me toward him. There was a need to make the things he voiced real, because I wanted him to feel good. Bane deserved everything good in this world. He was a one in a million kind of guy, and I was... I was nothing. A no one. I had nothing to offer him. I wasn't normal.

Not worthy of him.

And I never would be.

"I can see you're thinking it over. Just let me send him in and... and let him talk." She choked down a sound trapped in the back of her throat. "You've never spoken in front of me, but he tells me you can when you feel safe enough. He's that for you, isn't he? Your safe place?" I nodded slightly, or at least I tried to, and grimaced as I bit back the wave of pain that washed over me. "Good. Don't let that go, River. If he lost you, I don't think he would survive. You're, as far as I know, everything to him. He's never..." She tapped her lips, silencing herself like she was holding back something she knew. "This is all new to him, too."

My eyes tracked her as she left me alone, the door snicking shut behind her. I didn't know what to make of everything she said. I was everything to him? Why? How? What does he see when he looks at me? I wasn't a person anymore; I didn't know how to be like everyone else. I should take this opportunity to push him away, save him from me, before it was too late.

Look at what happened the one night I tried to help him. All I'd succeeded in doing was bringing the devil to his door, and Bane was the kind of guy who would ride to certain death if it meant saving someone he cared about. How he could value my worthless life over his didn't compute. He was a million times the person I could ever dream of being.

I was a rogue shadow, a memory that would fade with time. Footsteps in the sands of time that would be washed away.

A mistake.

That was what he'd said, and he wasn't wrong.

When he lost control of his cast-iron emotions that morning, Bane saw the truth that his pure heart blinded him to. I had to prove to him I wasn't worth his time, no matter how much my soul cried out for his. He was safer without me. He would be better off without me. I belonged to the dark. It was where I was reborn.

I didn't need psychic abilities to know he was standing on the other side of the door. I felt him. It was a physical reaction I had any time I was in his proximity. The air thickened, and electricity danced across my skin. The small hairs on the back of my neck and my arms stood on end, and goosebumps prickled across my skin. I was attuned to him so well, I'd be able to find him even if I was blindfolded. I could crawl across burning coals to the edge of the world without deviating course. He was my center, my true north. My internal compass would always lead to him.

Because Bane was my heart. Without him, nothing else existed.

Blood rushing through my ears masked the sound of the door opening. I couldn't swallow, because I felt paralyzed by his presence. I was fighting an internal war, and there would be no victor. To save him, I had to sacrifice myself. I wasn't a martyr; I was a realist.

"Oh, fuck." His broken voice tore through me, wrenching the still-beating muscle from my chest as he collapsed on the floor with a heavy thud. The sound reverberated through the room, a painful echo of that first moment he laid eyes on me just weeks ago. Exhaustion weighed down every part of me, pressing like a shroud, and I couldn't summon the strength to turn and face him. If this was my last breath, then let it be.

"River?" He sounded closer, but I couldn't feel his looming presence sucking the air from my lungs like it so often did when he towered over me. Was he crawling to me? How I wished I had the strength to move to see him. My eyes searched, even though it was futile. "Angel?" He gasped. "Fuck! Please, a-angel." His cracked voice shattered me. "I-I'm..." The bed dipped, and a chair scraped across the floor. My fragile heart fluttered in my chest, as delicate as fractured glass that a breath of wind would turn to dust.

Cedarwood and leather surrounded me. His scent called me back from the ledge where I stood, my toes over the precipice. Strong arms wrapped around me and pulled me back just as I pushed myself over and into the void of no return.

"Don't leave me, River. I couldn't survive without you, angel. I said things I didn't mean. I-I wasn't thinking, I was..." Hot tears hit my skin like acid as he confessed his sins against me. "I failed you, a-and now...now you're in here because of me. You're h-hurt because of me...my actions."

No! I screamed internally as my trauma locked my voice deep inside my mind. *No, Bane. You have never done anything wrong. I was wrong to touch you without your consent. I was wrong to take something from you that you weren't willing to give. I never asked.*

I'm sorry. I'm sorry.

I'm so, so sorry for coming back into your life.

"River..." His large hands cupped my face, his rough skin grounding me as his thumb cleared the torrent of tears off my cheeks. "I never should have walked away. I should have stayed and explained why I jumped away from you." I shook my head in tiny increments, pushing through the pulsing ache in my neck. I'd suffer for him, to bring him a momentary reprieve from his self-flagellation. An inhuman sound pulsated from his chest into me; it sounded like failure. It tasted like regret. A shattered future that had never had the chance to have life breathed into it.

"Are you listening to me, angel? Please, please look at me. River, please!" Panic rose in his voice, and it felt like ice coating my skin.

Confused, I blinked up at him through water-logged lashes. When did my eyes close? I didn't remember. I didn't... I didn't... I was struggling to grasp what was real and what was a figment of my imagination.

"Shhh, Riv. I'm here. I'm not going anywhere. I won't let them hurt you again. You're safe."

Bane's voice faded away, and I gave into the oppressive bleakness of my broken mind. I found myself in that special place where I'd sent myself so many times before to save myself from reality. The place where the guy of my dreams held me like I was a person. Someone he loved, who was whole and fully formed. He smiled at me like he loved me, and I loved him in return. Eyes I could get lost in looked at me like I was the sun that chased the darkness away.

But now even this world was tainted, cracked and broken. Rotten to the core. I was an infection that needed to be terminated. I hurt everyone I came into contact with. Even in the elysium my mind had created to keep me safe, I still destroyed the one soul I'd ever loved. His fingers slipped from my cheeks stained with blood, agony etched into his face. Was this how it ends? My blood on his hands would destroy him.

"I'm sorry I failed you, angel. I promised to keep you safe, b-but when you needed me, I wasn't there for you. Why did you leave? Was it because of me? What I said? What I did?" His pained cry sliced me open, revealing my rotten core. I hated that I was causing him pain without saying a word.

I forced my eyes open, and they locked on his. One a brilliant sky blue, the other the darkest depths of the forest, wild and free. They glistened like a fractured mirror, reflecting the maelstrom of emotions inside me. Pain and regret. Shame and guilt. Love and hopelessness. So much fucking pain it filled my lungs and drowned me.

My lips tasted of betrayal and salt. Here he was, begging for my forgiveness, when I was the one who'd put him in the most compromising position. "I-I...m... I'm...s...s-sor—"

Bane's lips brushed mine, silencing the words I tried to breathe life into, but they were barely audible even to my ears.

"It wasn't your fault. I-I—" he started.

I bit my tongue hard enough for the metallic tang of blood to burst across my taste buds and forced my arm up so I could cover his mouth. Bane deflated against me. His eyes fluttered shut, and he moved until he could nuzzle against my hand. My heart stuttered in my chest. Soft kisses whispered across my palm and onto my knuckles as he took control of my appendage and kissed my fingertips.

"Angel." He cleared his throat like he was about to make a proclamation that would change the course of history. "I. Love. You."

Who knew three words had the power to destroy me? A fresh wave of tears spilled from my burning eyes. It was too late. I was too late to save him from my cancerous self.

"N-n-n-no." I formed the word with trembling lips, but they were nothing but rasping air.

A watery smile lit up his face. "You don't get to tell me how I feel, Riv. You need to listen to me right now. No, you don't get to hide from this." He pulled my arm away from my face where I'd thrown it over my eyes.

"It's my truth, and I'll tell you every day until you believe me. I love you." He expelled a powerful breath. "I know I left things in a less than desirable way, and I will spend the rest of my life making it up to you, but the god's honest truth is I freaked the fuck out. I wanted you. I need you." His lips brushed over mine. "I was dreaming about you. I have dreamed about you since I brought you home. And waking up to you doing exactly what you were doing in my dream was heaven and hell, all rolled into the most devastating explosive experience I've ever had. I've never felt for anyone else what I do with you. But, even though I felt like I was floating among the stars, I also felt like I'd broken your trust. You were living with me for your protection. You were finally free, and I turned you back into an object."

"No." The word punched past my lips with a rawness that shredded my vocal cords, but I didn't care. I refused to let Bane make himself into my villain.

He was my protector.

My home.

My safe place.

"But—"

"No... y-ou...s...sav...ed...m...eee."

"I will always save you, angel, because I love you—whether your heart and mind can accept that or not. I'm irrevocably in love with you. Words might not mean much to you, but there are many ways I can show you what you mean to me when we get home."

He sniffed, wiping away his tears with the back of his hand before his red-rimmed eyes fell on me again.

Home.

One syllable that meant as much to me as love. Bane was offering me everything I'd ever deluded myself I could have. But was I really worth it?

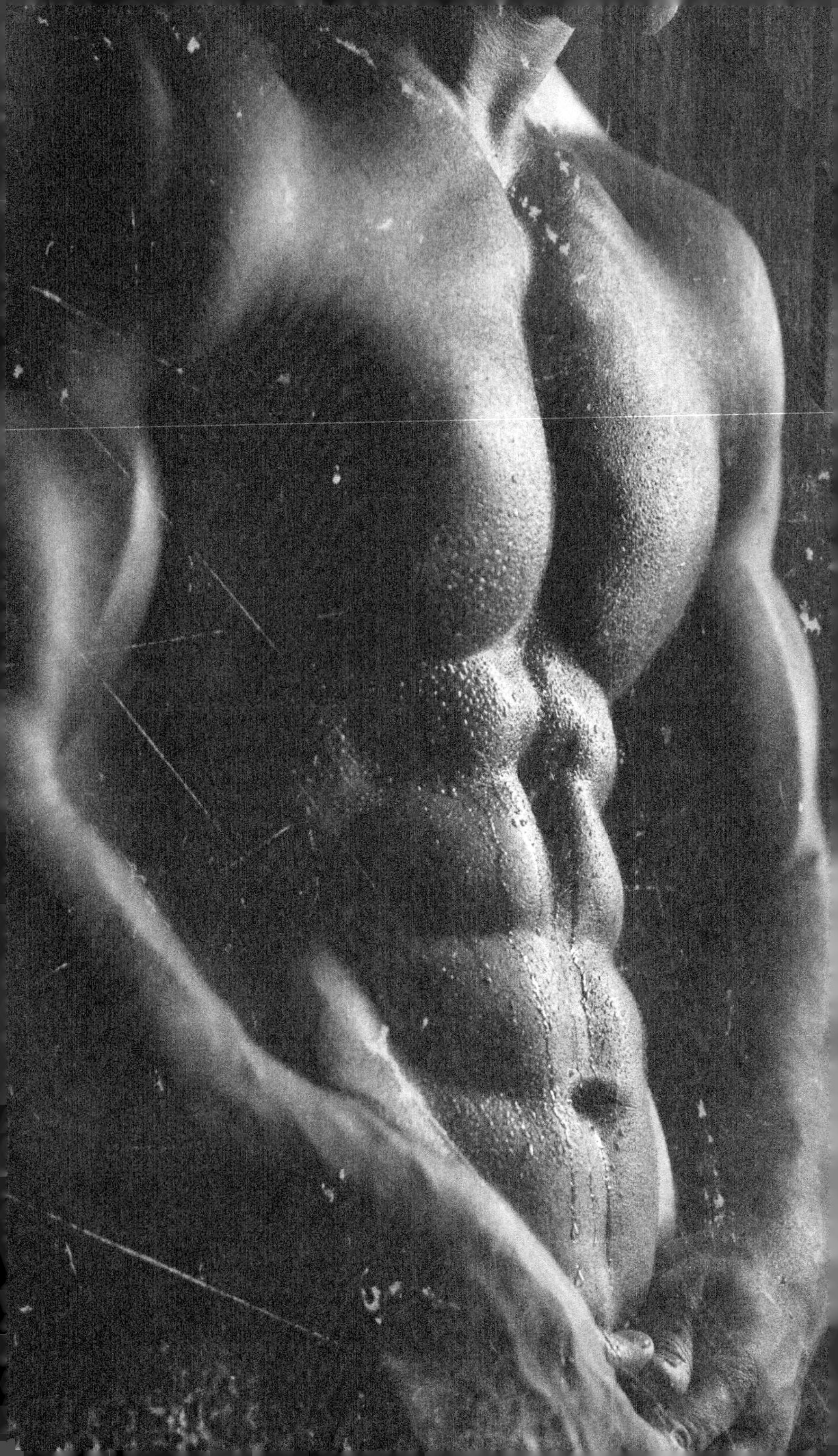

CHAPTER TWENTY
Bane

Seeing River lying in that bed, beaten and bruised, and trying not to lose control, was almost unbearable. One side of his face was swollen, with deep cuts marring his cheek, and his skin a stained watercolor of blacks and blues. I swallowed hard, but my throat felt tighter with each attempt, my lungs constricting as if I couldn't draw breath. I had just bared everything to him—heart, soul, and all the unspoken pieces I'd guarded for so long, offering them up at his feet. And now, silence. Deafening silence that stretched into an ache with each second he stared back at me through eyes that saw right past me.

Unable to handle the trepidation leaching into me, I pushed up from the chair, leaned in, and brushed my lips across his forehead, hoping he'd feel the tenderness I couldn't put into words. Then I turned and walked out of the room, the weight of his unspoken rejection pressing down on me, heavier than the guilt I already carried for abandoning him to his current fate. I'd given him all of me, but the hollow ache left from his silence was consuming me, filling me with the painful realization that even after all I'd said, it still might not be enough.

I might not be enough.

Montoya launched out of her seat in the corridor as I closed the door behind me. My eyes were wet with tears of fear as her gaze assessed me from head to toe. "How did it go?"

A shuddering breath rocked through my body as I tried to force the words from on my lips. "I-I don't know." My shoulders dropped as she stepped up to me and wrapped her arms around me in comfort. We must have looked ridiculous to passersby, but I didn't care about anyone else at that moment, only the boy who owned my heart, the one I'd left in the other room. He would forever be its keeper, even if he didn't want me.

Was it too much to ask for him to want me the same way I wanted him? Right now, I didn't care about my job, the case, or the career I'd spent my adult life forging from the ground up. All the things I'd sacrificed for meant nothing to me now. All I wanted was him. Without River in my life, I didn't think I could go on. The grief I'd felt when I lost my family didn't hold a flame to the devastation that wanted to swallow me whole.

"Give him time, Jacob. You just dumped a hell of a lot on him when he should be resting and recovering." I sighed and dropped my head until it rested on hers. The vanilla scent of her hair that once used to bring me comfort now left me feeling adrift.

"I know, but... I wanted him to know. No, I needed him

to know that he's not a job to me. He's... he's everything. And that might have come as a shock to him, but..." I licked my lips and extracted myself from her embrace. "We've had these moments where it's felt like time stopped when he looked at me, and I swear I saw the same want mirrored in his eyes."

"I don't think you're wrong," she said softly, like you would when speaking to a sad child. "I saw it that morning in your kitchen when he all but pissed on you." A smile tugged my lips at the memory, but it faded quickly. "He's spent his whole life being treated like a commodity. It'll probably take him a while before he can trust your words aren't pretty lies. The lies we believe are the most dangerous, especially when the truth is so hard to hear."

"Since when did you become so fucking wise?"

She smiled at me and tapped my nose. "Come on, let's grab a coffee and get an update from the doctor. Then you can go back to him and take him home."

I looked at her with indecision, my eyes darting between the door to his room and her. My feet had grown roots and refused to move. I was right where I should be, but not right where I needed to be.

With a huff, she crossed her arms over her chest, her sassy side roaring to life like a fire in her. "Fine. I'll go get us three decent coffees. You speak to the doctor, then go sit with River. But don't," she pointed her finger at me, jabbing my sternum for extra emphasis, "push him for an answer to anything other than questions about how he ended up where he did and what happened. Even that might be too much for him right now."

"Alright," I ground out, but I didn't miss the warning laced in her voice.

"Promise me, Benson."

I threw my hands up in the air in exasperation. "I promise."

"Good." With that, she spun on her heel and stalked away from me.

I found Dr. Morris at the busy nurses' station, and as he explained the state River was in when he was brought in, it took everything in me not to punch my fist through the wall. The only good bit of news was that once River had eaten, I'd be able to take him home. Acting as his guardian, I completed all the relevant release paperwork he handed my way, so once he gave the all clear, we could get out of this place.

"He will be fine," Dr. Morris said, pulling me from my memories. "He just needs to rest and take it easy. I'm sure you're aware that his body is still recovering from years of abuse and neglect. I urge you to make him see a therapist. The physical symptoms will heal and scar, but the mental toll will live rent free and fester in his mind, until it pushes him to the brink."

"I know."

He shuffled on his feet and looked like he'd swallowed something sour before pinning me with a steely gaze. "I'm not saying he is, but..." I held my breath, not willing to hear the words that would come out of his mouth. "I don't think he is coping, and his mutism is a sign that things may be far worse than you think. Tread carefully, officer."

"Of course, I will," I said, adding every ounce of authority I could to my voice as I passed him back the completed paperwork. "There is nothing I wouldn't do to see him happy and healthy." The doctor's eyes widened at me as I left him with his mouth gaping and headed back to River's room.

"Are you comfortable?" My voice was low and gentle as I pushed the door open and closed it softly behind me. His deep forest-green eyes glimmered in the dim light as he tracked every step I took until I was clutching the bottom of his bed.

A wan smile flickered at the corners of his lips, the swelling on his face stark even in the low light. "Mmmm." River made a noise in the back of his throat, which I took as an agreement.

"I need to talk to you about what happened. Why you left and where you went."

"I know." It was lucky I'd picked up some words through lip reading, because he was barely audible to my ears.

"It shouldn't take too long, but I need you to be honest, River. It doesn't matter about my feelings. I just need to know what went through your head and why you did what you did, especially since you were in protective custody in my house." By the time the last words left me, my control had snapped, and I was basically shouting at him. My frustration and unbridled fear boiled over so much that a young nurse stuck her head through the door and glared at me.

"I don't care who you are." She pointed at me. "But he needs to rest. Shouting at him won't help. You might be an officer of the law, but I will have you removed from his room by security if you can't operate in a professional manner."

"I'm sorry." I looked down at my feet and then at her. "Emotions are getting a little high in here."

"You're wrong. It's your emotions that are getting the better of you, officer. And it's not me you should apologize to, but my patient."

River scoffed, and I turned my gaze back to him and smirked suitably chastised. "I apologize." Then to the nurse, I said, "We'll be fine. The doctor said he can go once he's eaten. Can we get him some food?"

"We serve dinner at five p.m. He'll get it then." With that, she shut the door and a tenuous silence filled the room.

"Well, she was fun," I said to break the ice, and flexed my fingers around the rail at his feet. "Is it alright if I sit and start again?" River dipped his chin and my heart skipped a beat. With a calming breath, I grabbed the chair and slid into it, momentarily forgetting what I should do as my eyes traced over every blooming bruise on his face and the way they decorated his neck and arms.

"T-tal..."

I nodded and pieced myself back together. I couldn't afford to break in front of him. Not now. I had to find the strength to ask the hard questions and face the truth I'd rather run from. Childish? Maybe. But I'd never been in this position before; caring so deeply about someone who was involved in a case, enough for me to want to choose their happiness and health over the importance of my job. I was so screwed when it came to River, but in a way, it made me feel lighter. I had something to fight for now that was mine. He was mine. I'd make damn sure of it.

Bower's voice rolled through my head. *Only do this if you can keep your emotions out of it. He is a witness in this case, nothing more. Got it?*

I rolled my eyes at my own naivety. From the very beginning, I knew my emotions were too entangled with everything that was River Lane. Yet, I'd foolishly convinced myself that I was professional enough to keep them neatly compartmentalized.

"Here." I slipped my hand in my pocket and pulled out his phone, desperately wanting to scold him for leaving it behind and making himself untraceable. *Maybe that was the point?* I was almost certain he didn't know it had a tracker, considering he'd never had a phone before. I'd buried it in an obscure folder that I highly doubted he'd even looked at. But he wasn't an idiot, and probably knew his location could be triangulated through cell towers. Possibly?

River held out his hand and took it from me. His face paled as he flipped it over and turned it on. Guilt flashed deep in his eyes before they shuttered closed and his walls solidified before me.

"I thought it would be best if we did it this way," I hedged. "I'll ask the questions and you can type your response, okay?"

> K

"I need you to be honest with me now, River. This is for your own safety and protection, but also for the case."

He flinched at my words and fuck, how I wanted to kick myself in the ass for being a heartless dick. With trembling hands, I latched onto his arm. The feel of his skin beneath my fingertips was like a brand on my heart. River held himself still as I touched him, but the fear lingering in his pinched eyes made me feel like I was splintering at the seams. I was a mixed up cocktail of emotions, and I didn't know which one was going to come out on top. Christ, I was giving myself whiplash, let alone him. Gently stroking my thumb across his arm, I took the time to order the chaotic thoughts in my head. Fear, desire, and the need for control were all warring inside me.

"I'm sorry, that came out wrong." River blinked glassy eyes at me as he waited for me to continue on bated breath. "Everything I said before was true." My eyes fluttered closed, and I focused on the sensation of my skin on his, trying to ignore the intrusive thoughts every time I touched a fresh scab. I'd never admit to having them, but oh, how I wanted to fuck up those who hurt him. My phone buzzed in front of me, drawing my attention.

> Just ask me so we can go home.

My brain froze from shock as I read and reread his message. *Home?* I wanted to jump up and wrap my arms around him as waves of joy and humility washed over me. It was amazing the impact four little letters could have on my mood, but they made me feel like I was soaring above the earth.

A beatific grin spread across my face. I felt more settled and solid in my skin than I had in hours. Days, even. It wasn't an outright declaration that he felt the same way as I did, but it was a beginning. It was a start that I would hold close to my heart and nurture every day until he saw in his reflection what I saw every damned day.

Time seemed to pass in a blur as he answered every question I threw his way. I couldn't escape the feeling he wasn't being completely honest again. What he said was plausible, and most would have accepted it without question. But like a monster looming over the hill, every word he typed was laced with regret. The way his emotions were displayed so openly on his face was everything I'd wanted for weeks, but now it felt like I'd threaded a noose around my neck.

Even though he didn't say a word to me, I could hear every husky one in my mind, along with all the ones he left unspoken. He said he'd left because I'd hurt him and that rang true, but that wasn't the only reason. My notebook was filled with details about what had happened to him, but it was what he said when I drew our conversation to an end that rocked me to my core.

There's something I need to tell you.

"Okay. You know I'm here to listen. Always."

He gave me a wan smile that somehow seemed to intensify his sombre mood.

> Just don't get angry with me.

"I won't. I promise. Just please..." I ran my hand through my coarse hair for something to do. My fingers twitched with the need to haul him back into my arms and kiss him until he forgot every ounce of his pain.

> She sent someone to collect me. To take me to her.

"As much as I don't want to think about it, that makes sense. She knows she's under the spotlight. It wouldn't make sense for her to—"

> Please just stop and listen.

"I'm sorry." I shrugged as a wave of trepidation rolled though me and coiled in my gut.

> It was a cop.

"Are you serious?" My stomach dropped through my feet. I jumped up, sending my chair flying backward and started pacing. Out of everything he could have said, I wasn't expecting that. "Do you know who it was?"

He nodded and cast his eyes back down to his phone.

> Davis.

Shit, shit, fucking, shit. "I hate to ask this, but are you sure?" I waited with bated breath, praying for an answer a part of me knew would never come. River had no reason to lie to me.

> Yes. He came to the house with that other guy who did the security system. I recognized his voice from before. I didn't know his name until you introduced us.

Tears carved a path down his beautifully destroyed face as he looked up at me through eyes that were filled with shadows and fear. I sat on the edge of the bed, took his phone from him, and wrapped my hands around his.

"I know that can't have been easy for you to say." He shook his head, making salty tears fly, stained with his pain and fear. I leaned into him so my lips brushed his ear. "Thank you for trusting me, angel."

River sucked in a stuttering breath. "Y-you believe... me?" Wonder coated his voice that I was only able to hear thanks to my proximity. My heart bled through its cracks for all he'd suffered and his honest confusion that I wouldn't question something he said. He'd been led to believe his voice was powerless. Inconsequential. But I would listen and hear him. I would believe him. Always.

There were layers to River, ones he tried to keep hidden. The more I thought about it, the more I knew he needed Joelle's help. As much as I hated to admit it, River wasn't just running from me; he was running from himself. Years of experience had taught me you couldn't outrun the darkness inside your mind. It was relentless, waiting patiently for the smallest crack to slip through before it sunk its claws into you, leaving you unable to escape.

Right now, I was River's only anchor, but I didn't believe I was strong enough to keep him here on my own. I could protect his body, but his mind? That was beyond me. I hadn't told him yet that I'd been back home, and seen the message he'd scrawled on the mirror like we used to when we were younger and shared hidden secrets. In a world where we had nothing, those secrets became everything.

I'd burst into his room, ready to tear into him, to lay my heart bare—and found his bed empty, half his clothes gone, and Shadow sulking in his crate in the kitchen. I'd checked the CCTV and, after finding no sign of him leaving, punched a hole clean through the drywall. Not my finest moment, but the thought of losing him, of not getting the chance to set things right between us, had left me untethered.

Montoya walked through the door, injecting some much-needed oxygen into the room. "Sorry it took so long, but when I got downstairs and smelled the burned crap they call coffee, I knew I couldn't subject any of us to that. So, I went for a walk and found this adorable little place a couple of blocks away."

"Amazing," I grumbled and huffed a breath. "River's brought something to my attention that we can't ignore. I'm just not sure how Bower will take it."

Montoya glanced between me and River, curiosity burning in her eyes. "What?"

"Davis is compromised. He's involved with Dahlia." I shook my head, disbelief warring with that feeling of rightness in my gut. "He was the one who took River to her."

"Fuck! That doesn't surprise me." She shuddered. "He's always given me a bad feeling, you know?"

"Yeah." I sighed and rolled my head back on my shoulders, trying to work the tension out of the muscles. "I thought he was just a homophobic racist, but apparently, it goes far beyond that."

"You'll have to speak to Bower at the station. There's no way he'll believe you if he doesn't see the truth in your eyes."

She hit the nail on the head. The old guard all came up from the academy together, and it's going to take evidence, hard evidence, for Bower to believe us. "Now give it to me." I reached out for my coffee with a trembling hand and turned to River. "I don't know about you, but I could do with a drink." With a slight dip of his chin and a soft smile on his lips, he agreed.

"Ah, before I hand it over, raise the poor boy up so he can actually drink it, Benson."

Confusion washed over me before my brain kicked into gear, and I grabbed the control for the bed and raised River up. His breath punched out of him as it manipulated him into a sitting position. He squeezed his eyes tightly shut as lines of pain carved their way onto his beautiful face. After a couple of deep breaths, he locked his emotions down and pulled a mask of indifference over his face. He tested out the range of motion in his right hand, slowly clenching and unclenching his fingers before gingerly reaching for the disposable cup Montoya held out for him.

"I added a dash of caramel creamer to it for you, too," she said with a bright smile as River wrapped his hand around the cup. "Yours is just as bitter as you," she snickered and handed me a cup.

The bitter taste of freshly ground coffee was a welcome distraction from the painful conversation I'd been trying to have with River. Every question was one step forward, three steps back with him, but I'd give him this small reprieve before I continued.

My phone lit up with a message before I could pick up where we'd left off.

I want to go home.

"We can as soon as you've eaten something."

No. Now! I don't like being here.

"I don't like it either, angel," I soothed, reaching for him. I laced my fingers through his. That simple contact settled a part of me I hadn't realized was fracturing. It gave me hope we would come out of this on the other side.

> I need my clothes.

"They probably trashed them, considering the state you were in." My off-handed comment seemed to snap something in him, and he lurched forward, the cup slipping from his grasp. Luckily, Montoya caught it with her lightning-quick reflexes as I tried to hold him back from throwing himself off the bed. Color drained from his face, and his eyes became intensely focused on the bed.

"Oh, shit." Montoya's breathy gasp caught my attention, and I followed her line of sight to where River's right leg was now exposed. An all-consuming rage boiled my blood, and a red haze settled over my vision.

The sight of River's leg stole the air from my lungs as he scrambled to cover it and pushed me away. A sound like a wounded animal escaped his throat as his hand latched onto my face and pulled me so my eyes were on his. What I saw emanating from them was a sucker punch to my bleeding heart. His lips trembled as tears stained his bloodless cheeks.

"P-p...lease." Fear and agony coated the single word. "D-don't...l-leave..."

My breath whooshed out of my lungs like a collapsed dam. I scooped him up in my arms and buried my face in his neck, shaking with the force it took to hold my tears back. Images of his legs covered in stitches and bandages over still-oozing raw flesh flashed behind my closed eyes. Inhaling his sweet cinnamon and orange scent was a gift from the gods, one I'd never let go of.

"Never, River," I breathed into his neck and peppered kisses on his fluttering pulse point. "Never." I shook my head and sunk my hands into his wild hair, trying to imbed myself into him. "I'll never leave y-you." I hiccuped, fighting back a mournful cry trying to force its way up my throat.

"I'll, uh, go speak to the doc and see if I can get his... ah, clothes and get us out of here."

I didn't hear Montoya go. My every thought and action was consumed by the broken boy convulsing in my arms. I held him tightly, hearing the frantic thud-thud-thud of his heart against my ear as a river of tears flowed from him, drowning me.

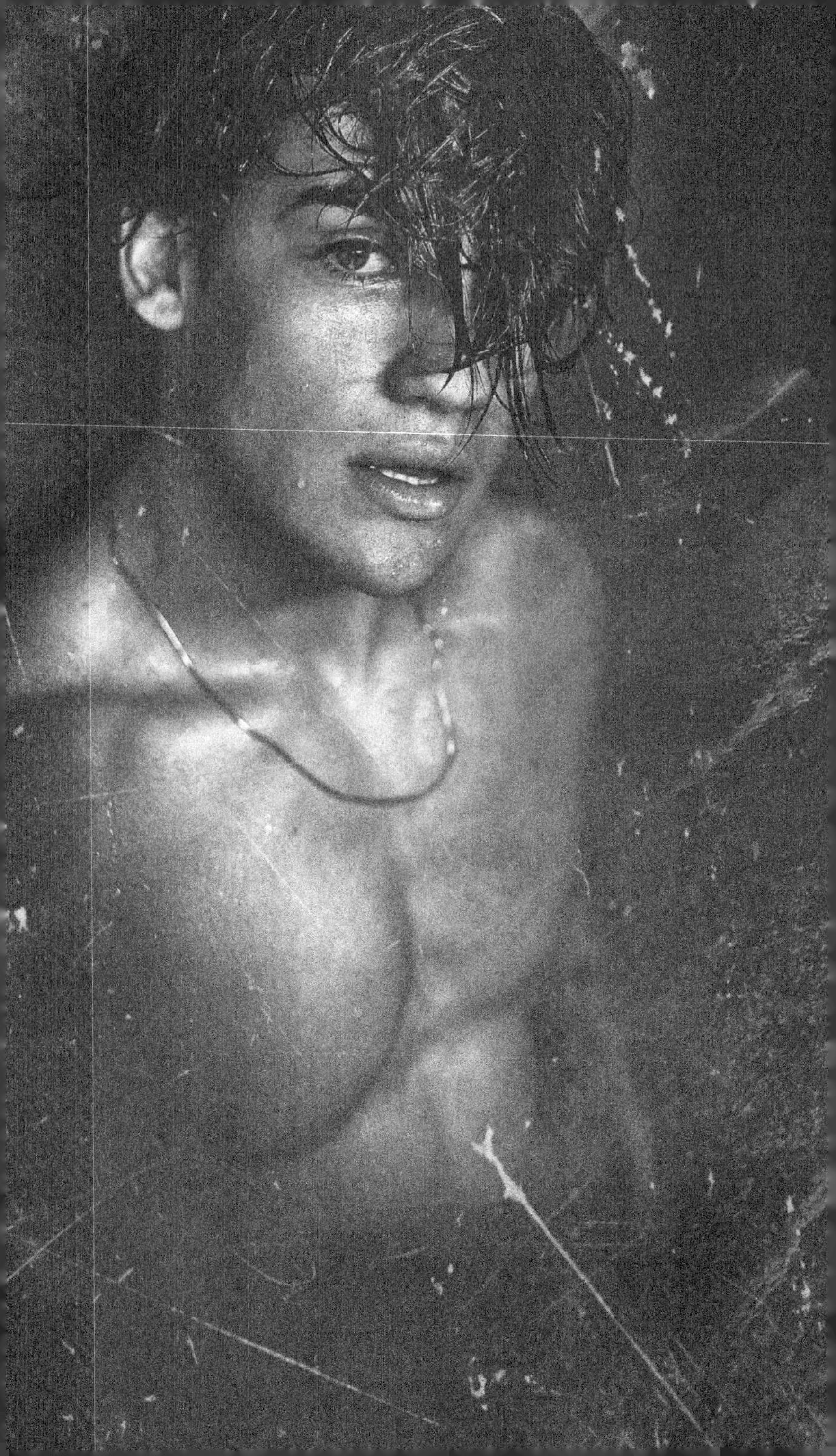

CHAPTER TWENTY-ONE
River

This wasn't the first time Bane had held me, and the safety and security I'd always felt was undeniable. But something between us had shifted on a seismic scale. We'd always been pieces of the same puzzle, but our splintered edges never quite fit together. Now that our truths were being laid bare at our feet, our broken parts could heal, and it felt like we were slowly fusing together in a way I prayed was unbreakable.

When I left his house, I was happy to die. Instinctually, I knew it was the best outcome I could have hoped for, but today I had hope. Fresh oxygen filled my lungs rather than dissipating when I inhaled. The darkness that shrouded me was lighter. Shadows danced where once there was nothing, and my heart felt like a smoldering ember I might nurture back to life.

Bane offered me everything I'd thought was an impossible dream, but no matter how much I wanted his heart, his love, to be with him... one question remained. Was I worthy of him?

"Shh. I've got you, angel. I promise I'm not going anywhere. I meant what I said." My breath hitched as his words wove themselves into the fibers of my being. "I love you, and I will spend every day proving to you that you're worth everything I have to give." I shook my head, refusing his words, my brain screaming at me to push him away before I ruined him. Lifting a trembling hand to his nape, my fingers sunk into his hot skin, hauling him closer to me.

"I-I..." I licked away the salty tears from my lips, exhaling heavily, unable to find the words for my tumultuous emotions.

Bane linked his fingers with mine, peeling them off his neck and pulled back. My heart froze, fear icing my veins. This was it. This was the moment he realized I was too much. That he'd leave, because no one wanted to tie themselves to a mess like me.

"River. *Angel.*" Bane's gravelly voice was raw and unfiltered. His hands cupped my slick cheeks, his left still entwined with mine. "Look at me, baby."

My eyes fluttered open at his heartbreaking plea. I looked up at him through wet clumpy lashes and even though he wavered in front of me, nothing could hide the depth of emotion painted on his face. His contrasting eyes were wells of honest love, and the sweet smile that lifted his full lips breathed life into me.

"I know you're scared." He brushed the still falling tears from under my eyes. "I know you don't believe me, and you have good reason to doubt me, given everything you've been through. But I will never lie to you." I tilted my head to the side in question, and Bane chuckled. "Not when it comes to matters of my heart. With that, I will lay every god's honest truth at your feet."

Chewing the inside of my cheek, I let my eyes trace every detail of his face and committed them to memory, searing them into my soul. Never had I felt so cherished as I did right now, even if it did feel like I was standing at the edge of a cliff with everything I'd ever dreamed of waiting for me at the bottom, if only I was brave enough to jump.

The sound of the door clicking open made me jump, but Bane didn't release his hold on my face. Instead, he leaned forward, brushed his lips over my clammy forehead, and whispered, "I would love you in any form, in any world, in any time, with any past. All I want is you. Never doubt that I would lay my life down for yours without a second thought, because you are worth fighting for. You, River, are everything."

His words settled into my soul, etched in starlight and dreams. And I knew at that moment that I would not let this chance slip through my fingers like the sands of time—I would fight for the ember coming to life in my heart. I had never known love in any form, but what I felt for Bane was what I believed love to be. I would love him like the world was ending, because I knew what a lifetime without it was like.

Resting his forehead against mine, he took a shuddering breath. "We do this together." His words melted into my skin and fused in my bones. His certainty took hold like roots in the darkest parts of me and pulled me toward his light. I could do this if he was beside me every step of the way. I wasn't strong enough to fight on my own, but with Bane in my life, I wasn't alone anymore.

"Together," I mouthed against his lips and felt him breathe them in as they curved in a tentative smile that I mirrored. He slowly pulled back, and I saw a lifetime with him moving like smokey shadows in his eyes. All we needed to do was give them life, color, and form.

A throat clearing made us both turn. Montoya leaned against the door, ankles crossed and hands shoved in her pockets. "Sharon's bringing you something to eat. She's also completed your paperwork."

My eyes darted back to Bane, and he shrugged. "I knew you wouldn't want to stay here any longer than you had to."

I snorted. Even though every inch of my skin burned with pain and every movement felt like my bones were crumbling to dust, I was climbing the walls being trapped in another cage.

"T-true," I rasped. I felt the weight of Montoya's gaze on me as I slicked my bottom lip. "I-I...m...my...bag?"

"They said—" Bane began, but Montoya swiftly cut him off, reading something in me Bane couldn't.

"I'll go check with Sharon about what happened to your belongings." With that, she slipped from the room again without another word. I struggled to get a read on Montoya. She seemed nice, but I still hated her for every day she'd spent with him that I hadn't. Whether or not my jealousy was warranted, it slithered through me, completely unrepentant.

After eating some dry toast and orange juice, Sharon changed my dressings and promised she'd pay me a home visit to check on my progress. I had a feeling it was more of a favor to Bane, who lost his shit when he saw the extent of my injuries. I reminded him this was nothing I couldn't handle. He'd scoffed, balled his hands into fists, and left in a cloud of frustration.

"He'll be okay, sweetie. He acts like nothing affects him, but still waters run deep." When I'd looked up at her in confusion, she snickered. "He's like an iceberg when it comes to his emotions. What he shows you is nothing compared to what he buries inside. Officer Benson has always been so very careful with his words and actions, not just because of his size, but also his position. But mark my words, that man has the softest, purest heart."

I'd smiled at her while she gave my dressings a final once over before she helped me into some of Bane's clothes and told me she'd keep searching for my belongings. I wasn't worried about my clothes, but there was something I needed, something I'd been willing to sacrifice my life for that I needed to give to Bane. Without it, I feared we'd both be living on borrowed time, and now that I had him, I wasn't prepared to lose him again. Dahlia wasn't one to give up control, and once she realized I had something vital to her operation, it was only a matter of time until I took my last breath.

Night had turned the sky pitch black. Even the glow from the streetlights seemed to be swallowed by the ominous darkness. Montoya pulled the car to a stop in front of Bane's house. My gut dropped as guilt overwhelmed me for everything I'd put him through, but I'd done it all with the best of intentions.

Bane slipped from the car, unlocked the house, and stepped inside, weapon drawn. I watched enraptured as the lights slowly flicked on in room after room as he checked to make sure it was safe. A weighted sigh slipped from my lips at all the extra stress my reappearance had brought to his settled life.

Montoya's gaze caught mine in the rearview mirror as I stared longingly at the house. I winced as her eyes narrowed. "They say the road to hell is paved with good intentions, kid. I don't know why you did what you did. Why you left..." A sharp inhale caught in the back of my throat as I struggled to find the words to justify what I'd done, but she held her hand up. "I don't want your excuses." My shoulders slumped, and every reason why I was a poison to Bane flared to life in my head. "I know you had a reason. I just hope the pain you've caused both of you was worth it."

Luckily for me, Bane appeared at the front door before her words could flay the skin from my bones, his strides devouring the distance between us. He opened the back door, wrapped his hand around mine, and helped me out within seconds. Instead of aiding me to walk the short distance, he hefted me into his arms with an unnatural gentleness for a man of his size, cradling me against his chest like I was something precious. The steady beat of his heart soothed my ragged edges as his body heat seeped into me through the layers separating us. His warmth filtered through my veins and lulled me to the edges of unconsciousness. My eyelids turned heavy, and after a few steady beats of his heart, the world fell away.

I woke with a start, sheets tangled around my legs, gasping into the near darkness of my room. It felt like the air from every breath dissolved before it reached my lungs. My throat was raw, and the fading echo of a scream hung heavily in the air. Before I could blink, my door crashed open, ricocheting off the wall. Bane stormed into my room, gun raised, eyes darting around, before his stormy eyes met with mine and the violence melted away, leaving only concern behind.

"What's wrong, angel?" he rasped, sleep wrapped around every syllable.

Clutching my throat, my mind spinning a mile a minute, my nightmare refusing to release me, I sobbed out unintelligible sounds. *I need you. Please don't leave me. I'm scared she's coming for me. I'm terrified she's going to kill you and burn everything you love to the ground.* Bane locked his gun and placed it on the nightstand, then slipped onto the bed like it was second nature, gently pulling me into his arms. I felt like I was falling, spiraling out of control, only seconds away from crashing into the ground and splintering into a million irreparable pieces.

"It's okay, Riv. I've got you. You're safe. Nothing can get you here." His deep voice flowed over me in a wave of comforting warmth that thawed my frozen bones, but did nothing to stop the unending deluge of tears falling down my cheeks. "Shh, baby. Please don't cry." The rough skin of his thumbs sent shockwaves over my flushed face as he swept away the tears that continued to fall.

The tension in my muscles eased as time passed unmeasured, and Bane's presence—his embrace—became a metronome I could set my soul by. Deep purples bled into the dark night sky as dawn approached, but I wasn't ready to be alone. I never wanted to be on my own in the dark again. And as my body slowly relaxed, exhaustion taking over, my mind clung to the fear that everything I'd dreamed of was moments from being ripped away.

Soft lips brushed across the nape of my neck, startling me. "I should go and let you get some sleep."

Fear slithered down my spine. "N-no S-stay...p-please." His heavy exhale ghosted across my skin, making goosebumps prickle across my neck and shoulders.

"I'll stay if that's what you'd like." *Always.* I had never felt safer than when I was cocooned by his body. It was irrational, but logic had no place in my life.

"T-thank...you," I breathed out. Bane's arms tightened around me, a silent acknowledgement. His thick thigh pushed between mine, and I locked it in place by wrapping my ankle around his.

"Anything for you, angel. Now sleep."

Heavy even exhales ruffled my hair as Bane succumbed to sleep, the arm wrapped around me becoming heavier every minute that passed. As the first rays of dawn filtered through the open blinds, my eyes fell closed, a small smile on my lips.

When I woke, my arms searched across the bed for Bane, but the sheet was cold. Blinking awake, I could still see the indent his head had left on the pillow. *It wasn't a dream after all.* The last few days had been a cluster fuck of epic proportions that had nearly ended my life, but the devil had spared me so I could act as a warning and to deliver a message. That was before she had even realized what I'd taken.

"I'll spare his life..." Her voice circled my mind like a cruel joke. I braced my arm against the tiled wall in the shower, my head hung low, defeated. Hot water pummeled my aching muscles as it sluiced down my body, staining the shower floor red as the remnants of my blood washed away down the drain.

I knew it was a lie. Dahlia was incapable of telling the truth. She stacked everything in her favor and used people's weaknesses against them. For Bane, that was me. For me, that was Bane, Max, Dale, and Gabe. The longer I defied her, the more people she would hurt or kill. I couldn't play what if with people's lives.

I was too weak, and she knew it.

"Here you go," Bane said when I stepped into the kitchen, a steaming cup of coffee in his hand. "How are you feeling?" I shrugged and winced in response before shuffling onto the bar stool at the counter. "That good, huh? I've got your meds." He slid a small pile of white and blue pills over, depositing them next to a bottle of water.

I hated taking tablets because I never knew what was in

them and feared being poisoned or drugged. But I trusted Bane, and he trusted the doctors at the hospital. All I could do was take them and hope for the best.

"They won't kill you, Riv. I checked them over," he muttered as I eyed them warily. "I know how you feel about taking things."

"Mmm." I hummed as I swallowed them down, my eyes tracking Bane as he took bacon and eggs out of the fridge. If I hadn't been paying close attention, I'd have missed the way his shoulders bunched and his breath hitched when he set them down on the counter by the stove before turning back to face me.

"Riv." His hands wrapped around the edge of the counter in a white-knuckled grip. "There's something I need to tell you."

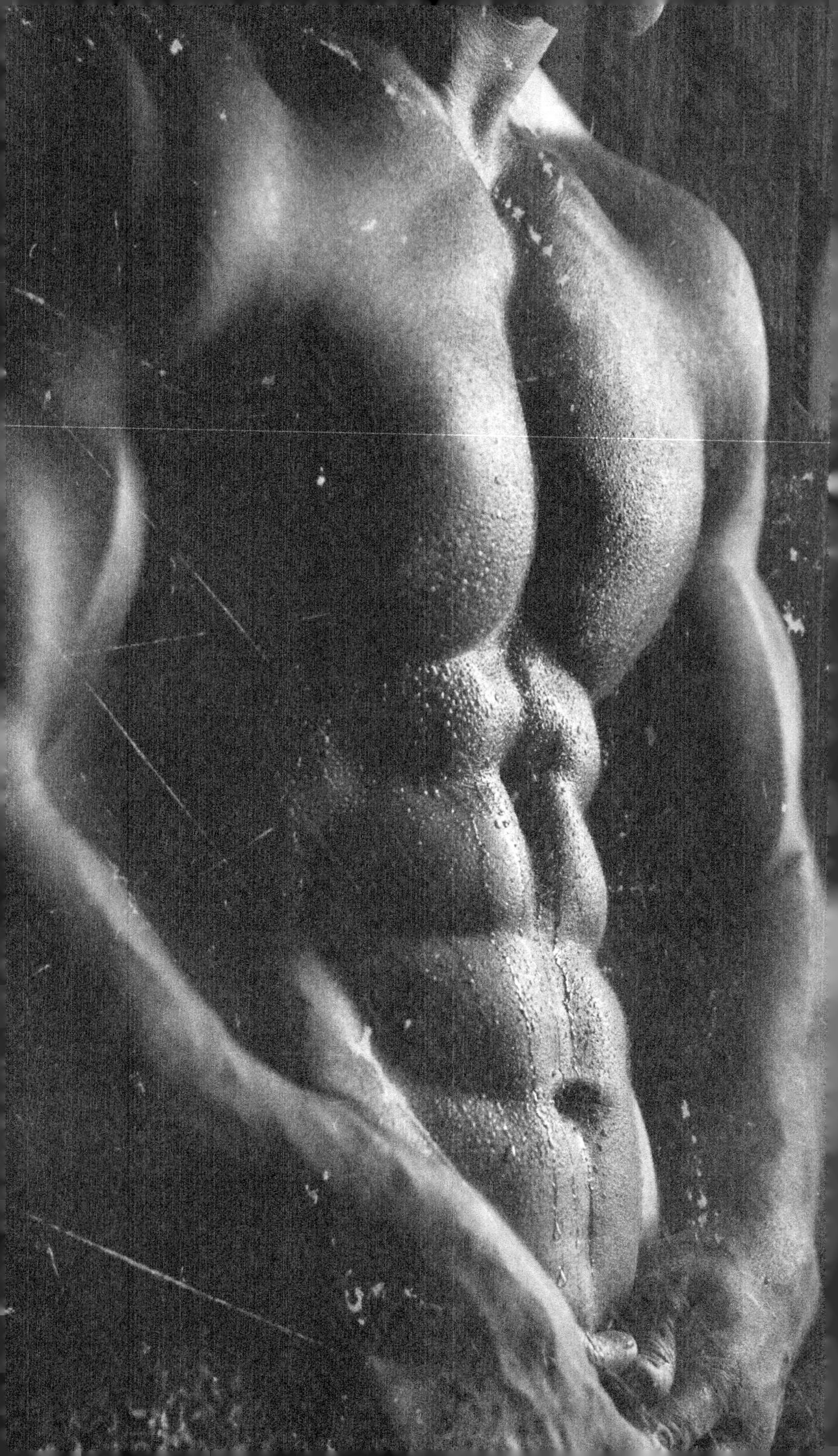

CHAPTER TWENTY-TWO
Bane

I watched the color drain from River's face, leaving his bruises in stark relief, making them look even more ghastly than when he'd walked in. He blinked wide, red-rimmed eyes up at me. I didn't know how many more hits he could take, but for now, they were going to keep coming until this case was closed and Dahlia was either behind bars or dead. I knew which outcome I preferred. Fuck my job and duty of care for my profession. My world had narrowed down, and now my purpose existed for only one man. River was at the forefront of every errant thought that went through my mind.

River swallowed and wrapped his trembling hands around his mug like it could shore him up and keep him safe. I didn't know how to say this, how to tell him one of his friends had been beaten, assaulted, murdered, and dumped in a container. I owed him the truth; he'd survived for so long in this life that sugarcoating it wouldn't do him justice. He was stronger than he believed. Very few people could have lived the life he had and still have so much love to give.

Shadow's claws tapped across the floor as he ran to River's feet, a pathetic whine following in his wake. His erratic tail thwacked against the counter as his head appeared next to River's arm, tongue lolling out the side of his mouth. I chuckled at the momentary reprieve. A beatific smile lifted River's lips as he stroked Shadow's head before his gaze sliced back to mine. The temperature in the kitchen seemed to drop.

"I..." I rolled my bottom lip between my teeth, my heart pounding its way up my throat. "I don't really know how to say this, but—"

River's face was void of all emotion, the sight stealing the air from my lungs. "W-who died?" he rasped. His voice sounded like broken glass.

I shook my head as shock rocked the ground beneath my feet. "How did you know?"

River screwed his eyes shut. A single tear stained his mottled skin, glittering in the subdued morning light. He pulled his phone out of his pocket. I mirrored his actions, setting mine on the granite in front of me.

> You looked like every officer and doctor on the TV when they tell a relative someone they love died.

My head dropped between my shoulders, and I sucked in a shaky inhale before lifting my eyes back to his glassy ones. "Max."

River gasped and bit his fist. His shoulders rocked as shudders rolled through him, and the dam burst, tears flowing in a viscous current down his face. "No. No. No. No." He repeated that one word, over and over again. My heart broke for him. I couldn't bring his friend back. All I could do was be there for him.

Without conscious thought, my feet carried me to him, and I wrapped my arms around his trembling shoulders. River buried his face in the crook of my neck, his stuttering gasps clawing at my skin as his pain became mine. His fingers laced through my hair, tethering me to him like he was afraid I'd vanish as he clung to me.

"I'm so sorry, angel."

River shook his head as tears and snot soaked into my henley. I didn't care. All I wanted was to be there for him in any and every way he'd let me.

"H-how?" he whispered against the shell of my ear. I shook my head as the images of Max's body flashed behind my eyes. "I-I n-need...to...know."

My fingers flexed against the hoodie he wore—my hoodie —until I felt his solid form beneath them and closed my eyes as I relayed the events of the morning Max's body was discovered. I promised him we'd make sure whoever killed him was arrested and held accountable for their crimes.

A hysterical laugh tore its way from River's lips. I released him and cupped his blotchy face in his hands. "I promise. I promise you, River," I vowed, staring into his eyes, forcing my way beneath the agony he was drowning in.

"S-she s-said..." He chewed on his lip as his rough voice cracked and gave out before trying again. "She s-said...I-I'd have m...mor...t-time."

"Who did?" I whispered, not wanting to hear the name I knew he was going to say. The hurt and betrayal was written into every line, cut and bruise on his beautiful face.

"D-Dahlia—"

My grip tightened unintentionally, holding him in place with more force than I'd intended. "That's why you left?!" I demanded incredulously. "You left me to go back to her?! After everything she'd done to you," I bellowed, fear and rage consuming me. "Why, River? Why the fuck would you do that? Why put yourself at risk like that?"

"B-b-because," he choked out.

"Because what? Am I not enough for you? Is this house —my home—not enough?" I threw my arms out wide, gesturing to the walls I'd spent my life trying to afford. My hands felt the absence of him like a missing limb.

"N-no...t...that's..n-not...it."

"Then what is it?" I growled, my sanity clinging on by a tattered thread. "I would give you the world, and you walk through fire back to the woman you described as the devil."

"No!" River's hands sunk into his wild hair, pulling and yanking at the dark strands out until they clung to his clammy fingers. Snot and tears mingled on his face and coated his blood-red lips. "I went to her FOR YOU!" he screamed. His shattered voice knocked the wind out of my sails, and I collapsed on the floor, shattered and broken.

I stared up at him from my prone position. "Why?" I whispered, too scared to even speak. Why would he put himself in her path and face her wrath again? It didn't make a lick of sense. The more we'd learned about Dahlia, the more depraved and dangerous she'd become. The more I thought about it, the more unstable his actions seemed.

River all but fell off his stool into my lap. The impact must have been agony when his shredded skin crashed into my legs, but he didn't make a sound as he crawled up my legs and wrapped himself around me until his wet lips brushed my ear.

"I did it for you," he breathed. "I knew she'd be watching for me. I wanted to help." His words spilled at an unintelligible speed, as silent as the grave, but I felt them all the way to the marrow of my bones. "I wanted you to win. I needed you to be safe. I was prepared to die so you could end her and save countless lives. S-so you could save others from ever having to experience the life I've had."

Shock rippled through me. Every word landed like a bullet ripping through my skin. I wrapped my hand around his throat and maneuvered him until I could look him in the eye. "Why would you sacrifice yourself for me?"

"B-be...cause y-you're m-my...h-heart."

Fuck. Me. The world stopped turning. We hung suspended in our own timeline as his fractured words echoed in my head. Tentative hope bled from him into me, stealing the air from my lungs. I didn't have pretty words gilded in gold. I couldn't offer him the world. All I had was raw, pure, unadulterated emotion, and the only thing standing between us and our happy ending was reality.

I crashed my mouth to his, tasting his tears and his pain, and swallowed them down. My tongue teased across the seam of his lips, making him gasp and open so delicately for me. My tongue wrapped around his, and it was like our souls reunited. Every wild and turbulent emotion in me faded away to a gentle ocean lapping at the shore.

River was my safe place.

My protector.

My home.

He was everything I needed and everything I never knew I did. We were night and day, but it was as if every road I'd taken had led me back to him. My true north. The only person in this world who could truly understand me, who fought for me even when he'd given up on himself. He was precious and pure. He was worthy of love and deserved to be cherished above anything—no, anyone—else.

His unique taste exploded across my tongue, and he

melted in my arms, fusing himself with me. His grip tightened around me as his arms wrapped around my neck, his legs locked around my waist, and we lost ourselves in a synchronicity of reunited lovers. We gave confession to each other, bared our shortcomings, our sins, and our failings through this union of flesh that went so much deeper than a mere kiss. Every brush of his lips resonated with my soul, binding us together in perfect symbiosis.

"Angel," I murmured against his kiss-swollen lips. "We need to move. This can't be comfortable for you."

River snorted indignantly. "I-I d...don't...c-care." Tension filled his arms as he forced every painful sound from his mouth.

"Stop being a martyr." Brushing a chaste kiss against his lips, I tucked my feet under us slowly so I could lever us up off the floor and walked over to the couch. "What do you need, Riv?" My lips teased across his damp forehead in a show of affection that was not quite a kiss.

River sighed, releasing his death grip on my hair and settled his still-trembling hands on my shoulders. I watched them rise and fall as he focused on getting his staccato breathing under control. His eyes, although closed, moved from side to side like rapid fire until a full-body shudder worked its way through his body from his head to his feet.

Bottomless forest green eyes fluttered open, a maelstrom churning in their depths. I felt like I was drowning and flying in them, in him, simultaneously. "S-stay...w...with me. H-hold...m...me."

"I'm not going anywhere." I brushed back the dark stands that clung to his brow before they fell in his raw eyes. "I'm so, so sorry about Max."

"I-its m-my f...fault." I looked at him in confusion. Had Dahlia twisted his mind so much he believed every one of her actions was his fault?

"It's not your—" He held his hand over my mouth and shook his head.

His Adam's apple rolled in his throat as he swallowed. "I-I failed." He huffed a frustrated breath and tapped his throat.

"Hang on," I said, sliding him off my lap. "Let me grab you some water." A whimper worked its way up River's throat as I headed to the kitchen, but I was back before he could make another sound. I pulled him back onto my lap, holding him in my embrace where he belonged. His small frame fit perfectly in my arms, like he was made to be there.

Uncapping the bottle, I lifted it to his lips and tipped it so he could swallow the warm water down easily. "T-thank you."

"Any time," I said.

"S-she g-gave ... me a...m...mess...age." I arched my brow and ground my molars together. "Y-you...h...ave...t-to...st-stop—"

"I will not stop until that monster is behind bars and can't hurt you anymore, River." He flinched as my anger bled into my voice. No matter how much I tried to control my emotions, I was a fractured vault about to erupt. My hands coasted up his arms, gently massaging his tense muscles. "I'm sorry, angel. Continue."

The semblance of a smile flickered at the corners of his lips. "T-that's...the...o...only...w-way." His voice gave out and his breath caught in the back of his throat like he was choking. "Y-you...l-live."

I mulled his words over while my fingers dug into his traps and continued down to his obliques before resting on his hips. "She said she'd kill me?" Riv nodded, just a slight dip of his chin, but the fresh wave of tears that carved their way down his cheeks told me everything. "Did she threaten anyone else?"

"Yesssss," he hissed through clenched teeth.

"Who?"

"E...every...one...I-I...care...a-about."

"Oh, angel." I brought my hands up so they could wrap around his shoulders and pulled him into me. River buried his head against my neck and inhaled deeply as my fingers teased the short hairs on the nape of his neck. "I won't let her hurt anyone else you care about. I prom—"

"No." His voice rang out loud and clear, cutting me off with its assertiveness. "D-don't m...make pr-promises y-you...c-can't..."

With River in my arms, I deflated into the soft cushions of the couch and tipped my head back, comforted only by the sensation of his exhales ghosting over my skin. I knew what he said was the truth. I couldn't promise to keep people safe, especially when I didn't know where they were, but goddammit, I wanted to. I wanted to be his knight in shining armor, but when you were fighting someone as sadistic as the devil, only another monster could outsmart her.

"I will do everything I can to protect them and you. To make this world a safe place for you to live." Cool lips worked their way up the column of my throat, along my jaw, and up to that sensitive spot just below my ear.

"Thank you." I felt the shape of his lips more than heard his voice over the pounding of my heart and then chuckled when a yawn pried his lips apart and he grew heavy in my arms.

"Sleep, angel. You need it to heal." I kissed his sweat-dampened hair and inhaled his cinnamon and orange scent like it was the only thing keeping me going. His scent was like a drug to me. It was better than air.

After River fell asleep and was a deadweight in my arms, my phone vibrated in my back pocket. It took a hell of a lot of wiggling River's weight around in my arms before I could yank it free, and by then, the call had gone to voicemail. Placing it on the cushion next to me, I waited for either a message alert or for it to start ringing again.

This time, I answered before the first vibration had finished. "Benson."

Harsh breathing echoed down the line. "It was a bust." A bust? Oh shit. There was a raid planned on Christine Hamilton's—the Dahlia's—today.

"Crap. I forgot."

"Ha. No shit." Montoya cackled. "It's alright. I told Bower what had happened, but he wants answers."

"I know " I pushed that point aside for another time because that wasn't what worried me right now. "What do you mean, it was a bust?"

The raucous noise of the station locker room disappeared when a door slammed shut, and Montoya groaned. "The place was deserted, Benson. Not a print or hair to be found. Every room had been whitewashed, every floor and surface deep cleaned. You could have operated on the ridiculously large dining room table, it was so sterile." She cleared her throat. "He's still stewing over what you told him about Davis. He just won't accept it. I don't understand. The guy is all kinds of wrong."

"I agree, but sometimes we can't see what is right in front of us. He's spent years working and training with Davis. All we can do is keep an eye on him and report back about any red flags. I don't trust him as far as I could throw him."

"You don't think *he* had anything to do with the failure of this one?"

"Shit." I pinched the bridge of my nose in frustration. "This day just keeps getting fucking worse," I muttered. "I guess only time will tell. If the next one goes the same...it's a pattern that even Bower can't ignore. Right?"

"I'd say so, but I bet he slips up before that. Is the kid alright?" The concern lacing her voice gave me a beat of levity. She might be a hardass, but when she cared, she was like a mother hen.

"Yeah, kinda," I huffed. "We kinda got into it over why he left—"

"And?"

"He said he did it for me—for us—to help with the case. Said he was willing to die if it meant we could take her down."

"What did he get?"

"I don't know, but..." My voice trailed off as pieces started to click together in my mind. "His clothes. Whatever he got must be with his clothes."

"Leave it with me. I'll check back in with Sharon."

"Thanks. I owe you."

"You always owe me, smartass. But, Benson?"

"Mmm?"

"Don't be too hard on him. I know what he did was stupid and reckless and scared the shit out of you, but his heart was in the right place. I can't imagine how powerless he feels. How powerless he's always felt. So while it might seem like he's grasping at straws, that boy is trying to change his stars and those of others like him. It was a noble act, even if it turns out to be fruitless."

"I know he meant well, but he's not a cop."

"No, he isn't. He's a survivor, Jacob. He's lived through things we can't even imagine." I sighed as her words laid more guilt on my shoulders than I already felt for shouting at him and losing my temper. "Take care of him. He's something special. Happy looks good on you."

"It'd look good on you, too."

"Hell would have to freeze over first. I don't need a man to make me happy when I have batteries and Tinder."

"I don't need to know about that," I snarked. "I'll talk to you later." I hung up before she could respond and cradled the broken boy in my arms, pulling him closer to me like I could peel back his skin and live right next to his heart. But that still wouldn't be close enough to satisfy this yearning inside me that wanted to consume him.

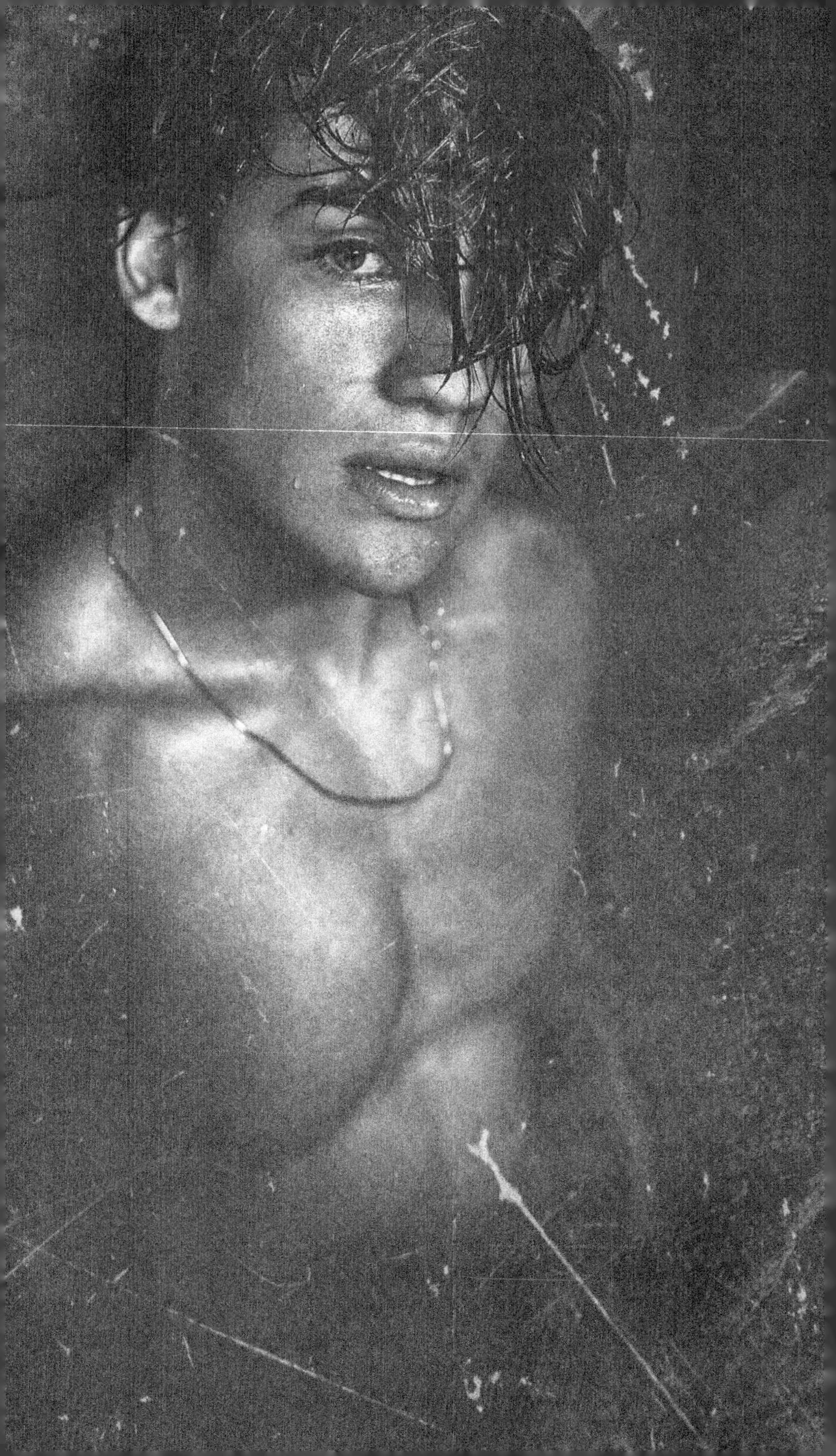

CHAPTER TWENTY-THREE
River

"Morning, angel."

I sighed as Bane's lips kissed a path across my exposed shoulder, sending delicious waves of electricity across my skin that made all the little hairs on my skin stand on end. A shudder rolled through me, and he chuckled at the nape of my neck as his hands massaged the tension from the tight muscles of my back, making me groan.

"Does that feel good, baby?"

"Y-yes," I breathed and buried my head under my pillow to hide the flush heating my cheeks.

Waking up to Bane's undivided attention was one of the best feelings in the world, even if my mind still struggled to accept what was happening between us. I didn't deserve to be this lucky. My body begged for more from him than he'd given me over the last two weeks, but every kiss we'd shared had been filled with tension, need, and love. I was drowning in an intensity I didn't fully understand, having never felt anything like it before. It was more than just a physical thing; every touch of his hands or lips felt like it was rearranging me on a cellular level. It was like Bane knew things about my body and psyche I hadn't even known existed. I wanted more with him, but every time I found the words, they died on my tongue and fear coiled around me. What if when we did more, he realized how used up and disgusting I was?

Would I survive him rejecting me now when he'd filled my head and heart with hope? Life felt too good to be true with everything I'd ever dreamed of right at my fingertips, but they were stained with blood as I tried to cling to this dream-like reality I'd found myself in. Reality was breathing down my neck and knocking on the door I'd bolted shut. But I could hear the countdown timer every time my eyes shut, and when it reached zero, my hopes and dreams would turn to ash.

"Bane?" I whispered. I felt more and more unmoored as he lavished every part of me he could reach with sweet, tender kisses. It felt like my throat was closing up, and even though I knew he was right here with me, he felt farther and farther away. The world was fracturing around me like a kaleidoscope, taunting me, reminding me I was unworthy. That happiness wasn't a thing people like me deserved.

"What's up, Riv?" he asked softly, maneuvering us until I was sitting in his lap and we were chest to chest. My legs were braced on either side of his hips, my hands resting numbly on his shoulders. "You know you can ask me anything, right?"

A shaky breath passed my lips, and I swallowed, my throat so dry it felt like it was stuffed with cotton. As I stared into his bright sky blue and dark bottomless eyes, I saw my hopes and fears reflected back at me.

"Angel, what's on your mind?" He trailed his knuckles down my cheek and sunk his fingers into my wild strands, pulling me closer. "Talk to me," he breathed against my lips, his taste invading my mouth. Soft kisses rained down on my forehead, eyes, down the bridge of my nose, and across my cheeks. My heart was doing somersaults in my chest that grew tighter with every beat as beads of perspiration grew on my hairline and top lip.

"I—" I licked my lips and shook like someone had walked over my grave. "Do you... w-want me?" My voice was small, the voice of a scared little boy who'd been given access to a candy shop but was too scared to step inside, fearful that with one wrong move, he would end up locked away in the dark. Abandoned and alone.

"You're safe with me, River." His lips brushed my lips with the lightest of touches. Not a kiss, but in comfort, seeking connection and trust.

"D-d you... want me?" I rasped and screwed my eyes shut, unwilling to see the look that crossed his face as fear of rejection churned in my gut.

"River? Look at me." I shook my head and tucked my chin against my chest, heat building in the back of my eyes. "Angel." Bane pinched my chin between his thumb and forefinger and lifted my head. "Look at me."

His smokey sleep-filled voice took on a commanding tone I'd never heard from him before. It made my spine stiffen and my shoulders pull back as my walls solidified around me. Echoes of men from the past ordering me around like I wasn't human filled my mind in a deluge of memories, and my heart started pounding for a whole other reason. My lungs burned, because no matter how many breaths I took, air didn't fill my lungs.

"River." A sense of urgency took over his voice, like I wasn't the only one who had become untethered.

It was a mindfuck how quickly I could spiral out of control and revert back to who I was before Bane. Someone who needed to disassociate at any given second because another moment in the present would be what sent me over the edge. An edge I'd been balancing on for far too long, and one I'd made my peace with that would eventually claim me. But these last two weeks had made me think that maybe the impossible was possible.

"Angel, shh. I've got you, okay? Just listen to me and breathe." I could feel his phantom touch surrounding me, but his voice sounded so far away. It was fading with every word he spoke. "Feel my heart, feel my breaths, and copy me." My hand felt suspended, adrift.

What was happening? Everything was like a dream. A beautiful, perfect dream. One I didn't want to wake up from. *Oh, god, please, please don't make this be a dream or an illusion my mind had created to keep me safe. Oh, god, please! Please make it be real.* Tears burned my eyes, but I couldn't open them. I didn't want to. I didn't want to see where I really was. I didn't want to know for certain this wasn't real. *Please, please, please. Oh, god, please.*

"Open your eyes for me."

No. No, no, no, no. I didn't want to. I wanted to stay here in my dream. It might not have been perfect, but it was perfect for me. Bane was here. He was here, and he wanted me. All of me. He'd said I was worth fighting for, and I refused to let that go. Fuck me. Kill me. Ruin me. I didn't care as long as I was here with him. If my eyes never opened again, that would be okay. I would be okay here with him. Here where I wanted to be.

"Bane." His name tore its way out from my heart, leaving a gaping wound behind. I wasn't whole. I was fractured into pieces that were splintering into fragments that couldn't be put back together. I thought death would hurt, but even as my tears carved their way down my cheeks, I didn't feel a thing because finally, finally I'd be free from this torment.

"Angel. Don't let it consume you. Fight it. Feel my heartbeat beneath your fingertips."

The world was a cruel, fucked up place, but it had nothing on my mind.

"That's it River. That's it. Feel me. Keep breathing."

His usual gravelly voice sounded unhinged and frantic in a way I'd never heard before. A hysterical cackle grew from my chest. My Bane didn't sound like this; he was cool, calm, and collected. Always in control. He was strong and dependable. He was the light in my darkness, the goodness to my sullied body and soul.

"I've got you. I won't ever let you go."

I scoffed. No one wanted me enough to never let me go, so I'd had to create someone to love me in my head—the only place I could find acceptance. But it also had the power to twist and crush me.

"You're doing so well, River. Open your eyes for me, please." His voice cracked and broke on that heartfelt plea. Phantom fingers ghosted over my face, stroking my hair back, brushing away burning tears.

"Open those beautiful forest-green eyes for me?"

My heavy eyes fluttered open, and he was there, cradling my face in his hands. What was real? What was reality, and what was a delusion? How could I tell when everything seemed to meld into one?

"You haven't lost it, baby. You're struggling. You've been through so much, your mind is trying to process it all. I promise I'm real."

Well, at least my mind was convincing. My lips twitched as I snickered, tasting the salt of my tears. "I-I don't know what to…b-believe," I whimpered, my throat aching like I'd screamed for hours. A quick check of my body reassured me I had no new injuries, just the ones that were healing.

"Thank god you're back with me." Bane sighed and cradled me lovingly in his arms, with my head tucked into the crook of his neck. He carded his fingers through my hair in a soothing motion as my tears slowly dried, leaving salty tracks on my skin.

"You had a panic attack." His chest deflated as he exhaled, like a weight had been lifted off his shoulders. "Something triggered you. Do you know what it was?"

"I…I don't…" I thought back through the hazy quagmire of my mind, and even though I was exhausted, a thread appeared. I followed it, and it all became clear. The question I'd wanted to ask materialized, but I didn't know if I was strong enough to ask it.

"Mmm. You know, don't you?" Bane murmured.

I inhaled his scent, using it to help calm my racing heart. "I-I do." Clearing my throat, I squirmed under the weight of his intense gaze. "I wanted to ask you s-something, but I…"

Large hands wrapped around my hips as he shifted beneath me like he was afraid I was going to disappear. It was like he could read my mind, because I needed distance between us before I could give credence to the question growing louder in my head. Pushing his arms back, I scrambled off his lap and across the bed, settling on my pillow. With my back resting against the headboard and legs pulled up to my chest, I glanced at Bane through my lashes. The concern marring his beautiful face was like a knife to my heart.

"I'm here when you're ready." The resignation in his tone and his hunched shoulders hurt to see. It reminded me I was a cancerous thing in his life, taking and taking until there was nothing in him to give me. I'd bleed him dry if he let me. He'd be better off without me around, but I had to know once and for all.

"Do you want me?" My voice was barely audible to my own ears, even as I hid my face in my arms as I waited.

Silence stretched between us, growing more palpable and suffocating the longer it continued. What I heard could have shattered adamantium. Soft sniffles reached my ears and my racing heart lurched into my throat. After a shaky inhale, I turned to find Bane, the immovable mountain, with tears streaming down his dark skin.

"W-why would you ask that?"

I was so lost in his wet lips moving that it took me a beat for my brain to register his question. "B-because...y-you don't... t-touch me..." My reasoning sounded weak because he did, but not in the way I expected and had become accustomed to. I was used for pleasure, a hole to be filled, a cum dump. But with Bane it was so foreign, his touches alien.

Shaking his head, he wiped the tears off his face with the back of his hand and when he looked at me, the heat in his eyes melted the ice coating my skin. "Is this because we haven't..." A deep blush stained his dark skin, heating his cheeks and making him seem younger while I felt decades older.

"Yes."

"Oh, angel." Bane launched himself at me and buried his head in my stomach, his arms wrapping around my waist as he wept. "I want you like I've never wanted anyone in my life. I...I don't really know how to explain it." He stuttered a breath. "With you, everything is different for me. The way I want you. The way I crave you." He snorted. "I've never wanted anyone the way I do you, River. You set my blood on fire and make my soul burn for you. I just..."

"You what?" I whispered into our bubble.

"I know what you've been through, what you have been

subjected to, and I don't want to be the same. I want you to want me too. I need you to feel pleasure as my every touch sinks beneath your skin. That it resonates with your soul. You are it for me, angel, and even if we never have sex, calling you mine would be enough."

"Oh, Bane."

"I don't want you to feel forced to do anything with me. I don't want to be like *them*."

Tears welled in my eyes, making him shimmer before me in the light of the morning sun as it streamed through the blinds. "You could never be anything like them."

"I wake up every day wanting to be worthy of your love. To be good enough to show you what you mean to me. I want to show you love and pleasure."

That word hung in the air between us as I turned it over in my mind because it was one I didn't understand, having never felt it. "C-could you teach me?" I asked timidly.

"Teach you?"

"I-I've...I d-don't..." I cocked my head to the side as he drew back and knelt in front of me like he was at confession. "I... t-the only times I've come was because I was forced to as a p-punishment. It was used as a way to humiliate me. T-they used my body against me. I don't know..." I cleared my throat. "I've n-never experienced pleasure."

"Do you trust me to show you?" Heat filled his glassy eyes and licked across my skin. We were like magnets drawn together. His lips moved closer to mine until every exhale filled my lungs, and when I spoke, they brushed mine.

"I trust you with every part of m-me. I trust you to guard and cherish my heart. I trust you to keep my body safe, and I trust you to show me things I've never experienced."

A blinding smile lit his face. The sun's rays created a halo around his head, and I felt reborn. This man, this titan, wanted to show me the wonders of the world, and I found every one of them in his eyes—all the promises he made, all the sunrises that stretched before us, all the moments we'd share where we'd learn each other better than we knew ourselves. All I had to do was believe.

Bane kissed the lingering fear from my skin, one sweet touch at a time, until his lips finally melded with mine. The first swipe of his tongue against the seal of my mouth felt like a match thrown into kerosene, heating the blood in my veins and bringing my body to life in a way it never had before. When I opened for him, he kissed me with an intensity that altered my perception of reality. He broke me apart, took my pieces, and healed me with the golden goodness in his heart.

Every tantalizing brush of his tongue brought us closer, like we were trying to fuse our bodies together. He removed every layer that separated us until his hot skin touched mine, and goosebumps prickled across my body everywhere we touched.

We kissed until our lungs screamed, and fireworks danced behind my eyelids. Gasping for air, he wrenched his mouth from mine and laid me face down on the bed, gently removing the sleep pants that hung off my hips with a tenderness that had my heart skipping a beat as it started to freefall.

"Such a good boy," he cooed.

Bane left a trail of wet opened-mouthed kisses from my ankle to my knee before nudging my legs apart. I gasped as the cool air met my entrance. A shock of fear ran up my spine that made my muscles tense. The automatic response had me gritting my teeth hard enough to crack them.

"Shh," he murmured into my skin before he kissed and teased his way up my thigh with his lips and tongue.

Thick fingers dug into the flesh of my ass, kneading the lingering unease away as he followed every burning touch with a soothing kiss. I shuddered as he parted my cheeks, the heat of his exhale coasting over the sensitive skin. I waited with bated breath for his next move. The bed dipped, and unable to take not knowing what he was doing any longer, I pushed up into my elbows and looked over my shoulder to be met with a sight that didn't seem real.

Bane was lying between my spread legs, staring at the most intimate part of me with a look of wonder on his face. I watched, mesmerized, as he parted my cheeks and buried his face in my cleft. His hot breath so close to my entrance had me clenching reflexivity as need and fear warred inside me. The unknown made my heart pound hard enough to tattoo itself on my ribs.

"So beautiful." Bane's voice was muffled by his position, but I felt it like he'd whispered it in my ear. "I bet you taste as good as you look."

With that, he kissed my hole and ran his nose along the length of my crease and groaned. My neck heated at the intimate act. I'd been fucked by a million different men, but not one of them had ever put their faces there, let alone kissed me. I didn't know if I wanted to pull him closer or push him away, but I knew if I asked him to stop, he would.

"Have you ever been rimmed, angel?"

"N-no?"

Bane chuckled. "Let me show you." The smile in his voice was unmistakable. "I want you to only feel pleasure with me, but if it gets too much or you want to stop, let me know."

"A-are you psychic?"

"No, baby, but I can feel the tension radiating off you. You're safe with me."

Before I could answer, the wet heat of his tongue seared against my skin from my taint up to the base of my spine. "Oh god," I groaned. "T-that's so good."

Bane hummed into my skin as he kissed my hole with slick lips and tongue, like he wanted to devour me. He ate my ass with the same fever he kissed me. He moaned and groaned like he loved the musky taste of me and slowly, with each pass of his tongue, I melted into the mattress. Bane stiffened his tongue and teased it around my rim, taunting the tight ring of muscle until it softened enough for him to push inside me.

"Fuck," I bit out and dug my hands into the sheets. My blood vibrated through my veins, my body so sensitive and receptive to his touch, unlike it had been with anyone else.

"That's it, baby. Open up for me."

My teeth sunk into my bottom lip. Uninhibited sounds wanted to spill from my lips as he lavished my body with an intensity I'd never experienced. I was lost to his fevered touch, my hips rocking, pushing back against his tongue as he surged inside me. The friction of the soft cotton sheet against my shaft felt like bolts of lightning in my groin.

It was too much and not enough. I wanted more, and I wanted to stop.

My orgasm grew deep inside me, organic and pure as lust fried my brain. I felt Bane everywhere. I was cocooned in his scent, the smell of our arousal saturated every inhale. His touch echoed through my body as he brought me closer and closer to the brink. Euphoria beckoned me, but something held me back.

Fear.

It tried to wipe out the pleasure Bane brought me. I whimpered as heat prickled the back of my eyes. My hips stilled as it started to sink its claws into me, pulling me into the darkness where he couldn't reach me.

"Come back to me, angel." His lust-drenched tone was the life raft I needed to pull me back. "I've got you." I groaned as he worked a finger inside me. "I can feel your walls rippling around me."

"I-I'm...c-close."

"I know, baby."

He pumped his finger inside me, the stretch and simmering burn as he entered me over and over, pushing me further toward the precipice of no return. My blood was liquid fire pooling in my balls as they drew up closer to the base of my thickening length. I couldn't hold on to my control any longer when he hit that magic spot.

"Oh my god, Bane," I cried. Tears spilled from my eyes as I reached back for him. I needed him to hold on to me, afraid I was about to be swept away. Linking his fingers with mine, he continued to stroke that place deep inside me.

"I've got you, angel. Come for me."

"I-I... c-can't."

"Yes, you can. I've got you and won't let go."

I wailed as my orgasm ricocheted inside me, detonating, sparking every nerve ending and catapulting me out of my body. "Bane." A kaleidoscope of colors danced behind my eyes, and I floated somewhere among the stars.

Soft kisses covered every inch of my face as I slowly came back to myself. Bane's cedarwood and leather scent was everywhere, and I swear I could feel a warm cloth against my groin.

"W-what's t-that?"

"Welcome back, baby." My heavily lidded eyes fluttered open. The image of Bane's smile will be forever etched into my mind. "You okay?"

"Mmmm." His fingers stroked down my stomach as he continued to gently wipe my release from my skin. "S-sorry," I muttered, shame heating my cheeks.

"What for?" Concern filled his eyes as they traced over my face.

"F-for making a mess."

Bane snickered. "If you didn't, I'd have been worried you didn't enjoy yourself. Sex is messy, but this?" He dragged his finger across my stomach and held it in front of my face, showing me my release. "This is delicious. Mmm." He sucked his finger clean, then leaned forward and kissed me, pushing my release into my mouth with his tongue.

Jesus, he was filthy when he got going and tasting myself when his tongue wrapped around mine was surreal. It bound me to him in the most unexpected way as I melted into him.

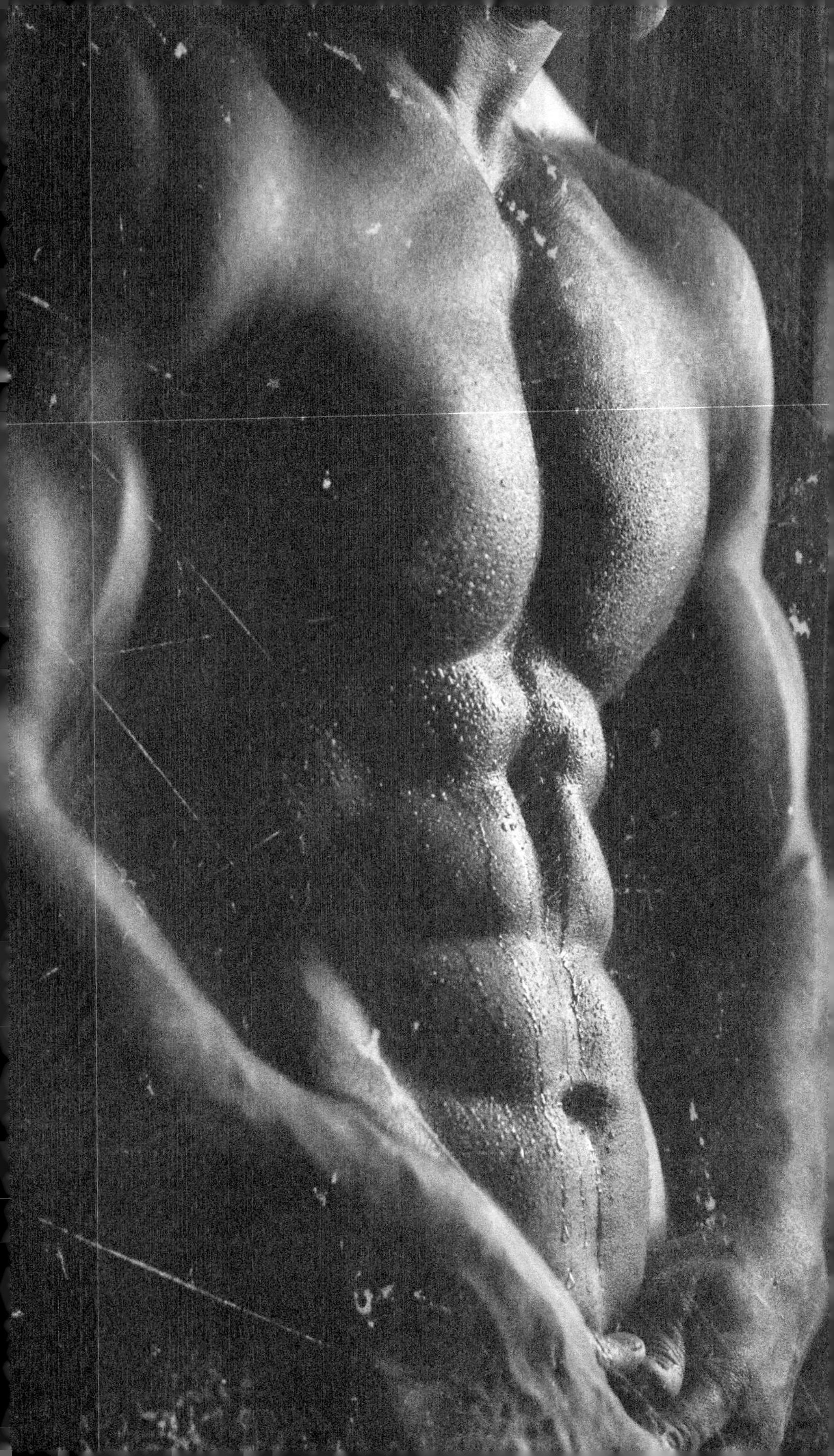

CHAPTER TWENTY-FOUR
Bane

"Coffee?" I said brightly as River shimmied into the kitchen, hitching the leg of my borrowed sweats up. He looked absolutely adorable drowning in a pair of my sweets and one of my hoodies. He'd refused to let me buy him any more, saying he preferred wearing mine. Who was I to argue when seeing him in my clothes settled that possessive part of me?

Never before had I acted this way about one of my exes. I didn't care what they wore. I suppose if I thought about it, I didn't really care what they did or the time we spent together. Nothing had ever felt so right as it did with River.

"P-please." He slipped onto his favorite stool at the end of the breakfast bar. Shadow darted out of his crate to greet him. These two had become inseparable recently, but I didn't begrudge the dog much, even if it did make snuggle time on the couch challenging.

Knowing someone was here for River when I had to head in to the station was a comfort, especially when I worked nights. Shadow slept on his bed, curled up at his feet, or beside his chest when his nightmares were particularly volatile.

"Here you go."

I pushed River's mug across the counter before pouring my own. I made my way over to him and spun him so he faced me and stepped between his legs. "How are you feeling about today?"

"Umm." River chewed on his abused bottom lip. When his anxiety spiked, he struggled to maintain eye contact with me. We'd had hundreds of difficult conversations over the last few weeks, so I'd learned his tells when he was struggling to process everything. Today was pushing him to the brink.

"I can stay if you'd like me to?" It wasn't a hollow offer; no matter how important it was for me to be at the station today, I'd drop it all for him. I think he was finally starting to believe me when I told him he'd always come first.

He sighed, and some of the tension eased in his shoulders. Looking at me through his thick lashes, he tried to smile, but it resembled a grimace. "I-I know...but...I-I will be okay. I think?"

"You sure? It's not a problem." It would be to Bower, but fuck him. He'd used our relationship to further his own goals, and it had put River in danger. Regardless of whether it was his fault, I was struggling to reconcile a positive working environment with him at the moment.

"Uh huh, yeah?"

"I'll have my phone with me, so if you need me, just call." River nodded and wrapped his hands around his steaming mug. He was putting on a brave face for my benefit, but trepidation shone in his dark-green eyes.

"I'm sure it'll be fine."

"I am too. It's not like you haven't had video calls with Joelle before." I shrugged, trying to lighten the mood. "It'll just be the real-life version of that today, but at least you can curl up on the sofa with Shadow, unlike me. I don't get puppy cuddles at her office."

River snorted, and a mouthful of coffee sprayed across the granite. I'd take the win, even though it caused a mess. His momentary smile gave my weary heart wings. They were still few and far between, but healing was a marathon, not a sprint. He needed my patience and love above everything else. And those, I could give him in bucket loads.

"You're amazing, you know?" I brushed a kiss on his forehead and inhaled his sweet cinnamon and orange scent.

The toast popped before River could respond with some of his derisive snark that seemed to be his new defense mechanism. Luckily for me, Joelle dealt with the brunt of it, now that he was feeling comfortable enough to speak in front of her. Montoya, on the other hand, was still a work in progress. I didn't know what had happened between them the day she'd driven us home from the hospital, but it'd put him on high alert around her.

We chatted aimlessly while we ate our breakfast and consumed copious amounts of coffee. So much so, I swore my blood was pure caffeine by the time I grabbed the keys for my bike. The sun was shining today, and although it had been a rough night, I was feeling positive about today for the both of us. Life with River was like balancing on a knife edge—it was as exhilarating as it was terrifying. Experience had taught me that when things felt like they were going well, it was only a matter of time until the tables turned and we were drowning again.

River was rinsing the dishes as I pulled my boots on,

whistling to a tune playing on the radio when my phone rang. It was like time froze as we both turned to look at it vibrating on the counter. His eyes tracked every step as I walked over and picked it up.

"Benson."

"How long until you're in?" Montoya asked. The edge to her voice had me standing up straight.

I looked over at River as he closed the dishwasher. "I'm taking the bike, so twenty minutes? I was just waiting for Joelle to arrive. She should be here any minute."

"That's... that's good."

"Montoya, you sound distracted. What's going on?" I jumped as River wrapped his arms around me. His touch was just what I needed to soothe the rough edges forming in my mind.

"Is he there?"

"Mhmm." I tugged his body in tighter to mine, knowing he could hear her loud voice even though I had the phone pressed to my ear.

"Shit. There's been another body—"

"Has the vic been identified?"

"Yes. Davis was first on the scene." River stopped breathing and went rigid in my arms while my mind was running a hundred miles an hour. Davis was first on the scene... that was pretty convenient. Releasing a heavy sigh, Montoya continued. "Dale Underwood."

"Noooooooo." River's harsh cry ground my heart to dust as he collapsed at my feet. Shadow crowded around him and I hung up on Montoya.

"Fuck, angel. I'm so, so sorry."

He shook his head, tears streaming down his beautiful face. I knelt in front of him, scooped him up into my arms, and carried him over to the couch. River buried his face against the column of my throat, his tears slicking my skin and soaking the collar of my shirt. I didn't care, as long as being in my arms brought him even a modicum of comfort I'd stay here until I was soaked.

"Y-you need to s-stop..." An inhuman sound got caught in the back of his throat as his fingers sunk into my shoulders. "I... I can't lose you, B-Bane."

I ran a soothing hand up and down his back. "You're not going to lose me. I promise you." I cupped his face between my palms and brushed away his tears from his cheeks. "I promise." I kissed his red nose, his eyelids, and his forehead before resting mine against his.

Each of his shuddering breaths rocked through me, slowly unmooring the control I had over my emotions. In my line of work, I had to remain detached, compartmentalize my emotions while retaining empathy, but seeing someone you loved hurt so much made it almost impossible.

"D-don't m-make promises you c-can't k-keep."

"I would—" The doorbell rang, drawing our attention. "Let me get that," I said, setting River down on the couch and pulling a blanket over him. Shadow jumped up and curled himself into a little black ball behind River's legs where he had them tucked up on the couch.

"Morning," Joelle greeted cheerfully when I opened the door. Her smile quickly fell when she saw my face. "What's happened?"

"River's had some bad news, but I'm sure he'll want to talk it through with you."

"Of course." She gave me a facsimile of a smile as I motioned her inside and made her way over to River.

"Would you like a coffee before I head out, Joelle?"

"If you've got some made, sure. If not, I'll take some water."

"Sure."

Once I'd made them both a coffee and set a couple of bottles of water on the coffee table, I kissed River goodbye. Joelle was fully aware of our relationship, even if she didn't approve. I refused to temper my love for River around her. I wanted to reassure him at every turn, so he wouldn't allow his intrusive thoughts to creep in and twist our reality until it was something dark and depraved. He'd had enough of that in his lifetime. I wanted to be his safe harbour.

Holding his face in my hands, I brushed my thumb over his bottom lip. "I can stay if you want me to."

Blinking through bleary eyes, River shook his head. "N-no. Joelle is here. Sh-she'll take care of me until you…" His voice fractured and broke, and my heart stalled as emotion stained his face. When would the hits stop coming so he could truly heal and find peace?

"If you're sure?" I whispered and ghosted my lips over his forehead.

"I am."

His strength astounded me. This was the second friend he lost, and even though neither of us had said what this meant, we knew. Dahlia wasn't giving up, and time was running out. We had to take her down before she took us out. With the stakes as high as they were, I would do anything to make that reality come to fruition as soon as possible.

"I'll be back as soon as I can." I squeezed his shoulder before I stepped back and headed to the garage. With a final glance over my shoulder, I saw Joelle hand River a box of Kleenex.

She mouthed, "I've got him." I nodded and headed through the door.

My bike rumbled to life beneath me as I waited for the garage doors to open. The bright sun that had streamed through the blinds earlier was hidden by thick gray clouds, as if the world was mourning another innocent life lost on the battlefield of this underground war that raged unseen by the general population.

The blacktop fell away as I weaved through the downtown traffic, and before I knew it, I was pulling into the station's parking lot. Montoya leaned against the wall by the back entrance, her right foot resting against the wall as she spun the squad keys around on her finger.

"Be quick. We need to move before the press arrives on the scene." I nodded in acknowledgement and headed to the locker room to grab my vest. Luckily for me, everyone was preoccupied and focused on their own tasks, so I was in and out in a couple of minutes. It gave me enough time to focus on the job and stow my worries about River away. Joelle would take care of him and would call me if he needed me.

I pushed the door open and Montoya jumped to attention and fell into step beside me. "What do we know about this one?" I asked and held my hand out for the keys.

She deposited them in my hand before running a hand over her slicked-back hair and let loose an exhale. "Davis was out on patrol with one of the rookies, and a call came over the radio about a fire. They were the first ones on the scene."

Suspicion weaved its way through my mind. Ever since River told me about Davis, my mind hadn't been able to let go of it. I watched everything he did under a microscope. I just needed to trust my gut, see it through, and get to the bottom of his betrayal.

"Why do I get the feeling you're not telling me everything?" I yanked my door open and slipped behind the wheel and buckled in. I checked to make sure Montoya had clipped her seatbelt in and raised my brow, waiting for her to give me the full details.

"You're not wrong. I'm not sure I can believe it until I see it for myself."

"That makes no sense," I muttered as I started the engine and pulled out of the parking space and headed to the exit. "Where to?"

As Montoya relayed the address to me, a sense of déjà vu struck, but I shook it off. We merged into the traffic and hit every red light, making her chuckle as my frustration grew. A few minutes passed before my brain finally caught on to the errant thought that had struck when she mentioned the address.

My eyes widened, and I gasped as we hit another red light. "That was the property we raided the other day? But wasn't Davis's patrol route on the other side of town?"

"It was," Montoya confirmed. "Interesting how it's suddenly nothing but smouldering rubble, and our vic was one of the guys that came in with River. And Davis just happened to be there as it went up in flames?" She glanced over at me, wariness shining in her eyes. "Davis said there was more at the scene, but he wanted to talk to you in person."

That little bit of information piqued my interest. "Any idea what he meant by that?"

"Not one. You know he can be a skeevy guy and likes to play power games. I think he likes knowing information we don't."

"I guess we'll find out any second," I muttered as we pulled off onto the driveway of the big house that had belonged to Christine Hamilton, a.k.a. Dahlia. The wrought-iron gates were wide open, and the sweeping driveway curled through woodland before it opened out to where the large Hamptons-style home had once stood. Flames still licked at the western side of the massive structure. Luckily, the fire department was now in attendance and had jets of water dousing what remained of the fire.

We took the secondary driveway where it forked to the left of the main house and drove around to the guest house. Davis's car was parked in front of the chalet-style apartment that sat over the three-car garage. Smoke from the fire carried thickly on the wind, but I could make out Davis pacing across the grass, having an animated conversation on his phone, when he should have been working the scene with his partner—even if he was a green rookie. What could have possibly been so important that he had to take a personal call right now? As far as I knew, Davis didn't have a romantic partner or any dependents. The question niggled at my brain. I spotted his rookie leaning against the side of his squad car, staring intently at the open door to the guest house, his green tinged face filled with trepidation.

We pulled up and parked behind Davis's car and crossed the brick driveway to the rookie, who now stood to attention. His wide-eyed gaze darted between us and Davis as he shuffled on his feet.

"Barnes, how are you doing?" Montoya enquired and shook his hand. Feeling on edge, I folded my arms over my chest and waited for him to respond. The poor kid was white as a sheet, visibly shaken, and struggled to string a sentence together as he explained the sequence of events that preceded our arrival.

"Is Daniel on his way?"

"Yeah? I-I think so? Davis is on the phone to him now... I think? Told m-me to wait for you here."

"So our vic hasn't had a positive identification yet?"

"Y-yeah, well, Davis said—"

"If Daniel and his team haven't run it, and the vic doesn't have any ID on them, how did you confirm who they were?"

I was losing my patience with the kid. It wasn't his fault, but I was spiraling. River was at home, grieving another friend he believed was dead, and now there was a chance they might not be.

"D-Davis said he was brought in the night of the hotel raid a-and that was enough for h-him."

"Alright, Barnes," Montoya said. "Why don't you wait here for Daniel to arrive, then send him up to us. We're going to check out the scene."

"Sure." Barnes kicked a stone and shoved his hands into his pockets. But it was the way his eyes kept darting over to Davis that made my hackles rise.

"You got gloves?" she asked and turned in my direction, her brows pinched together in the gloomy light.

"Here you go." I passed her a pair and turned to Barnes. "Just to confirm, is our victim in there?" I nodded toward the guest house and waited, growing more and more agitated the longer it took him to answer. It was like he was scared of us. I refused to believe it was the crime scene that had put him so on edge.

Chuckling, Barnes eventually responded to my question. "Oh, y-yeah. He's up in the bedroom, second door on the left after the kitchen."

Without another word, Montoya and I entered the property and took the stairs up to the first floor.

"Wow. Even with the smoke obscuring it, that view is still gorgeous," she said as we stepped into the open-plan living room where the floor-to-ceiling glass windows overlooked the grounds and further in the distance the lake I'd taken River to on my bike.

"Benson? You need to come and see this. Now!"

I blinked and realized Montoya had ventured deeper into the apartment, and judging by the alarm in her voice, she was looking at our victim. Turning on my heel, I headed down the tiled hallway in the direction of her voice at a fast clip. Just as I was about to enter the room, she stepped out and stopped me by putting a hand on my chest.

"What?" I grit out through clenched teeth. The set of Montoya's shoulders put me on edge even more. "Why are you blocking my way?" I tried to sidestep her so I could get into the room, but she anticipated my move and continued to block me. "What the hell?"

She dropped her head to my chest and let loose a harsh breath that chilled me to the bone. Montoya was a hardened cop for a crime scene to do this to her it had to be bad. "Just stay calm, alright? I know why Davis didn't share this with us, and I think it's because he wants you to react."

"What the hell are you talking about? Just let me in there. We have work to do."

She narrowed her eyes at me. "Jacob." I snapped to attention at the use of my first name. "Trust me when I say this is going to be hard. You need to stay calm. He's pulling something, I just don't know what."

I nodded. "Alright." She grimaced like she didn't believe me, and to be honest, I didn't either, but I said what she wanted to hear.

"I'm here for you, okay?" The soft tone of her voice had the hairs on the back of my neck standing on end. What fresh kind of hell was I about to walk into?

Montoya stepped back. I moved into what I assumed was the primary bedroom, judging by the expansive floor-to-ceiling picture windows. That should have been the detail to grab my attention—but it wasn't. My eyes were riveted to the wall behind the bed where red writing—god I hoped it was spray paint and not blood—dripped down the wall in stark contrast to the bright white paint.

"Jesus fucking Christ. Am I seeing things?" My stomach turned to lead as I read the words over and over, then glanced over my shoulder at Montoya, who solemnly shook her head.

"Unfortunately not," she murmured and stepped over to the body lying sprawled on the bed. "Looks like he was flayed alive." She cleared her throat, gagging twice. Her golden complexion had paled, perspiration glistened on her skin and at her hairline.

"Are you okay?" I asked, my voice taut with rage, as I forced my gaze to remain fixed on the body, determined not to let the words scrawled on the wall provoke me. The bitter taste of bile rose in my throat, and I clenched my jaw, grinding my molars to hold back the torrent of vitriol threatening to escape. I knew exactly who had left that message—and precisely what it meant. Blinking away the sting of tears, I fought valiantly to wrestle my emotions under control.

> *You kept him, didn't you?*
> *Time is running out.*
> *Tick tock. Tick tock.*

"Y-yeah, this..." She gestured toward the mutilated body. Even though dried blood covered his face, it was unmistakably Dale. "This is some twisted shit, right? He looks like his skin was either sliced, or—"

"No, the cuts aren't clean enough for a blade. These look more like whip marks that split the skin." I sighed. I wasn't an expert, but I'd seen the work of a sadist Dom that had gone too far once, and the wounds were eerily similar. Hauntingly so.

"The most disturbing thing is the lack of blood on the bed. Judging by the amount covering his face and the wound to his neck, I'd say they tortured him before hanging him by his feet." She gestured to the deep purple-black bruises ringing his ankles. "Then sliced his throat open and drained him dry. Again, this isn't where he was tortured or killed, but judging by the coagulation of the blood, this was recent."

"I think it's safe to assume that he was tortured and killed in the main house, then brought over here and presented like this... for us to find."

"That would explain why it's currently a burning pile of rubble," she said. "For the fire to have consumed the building that well so quickly, I'd be willing to bet they used accelerants to remove all traces of evidence."

"Ahh, there you two are." Davis sauntered into the room looking cool, calm and collected and stood at the foot of the bed next to me. "Interesting one, isn't it? Any idea what that's referring to?" He gestured with his head toward the wall, an almost taunting tone to his voice and a smirk on his lips.

With my emotions locked down, I slid on my professional mask. "Not a clue. Have you heard from Daniel? We could use his expertise on this."

Davis grunted. "He's on his way."

"Good. We'll stay until he gets here and get a preliminary report from the fire chief then arrange a follow up. Do you think Barnes is up to manning the gate?"

"Nothing like throwing them in at the deep end." He chuckled and clutched his gut. "I heard there are reporters gathering down there already. It'll be a good experience for him." Slapping me on the back with a little too much force, he continued, "Alright, well now that you two are here, I'm heading out." Davis shot me a salacious grin that made my skin crawl, saluted Montoya, and left, leaving a foul smell in his wake.

"Today's going to be a long one," Montoya muttered under her breath as she stepped out of the room, leaving me alone with a message written in blood that threatened the safety of the one person I cared about more than my job.

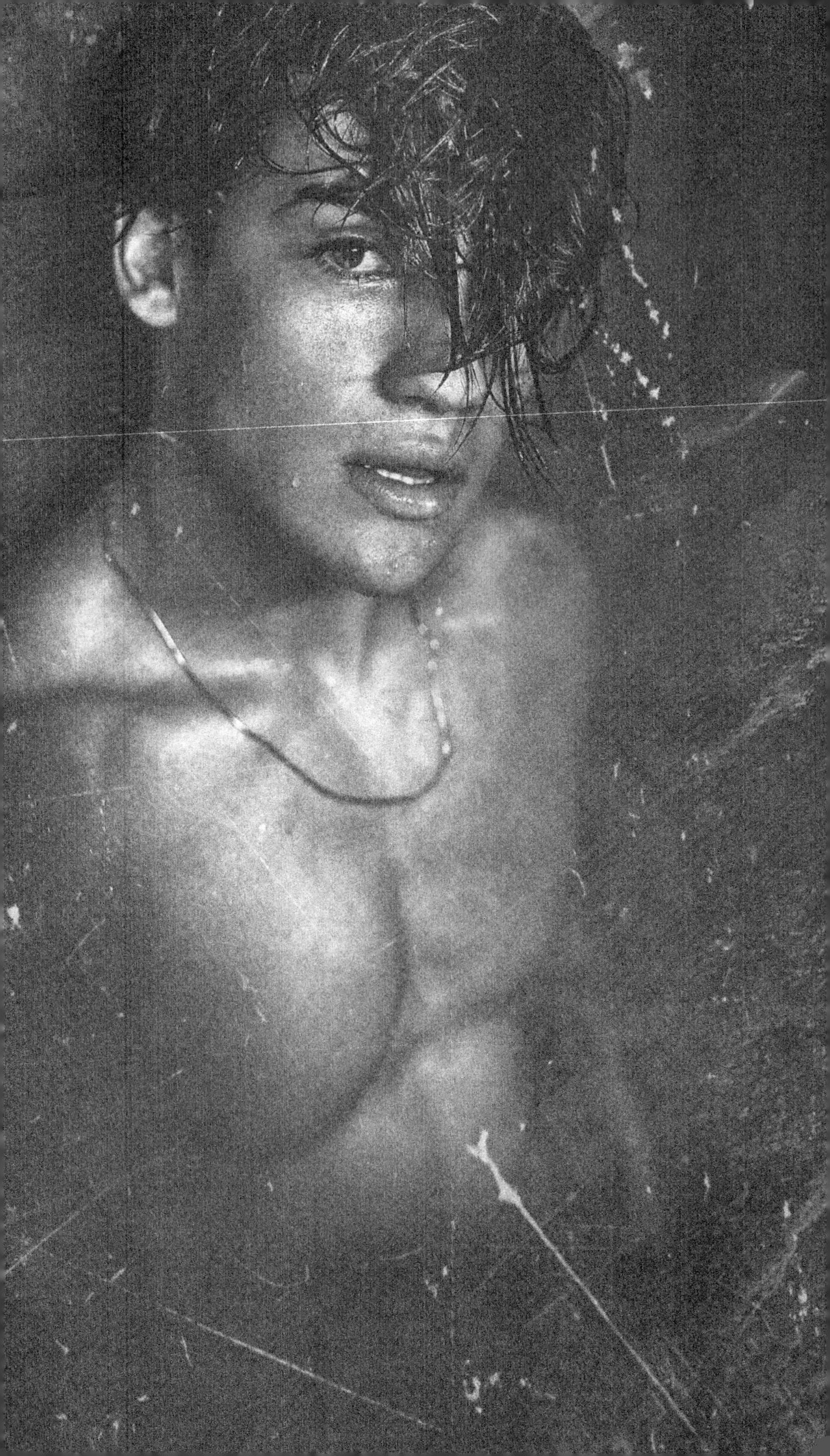

CHAPTER TWENTY-FIVE
River

I'd spent a lot of time working with Joelle, discussing and dissecting my life experiences and the methods I'd taught myself to cope. The main one she'd focused on has been my selective mutism and why I felt that was the best way for me to handle the life I had been forced into. She suggested cognitive brain therapy and explained how learning new coping mechanisms would foster a healthier way of dealing with situations that would ordinarily make me shut down and take the shit that came my way.

Joelle said I wasn't weak, that I'd just been in survival mode for so long it had become as easy as breathing. But now I have the opportunity to grow and heal, and I shouldn't shy away from the good things I deserve. Whether I believed her or not was another thing, because my cynical mind found it difficult to understand that things could be good after surviving such a violent and depraved life.

Over the weeks, she'd instilled a glimmer of hope in me that I wasn't totally broken or irreparable. Although I found her positivity hard to manage most of the time and have questioned more than once if she was as screwed up in the head as I was. Joelle was a relentless force of good, and even though I found it hard to admit, she had helped me find my voice again. I may only be able to string small sentences together when in the company of those I trust, but it was a start. And it's helped Bane and I build a solid foundation to our growing relationship, rather than one that resembled a house of cards built on quicksand.

The hardest battle I'd chosen was my inability to trust that the drugs she'd prescribed to help temper my gnawing anxiety and ever-present depression weren't going to kill me after watching many of the guys under Dahlia's care die from accidental overdoses taking coke cut with rat poison. It had been an insurmountable mountain that I'd kept trying to scale, but inevitably ended up failing and falling back down.

"Every day is a fresh start. What happened yesterday doesn't control me or influence today. I am worthy of happiness. I am worthy of love. I deserve to live." I scoffed at my reflection in the mirror as it stared back at me as I spoke my daily affirmations. I didn't see the point of them, but it was all part of the CBT Joelle had me on.

"What are you up to, angel?"

Bane stepped up behind me and wrapped his arms around my waist before nuzzling tender kisses on my neck. I tipped my head to the side to allow him better access and sighed, relaxing into his hard body.

"Just saying my daily affirmations."

"Mmm." He moaned as the tip of his tongue teased my pulse point. I shuddered as he nudged the sensitive spot just below my ear with his nose and inhaled, his chest rumbling behind me.

Lost in the beauty of our reflection, my mind wandered. The contrast between us was striking. Bane might have been only five years older than me, but where I still looked like a teenager, he was all man. He towered over me effortlessly, looking like he could scoop me up like I weighed nothing. I couldn't deny how much I loved the way he could maneuver me with just a flick of his hands, even if it sometimes stirred something deep and uncomfortable in me.

His broad shoulders, carved with deliciously defined muscles, flowed down to powerful arms and a chest that commanded attention, leading to abs that would make any bodybuilder green with envy. His forearms, thick and veined like something out of a fantasy, guided my gaze down to where his large hands rested. They skimmed teasingly across my exposed stomach, leaving a trail of goosebumps in their wake. They made me feel delicate, precious even, and lit a fire in me that traveled through my veins and spread out to my fingertips and down to my toes.

"What would you like to do today, angel?" Bane's lips brushed the shell of my ear, the heat from his exhale making me shiver.

There were so many things I wanted to do, and all of them involved him. The last few weeks had pushed us individually to our limits and tested us as a couple. After Dale's body was discovered alongside the fire that burned down any evidence of the crime, Bane had been relentless in his work. The hours I'd spent alone had me feeling like I was caged once again. Luckily, I had Shadow, and after much coaxing from me, Bane allowed us out into the yard to play for a couple of hours a day.

"Well…" My breath caught in my throat as I watched his

hand slide up my stomach and tweak my nipples before gently collaring my throat with a possessive hold.

Bane chuckled huskily in my ear. "Well what, sweetheart?"

My tongue toyed with my bottom lip, and my mouth curved into a grin when I caught his eyes tracing the movement in my reflection. His comforting weight became more present as he pinned me against the counter, and my head fell back against his chest when the weight of his hard length rested between my cheeks.

"I was thinking..."

"Yes?"

His thumb brushed over my slick bottom lip and pulled it down until it bounced free, and I felt more than heard his deep groan. I pushed my ass back against his hardness and slowly rotated my hips in a figure of eight motion in the limited space. After everything we had done, we still hadn't had full penetrative sex, but that need had become a craving I couldn't ignore.

I wanted Bane in every way, needed him to replace the touch of everyone who had stolen their pleasure from me at the expense of my suffering.

He had promised he'd teach me what pleasure was, what it felt like to feel a connection with someone that defied the laws of physics. Bane had succeeded and made sex a religious experience. There were no words to describe how he made me feel, and if there were, I had yet to learn them.

Panted breaths heated my cheek, and Bane's eyes filled with a lust-fueled fire as he stared at me through our reflections.

"I-I thought...m-maybe we could watch..." My bottom lip rolled through my teeth as I fought to smother the grin trying to break free. Bane arched his eyebrow in question and pinched the pebbled nubs on my chest until I was squirming against him and lost the rhythmic roll of my hips. "We could watch *Is It Cake?*"

Slack jawed, his hold on my throat loosened. "Watch *Is It Cake?* You are a devious little deceiver, angel." Bane growled and nipped at my earlobe. "I can think of something else we should do to work up a suitable appetite before we watch that."

Large hands coasted down my arms, one bracing around my back, while the other hit the back of my knees as he bent down and scooped me into his arms and marched out of the bathroom.

"Bane, put me down."

"I'll put you down, alright." He smirked when I glanced up at him. In a split second, I was sailing through the air and landing with an undignified thud on the bed. "Out." Shadow's head snapped up from where he was basking on the floor in the sun's rays. I swore he pouted as he left the room with his tail between his legs.

Bane crossed over to the door in two powerful strides and locked it before the weight of his heady gaze pinned me in place. "Now then, as I have the weekend off, I thought we could spend some time getting reacquainted? What do you say, angel?"

Enraptured, I watched him stop at the foot of the bed and work his grey sweats down his ass before kicking them across the floor. His long, thick cock slapped against his abs, a glistening bead of precum leaking from his slit.

Licking my lips, I crawled down the bed toward him. My eyes traced the slow stroke of his hand as he worked himself from root to tip. Saliva pooled in my mouth as arousal flooded my veins and my cock thickened beneath my boxers.

"Come here, angel." Bane beckoned me with a curl of his

finger and patted the foot of the bed. "Lie down on your back with your head over the edge and open that pretty little mouth for me. I want you to get me nice and slick before you finally welcome me home."

A shiver rolled through me as I got into position. Luckily for Bane, his bed was high, so he'd only have to bend his knees a little to lay his glorious length on my tongue. In position, I tipped my head back far enough to swirl the tip of my tongue over his heavy balls that hung above me.

Bane jolted like he'd been struck by lightning, and his large body collapsed over me, hands braced against the bed by my knees. "Fuck me," he groaned as I sucked one of his balls into my mouth and laved my tongue around it. "I wasn't expecting that." The gravelly texture to his voice had deepened a few octaves, making it a palpable entity that caressed my skin and heated the blood in my veins.

"So fucking beautiful." I felt each word form against my thigh as soft kisses glided over my skin to my groin. My dick twitched as he mouthed my cloth-covered erection from the base to the head, where he lapped at the wet patch formed from my precum.

"B-Bane," I whimpered as I released his other ball and wrapped my hand around his steely length, trying in vain to position it so I could wrap my lips around its swollen, glistening head. "I-I need..."

"I know what you need. Just hold still for a second." I glanced up when his fingers sank beneath the elastic of my boxer briefs. I tensed when the cool air hit my length as he peeled my underwear down my legs. Without thought, I stroked his length and enjoyed the show as his abs contracted and extended above me as he finally divested me of the only item of clothing I was wearing.

Bane's fingers danced up my legs, traced the juncture where my thighs met my groin, and followed the slight gullies that hinted at abs across my stomach until the heat from his palms massaged my pecs. He tweaked my nipples, and my body vibrated under his ministrations, my hips eagerly lifting off the bed, seeking him out.

"Open for me, baby."

I blinked, dazed and drowning in my want for him. It felt like a drug, his every touch cementing my addiction, ingraining it in my bones. He dipped his thumb into my mouth, gently pulling my chin down, opening me further as he positioned himself and rested the head of his dick against my lips. The salty flavor of his precum dripped into my mouth and burst across my taste buds. A needy moan vibrated in my chest. I wanted to swallow him whole, but I'd relinquished control to Bane, because I knew he'd take care of me, always putting my needs before his own.

With his hands cupping my cheeks, Bane slowly thrust into my mouth, holding my jaw open while I adjusted to the stretch before pushing in. The silky texture of his erection glided down my tongue until it hit the back of my throat, and I swallowed around him, pulling his dick farther down.

"Fuck. I forgot you have no gag reflex."

My lips twitched. I wanted to smile, but they were stretched to capacity around his girth. One of Bane's hands moved down to my throat and tightened until he would have been able to feel his cock buried deep inside me. I loved the possessive hold he had on me, but I also knew he did it so he could monitor my pulse as I lost myself to my submission of him.

By the time his heavy balls rested on my chin, my throbbing cock was leaking like a fountain. Precum smeared across my lower stomach, so sensitive that even the air moving had my balls drawing up close.

"Such a good boy for me, angel," he cooed as he worked his length in and out of my throat.

Saliva seeped from my lips every time he pulled back, so only the glans stayed in my mouth. I sucked in a much-needed breath. I dipped the tip of my tongue into his slit, seeking the next salty drop before he sunk back down into my throat.

I braced my hands on his muscled thighs, my fingers sinking into his flesh hard enough to leave bruises as his tempo increased and he started to use me the way I wanted him to. He owned my heart, body, and soul. There was nothing I wouldn't do for him—even dying with his cock lodged in my throat. The limited supply of oxygen to my lungs was affecting me. It felt like flying, like I was slowly leaving my body behind, blanketed in a warmth only Bane could give me. The never-ending buzzing in my mind quietened as I gave myself to him.

Hot kisses rained down my spine, and when I opened my eyes, the world slowly came back into focus. I found myself lying on my front, my head resting on my folded arms, my knees tucked under me and my ass in the air. Bane's hands held the globes of my ass apart, his heated touch a brand on my skin as his tongue circled the divots at the base of my spine.

"You're so perfect for me, Riv," he murmured against the base of my spine. "I need a quick taste before—" I missed what he said as he licked from my taint to my entrance. His hot, wet tongue circled the tight ring of muscles, stoking the burning need that thrummed below my skin and pooled at the base of my spine. Bane lapped at my hole using his tongue, lips, and teeth to tease the sensitive skin until it softened enough to allow his stiffened tongue inside me.

"M-more." I reached back and sunk my hand into his thick hair and pulled him closer. Holding him in place, I rocked my hips and pushed back, forcing his tongue deeper inside me as I rode his face. The rough abrasion of his stubble only heightened my pleasure, but it wasn't enough. My channel ached to be filled.

"I n-need you."

"Are you sure?"

It was sweet that he checked in. It was obvious my body was on board—it was practically begging him to get inside it, but Bane loved me. He cherished me in a way that was still foreign. It felt alien to be desired as more than a hole to be used and discarded. He cared enough to check that I was mentally present and consenting.

"Y-yes." Arousal consumed me to the point it was getting almost impossible to form coherent sounds. Sweat slicked my skin, and I felt like I'd claw my skin off if he didn't get inside me. "Now."

My arm flailed, feeling like jelly as it stretched toward the nightstand to get the lube. My fingers clutched the blankets, unable to get close enough. Bane chuckled above me, heat pouring off his skin as he leaned over me and smoothly retrieved it. I rolled my eyes. Of course, even on edge, he could still do everything with a fluidity I'd never possess.

"Shh, angel," he murmured when I flinched as cold drops of lube landed at the base of my spine and slid down my crease. "I've got you." His talented fingers swiftly worked me open and sunk inside me before I could beg for more. The head of his cock notched against my entrance. He dragged it around the softened ring of muscle, pushing against it but not breaching it and sinking inside me.

"Bane," I mewled, desperately needing him.

"No." I froze. His hands gripped my hips, his fingers flexing into my skin. "Not like this. When I finally sink inside you, I want to watch every emotion flicker over your face. I want to watch you come on my cock. I need to see you fly." My head spun at his beautiful words and the meaning behind them. The sentiment stole the air from my lungs as he flipped me over.

"B-Bane," I breathed as he pushed my knees up to my chest and bracketed my hips with his legs and tipped my pelvis up.

"Hands behind your knees." I obeyed immediately, mesmerized by the frantic rise and fall of his chest and the way his dark skin glistened in the beams of sunlight cutting into the room. His sweat glistened like diamonds, casting fractals of light around us.

My head rocked from side to side, trying to clear the lust from my mind so I'd remember this moment forever. I'd be able to relive it whenever my eyes closed. "P-please."

The most serene smile lifted his swollen lips, and his mismatched eyes burned with the power of a thousand suns as he looked at me. It felt like time stood still, a silent sentinel to this moment. One that could never be taken back, one that would change each of us irrevocably. One that would finally heal the cracks in my soul with his golden light.

Bane was about to become part of me, and I'd never forget it.

The intensity of our connection grew, and the air thickened with our combined arousal. I shuddered as the head of his cock circled my entrance before he tapped it against my rim and pushed inside.

"Oh my god," I breathed out, and bore down as his thick head slid inside me. Bolts of electricity pulsed beneath my skin, and Bane released a shuddering breath as another inch worked its way down my channel. My head tipped back, and my eyes fluttered closed as the sensation overwhelmed me. The burning stretch, the heavy weight, the pain that turned to pleasure as another inch entered me, my body eager for more.

"You're doing so well, angel." He kissed my forehead, then sealed his lips to mine and licked inside my mouth, tasting himself on my tongue as his hips thrust forward again. "That's it, baby. Half of my length is inside you."

I felt so full, so owned, but not quite complete. I needed him fully seated inside me for that to happen. Releasing the grip I had on my legs, I locked them around his waist and dug my heels into the globes of his ass and pushed his deeper inside of me, refusing to stop until his groin was flush with my ass and I could feel the heavy weight of his balls.

"Fuck! River," he growled. "I'm going to come if you keep doing that, and I want to make it so good for you." Ownership laced every syllable as he possessed me wholly.

I could see his need in his eyes. It echoed mine.

"I'm so close," I breathed against his lips as I pulled him back down for another soul-affirming kiss. As my tongue wrapped around his, he pulled back the head of his cock, dragging it over that sweet spot inside me only he'd ever been able to find.

"You're so fucking tight."

He rolled his hips, slowly keeping as much of his length inside me as was humanly possible. He settled into a languid rhythm that had our slick bodies locked together in delicious torture, sending waves of pleasure surging through me. I felt like I was soaring with Bane right alongside me. My balls drew up tight, hugging the base of my cock as it throbbed and pulsed, trapped between our bodies. Every thrust of his hips, the friction of his hard abs against my sensitive skin, had me thickening and precum leaking from me with every pass.

"Angel." His lips brushed mine. Not for a kiss, but for the electrical connection that hummed between us.

"Bane...I-I'm..."

"I know." He smiled, pure love shining in his eyes. His hands cupped my face, and he rested his forehead against mine. "I can feel your body cling to me every time I try to pull back. It's magical, the way your walls ripple around me. You're perfect, River."

He thickens inside me, pushing my body to its limit. I felt raw and undone. Bane's control fractured, and his thrusts became animalistic. Primal. His cock pulsed inside me as he filled me with his cum. I finally felt free.

"Come for me, angel." Bane's body shook as his release stole him away and separated his soul from his body. "Fuck. Yes. Yes, River, that's it. Come on my cock, angel."

My orgasm obliterated me as it detonated, incinerating me from the inside out. Every muscle froze as thick ropes of cum sprayed across my stomach all the way to my chin. Every color in existence burst behind my eyes as the world faded away.

Sweat dripped from Bane's face as he clutched me to him, still lost in the aftershocks of his orgasm. Every shockwave made his still hard cock twitch inside me, eliciting a groan deep within my chest. My muscles refused to work, and my arms and legs felt like jelly. I was high on my post orgasmic haze, my body and mind finally sated.

I felt kisses all over my face and sighed, sinking into the mattress. Rough fingers kneaded the lax muscles in my arms, while Bane whispered sweet words of love and affection into my ear. He rolled us until I was sprawled on top of him and drew the blankets over us.

"Shh, angel. Sleep. I've got you."

My head weighed a ton, but I managed to lift it enough to rest my chin on his chest. After a couple of deep cleansing breaths, I said, "Stay inside me...for...as long..." Sleep claimed me before I could beg him to stay there, plugging me. I didn't want this magical connection to ever end.

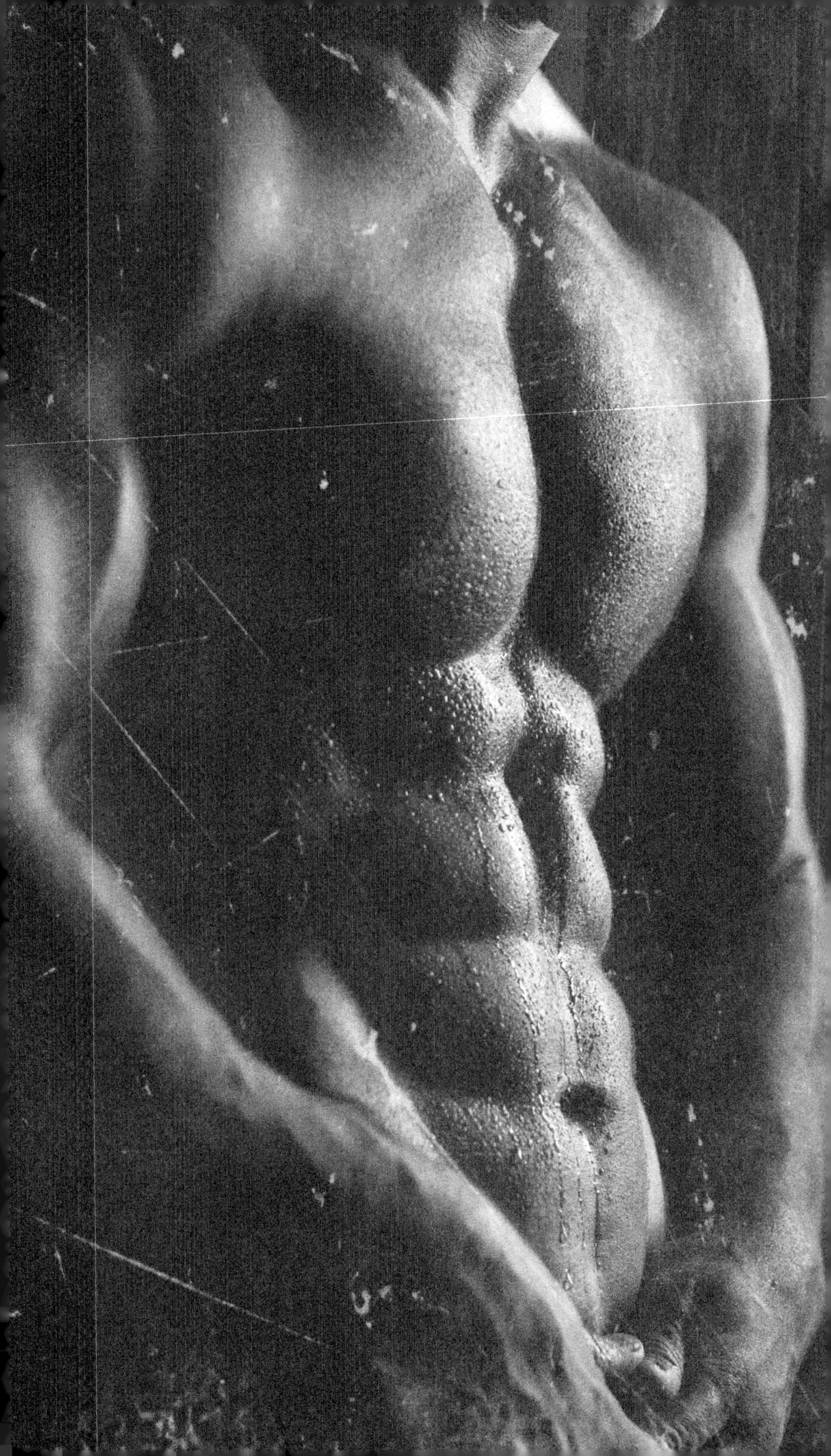

CHAPTER TWENTY-SIX
Bane

"How are you feeling about today?" River asked cautiously as I sifted through the folder laid out on the counter in front of me. I took a beat to digest the question. We'd spent a month putting everything together for the raid we had planned for today, and I had the job of checking and cross-checking every lead and piece of information the team had pulled together for it. From who would attend, to the location, security, and most importantly, what was up for auction. The products on the docket for tonight were children, none of whom were older than twelve. I'd even liaised with the alphabet agencies before Bower took that off my hands. That man had his sights locked on a promotion. Word had it there was a head of title up for grabs with one of them if he could pull this off.

Miraculously, we'd managed to turn one of the lower level guys—Marco—in Black Dahlia's network. The promise of full immunity in relation to the case had him singing like a lark once the paperwork was signed and sealed. What the idiot didn't know was we had enough dirt on him for unrelated activities that he'd never see the light of day once the night was over.

The guy didn't know a thing about loyalty, which benefited us exponentially. He worked security for Dahlia's establishments, namely the strip joints that acted as backstreet brothels, and had a tendency to sample the merchandise with a rather rough hand. We'd acquired several statements from the girls that ended up in hospital because of him.

Fortunately for us, he played poker with guys who were higher up the food chain. And it turned out once those men got some hard liquor into them, they let slip about upcoming events like auctions or big clients that were coming in to sample product.

"I'm cautiously hopeful." I glanced up at him when a mug of coffee brushed my fingertips. "Come here, angel." River slipped into my open arms like he was made for them, and when his wrapped around me, I felt settled for the first time in nearly forty-eight hours.

"When do you l-leave?" He tried to hide it, but I heard the tremble in his voice and so did Shadow, who appeared at his feet, his head butting into River's calf, making him chuckle. It was like that dog could sense when his anxiety spiked and was there instantly, demanding attention and distracting him.

I checked my watch and gulped down my coffee. It seared its way down my throat, but I welcomed the pain and the much needed hit of caffeine. "Montoya should be here in ten." A sigh slipped past my lips, and I buried my face in his unruly hair. River's cinnamon and orange scent infused me with a much needed sense of calm and clarity.

"I promise I'll be back." I knew what he was thinking,

even if he never said it. His fear of me not returning was a palpable thing. It was written in his forest-green eyes every time I caught them. He'd come so far with Joelle's support, but the fear of abandonment was deeply ingrained in both of us. I wasn't sure we'd ever get its hooks out of us.

"I know," he murmured into my chest and tightened his hold on me.

"Cooper's coming round, isn't he? Bringing the new pup to play with Shadow?" River tipped his head back and grinned up at me, a childlike wonder sparking in his eyes.

"Yeah. It's a pom-pom or something."

I snickered and nodded my head. A dog breed specialist I was not. "Or something, alright." My lips brushed his forehead in a tender kiss that melted into a smile when River's fingers traced patterns across my back. My eyes shuttered closed, and I focused on their path. It wasn't random shapes; he was writing something. A shiver skittered down my spine as my brain tried to piece it all together, but if the thudding of my heart was anything to go by, my heart and body knew already.

"You got it?" he whispered softly.

"No. Again?" His husky laugh heated my face, and his answering smile warmed my insides.

"Now?"

I closed my eyes and focused intently on the path River's fingers took, like they were painting the darkness with the light of his love. First there was an I, followed by an L, then an o?

"I love you." My voice shook as emotions overwhelmed me. Although River had become more vocal and confident, he still struggled to say those words, so he found as many creative ways to show me how he felt.

"That's not all," he breathed against my ear.

With my face in the crook of his neck, my lips brushing

against his silky soft skin, I let my mind drift as he started again. This one wasn't so easy to decipher, and when I asked him to repeat it, something changed, but the meaning was still the same.

"You did a symbol instead of a word the second time."

"I did." He shrugged. "Did you work it out?"

"It took me a minute, but I did."

River stepped back so he could look at me. Eagerness and excitement lit up his beautiful features. "Well?"

"My heart."

My voice cracked and broke on the last word as I took him in. If someone had told me a year ago I had found the boy who became my anchor during some of my darkest days and that he would become my lover, my life, the centre of my universe, I would have hit them up the backside of the head and asked how much they'd had to drink.

My hands cupped his face, thumbs brushing over his flushed cheeks. I could admit I was drowning in River, suffocating on him, but who needed air when I had him? This moment felt pivotal, but I couldn't fathom why. Overcome with desire, I sealed my lips to his. His sharp inhale allowed me access, and my tongue wrapped around his as a fresh wave of his taste burst across my tongue. River surged forward as he pushed up onto his toes, and his hand snaked around the back of my neck, his blunt nails trailing across my skin. Before I could deepen the kiss further and pull him into my lap, we were interrupted by someone hammering on the door.

River broke away, mirth dancing in his eyes. "No," I grumbled and pulled him back to me. I felt his wicked smile against my mouth.

"Put that boy down, and get your ass out here, Benson!" Montoya yelled through the mailbox, making River snicker as I groaned and nuzzled into his neck.

"Why? Why me?"

"Shut up, you big softie. Today is the day. I'll be in the car. You've got two minutes."

My gaze swung to River, who looked suitably rumpled and good enough to eat. I leaned forward, but his finger on my lips halted my progress.

"But..."

"No." He chuckled and shook his head. "The s-sooner you go, the sooner you can come home to m-me."

"Fine." Rolling my eyes, I pressed a kiss to his forehead, nose, and eyes before he pushed me away and ordered me out of the house, stating he had puppy cuddles to look forward to.

THE STATION WAS A HIVE OF ACTIVITY WHEN WE ARRIVED. WE headed to the situation room where everyone that was involved in tonight's op was already waiting. Bower stood at the front of the room. The whiteboard behind him laid out our movements and locations down to the minute. He went over every detail with a fine-toothed comb before dismissing us with the order to get our heads on straight and gear up for the op.

Unusually for Davis, he had been quiet during the briefing, focused on his phone with a furrow between his brows. Warning bells rang in my head and got louder the closer I watched him.

Bower had saddled him with a couple of rookies, who would monitor the wider perimeter and notify us of any unexpected arrivals. Keeping Davis out of the action was an intentional move on Bower's part, now that his suspicions had been raised after the fire and Barnes's sudden resignation.

Montoya and I made our way to the locker room and did a final check of our equipment. A heavy sense of foreboding hung over us as the rest of the team slowly ambled in and did the same. This was our third raid, and I hoped against all hope this one was successful after the first two failed.

Dahlia herself had become a ghost and vanished off the face of the earth. River had said she had eyes everywhere, and I was starting to think he was right more than he knew. I couldn't help but think Davis wasn't working alone.

The two messages she'd sent me had upped the ante, and it had been harder than ever to get approval for this operation. If it failed, I feared it would all come crashing down on my shoulders, and then where would that leave River?

"Don't go there, Benson." Montoya's hand latched onto my shoulder with a nail-biting squeeze. "We need to think positively, or that bitch wins."

"I know." My head hung forward as I braced my elbows on my legs. "I just...I'm—"

"Scared?" I nodded. She sat down next to me, her shoulder brushing mine in support. "I get it. You've got more than any of us riding on this."

"Mmmm." I finally had someone to fight for and everything to lose. I refused to allow that reality to come to fruition. Our time was finite, and I wanted to spend every moment I had left with River. To love him through all the seasons of his life, to have the honor of watching him grow and discover new things and experience this blossoming love between us.

That's why this raid had to work. I refused to accept failure.

"Bower won't put you on parking duty if it turns out to

be a bust." She glanced around, a shifty look in her eyes. "I have—"

"Don't. I have a feeling I know what you're going to say, and I have the same feeling. If the worst happens tonight, come to mine and we'll talk it over before going to Bower." She gave me a nod and left the room to grab one more hit of caffeine before our long night.

As night fell, a cold, starless sky watched as all the teams moved into position and checked in. Montoya and I sat on the roof of a nearby farmhouse, watching the high rollers come in their droves. Their blacked out cars crunched on gravel as they formed a line resembling a uniformed army of ants, crawling along after one another until they disappeared into the underground parking garage. The windows of the mansion were blacked out, and if it wasn't for the guards patrolling the site or the torches lining the driveway, you would think the place was deserted.

A biting wind whipped up off the vast expanses of arable land surrounding us, burning my cheeks. I rubbed my hands together as my fingers slowly turned numb. I knew there was money in the skin trade—big money—but seeing the breadth of wealth that had arrived had my stomach churning like a savage ocean. Acid burned the back of my tongue, decimating River's sweet taste. My heart was in my throat, and it felt like I was choking on air at the thought of the depravity taking place inside those stone walls.

I wanted to throw caution to the wind and storm down the gates with my gun raised, catching every one of them and making them answer for their crimes, but we had our orders. And orders were always followed. Our watches were synchronized, and tension bled into the air, thickened with anticipation and something I couldn't quite pin down with each passing minute.

"The auction is about to start," I murmured. Montoya glanced up at me with her binoculars in her hand as she tracked the guards' movements. The night was deadly silent. The only sound apart from our shaky exhales was the eerie whistling of the wind.

"Go time can't come soon enough. The wait is excruciating." I hummed in agreement and flexed my fingers. "It seems too quiet, too calm," Montoya mused, and the hairs on the back of my neck stood on end.

My hand shook where it rested against my gun. I couldn't have agreed with her more, but we had to stick to the plan. Otherwise, mistakes would be made and lives put at risk, both those of our officers and the innocents being held inside. Casualties were bound to occur, but we wanted to keep blood spill to a minimum. It wasn't long until Bower's voice sounded through our comms as the first team moved into position to take down the guards covering the perimeter. We watched as each one was taken out silently before an alarm could be raised and alert those who were inside.

"Time to go." I tapped Montoya on the shoulder, and we swept down from our vantage point. "Moving to hand signals. Stay on my six."

Montoya became my shadow as we melted into the night and made our way at a clipped pace to our meeting point, where we convened with the rest of our group. Beta team would enter the back of the property through the cellar entrance with the intention of liberating the children who were being held. A couple of clicks out, we had vans and an unmarked ambulance on standby to move them to a safe house and administer any required emergency first aid.

Alpha team would breach the property by the side entrances to the east and west of the mansion and lock down all entrances to the ballroom. If everything went according to plan, we'd walk out with Dahlia and her associates in cuffs. My eyes were on the prize. I'd leave every other sick fucker who was present to the rest of the team, but that bitch was mine. She'd made it personal, and I could be as vindictive as the next person. I wanted my face to be the last one she saw when she took the last breath of fresh air she'd ever get as a free woman.

"Split. Split. Split," Bower ordered. The teams divided as we reached the property line. Things moved swiftly, and my heart thundered like a war drum. My blood whooshed in my ears as adrenaline flooded my veins, sharpening my senses and bringing the world into focus around me.

Once we were in position, we waited for the signal to breach the property. We had to time it perfectly, so each team entered the building at the same time, leaving no exit unmanned if anyone tried to run. Trepidation skittered across my skin, and it felt like time slowed as we waited with bated breath for the go sign.

"Go. Go. Go." Alpha team moved as one as Montoya opened the unlocked door. The others swept in, making sure the coast was clear. I scoffed at the arrogance of the monsters who thought they were untouchable. A malicious smile lifted my lips behind my mask as I entered the building and closed the door behind me.

On silent feet, we followed the blueprints we'd memorized through reception rooms and libraries, then down the grand hallway that led to the ballroom where tonight's activities would take place. We lined up, four agents on either side of the door, and waited for confirmation everyone was in place.

Focused on regulating my breathing, my fingers flexed

around my grip. Someone tapped my shoulder. I glanced up to see Montoya waving her hand in front of her neck before tapping her ear. After a momentary confusion, I got what she was getting at, and strained my ears, trying to hear anything above the breathing of our team, but the house was silent. Surely, if there was an auction going on, we'd have heard them by now.

Lead filled my feet as the truth set in. My jaw clenched, and I ground my molars while we waited for the signal to enact the final part of tonight's plan. It took every single year of my training not to allow my growing disappointment to derail my focus. *Lock it down, Bane. Focus on the now. You can't fuck up.*

"Abort. Abort. Montoya and Benson, remain there. I'm coming in. The rest of you, clear out."

"What the fuck?" Henderson hissed as he turned to me, his eyes narrowing. "What's going on?"

My shoulders slumped, and defeat washed over me. "I have no idea. Head out to the designated meeting point and wait for further instruction."

Henderson stuck his middle finger up at me and followed the rest of the guys out the way we had come. After a few minutes, Davis's voice filled my ear, and I cringed at his smug tone.

"Beta team found thirty men downstairs, all drivers who were hired to collect a Mr. Jacob Benson and his team. There is no one else in the property."

"I've taken statements from all of them—it was a rush job that came through tonight. I'll liaise with the company owners tomorrow, and once I've got my hands on the payment details, I'll trace the sender and see what I can find out," Jordan said next, sounding as deflated as I felt.

Montoya looked at me, confusion clear on her face. I kicked the wall and threw my mask on the floor. "FUCK!"

"What's wrong? What do you know?"

"D-Davis." Anger consumed me as his words played over and over in my head. "He said the drivers were all waiting to collect me and our team, and confirmed the building is empty."

"Shit."

"This is so fucked up. She used me. She fucking framed me, Montoya. There's no way Bower will let me continue working on this case. W-what's going to happen to River if I'm pulled from his protection?" Fear lanced through my heart like a bolt of lightning, turning it to dust.

"Don't. Don't go there." She growled and yanked my head down to her level. "Don't let that bitch get inside your head. Do not let her win."

Before I could answer, the clacking of shoes echoed down the hallway from where Bower had entered through the unlocked front door. The flashlight in his hand swung wildly, the bright beam carving a blinding arc of light in our direction. My hand shot out to cover my eyes, and he was standing in front of me before I could even blink.

"What the fuck happened, Benson?"

"I-I don't know, sir." I hung my head, and focused on my booted feet. My hands balled into fists, then relaxed at my sides as I drew in a deep, calming breath. It took every ounce of self-control to swallow the vitriol on the tip of my tongue. Arguing over something beyond my control would accomplish nothing. But having my integrity questioned? That was dangerously close to crossing a line. I could only hope Bower would see reason before I reached my breaking point.

"You were played. Clearly, your turncoat is more manipulative than you thought. He. Fucking. Played. You. Do you understand how much this raid tonight cost? Our department can't afford to keep blowing the budget on failures like this."

"That's not fair, sir. If you look at it logically—"

"Do not question me, Benson. I have given you a hell of a lot of latitude in this case." What he meant was he'd given me enough rope to hang myself if it failed, which it looked like it had. I couldn't dispute that.

I cleared my throat, steeled my spine, and pulled my shoulders back. I looked Bower straight in the eye. "I'm certain it was Davis, sir."

Bower eyed me. I felt the glacial weight of his gaze drag from my head to my feet before it returned to my face. "And what do you have to support that claim?"

"He was the only one on his phone during the briefing. There was a two hour window between it and when we left," I explained. "He had plenty of time to notify his contact so they could change locations. That, and the drivers were waiting here to collect me and my team."

His hand ran down the side of his face. I could see him weighing the odds of what I was saying, but he wasn't willing to give me an inch and changed tack. "Have you at least scoped out the ballroom?"

"No, sir. We waited here like you ordered." Montoya stepped up next to me, turning her glare toward Bower. He might have been our boss, but she never backed down when she felt someone was being treated unjustly. She was my best friend, but my partner first and foremost. We protected each other. We were loyal to a fault.

"Do I have to do everything myself?" he grumbled and pushed the doors open to the grand ballroom. His anger made them fly back until they crashed into the walls, the sound echoing in the vast space.

What we saw when he did would be burned into the inside of my skull forever. The cavernous room was deserted except for two bright spot lights that were directed at the floor in the middle of the room, illuminating the macabre scene displayed for our—or my—viewing pleasure. The coppery taint of fresh blood filled my lungs as I sucked in a sharp inhale. In the middle of the illuminated circle lay another body. I didn't need to get a good look at the unfortunate soul to know who the victim was. Devastation rocked through me at the thought of having to tell River that another one of his friends had lost their life in a war they'd had no choice but to be sacrificed in.

"I wasn't expecting that," I muttered under my breath as Bower and I stepped into the bright circle of light. "Stop!" I flung my arm out in front of Bower, halting his progress. He turned to me, his irate face a deep shade of puce.

"You better have a good reason for this, Benson. There's another dead body in here!" he ground out and crossed his arms over his chest, turning the full weight of his accusatory gaze on me. I refused to cower. I would not crumble or give him any reason to think I was guilty, even by association.

My shoulders rose and fell as I took a moment to get my rapid breathing and flaring temper under control. "I do, sir. If you look closely at the floor, you'll see why." I gestured with my hand, and his eyes followed to where I was pointing. His head tilted to the side, and his hand flew up to cover his mouth.

"Thank you." Bower's genuine tone surprised me. "I couldn't see it from where I was standing."

"I was lucky the light caught on the blood. This is just like the one the other day," I continued. "The victim's body had been brutally tortured, his skin flayed from bone. Neck slit and blood drained. The MO matches perfectly, even down to the blood used to leave a message. The only difference this time is that it's on the floor and not a wall."

"Montoya, get Daniel down here now." She jerked her

head in acknowledgement and spun on her heel. "Wait," Bower barked, holding out a burner phone. "Take this, and tell no one. Make sure Daniel understands this stays between us."

"Yes, sir." Montoya slipped the phone into her pocket and headed into the hallway to call Daniel.

I crouched down, inspecting the floor, and pulled out a pair of gloves. Snapping them on, I dipped my finger into the viscous liquid. It was cold to the touch and tacky, but still fresh. Poor Gabriel hadn't been dead for long, that was for sure. Daniel would be able to confirm the time of death for us. This game of cat and mouse was getting old. It felt like we were chasing our tails rather than making any headway, and each warrant we applied for was harder to get. We had a limited window left to solve this case before it went cold and Black Dahlia won.

"Can you see what it says, sir?" I peeked up at Bower as he paced the circumference of the circle with his cell in his hand and was momentarily blinded by the flash when he snapped a photo.

"Next move. You lose."

"Huh?"

"That's what it says." He exhaled heavily and scrubbed his hand down his face. "Does it mean anything to you?"

Bowing my head, I answered. "Yes. It's personal, just like the last one. Dahlia is targeting River, and by extension, me. She seems to think he can make us stop the investigation. That's why she's killing off River's friends."

The sound of Bower's shoes on the hardwood floors echoed in the cavernous space. "This isn't a bad thing. It means we're close, Benson. We've got her rattled, and it's just a matter of time before she makes a mistake. We need to keep pushing."

"I agree sir, but..." I glanced over my shoulder, looking

for Montoya. It was time to put forward our theory and see if he agreed. I had an idea, but I didn't know the why.

"What is it?"

"Daniel will be here in thirty, sir," Montoya said as she stepped up beside me. "Oh, shit." Her eyes widened as she took it all in. "That's the same MO as—"

"Yeah, it is," I agreed and cleared my throat. "Montoya and I have a theory about why Black Dahlia keeps slipping through our fingers."

"Alright, let's hear it."

"Oh, Daniel also confirmed that some of the evidence he's been working on has been tampered with. Luckily, he has trust issues, and made duplicates of everything."

"That's just fucking awesome." Bower narrowed his eyes in exasperation. "This is the biggest case I've ever worked, and it's going to shit." He shook his head before turning back to me. "What's your theory?"

"We've got a mole." The color drained from Bower's face, and I could see the cogs turning in his head. "The only people that have known the finer details of this case—dates, times, and locations—are the team directly involved. This raid was only confirmed this afternoon. No one left the station, and all the phones were locked."

"No!" Montoya shouted. "Remember, you commented about someone on their phone during the brief."

An evil smile curved my face. "I know who our rat is, sir, and just how to catch him."

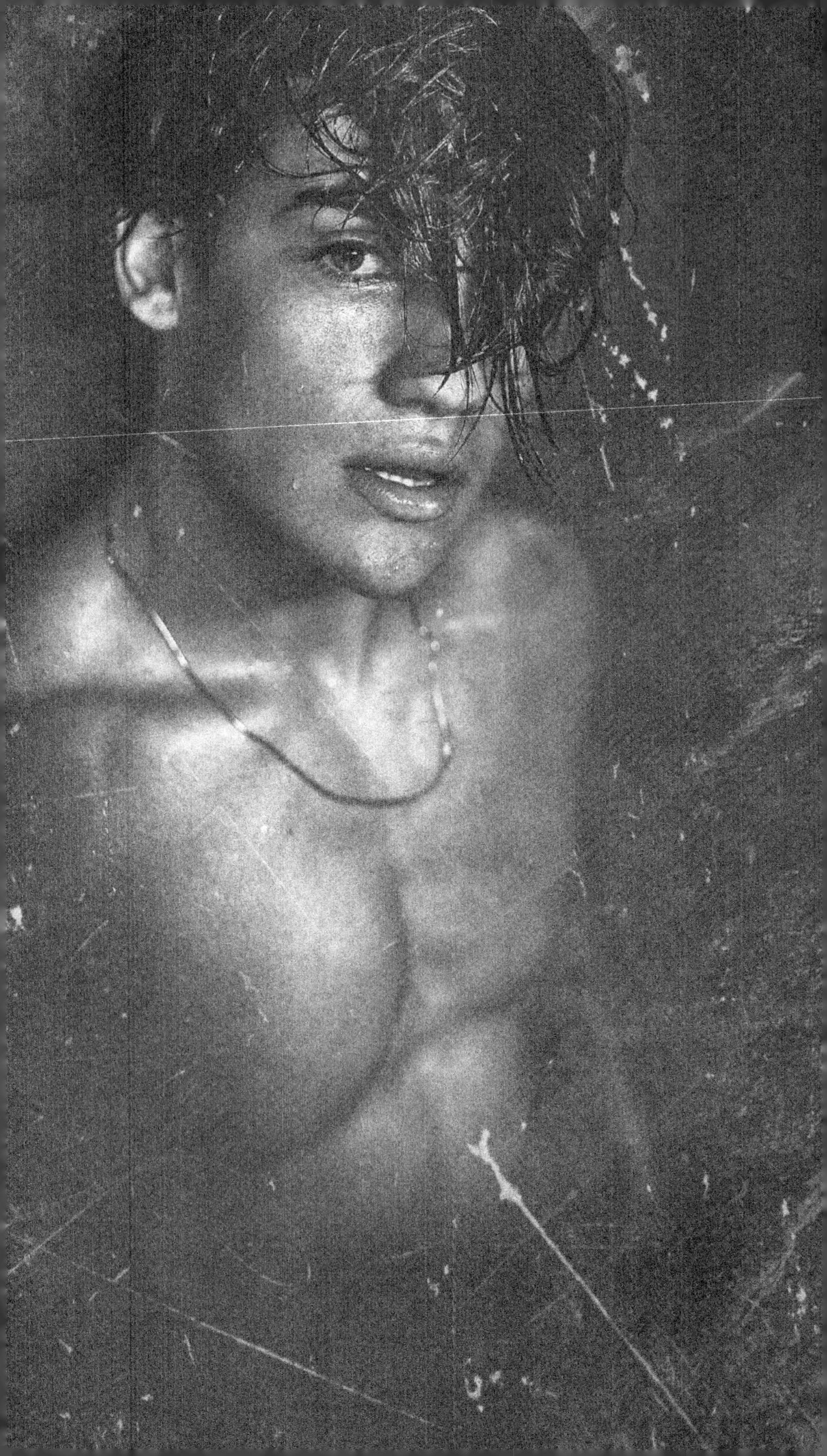

CHAPTER TWENTY-SEVEN
River

"Ugh, g-get off. It's too early for kisses," I groaned as a rough tongue lapped at my face. "Shadow, no more. Stop. Ugh, p-please?" I batted him away until he left me to sulk alone at my rude awakening. "I'm awake, alright?"

With my eyes still closed, I pulled the blankets up over my face and inhaled Bane's cedarwood and leather scent that was ingrained in the material, needing some kind of connection with him. Since I'd been staying at his house, I could count on one hand the number of nights I'd spent without him under the same roof, but none had been as tough as last night.

After Colton left with Snowy, his little white pom-pom-whatever-it's-called puppy, the house had felt like a crypt. Shadow had kept me company as I curled up on the gray couch and watched a few episodes of *Is It Cake?* Then acted as an emotional support dog while I'd bawled my eyes out when Domitianus found his sex slave Hermes in bed with one of his guards and lost his ever-loving shit. I wouldn't say he loved Hermes—I didn't think he was capable of it—but he felt an entitlement over him. Ownership. Something I knew and understood all too well. Eventually, he'd had poor Hermes strapped to the front of a boat and watched as a giant crocodile ate him without shedding a tear.

People with power were heartless assholes the world over, and it didn't seem to matter if it was part of humanity's history or the present day. People seemed to be addicted to power, control, and ownership. History was doomed to repeat itself, and it made me sick to my back teeth.

Nothing I had done had kept my mind off missing Bane. He was like a phantom limb. An intrinsic piece of me was gone, and I felt its absence with every breath. Was I codependent on him? Without a fucking doubt. Bane was my tether, the one thing that grounded me and stopped me from spiraling out of control. He kept the darkness that controlled my mind at bay. He was my light. My heart.

No matter how hard I tried to implement all the things Joelle suggested, I still struggled. Every single fucking day. My intrusive thoughts grew louder when I was alone and I'd find myself thinking of all the ways Bane's life would be better if I wasn't there dragging him down.

He deserved so much better than me.

I didn't regret a single second I'd spent with him since he'd walked into that interrogation room and had collapsed on the ground at my feet. He'd brought me back from the brink and saved my sanity. I'd been fracturing at the seams, and it was his love and support that pieced me back together. But still...

A loud bark right by my head made me jolt up so fast the room spun. I peeled my eyes open. "What?!" The little shit sat next to the bed, wagging his tail. "You need to go for a pee?" If a dog could nod, Shadow did. "Fine!" I groaned, kicked the blankets off, and shuffled toward the door, pausing only to yank Bane's ridiculously larger sweatpants up before I tripped over them and headed downstairs. "You and me both, buddy. You and me both. Now go out and do your business while I do mine."

A yawn stretched my mouth as I opened the back door for Shadow and left it a jar so he could get back in, then hurried upstairs for a piss and a quick shower. Once I felt human, I'd call Bane and find out what was going on. Worry gnawed at me, making me feel all kinds of lost and unsettled.

Water clung to the glass as I stepped out of the shower and grabbed a towel off the heated rail. I smiled despite feeling myself starting to spiral. I'd used Bane's shower gel so I could smell like him. His scent was intoxicating, but this was a poor imitation. It was missing something fundamental—him.

Steam coiled in the air so thickly, I could hardly see a foot in front of my face. I was slightly obsessed with having a shower hot enough to melt your skin from your bones. It was a novelty and a privilege I'd never take for granted. Having spent so many years showering in a filthy cubicle with water that felt like fresh glacial melt, I appreciated everything being here had afforded me. Things most people took for granted were like a blessing from the gods.

I glanced up at the mirror that was covered in a glistening sheen of condensation, and tears stung my eyes at the message emblazoned on it. He must have left it yesterday before leaving for the station. "Oh, Bane," I whimpered, my finger tracing the letters on the glass.

*You own my heart,
so I've left it with you.
Keep it safe until I come home.*

"I can't believe you've made me cry. And you're not even here, so I can yell at you for it." Not that I would—my voice was still far too brittle for that—but the thought burned brightly in my brain, smothering the crushing loneliness I was feeling. It was devastating. I'd never felt so pathetic in my life. I had everything I'd ever dreamed of, but right now, I was miserable.

"You're p-pathetic. What does he see in you? You need to be stronger than this." Scoffing at myself, I shook my head and brushed my teeth, trying to think of anything other than the wound festering in my heart.

By the time I'd finished up in the bathroom, gotten dressed, and grabbed my phone off the nightstand, Shadow was waiting for me in the kitchen. His tail thumped on the hardwood floor as he stared forlornly at his empty food bowl. "Seriously, a-anyone would think we didn't f-feed you." I chuckled and scratched his head, topped up his bowl, and flicked the kettle on.

While I was waiting, I checked my phone for missed calls or messages, but my screen was blank. I worried the broken skin at the edge of my thumbnail as I tried to work out what was best to do. Joelle's voice flitted through my mind with an unholy number of exercises she'd given me to do when I felt like I was drowning. *"This homework will really help cement everything we've been discussing over the last few weeks."* My eyes rolled back in my head. I wanted to yell back that I was trying, but sometimes it felt like I was still failing. I was angry at myself for feeling this way, but also with Bane, because I needed him and he wasn't here. He was my strength when mine failed, the light that sat with me in the shadows when they were too strong for me to fight back on my own.

With nothing better to do, I made a cup of chamomile tea, another one of Joelle's suggestions for when I felt like I was crumbling, and took my meds. My brain was foggy as I tried to remember if I'd taken my meds last night, but I came up blank. Maybe that was why I was struggling so much now. Maybe all I needed was time. Time for the chemicals to help rewire my brain so everything connected the way it should. I needed to learn to dance in the rain, because even this storm would pass.

The doorbell rang, and my mug slipped from my grasp and crashed onto the granite, spilling my tea everywhere. "Well, this is inconvenient," I grumbled as I headed to the door. I glanced through the peephole and saw Sharon with a warm smile on her face.

"I know you're there, River," she said softly. "I'm not coming in, I've got something..."

Unlocking the dead bolts took some time, but when I pulled it back, her shoulders relaxed. "S-sorry." I scuffed my foot against the door frame, struggling to hold eye contact with her and felt my cheeks heat.

"Hush now, dear. None of that. I've got something of yours that I've been meaning to return. Luckily for you, Montoya called this morning, and it triggered my memory. It's a funny story, really. One of my colleagues—Kirsty—picked it up and put it in her locker by mistake, thinking it was her son's. I put it down in my guest room and completely forgot where I'd put it. It's my age, you see." She chuckled, her eyes dancing with mirth. "But was in the neighborhood, so I thought I'd drop by and finally give this to you."

"Y-you're...n-not old."

The warmth in her smile went all the way to her eyes, and it felt like a warm hug. Other than Mrs. Wilkinson, no woman had ever looked at me like they cared, but Sharon did. She handed me a bag, and I peeked inside curiously.

"It's the bag you had with you at the hospital. I couldn't save the clothes you were wearing, as they were ruined." I shrugged, because I'd hardly had any clothing left on my body by the time Dahlia was done with me.

"T-thank you." I tried to smile, but it hurt. My emotions were a raging storm inside me, and I felt like a candle about to be snuffed out. Sometimes, just functioning was impossible, and today seemed to be one of those days. I needed to go before I said something that would upset her, and I didn't want to do that.

"Alright then." A look of concern washed over her face, but one of the things I liked about Sharon was that she didn't pry. She would listen if you needed her to, but never pushed, and I was so grateful for that. "Say hi to Jacob for me and try to have a good day, River."

She gave my arm a reassuring squeeze before carefully descending the steps and driving off. I stayed on the porch while her car disappeared down the street. A prickle of unease crept up my spine, the hairs on the back of my neck standing on end like someone was watching me. I glanced up and down the road, trying to pinpoint which car was the unmarked one, but it was pointless. I had no idea what I was looking for in the first place.

Letting out an exasperated breath, I kicked the door shut and locked it securely. Shadow trotted over to meet me before I could take another step, sniffing curiously at the bag in my hand. Carrying it into the kitchen, I set it down on the counter, avoiding the spilled tea, and turned my attention to the bag.

The bag was absolutely filthy and not worth saving,

which was a shame because I really liked it. The fabric reeked like a sewer, and I didn't even want to think about what might be clinging to the material. My chest tightened, and my heart pounded like a war drum as I rifled through the obvious pockets, praying nothing had been taken. Hidden inside the bag was something crucial—a USB stick I'd risked my life to get for Bane. I clung to the hope that it held enough evidence to finally bring Dahlia down, giving Bane the leverage he needed and me a shot at a peace I'd never dared to imagine.

I had long resigned myself to the idea that death was my only path to peace, but now, for the first time, I held something far greater within my fragile grasp—the promise of a future, of love. Reality stood between me and every one of my dreams. What I once dismissed as delusions, I now recognized for what they truly were: hope. I understood the difference now between a life resigned to despair and one fueled by the belief that dreams could become reality if I fought hard enough. This drive would hopefully tip the scales in our favor and help us win the war we—Bane—had been waging and finally end the suffering of thousands.

"Shit," I muttered under my breath, running my fingers along the inner seam of the bag, searching for the threads I'd carefully unpicked. My hands trembled as I rigorously searched for the hidey-hole I'd made. I felt a hard bulge under my fingertip and slowly traced it. A breath punched out of my chest, and a smile curved my lips. "Yes," I hissed, and slowly extracted the black rectangle from the inner lining of the bag.

"I can't believe it." My crazy plan had actually worked. I leapt off the stool, cheering as disbelief coursed through me. For once, something I'd set my mind to had succeeded. Joelle's voice echoed in my head, clear and reassuring. *You're capable of many amazing things, River.* The memory hit me hard, and I swallowed back a sob.

Tears blurred my vision as an unfamiliar emotion washed over me, overwhelming and impossible to name. Was this achievement? Pride? Whatever it was, it rooted me in place, making it hard to focus on what I needed to do next. Shaking it off, I slapped my hand across the granite countertop, searching for my phone. The moment my fingers found it, I dialed Bane's number without hesitation.

Each ring felt like an eternity, my nerves fraying more with every passing second. My confidence faltered, resolve crumbling as I prepared for disappointment. But just as I was about to hang up, his deep, gravelly voice came through the line.

"Angel?" He breathed a weary sigh. "Are you okay? I'm so sor—"

"I-I need you to come h-home. Now."

"River, what's wrong?" Something banged, and the echo down the phone made me freeze. I needed to reassure him quickly.

"N-nothing." I licked my suddenly dry lips and cleared the lump lodged in my tight throat. "Y-you remember when I said I w-went in search of her...f...for a reason?" I asked with a shaky voice.

"Yes, of course. You never told me what, though?" The hint of accusation in his tone made me wince, but I brushed it off. He was probably exhausted and stressed. All that pain and suffering was about to be worth it.

"W-well, I remembered you telling me about USB drives and t-that they stored i-important information."

"I did, yes." I could picture the confusion on his face as he pinched the bridge of his nose. "But what does that have to do—"

I didn't let him finish, knowing if I didn't get this out

now, I never would. Steeling my spine, I drew on every ounce of strength I possessed. "I-It's simple, really. After you talked to me about them, I remembered that D-Dahlia always carried a laptop and it had something that looked like the one you'd shown me so..."

"So you left me, put your life at risk, and nearly shattered my heart—all to get hers?" Bane's voice rose, thick with anguish. Each shuddering gasp revealed his pain.

"I-I'm s...sorry. I didn't..." I huffed out an anxious sigh. "I w-wouldn't..." I shook my head as tears pricked the back of my eyes.

"I'm sorry, angel. I...it just hurts so much. Every time I close my eyes, I see you lying in that bed. It reminds me of when..."

His words trailed off, but I knew exactly what he meant. It reminded him of his family and the day he lost them. "I'm sorry, I never meant—"

He interrupted me. "I know, angel." He swallowed audibly. "What did you—"

I cut in, sounding rather hysterical as I tried to regulate my chaotic emotions and relayed to him how Sharon had turned up with my bag. "I have it, Bane. Here in my hand. The one I pulled out of her laptop when..." I bit my lip, holding back my words. He didn't need me to rehash everything I'd gone through when she'd walked into the room. I never wanted to cause him pain, more than I already had.

The line was silent for a couple of beats, bar Bane's staccato inhalations. "Do you know what's on it?" he finally said.

"I don't have a clue, but it's got to have something incriminating on it, right?" I deflated like a burst balloon and sank to the floor. I pulled my knees up to my chest and wrapped my arm around them, needing support and comfort. Shadow appeared as if I'd summoned him and pushed his head under my arm. Just his presence eased my turmoil.

"I believe in you, angel." The dulcet tone of his voice soothed me. "And I think it might be the very thing we need to link everything together." I smiled so hard my face ached, even though tears still flowed down my cheeks. "I need you to put it somewhere safe until I get home, okay?"

"Yes." My voice trembled as much as the hand trying to hold my phone up to my ear.

He exhaled loudly. "I'm sorry I didn't make it home to you last night." His sincerity swelled my heart. "Once this case is over, I promise you things are going to change. You are the keeper of my heart. You are my sole priority, angel. I will do better for you."

"I-I...love you." The words tasted like levity and freedom. Hope.

"I love you too, River. But there's something I need to tell you, and I hate that I can't be there with you right now. It breaks my fucking heart. But you deserve to know. The raid was a failure. She knew, River. We definitely have a mole."

"D-Davis." I breathed life into the name and hoped it had the power to destroy him. "I said h-he was t-there..."

"Yes, you did, but Bower dismissed it when I spoke to him. Said he'd keep an eye on him because he couldn't believe someone he's gone through the academy with would betray him."

"He was the one who f-found me in the...w-warehouse and took me to her. I recognized his voice when he brought that guy over to the house to do the alarms," I choked out, feeling helpless. "I-I recognized him, but I'd never seen his face and assumed it was a coincidence, until..."

"I know. I know, River. I'm hoping he'll take me seriously now." Bane sighed, tired and weary, like the weight of the world rested on his shoulders. "I'm sorry for raising my voice at you. I just feel so damn frustrated right now. There's so much I need to tell you, but it's not the right time, the right place. I'll tell you the next time I see you."

Something in what he said felt off. I couldn't put my finger on it, but alarm bells rang in my head. He was always open and honest with me. But today, he was a vault, keeping something vital close to his chest.

"O-okay." I cuddled Shadow, needing him to be my mini Bane until I could be in his arms again.

"Keep yourself safe. Don't leave the house and keep Shadow close. We've had another lead, and I think this is going to be it angel. We're almost at the end." I gasped at the raw need in his voice. "I promise you, it's almost over. Just keep yourself safe for me and I'll explain everything when I get home."

"O-okay. I-I can do that."

"Good. Love you."

He hung up before I could tell him I loved him too. My eyes dropped to the USB in my hand. I knew exactly where to put it. The only person who would ever think to look there would be Bane, because he knew its secret.

My feet dragged as I climbed the stairs. Shadow bounced between my feet as I moved slower than molasses. I collapsed on my bed, emotionally wrecked, and picked up the wooden heart off the nightstand. It was a bit like a Rubik's Cube, made up of different coloured pieces of wood, each one with its own unique texture. But what you couldn't tell was that if you pressed certain pieces in the right order, it opened up and was just big enough to keep the USB safe until he got home. Wrung out, I pulled the covers over my trembling body and closed my eyes, praying the next time they opened, I would be wrapped in Bane's arms.

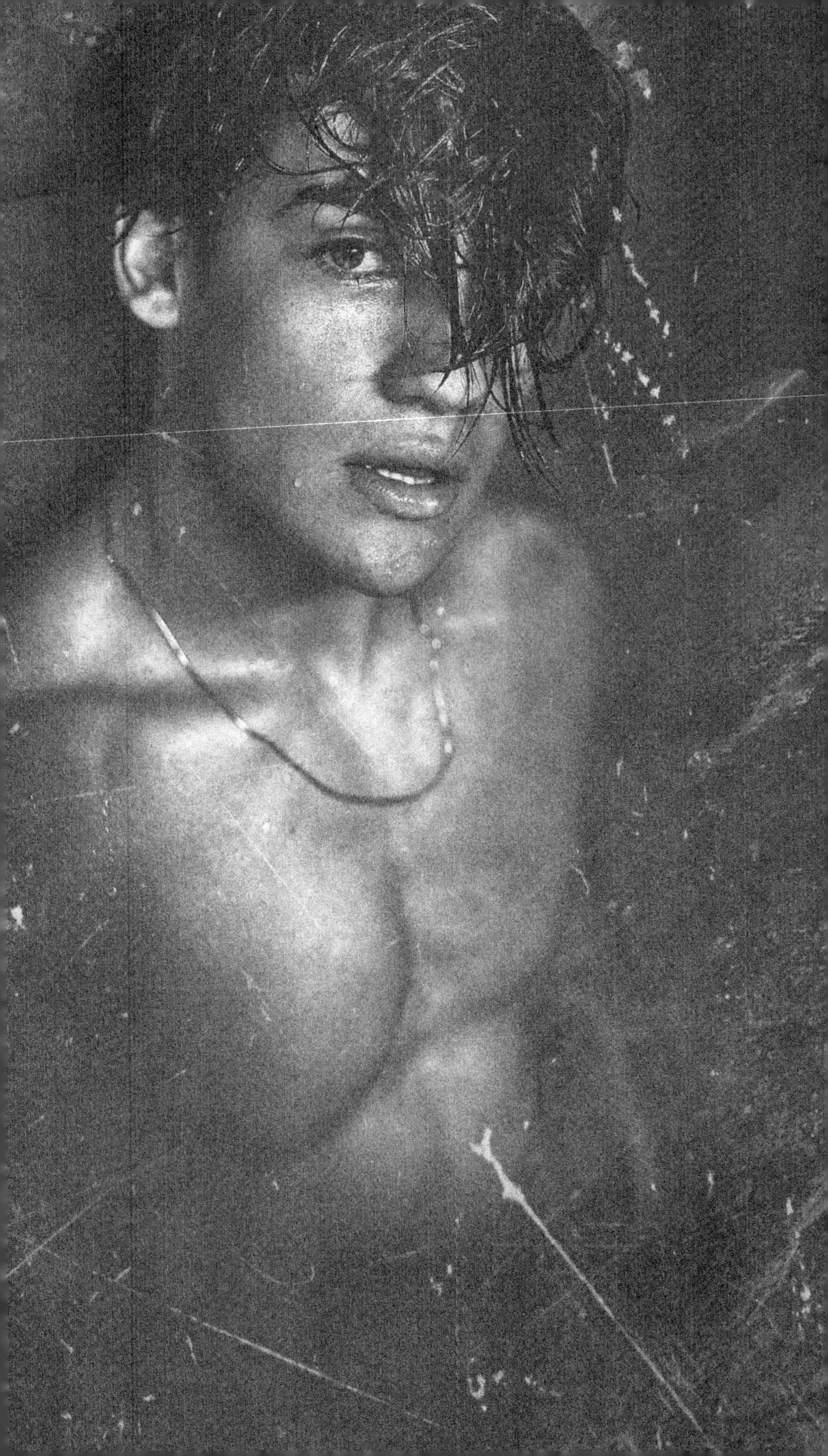

CHAPTER TWENTY-EIGHT
River

My eyes flew open, an indistinct emotion pulling me from unconsciousness. Ice cold air licked across my skin as the blankets were violently yanked off me. I tried to scream, but something leathery covered my mouth and pinched my nose. My eyes stung, and gut-curdling fear crawled all over my skin, turning the blood in my veins to ice.

A maniacal cackle had every muscle in my body locking up tight. My eyes darted from side to side as they slowly adjusted to the darkness. Night had fallen since I passed out, and with my blinds nearly closed, only a small amount of light seeped through them. The sound of blood thundering in my ears echoed the rapid beat of my heart, making it impossible to hear anything, but I could finally make out the three figures surrounding my bed.

The one immediately to my right had covered my mouth

with his gloved hand, and when I turned to look at him, recognition zinged through me like a ricocheting bullet.

"Hello, whore." He sneered and tilted his head to the side like a clockwork toy. It was creepy as fuck, especially when the other two mimicked his movements. The same unhinged, bloodthirsty look glinted in their eyes. There was no doubt about it. I was about to be dragged back down into the bowels of hell. Bile burned a path up the back of my throat. I'd never tasted fear in such an all-consuming soul-crushing way.

How did they find me?
How did they get in without triggering the alarm?
Did Bane know?
Was he on his way to save me?
Was he hurt?

God, I couldn't even face that thought. I screwed my eyes shut and felt myself go numb as the first tear broke through my lashes and carved a relentless path down my cheek.

Bane, please! Please help me, I screamed and pleaded in my head. I'd beg the universe if I had to, and sacrifice anything just to see him again. The Mitchell brothers had found me, and I knew what they were here to do.

This was it—the end of the road. The Mitchell brothers were about to cash in their promise with the devil. Dahlia had vowed she'd send them for me if I didn't comply. I guess she finally ran out of patience. Or this was a Hail Mary? Did she know Bane was closing in? Did she sense that life as she knew it was slipping through her fingers, about to be torn away? Maybe this was her parting shot, her final *fuck you*—ruining Bane's life by taking mine.

My worst fears were no longer whispers in the dark that haunted me. They were here, flesh and blood, unstoppable, and there was nothing I could do to fight them. For the first time in my life, I truly understood what it meant to be completely powerless.

There was nothing I could do to stop them when electrical tape sealed my mouth, trapping my screams. I was too weak when they wrenched my arms behind my back, binding my wrists and ankles with brutal efficiency. I couldn't fight back when I lay prone on our bed and a sickly sweet smell invaded my lungs, sharp and burning, making my vision tilt and my strength abandon me.

There was nothing left in me when I was thrown over their shoulders, my body limp and useless, my head cracking against a doorframe as they carried me through the house. The pain was like a bullet to my brain, making the world vanish behind a blinding white light. A hot gush of liquid slicked down my head, dulling the pain once the pressure eased. They slipped out the open back door on silent feet, unnoticed by the rest of the world. Not even the security light came on over the deck as they marched across the backyard under the cover of near darkness. The light of the moon hid behind the clouds like it was refusing to bear witness to the atrocities that were about to happen. They moved with a calculated efficiency that chilled me to the bone. Clearly, I didn't really know they were capable of.

I knew they were monsters who masqueraded as men, but I'd only glimpsed the depths of their depravity, even the times I'd thought I was at death's door. I guessed tonight their masks were going to come off, and I'd see who they really were. It was clear they didn't fear me being able to identify them, because everybody knew the dead couldn't talk.

They didn't make a sound until we passed through the wide-open back gate, now secured with a state-of-the-art biometric scanner and a brand-new lock. The system had been installed by the expert Bane hired to turn this house into a fortress. No one should have been able to breach these high walls—the very ones Bane had ensured were there to keep me safe. Yet, the Mitchells made a mockery of those efforts. Somehow, they had gained access undetected—a feat that should have been impossible. But clearly, it wasn't.

Shit, that would mean.... Davis wasn't the only snake Bane and Montoya had in their midst. It was too late to warn them. All I could do was hope they saw the truth before it was too late for them too.

"I'm out of here. If you get caught, I was never part of this. About a mile into the woods, there's an old quarry pit, if it's any use to you," a voice I recognized but couldn't place said nonchalantly.

Someone to my left—or at least I thought it was my left—scoffed. "We're not stupid enough to get caught. You, on the other hand, are a loose end we can't afford." No sooner had he finished talking, then the sound of two muted gunshots rang out into the night, followed by a loud thud as a body fell to the cold, hard ground. I'd know that sound anywhere.

"Carter, hide the body."

"On it."

"Help him, Eli, then the fun can really begin. This little whore is ours now."

Bile surged into my mouth, contained only by the tape. I tried to swallow it back down, but some seared its way up through my nostrils and trickled down my face.

I was about to die. I knew it with the same certainty I knew the sun would rise tomorrow. There was only one person I wanted—no, needed—to see before I took my last breath.

Bane.

It was the last thought that flowed through my mind

before I gave up fighting and succumbed to whatever drug was slowly coursing through my veins.

ONE MOMENT, I WAS CURLED UP ON THE COUCH WITH BANE'S hard body spooning me from behind, his hand draped around my waist, holding me close like I was the most precious thing in existence. The next, I was falling unceremoniously through the air and crashing into the frozen ground, smacking my already pounding head against a something hard as twigs and stones dug into my side.

Stars danced behind my eyes, and a scream tore from my chest, muffled by the tape covering my mouth. I jerked as hands grabbed hold of my hair and yanked my head back. A figure appeared in my line of vision, but the world swum around me, making it hard to focus. My face felt like it had been coated in gasoline as the tape was wrenched off my face, tearing the delicate skin off my lips.

"Open up, slut," the figure in front of me growled. The pressure on my scalp increased as he forced the blunt head of his dick between my bleeding lips.

Bane, I'm so sorry.

"That's it, you worthless whore. Take it. Take all of it." Without warning, he started to ruthlessly fuck my throat until my lungs screamed and all I could taste was a toxic combination of blood and piss.

Forgive me.

Never had I hated Joelle more than I did tonight. All the things she'd spent weeks teaching me did little to help me now. If anything, it made me more vulnerable, because I couldn't dissociate like I once could. I couldn't shut myself down, so I felt everything they did to me. I wanted to set my mind free and be with the boy with one eye as blue as the sky and the other like the darkest depths of the forest. With him, I was safe and free, surrounded by a dream-like world filled with possibilities.

But that safety net had been stolen from me in the name of helping me heal. With tears streaming down my face, I was forced onto all fours. Twigs and stone cut into my skin, but it had nothing on the pain ravaging my throat.

They ripped my sweats down my ass and sliced my hoodie off my back. The blade caught on every nodule of my spine as it went, and I mourned the loss of my layer of protection when it fell off my skin like water off a duck's back.

My head was floating the longer I was starved of oxygen. My lungs burned like an icy inferno as I was pushed to my limits.

Something solid and cold dragged down my spine. I could feel every rough splintered edge as it dug into my skin, slicing it until warm blood trickled down my sides. The burning pressure at my entrance stole the last of my strength, and the world went black.

I'll never be worthy of you now. I never was. You were always too good to be mine.

COLD WATER HIT MY FACE, FORCING MY HEAVY-LIDDED EYES open. Not that I could see anything. But I could feel every-fucking-thing. The rope that burned around my neck, the fibres chafing against my skin. The feel of the bark slicing against my back with every forceful thrust that stole the air from my lungs. The bite of something sharp around my wrists as it cut into my skin until I bled, and the ache in my shoulders from holding my body weight.

"Fuck you," a voice growled before pain exploded in my temple.

"This is the best fucking feeling ever."

The voice sounded like it was miles away. Everything hurt. My fingers wouldn't move, and I couldn't feel my legs. I wasn't even sure if I was breathing.

The steady beat of my heart was absent. There was just the occasional buh-bump, but it felt like minutes passed between the faint sound. I was so cold. So, so cold.

"What should we do with the..."

Voices faded in and out, just like the wind.

Don't give up.

"Leave it..."

"No one will find it..."

It's too late. I'm sorry I wasn't strong enough, Bane.

"Time to go."

If I had to do this all over again, I wouldn't change a thing because I got to meet you.

I love you, my heart. Please forgive me.

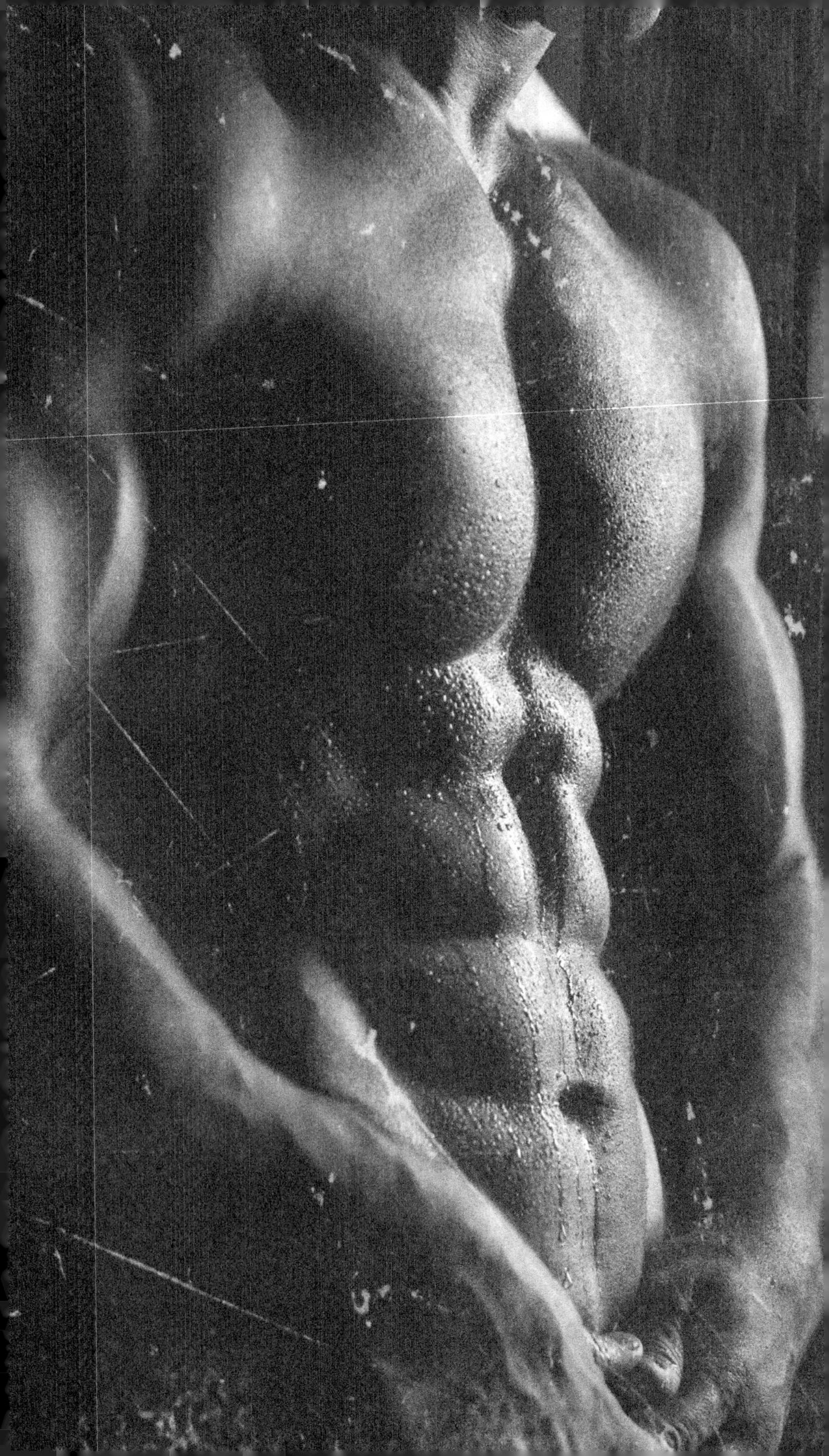

CHAPTER TWENTY-NINE
Bane

"Benson?!" Montoya burst through the door to the changing room like a bull in a china shop. "Get up and come with me. We've got a," she glanced around the room and lowered her voice, "visitor."

"Now?" Marco, our informant, was the last person I expected to see this morning, especially after last night's epic disaster. I looked at her in confusion, but pushed my sorry ass up and dragged myself over to her.

"Yes, he said you wouldn't want to miss this."

"I'll just bet he did," I muttered as I followed her through the station and out the back entrance to the parking lot.

We both checked the coast was clear and moved swiftly across the blacktop through the tree line that separated the station grounds from one of Holm Oaks rolling parks. "Did he tell you anything else?"

"Nope, but he said he wanted to go into protective custody."

I snorted. "I'm sure that can be arranged."

It just won't be the type he's expecting. There will be no twenty-four-seven guard or relocation to another state for this moron. I know Bower doubts his authenticity, but Marco doesn't have two brain cells to rub together. The only thing he cares about is coming out on top, and he thinks his deal with us will provide him with that. I can't wait for reality to slap him over the head.

"There he is." Montoya pointed to the lone figure sitting under the large weeping willow on a partially hidden park bench. "Should we bring him in after this, give him just enough to think he's safe, then book him?"

"I love the way your mind works." She turned a beaming smile my way. I was grateful for this moment of levity and prayed that whatever Marco was about to divulge, along with that goddamn USB drive River risked his life for, gives us enough to lock this case down. Then I can hand in my badge and start over somewhere with River.

"Marco." Montoya leaned against the back of the bench, facing me. To the casual observer, it looked like we were just chatting and had nothing to do with the guy in a puffer coat with his hood pulled up.

She was more than capable of handling this meeting on her own, but we were partners, and I'd never put her in a position of going out without backup. You could never be too careful in our line of work, especially when it came to informants and turncoats. If they were willing to betray the people they were meant to be loyal to, then they wouldn't have any qualms fucking us over either.

"What have you got for us?"

Marco shuffled on his seat and stuck his hand in his jacket pocket. I tensed, my hand circling my gun, poised to draw it at a moment's notice if it was required. "I know where she is and why you haven't been able to find her."

"How?" I bit out, tension rolling through the muscles in my arms.

"You've got a leak, a big one. The guy has been on her payroll for years. And there are others that will surprise you." He pulled a rolled-up magazine out of his pocket, opened it, then dropped it in the trash can next to him. "Names and locations are in there."

Montoya pulled some gum from her pocket, popped it in her mouth, and stepped over the bin. After casting a covert glance around, she lifted the magazine and tucked it under her arm before sauntering over to the edge of the lake bordering the park.

"If this comes through, we'll get things sorted for you. Until then, sit tight."

Marco scoffed and muttered under his breath before stalking off in the opposite direction. I stayed where I was and kept an eye on the few people walking around the park this early in the morning. When I didn't spot any suspicious activity, I whistled the tune to I Ain't Worried by OneRepublic and strolled back to the station, knowing Montoya was hot on my heels.

Once we made it back to the lot, I pulled the squad keys out and unlocked it. Once we were inside, I turned to Montoya. "So?"

She tipped her head back on her shoulders and looked at the roof, her fingers playing with the pages of the magazine. "He knows Davis is our leak." My eyes bugged out of my head in shock. A small smile flickered at the corners of her lips. "He also knows where Dahlia is, and you're not going to like it. If we take this to Bower, he's going to blow up."

"Why?"

"Because this goes all the way to the top. It's the perfect cover. She's a genius, really."

I shook my head. "Where is she?"

"She's staying at the mayor's log cabin in Lost River, about two hours away up in the mountains."

Completely dumbfounded by that revelation, we headed back into the station, straight to Bower's office to bring him up to speed and put in the groundwork to make sure the information was accurate before we put a plan into place. True to form, Bower's rage was incandescent. I was certain his bellows could be felt through the station as the foundations shook.

"The fucking mayor? Are you serious?! We need to make sure this is air tight, because if we do this and it's wrong, none of us will ever be able to get employment again."

It took three hours of digging and a call to a former colleague who had left the force a few years ago to start his own security firm—one that operated free from the constraints we were bound by. I chose to overlook the likelihood that he was skirting the law, focusing instead on the bigger picture. This was about more than rules; it was about the greater good. We were on a mission to bring down Black Dahlia and save thousands of lives.

"It's accurate. Thermal images show she's there with three guards. I like those odds."

"Thermal?" Bower raised a questioning brow, but I shook my head. He didn't need to know how I got them, only that they confirmed what we needed to know. "Alright then, we keep this between us. No one else can know. It pains me to say that you two are the only ones I fully trust at the moment. Plus, if we keep this one small, we should be able to slip out unnoticed and be back before anyone works out we're gone."

We were all in agreement and spent the next few hours

prepping for our trip to Lost River. Luckily for us, my friend also pulled the true blueprints for the property because the ones that had been registered with building control were extremely inaccurate. Bower would work out how to handle the mayor, as that was an issue for another day. Today, we were wholly focused on taking Black Dahlia out at the knees and making sure she would never rise again.

"Remind me again why we're in this heap of junk." I moaned as my knees crashed into the dashboard of Montoya's truck. The damn thing was ready to be scrapped. I'd had to fold into myself so much, my knees were up by my ears.

"Stop whining. You sound like an old man."

An ear-piercing alarm rendered through the air, freezing the air in my lungs. "No! No, no, no, no." My hands shook as I tried to get my phone out of my pocket, but it was almost impossible at this angle. "Fuck, no. This can't be happening," I growled and yanked at the fucking thing stuck in my pocket.

Montoya cast a wary glance my way as she struggled to keep her eyes on the road. We were halfway to Lost River, about an hour away from home. We were in the middle of nowhere, and I had no means of getting back to Holme Oaks any time soon.

"What's going on?"

I ignored her and flicked through the apps on my phone, pulling up the one I needed and prayed to every god in heaven and hell that existed that this was just a misunderstanding. False hope was a poisonous thing, because I felt the wrongness of this in the marrow of my bones.

"Stop the car," I barked and threw open the door before the wheels had even stopped turning, dropping to my knees on the grass verge and emptying the contents of my stomach.

I felt Montoya at my back. She was wisely giving me space, which I was endlessly grateful for. "What's going on, Benson?"

"I-it's River." I wiped my mouth with the back of my hand, removing any traces of vomit. There was nothing I could do about the stench or the taste. "He's left the house and gone beyond the perimeter boundary. His location shows he's at the quarry pit in the forest behind my house and has been there for over thirty minutes." I threw my hands up in frustration, fear licking at the edges of my mind. "He knew not to leave. He wouldn't do that again. He knew the risks...he wouldn't. He wouldn't..."

"Okay?" The look of confusion on her face was my undoing. The icy fear turned to fire as my anger flared white hot.

"He knows not to leave the house." I was aware I was repeating myself like a stuck record. The same thought repeating again and again, as if it would change the outcome. Stupid, so damn stupid, but there was no place for reason now. "He knows Dahlia has been murdering his friends. She threatened to kill him if he didn't stop this investigation. He stole something from her that could potentially provide enough evidence to make our case ironclad. Beyond irrefutable-fucking-doubt kind of guarantee."

"What does he have?" Her perfectly arched brow lifted, her inquisitive nature shining in her eyes as she regarded me, unsure if she should intervene or let me have a full on breakdown.

"He took the USB from her laptop." Her eyes glazed over as she processed what I had just said while I glared at the red dot on my phone, willing it to move. Something it didn't, and hadn't done in the last thirty-five minutes. Fuck!

"So when he was—"

"Yup."

"He went to her?"

"He did, in a roundabout way." I dragged my hand down my face, trying to work out what to do.

How did I get from here to there with no transport? Trepidation thrummed in my veins. Every solution that popped into my head fizzled out instantly. My mental capacity was shot. I was fucking inadequate. A failure.

I promised him again. And again, I'd failed him. I'd never forgive myself if he was hurt. I'd told him he was more important to me than my work—than this case—but how had I shown him that by being there for him? Hell to the no. No, I'd gone to work and not left for close to thirty hours. River deserved love, and he deserved someone who did what they said they were going to do. Not someone like me who fed him pretty lies. The lies we believed could destroy us, and I was terrified mine were about to do just that.

"For you?" Montoya eventually asked, snapping me out of my mental collapse.

"So he said."

"Oh my god, that all makes sense now," she said with a touch of wondrous awe in her voice. "Stay here. I'm going to call Bower. He shouldn't be far behind us. He can come with me, and you can take his truck and get back there, stat!"

I didn't possess the wherewithal to thank her for stepping up and taking over. Her ability to think logically could be the difference between life and death. Fuck! I hope that wasn't the case, but... *Nope, don't even go there, Bane!*

Forty minutes, a heated argument with Bower, and a bellowed "Fuck off! River's more important than any case!" while I liberated his truck later, I was tearing down the road, sirens wailing and lights flashing, as if clearing the way could silence the panic pounding in my chest. Ignoring speed limits, I pushed Bower's truck to devour the miles of blacktop separating me from the one person who made my heart beat. Taking the corner onto my street, I drifted into a wide arc at double the safe speed, the urgency in my veins growing stronger with every eerie, passing second.

The violent tremors rolling down my arms and legs weren't fear—they were pure chemical overload. My body didn't know how to process the chaos, but it harnessed the energy, fueling me for however long it took to reach River and make sure he was okay.

The tires hit the curb with a bone-jarring jolt, launching the truck into the air before it slammed back down onto my driveway, skidding to a halt. I flung the door open and vaulted out so quickly my legs buckled beneath me. My hand shot out, grabbing the doorframe just in time to stop myself from hitting the pavement. My stomach churned violently, like I was a ship caught in a relentless storm, the taste of vomit an ever-present reminder of my dire situation.

"Fuck," I gritted out when I realized I'd dropped my phone. It should have been easy to find under the security light that should have come on when I pulled into the driveway, but it was pitch black, almost like someone had cut the wiring to the house. I glanced around, noticing the blanket of darkness covering the entire street. Things were going from bad to worse. I couldn't see a damn thing.

"There you are." I breathed a sigh of relief when a notification of some kind lit up my screen so I could find it. Flicking the ad away, I tracked River's location. It had moved, but not far. Not enough. Alarm bells rang in my head.

Trusting my instincts, I called the local ambulance station and got Sharon's husband, John, on the line. I gave him the lowdown on the situation as I raced across the backyard, out through the gate that should have been impossible to open, and broke through the tree line into the woods beyond. Branches smacked me in the face, but I didn't feel them. I felt like I could walk through fire, and it wouldn't touch me. With only the app and the torch on my phone to guide me, I ran like the wild hunt was chasing me.

"Drop Sharon your location, Jacob. She's visiting a friend just around the corner. She'll come help you until we get there. Stay calm and look at everything—"

"Fucking stay calm?!" I bellowed and cut him off. How the fuck could I? Distracted by sending Sharon my location, I lost sight of where I was going for a split second. Ow! I tripped over something that took my legs out from underneath me. My momentum propelled me into the air before I could react.

Luckily, I managed to tuck and roll without injuring myself because if I had, I would have torn the heavens from the sky in my anger if anything had dared to stop me from finding River. The existential dread suffocating me grew stronger every second he wasn't in my sight. I turned my phone in the direction I'd come and found a poorly obscured body. This wasn't a good sign. What the hell had happened here tonight? I dusted myself off and quickly checked them over, horrified by what I saw until it registered who it was. Two bullet wounds, one to the head, the other to the chest. There was no way Davis could have survived that.

"Karma is having a hell of a day," I growled. "Because if she hadn't killed you, I would have. If you're the reason River is hurt, I will find you and make you pay, Davis." I shook my head and pumped my clenched fist. "Death is too fucking easy for you, you fucking piece of shit. You got what you deserved. Enjoy hell."

With one last dismissive look at Davis's body, I started running. I knew I should have called it in, but I had somewhere far more important to be, with someone who held my life in their hands. It was almost impossible to navigate my way through the wild and untamed woods, but they blurred as my vision tunneled, like I was looking through the sight of a gun, focused on the red dot on my screen.

My heart felt like it had detached itself and was furiously fighting its way up my throat, choking me every time I tried to breathe. Air in my lungs didn't matter, neither did the shallow cuts that littered my face and arms from thorny brambles that hung like coiled snakes. My legs burned as lactic acid built in the straining muscles. Blood coated my tongue where my teeth sunk into as I pushed myself beyond my capabilities.

I burst through a dense patch of shrubs, their tangled branches clawing at my legs and sweeping them out from under me. I hit the ground hard, knees slamming into the damp earth, as my phone skidded away, coming to rest against a large stone. Its faint glow illuminated the decaying trunk of a fallen tree ahead. My fractured mind struggled to process what I was seeing.

"RIVER!" I screamed, my voice raw as I clawed at the slick ground, scrambling to my feet. Dirt and debris clung to me as I launched myself toward him, my breath coming in ragged gasps.

"River? Can you hear me?" I collapsed beside him, trembling hands reaching to cradle his bloodied cheek. My emotions surged uncontrollably, a tidal wave I couldn't hold back. Hot tears spilled freely from my aching eyes, blurring the awful reality before me. My mind rebelled, screaming that this wasn't real. It couldn't be real. This had to be a nightmare, a cruel fantasy. Not him. Not like this.

"I'm here, angel," I sobbed, the words catching painfully

in my throat. "I'm here now." A hundred apologies crowded my mind, but they stuck to my tongue, choking me. *I'm sorry. I'm so fucking sorry, baby.* The words tasted like failure and grief. *Forgive me. I love you. I can't live without you.*

His eyelid fluttered weakly, revealing a single bloodshot forest-green eye that blinked up at me. But it wasn't looking at me—it was as though he was staring through me, the vibrant light that once filled it dimming by the second. His bloodied fingers twitched feebly at his side. Instinctively, my hand found his, drawn to him like a magnet. I wrapped my fingers around his and brought his hand to my lips, brushing desperate, trembling kisses over the broken skin of his.

"Y... y-you are my s-seven minutes," he whispered, blood painting his lips. His hand slipped from mine, fingers falling lifeless and limp against his side. One eye rolled back in his head while the other, swollen and black, remained shut.

"Riv?" The word tore from me, raw and broken. "RIVER?" My voice cracked into a garbled scream, shredding the remnants of my heart. "Come back to me! Please. Please, baby, don't leave me. I n-need you." I pressed my trembling lips to his, the taste of him—metallic and familiar—searing into my soul.

The world dimmed, collapsing inward until there was only him. Tears burned hot as they carved rivers down my cheeks, every drop a fragment of hell. With a ragged breath, I raised my shaking fingers to his throat, desperately seeking the faint echo of a pulse. *Don't leave me. Please, not now.*

We'd just begun, just started becoming *more*. I knew it was selfish, but I couldn't live without him. He was the air in my lungs, the beat of my heart. He'd fought so hard, so long, when anyone else would have let go. He'd clawed his way through every storm and now, when he was finally mine, the world wanted to take him away.

How I hated the world and every goddamn soul in it.

"Where are you?" I screamed into the night, my voice hoarse and desperate. For the first time, I understood why people cursed the emergency services. They were always too slow. Every second dragged like an eternity. Every moment they weren't here brought him closer to slipping away. His blood clung to my hands, sticky and cooling, leaking endlessly from wounds I couldn't close.

I didn't know how much time had passed; minutes, hours, a lifetime. Color drained from everything. I couldn't even fathom if the sun would rise tomorrow. If he didn't make it, there would be no dawn, only an endless night until I followed him into the void.

"Benson? Jacob!"

A hand landed on my shoulder, jolting me. I flinched violently, a low growl rumbling in my chest as I shielded River's limp body. My head snapped up, wild and unseeing, until Sharon's face came into focus. She knelt beside me, her eyes soft with empathy and laced with the same pain I felt.

"Let them help him," she murmured, her voice steady but urgent.

Sharon liked River. She'd said once that he was good for me, that I was better with him in my life. But now, her expression gave everything away—the tightness in her jaw, the pinched lines around her eyes. She didn't think he had much time left.

Time. The one thing we all believed was endless—until it wasn't. It slipped past us, unnoticed, until the clock stopped ticking and we realized how much we'd wasted. How much we'd missed. I would never waste another second with him again. Not if I could help it. If only I had the chance.

"Let them do their jobs, Jacob," Sharon said gently, her voice cracking just enough to betray her own fear.

"You can come with us to the ER. I'll radio ahead and make sure they're ready at the doors," John said as he stepped up beside her.

His words didn't register at first. The thought of letting him go clawed at my chest. Unbearable. Impossible. An inhuman sound ripped from me, raw and primal, as I slowly loosened my grip. My hands shook as I eased back, letting them take him away. Letting him go.

The emptiness as they loaded him onto a stretcher and carried him away was all-consuming.

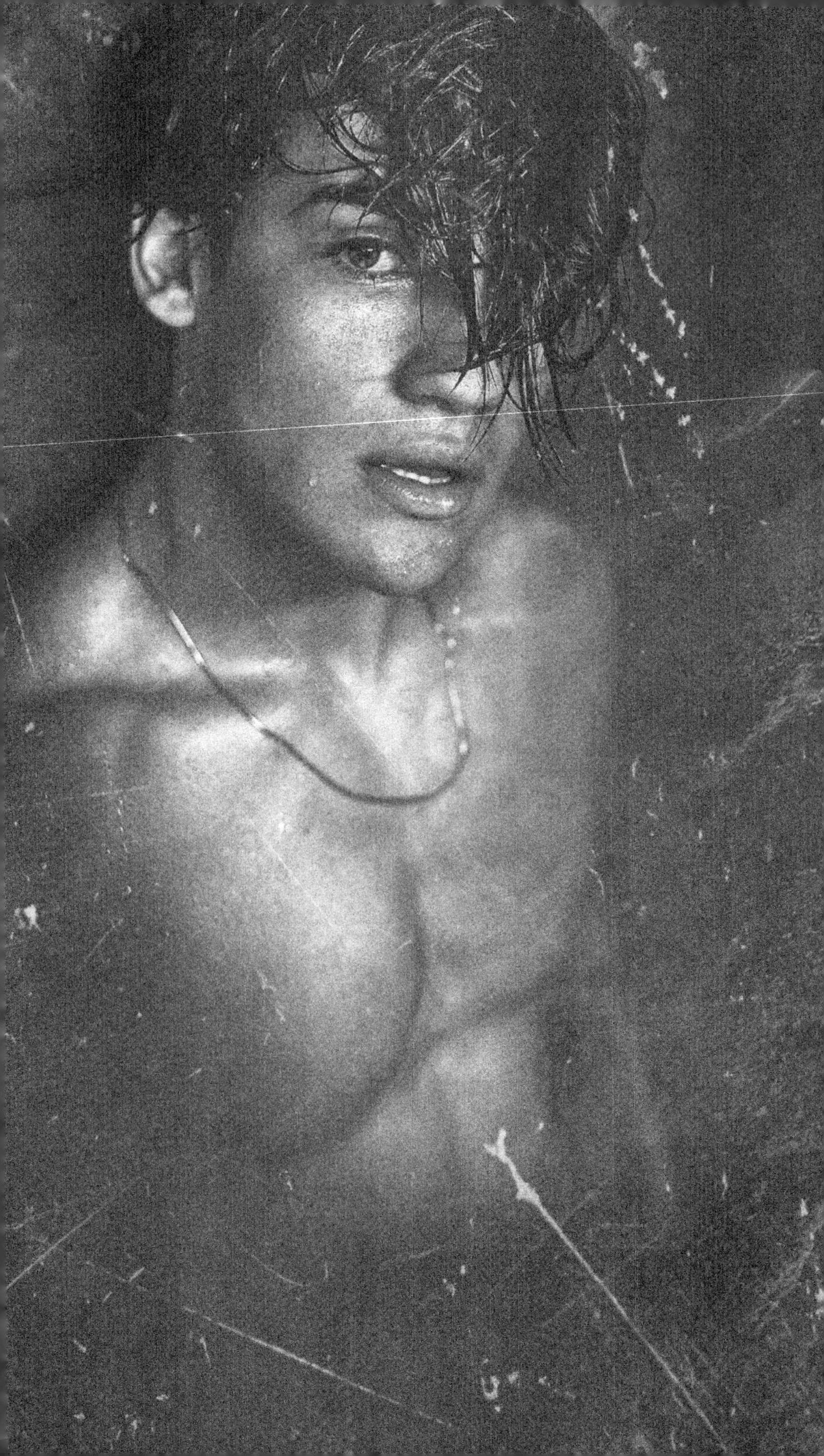

CHAPTER THIRTY
River

The tang of antiseptic, sharp and chemical, coating my tongue with every breath, pulled me from the drugging hold of sleep. The steady beep of a heart monitor pierced through the haze, its rhythmic sound reassuring, if not a little annoying. The soft hum of distant voices, the squeak of shoes on polished floors, added to the strange symphony confirming I was once again in the hospital.

My eyelid fluttered, heavy and reluctant, against the bright glare of light coming from above me. Blurred shapes slowly came into focus—the ceiling tiles, a bag hanging from a pole beside me. A large body folded over the bed, head resting on my thigh, hand tightly gripping mine like it was the only way to keep me here.

The sound of the door opening drew my attention as a young nurse walked in. The small smile on her face brightened when she saw I was awake. "How are you feeling, River? I'm Jenna, and I'll be looking after you today."

"Okay," I rasped and tapped my throat. My mouth was dry. I attempted to clear my throat, but it felt like I was trying to swallow sandpaper.

"Let me get you some water. It'll help with the swelling and hopefully make you a bit more comfortable." I tried to smile, but it hurt too much. Bane's soft snores rumbled against my hand, where his face was buried.

"He hasn't left your side since you were brought to the ward. He's a keeper," Jenna said.

My good eye rolled back in my head, agitation crawling under my skin at her words. I wanted to tell her to fuck off. That he was mine, and she could never have him, but I didn't know if that was true anymore.

I hated not knowing whether he would want to be with me after this. There was a difference between knowing what someone had been through and accepting it. A difference between seeing the evidence first hand and having to live through the lingering effects of it. I'd put him through so much already, and I was terrified this would be one step too far. There would be no blame if he decided being with me was too much hassle, that I was too much for him. It would hurt. It'd fucking gut me, but I'd understand. Most days, I couldn't stand myself, so I'd get it if that was what it came to.

There were a million questions dancing like fireflies in my head, but I locked them down. She wouldn't know the answers, anyway. Only the man asleep next to me would.

"I'll be back in a sec. I'll let the doctor know you're awake." She swept out of the room as quietly as she'd arrived. I savored the peace; it wouldn't be long until the circus arrived, and I'd had enough of people to last me a lifetime. The idea of living in a cabin in the woods was very appealing. But so was that eternal kind of sleep, the one you never woke from, where pain and suffering died as you did.

"Who was that?" Sleep coated Bane's worried voice as he blinked blearily up at me. "Ugh." He rubbed the back of his neck with his free hand, refusing to relinquish his hold on mine. He sat up slowly, rolling his shoulders in an attempt to get rid of the kinks from sleeping bent over the bed. "How had I forgotten how much it hurts to sleep like that? I'm not twenty anymore." He scoffed and shook his head.

A breathless chuckle caught in my throat, and I winced. Someone was cranky this morning, but nothing beat waking up to him next to me. Sadly, his presence did little to curb the spiraling fear coiling inside me and all the unanswered what ifs hanging around my neck like a noose.

"Stop, River." He pinned me with those hypnotic, mismatched eyes of his, and I felt like I was drowning in their depths. "I can see the cogs turning in your head so fast there's steam coming out of your ears." He wrapped his other hand around mine so it was cocooned by him. "I'm not going anywhere."

My answering smile was as brittle as I felt. The desire to believe him was overwhelming, but... there was always a but. Everything had been conditional in my life. If I did this, I'd get that. If I performed for a john, allowed him to beat and use me however he wanted, I'd get a hot meal. Simple little things at the time that have had a ripple like effect on my life. Even Bane's love had that "but" attached to it. I was his top priority, but first he had to close this case. I wasn't even sure if he'd realized that he had caveats dotted all over our relationship.

"Angel?" His large shoulders rose as he took a deep inhale, then shuddered and lowered as he let it out. "I'm sorry."

My good eye fell closed, and I turned away, not willing to

hear what he had to say. I could already see the shattered pieces of my heart bleeding across the off-white floor.

"River, please listen to me." He squeezed my hand to emphasize his words. "I'm sorry I wasn't there like I'd promised to be." His voice thickened as he kept talking. "I'm sorry I wasn't there to keep you safe and prevent you from getting hurt like I'd promised." A single tear fell and slid hotly down my cheek. "I'm sorry I promised you were my priority but focused on my job and the case before you. I'm sorry I made promises and didn't keep them. I'm sorry I let you down. I'm sorry I've failed you in every single way I promised you I wouldn't."

My teeth sunk into my bottom lip until the taste of copper exploded over my tongue. His heartfelt words felt like they were carving up my insides. I wanted to tell him it was alright, and that I understood. That I was a big enough person to see the bigger picture and the importance of the work he was doing. In a way, I could, but that was overshadowed by the crushing hurt his absence had caused, because if he had been at home, then would this have happened? Would I be here right now?

I was drowning in a suffocating agony that had me wanting to peel my skin off and sink into a vat of bleach to cleanse my ravaged soul. I had only just managed to start removing the touch of every man that came before Bane with the ever-growing physical part of our relationship. And I'd worked so hard with Joelle to work through my trauma and understand why I was the way I was. Why I said or didn't say the things I did and why I reacted to certain situations the way I did.

But now, every small step forward that felt like I'd crawled through a riptide to achieve was washed away, obliterated like it had never happened. I was once again a hollow shell, a skin-covered skeleton with nothing inside except an emptiness that suffocated every fleck of light, the outsider looking in on a life that could have been mine, and I didn't know how to process any of it. It was like my life had been ripped from my hands in the blink of an eye, and I'd woken up in an alternate reality where everything was the same, but different.

I was altered, and I didn't know if I could find my way back.

Hot, wet drops hit my hand. The feel of them on my cold skin was an echo of a memory I couldn't grasp. Glancing over at Bane and seeing the pain etched deeply into his face was a vise around my heart.

"Here you go, River," Jenna said and poured me a cool glass of water before setting the jug on the cabinet by the bed. "I even got you a straw to make it easier for you." She smiled sweetly as she handed it to me, then busied herself fiddling with the bags that hung on the IV pole.

The effort required to separate my hand from Bane's had been immense, but I needed some space to think and feel, to shore up my walls. Even though he'd said all the right things, I'd believed his perfect lies before, and I didn't want to be the fool that let history repeat itself.

"How's the pain, River?" Jenna glanced at me as she changed one of the hanging bags, her gaze intent and understanding. "Do you have a phone you can use if your throat is too sore to talk?"

Heat pricked the back of my eyes, but before I could answer, Bane spoke up and came to my rescue.

"I do, or I can grab him a pad and pen." He turns to me. "Whatever you'd prefer, angel." God, my heart couldn't take his sweetness, not when he blinked those wide puppy-like eyes at me. I held my hand out for his phone, and with a blinding smile, he set it in my hand.

> It's about a 7. My back is throbbing like a bitch and feels like it's stuck to the sheet, and my throat feels like it's closed up.

What I didn't tell her was that my head was pounding so badly the vision in my one good eye kept going black, and there was a high likelihood I was about to vomit everywhere. Sweat slicked my skin, and droplets dripped down the back of my neck.

"I'm not surprised. You've been through a lot. Dr. Miller is working his way up the ward. You should be next. I've just changed over your fluids and IV antibiotics. You're not due any more pain meds for a couple of hours, but I'll have a quick word with him and see if I can give you a top up after he's been to see you. Then you can get some rest." She turned to Bane. "You should go home, have something to eat, take a shower, maybe get some sleep. The doctor is going to want to have a sensitive conversation with River, so it might be best to give him some privacy."

"I'm not going anywhere," Bane bit out. He pushed the chair back and rose to his full intimidating height. "I'll be here right by River's side until he tells me he doesn't want me anymore," he leaned over the bed and eyed the tag on her uniform, "Jenna. If it's all the same with you."

Suitably chastised, Jenna shut her mouth with a snap, turned on her heel, and left the room. My head tipped back so I could look up at Bane, fighting the smile that wanted to lift my lips. I loved this possessive side of him, long may it continue.

> That wasn't very nice.

Looking down at the screen, Bane snorted. "She was trying to get rid of me." He shook his head and squeezed my hand, brushing his thumb over my knuckles. "I'm not leaving you, not again. Unless you order me away." I sucked in a sharp breath and welcomed the burning pain. "I want to be here to support you, no matter what the doctor wants to talk to you about. It's standard procedure for people who have gone through what you have."

> How do you know? How does that make you feel?

"What do you mean, angel?" He sighed and settled back into the chair after placing a reverent kiss on my forehead.

> To know that I was raped and beaten. Used and...

> I guess left for dead.

> But clearly those idiots didn't do that part right, because I'm here. Right?

Bane's eyes grew glassy. There was a hollowness in the shadows that haunted them. I wouldn't sugarcoat reality for him. If we were going to get through this, we had to face the truth in all its brutal rawness. I couldn't remember everything. I was certain they'd given me some type of drug that, coupled with the blows to the head I'd sustained, made my memory patchy. There were signs they'd violated me, like the dried cum between my cheeks, but most of it was a blur.

> I'll consent to anything if it means they finally get what's coming to them.

"They? You know who it was?" Bane said with a voraciousness that shocked me. He was normally so sweet and tender, a trait that seemed at odds with his bulging muscles and stature. I knew I was stereotyping him, but god, the things this man did to me.

> Yes. They taunted me about how good it would be to fuck me as I took my last breath and all the things they'd do to the body I left behind.

"You never told me." Hurt laced every word as Bane pulled his hand away from mine, folding his arms tightly over his chest. He leaned back in the chair, his expression sharp with accusation. "I thought you told me everything."

Tears welled in my good eye, and I tucked my chin against my chest, the tears spilling as I cried. Each sob felt like it was splitting me open, the pain radiating through my battered body, but not as much as the pain in my heart. I'd tried to protect, but in doing so, ended up hurting him more. By hiding the truth, I had betrayed the trust he'd so willingly offered me. Couldn't he see? I was a cancer, slowly killing him.

Summoning every last scrap of strength, I met Bane's beautifully broken eyes. His gaze was heavy with layers of pain and suffering—pain I had caused. "I...I'm sorry," I rasped. "I...I...w-was...tr...try...in...t-t..." My hand clutched my throat, a futile attempt to steady the broken pieces. "To...pr...pro...tect...y-you."

"Why, Riv? Why?" His voice cracked with anguish. "All I've ever wanted is to be here for you. To help you find yourself and heal. To fight back the monsters that haunt your dreams. To show you how loved you are."

He sniffed hard, trying to keep his composure, but I couldn't hold on any longer. My eyes fluttered shut as the room began spinning, tilting wildly, and a flashing white light drowned my vision. Waves of heat coursed through me, and my stomach churned violently, the nausea rising until it reached my throat. I retched, blindly reaching out for Bane, my last anchor.

"Shit! Riv, hang on." His chair scraped loudly across the floor as he sprang to his feet. My hand clamped uselessly over my mouth, trying to stop the inevitable. Vomit trickled through my fingers as Bane moved quickly. "Here." The rough texture of cardboard brushed under my chin just in time for another wave to erupt from my mouth.

Of course, it had to be right then that Dr. Miller walked into the room. He didn't miss a beat, though. He smoothly replaced whatever Bane had hastily shoved under my chin and administered anti-sickness medication. The violent tremors eased, and the searing light in my head dimmed as the doctor added a stronger painkiller to my rotation.

I looked at Bane, searching his reaction for the expected horror and disgust. Instead, all I found was unwavering support and understanding. He didn't flinch or falter. He questioned Dr. Miller at every step, advocating for me as I struggled to trust the medications and battled the paranoid fear that someone was trying to harm or poison me.

Dr. Miller confirmed I had needed multiple stitches to close the deep lacerations across my back and the tears to my rectum. He spoke about my treatment plan and how long they wanted to keep me under observation because of the nasty concussion I'd also received. Having more than one in such a short period of time meant I was more at risk of things going wrong, so they were paying close attention and I needed to answer honestly when questioned about my symptoms.

Once everything had calmed down and the storm in the room quieted, Dr. Miller perched on the edge of my bed. He explained the remaining exams they needed to perform and gently brought up the rape kit. If I consented, he said, they could share the results with the police to help ensure my attackers' conviction.

With Bane holding my hand, I lied as still as possible while swabs and samples were taken. When I asked, Dr. Miller confirmed that the stitches were dissolvable and would be gone within a couple of weeks. I'd suffered similar injuries before, but I'd never been treated with this kind of care.

Through it all, Bane never wavered. He stood beside me, unflinching in the face of cold, brutal facts. He didn't look at me with disgust or pity. Instead, he held me with his eyes full of love and empathy, anchoring me in a storm I might not have survived without him. By the time they left us to our own devices, the painkillers were finally starting to dull the pain, making me drowsy.

My good eye felt heavy and laden with sleep. Bane brushed my unruly hair off my forehead and brushed kisses to every part of my face he could reach. The semblance of a smile flickered at the corner of my lips. His soft, gentle touches were melting my insides, and the residual anger and resentment I'd been harbouring toward him lessened.

"Angel?" he whispered as my eye fluttered closed. The tension in my body eased as unconsciousness pulled me under. His hand wrapped around mine, his lips brushing over my knuckles as his hot breath ghosted over my skin. "You never told me who hurt you?"

His deep, gravelly voice echoed around my head. I couldn't be sure if he was really talking to me, or if I was dreaming. "The Mitchell brothers," I mumbled as I lost the fight to the drugs coursing through my system.

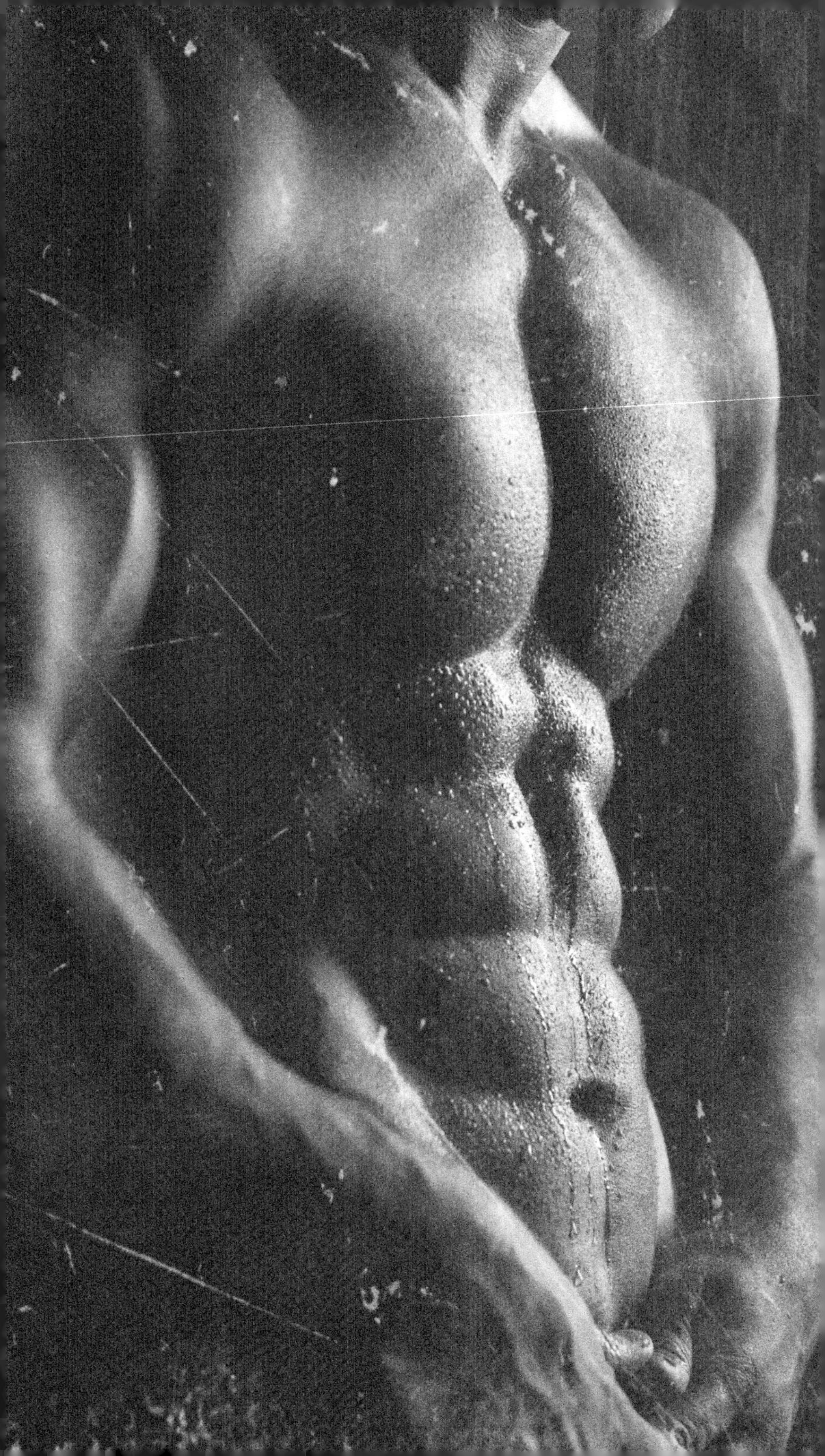

CHAPTER THIRTY-ONE
Bane

River was sleeping like the dead when the door clicked open. I took my gaze off him for a second to find Montoya in black jeans and a hoodie, striding toward me with two massive cups of coffee.

"How's he doing?" she asked softly and wrapped her arm around my shoulders, offering me some much-needed comfort. The last however many hours since I'd left her came rushing back to the forefront of my mind, and I shattered like a pane of glass.

Tears slicked my cheeks, and my body convulsed as pain and heartache swept me away. I'd come so close to losing him, all because I had my priorities in the wrong place. I'd learned my lesson, and things were going to change. It might cost me my job, but I had enough in savings and equity in my home to start over somewhere else. I wouldn't do anything without consulting River first, though.

"He's s-so fucking strong," I whimpered, my voice strained and raw. "I was t-too late…"

Montoya set the coffee cups down on the unit next to River's bed, grabbed an extra chair, and sat next to me, close enough so her shoulder butted up against mine. She shored me up physically and started picking up my fractured emotions. "You weren't too late, Jacob. He's still here because of you—"

"It never should have happened." My chest rumbled. Self-loathing was a vile cocktail to swallow. "I should have been there. If I had, he wouldn't be in here right now."

"He might not be. Or you both might be dead." She shrugged and handed me my coffee. "You don't know, because that wasn't the road that was travelled. There's no point in beating yourself up over what you can't change."

I scoffed. "When did you get so wise?"

She snickered. "I've been talking to Sharon a lot. Think she's rubbed off on me." Her hand rested over mine. "But in all seriousness, you can't keep beating yourself up. You need all your strength to focus on River. Fuck knows, he's going to need you now more than ever."

"If he doesn't hate me." I sighed and welcomed the rich, bitter liquid as it slid down my throat. Its welcomed warmth filtered through my body.

"He might be angry and hurt." I eyed her over the top of my cup. "He has every right. You promised him so much and…" She didn't need to finish that sentence, because I knew exactly where she was going with it. I'd spent every minute berating myself for the choices I'd made since I found him.

"That's going to change," I promised. "I've told River that too and apologized profusely. I can only hope he believes me and has enough faith in me to give us another chance. If he walks away, I don't know what I'll do."

"That boy thinks the world of you. I've never seen anyone look at you the way he does, the way he always has, even when you couldn't see it."

I let her words settle into my bones. I knew River loved me, but sometimes love wasn't enough. Actions spoke louder than words, and so far, mine had been the opposite of every word I'd said, every promise I'd made. But that stopped now.

"Do you know who did this to him?" she asked carefully.

"Yes. River said they were the Mitchell brothers. I don't know anything else about them but...actually." I turned to face Montoya. "Are you okay to sit with him for half an hour? I'm going to run home, shower, and grab the USB that's hopefully still hidden in the house. I'll bring my laptop back, and we can see what's on it once and for all."

"You don't have to ask. I'm assuming he's going to be out for a while?"

"Yeah, they upped the morphine as he was struggling so much with the pain." I brushed a kiss to the top of her head, and with a final longing glance at River's prone form, I slipped out of the room and headed home.

Not that this house felt like home anymore, not after everything that had happened here. It was a shock to the system to see police tape cordoning off my entire property, meaning I'd have to park on the street. But before I could, old Mrs. Burrows appeared on her porch and waved me over to hers.

"Thank you, Mrs. Burrows," I said and shut the door behind me. "It's been a hell of a time."

"I'm so, so sorry to hear what happened, Benson. How is the young boy doing?" I winced at her choice of words. River wasn't as young as he looked. "He's doing as well as can be expected under the circumstances. I won't be long; I'm just going to clean up, and then I'll be off."

She gave me a quick hug that almost had me breaking down again. After abandoning my car on her drive, I ducked under the tape and stepped into my house. It was just four walls filled with memories that had been tainted by everything that had happened. I'd never feel safe in here ever again, and I doubted River would either.

"We weren't expecting you, Benson," Daniel said when I stepped into the kitchen and put my keys on the counter.

"Oh, I came to have a quick shower and change. That's alright, isn't it?"

"Of course it is. They didn't go in your room, so as long as you're careful when you go up there, it won't interfere with my work."

"Great."

I'm showered, changed, and out of my room in ten minutes flat, not willing to linger in my own home. I crossed the hall into River's room, careful not to touch or disturb anything other than the item I came to collect. Bile lingered on the back of my tongue as I took in all the evidence markers that littered the floor, bed, and doorframe, where a bloody tuft of hair was caught between the splintered wood.

"Keep it together," I muttered to myself as I stepped over a marker next to a piece of cloth. If I had to make an educated guess, I'd say it was a soaked chloroform rag, or something of that ilk, and was used to either knock River out or disorientate him.

I had told him to put the USB drive somewhere safe, and there was only one place I could think he'd use—the beautifully crafted wooden heart I'd gifted him. If you didn't know what it was, you'd think it was just another quirky ornament, but I'd lay the outcome of this case on it being in there.

Careful not to leave any new prints, I snatched the heart up and tucked it into the bag I'd packed with some clothes and other essentials for River to use while he was in the hospital. By the time I made it downstairs, Daniel was working on the back door and the deck, going over every inch.

"Daniel?" I called out, and his head popped up from where he'd been kneeling on the decking. "The power was out for the whole street when they took River, but I believe a few of my neighbors have battery backup for their security cameras. Do you think you could get them checked to see if we've caught these fuckers' faces, in case they come for River again while he's in the hospital?"

He swept his hair back off his face, looking slightly flushed. "Of course. I'll get Anne on it when she's back from lunch."

"Thanks. Keep me updated if you find anything." I waved him off, grabbed my laptop from its hiding place down the side of the couch, and got back into my car.

By the time I'd parked at the hospital, an idea was crawling around inside my head like an earworm I couldn't catch. There were pieces of this puzzle that fitted together, but I wasn't able to find the right placement. I hoped once Montoya and I had gone through whatever was on the USB, that things would be clearer. Keeping River safe was the only thing I could focus on right now, and if I knew twisted individuals like I thought I did, there was a countdown running until they tried to come for him again.

The Mitchell brothers clearly had no issues or conscience when it came to killing. They were far too cavalier with Davis's body for this to be the first murder they'd ever committed. River's words from earlier echoed through my mind.

They taunted me about how good it would be to fuck me as I took my last breath and all the things they'd do to the body I left behind.

How long had he lived with that threat hanging over him? If Dahlia knew the Mitchells wanted to do this to him, why did it take so long? Was she using them for something? Did she have leverage on them?

I didn't know why anyone would want to hurt that beautiful boy. The more time I spent as an officer of the law, the more I learned about the depravities of human nature. The world was full of sick fucks, and I hated I was a part of it.

Jordan stood guard outside River's room and greeted me with a small smile when I stepped off the elevator. I breezed inside, closing the door behind me. "When did he get here?" I asked Montoya as I settled into my vacated chair. I handed her my laptop before searching my bag for the wooden puzzle heart.

"Bower sent him over after I told him you'd left."

"Ah." Guilt lanced through me when I realized I hadn't enquired how things went after I abandoned them on the way to Lost River. "I'm sorry, I—"

"I'm going to stop you right there." I huffed a breath as I poked at the heart, trying to remember the right sequence to open the damn thing. "You did the right thing, so don't you go feeling guilty for abandoning us, because you didn't. You went where you were really needed."

I snorted at her casual dismissal of me walking out of an operation, but who was I to argue with a woman's logic? "Alright, but how did it go?"

A brilliant smile lit up her face. "As luck would have it, your friend or whatever he is, Boston?" A flush stained her cheeks, and I hid a smirk behind my hand. "Where was I? Oh yeah, your friend Boston had been monitoring the property. When he noticed you didn't arrive with us, he helped out."

"He did, did he?" Her flush darkened, and she refused to look at me as she turned my laptop on and did everything possible to ignore me. "That's all he did?" I nudged her shoulder, but she focused on the collection of photos that made up my screensaver. "So, do you have her in custody?"

"Fuck yes, we do. Boston has some skills!" she said with a level of appreciation I'd never seen in her before. "She's on a seventy-two hour hold while we secure the evidence to officially charge her. Bower is already getting heat from the mayor, so we need to find something that will stick like shit. Otherwise, she'll walk, and half our department will be dragged into an investigation, if the Mayor's threats are anything to go by."

I glanced over at River, who was still sleeping somewhat peacefully, the little furrow between his brows the only indicator that he was still in pain, even in sleep. I didn't want to break my promises to him, but with the high possibility his life was still in danger, I had to do everything I could to protect him. "Got it!" Cautious excitement flowed through me as I extracted the USB from the heart and handed it off to Montoya while I stowed the heart back in my bag. Maybe one day I could use it to hide something much more precious for River to find, something he'd wear for the rest of his life.

That thought sparked in my heart as it took root. One day, when we settled somewhere new and recent events were nothing but a distant memory, I'd make River mine in every way humanly possible. It'd tie his soul to mine, so no matter how many lifetimes we lived, we'd always find our way back to each other.

"Pass it over. Let me log in and see what we've got."

"I hope River was right about this," Montoya murmured as I located the drive and opened it up. "Holy fuck. That's... that's..." Hearing her at a loss for words for the first time since we'd met floored me.

River hadn't been wrong—not at all. My chest swelled

with pride for him, for everything he'd sacrificed just to save others from the fate he'd endured for years. Any anger I'd clung to about him running and putting himself in danger melted away. I was in awe of him. Hundreds of meticulously organized files loaded onto my laptop. We had struck gold. Dahlia, or Christine Hamilton, as she had been known to many of the elite, kept details on everything and everyone she'd ever crossed paths with.

We had details of all the individuals on her payroll, from their basic details to where they lived and what part of her operation they worked for. Anything that could be used to incriminate and blackmail them, and details of their families, too. She had records of all the sex workers and slaves and where they worked. Addresses and details on associates and anyone who used her services. Davis was in there, and so was the mayor.

I was riding high when I called Bower and told him what we'd secured. He asked that I send it through to his encrypted server and confirmed he'd liaise with the alphabet agencies to coordinate a cross-country crackdown to take out the biggest players. He was overjoyed at what we'd been able to achieve in the last few days and reluctantly thanked us for all our hard work.

There was one bit of information I kept to myself, and that was the identities of Carter, Eli, and Killian Mitchell. We needed to tread carefully where they were concerned, because it had become apparent that Davis wasn't our only mole. I refused to risk River's safety when he was still in such a vulnerable position. I snapped a photo of them with my burner phone and stepped out of the room to talk with Jordan. He was already up to speed on what had gone down and was eager to prove himself.

"Take this with you and go to the security office. Review all the CCTV footage for the last twenty-four hours and see if these three crop up at all. Might be worth putting an alert out on them too, because when they step foot in this hospital, I want to take them down before they get on River's floor. Got it?"

"No problem. We'll make sure they don't get within a hundred feet of him." He slapped me on the back before marching down the corridor to the security office. My brain churned with a plan to make sure we caught them trying to clear up the mess they left behind.

My heart thundered in my chest, and my blood zinged through my veins. The end to all this shit was within touching distance. There was just one more loose end to tie up, then I'd be able to give the beautiful broke boy who owned my heart the happily ever after he deserved.

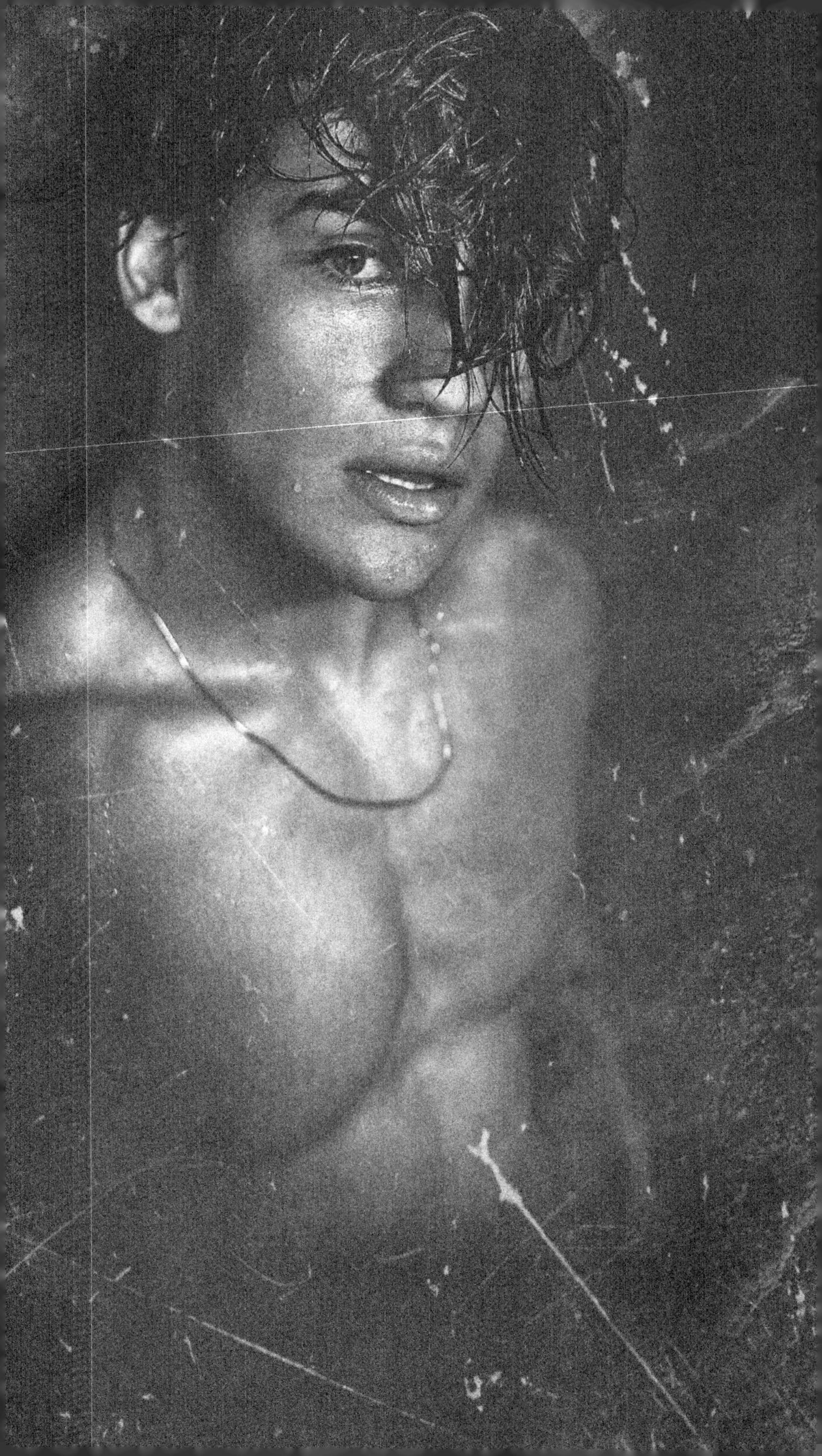

CHAPTER THIRTY-TWO
River

I woke up with a silent scream clawing its way up my throat, disorientated and terrified. Once my breathing was under control and I remembered where I was, I blinked my good eye open and found Bane and Montoya watching over me like sentinels guarding the gates of hell.

Bane gently cupped my face, his thumbs sweeping away the torrent of salty tears spilling down my cheek. His deep voice whispered soothing platitudes that calmed my ravaged soul. His plush lips pressed kisses across my face until I was shivering from the sweet intensity of his singularly focused affection.

"Can I kiss you?"

I snorted through my snotty nose and tipped my head to the side as I regarded him. Hadn't he been doing exactly that?

"You know what I mean, angel. A proper kiss." He

sighed, his hot breath ghosting over my dry lips. "It's been too long since I've tasted you, River..."

My tongue darted out and wet my lips, and his eyes hungrily tracking the motion. My body responded to his proximity, and my heart ached. Was I ready to reconnect with him this way? My head said no, but my heart and body were on a whole other page.

"Please don't overthink this, baby. I love you." He rested his forehead against mine, the move sending shockwaves of electricity through me. "Yes, I fucked up, and I probably will again, but there is nothing more I want in this world or any lifetime that is to come than you. I think it's always been you, angel, even when I didn't know what a love like this felt like. Even when I fought the way my heart ached and my body begged for you. There is nothing without you."

Fuck me. His sweet words and silver tongue weaved a spell over me that I didn't want to fight. I could spend days wallowing in the pain of betrayal or stoking the anger his broken promises made me feel, but I wasn't certain that was what I really needed. I wanted to drown in him. My safe harbor. My heart. My everything.

My right hand surged forward, circling his neck as I pulled him closer. Bane's lips sealed over mine and it felt like coming home. His tongue licked and teased across the seam of my lips, begging for entry. My lips parted, and his tongue surged forward and wrapped around mine. I sighed as his taste exploded across my tongue.

A groan rumbled in his chest as he took control and nipped my lips before sucking on my tongue. I reveled in the light teasing he gave me before he fucked into my mouth and owned me. The blood in my veins turned to quicksilver, and Bane stole the air from my lungs so he could sustain himself. We lost ourselves in each other, a perfect symbiotic relationship.

The world around us faded away until there was nothing but a single pinprick of light left, just us and the lust burning between us. I didn't think I'd feel like this ever again after what the Mitchell brothers stole from me, but somehow my heart, body, and mind had aligned and set me free.

A throat clearing made Bane jump, and he pulled back. Montoya stood at the end of my bed, cheeks flushed and a smirk on her face. "As much as I enjoyed the show because, boy." She waved her hand in front of her face like she was fanning herself. "Jordan has an update that I don't think you'll want to miss."

With a grumbling moan, Bane stepped away from me and folded his arms over his chest. My lips twisted into a smirk at the deep rouge tinging his cheeks. "I..." He shook his head. "Don't ever do that again," he bit out, but his words lacked heat. "Where's Jordan?"

"Coming." She smirked. "I sent him to get coffee from that place down the block, to give you...time."

"Seriously?" Bane rolled his eyes and retook his seat.

"Seriously," she parroted.

Bane turned back to me. "Are you comfortable?" He took my hand in his and ran his thumb over my knuckles. After I shook my head, he grabbed the bed control and raised me up so I could at least feel like I was part of the conversation.

Montoya hid a smile behind her hand. "I'm glad you two sorted shit out." I tipped my head to the side and waited. Chuckling, she glanced over at Bane, who seemed very interested in a loose thread on his jeans. "Let's just say he was a bit sulky when I got here."

A smile tugged my lips as Bane scowled at her. I was starting to see that the bond they shared wasn't a threat to what I had with Bane. The more I thought about it, the more they seemed like siblings.

"Ah, here is the man of the hour," Montoya said as the door opened and a guy I'd never seen before stepped into my room. His dark eyes twinkled as she lurched forward, reaching for one of the cups he had balanced in a carrier in one hand as he tried to close the door behind him.

"Get off," he grunted as she crowded around him. She lifted one of the cups and sauntered back to her seat. He rolled his eyes, then handed one to Bane. His eyes dropped to me. "I, um...shit. I didn't get one for you, sorry."

My chest ached as I held in a laugh and shook my head. Using Bane's phone, I tried to put him at ease.

> It's ok. Water is the only thing I want right now.

Jordan snorted, his lips twitching. He circled the bed and leaned against the wall opposite me and took a long swallow from his drink.

"Montoya said you had an update?"

"Yes, I've found a few interesting things." Jordan straightened up, looking all business while dropping the playful persona. "Once I found the right security room and gained access to their CCTV footage, I scrolled through everything from today, all the way back to River's previous stay."

I glanced up at him in confusion, not really understanding the relevance, but before I could ask, Jordan continued. "Bane said someone took your things. Your clothes were likely destroyed, but the nurse, Sharon, mentioned her colleague took it by mistake, right?" Unable to speak, I nodded. "I don't think it was an accident." He raised his fingers like speech marks to emphasise his words.

"What makes you say that?" Montoya asked.

"Well." He rubbed his hands together. "It didn't take long for these guys to appear on the footage. One of them was here earlier today, talking to a nurse. The conversation didn't last long, but it was intense, and resulted in her storming off. He waited around for a bit, then walked a circuit of the building while noting the cameras. After confirming with the guard on duty who she was—Kirsty Ambrose—I got him to look up her shift pattern and it turned up two things. One, she was on a lot of shifts with Sharon, and two, she was working the night you were brought in, too."

"So you think she's guilty by association." It wasn't a question, but Jordan nodded anyway. "She's here on shift today?"

"Yes, on this ward."

"Fuck." Montoya looked at Bane, and the silence stretching between them was suffocating. You could have heard a pin drop as they had a conversation that consisted of frowns, nods, and head shakes. No actual words passed between them, but by the time Montoya left the room like her ass was on fire, they'd come to some kind of understanding. Bane worried his bottom lip between his teeth.

"Want to share with the room what you've decided?" Jordan asked as he took the seat next to Bane.

"Sorry." Bane sighed and ran his hand over his face before his eyes flicked to me like he was making sure I was still here. "We've worked together for so long that sometimes we forget other people can't understand us." Jordan gave a semblance of a smile while he waited for Bane to continue. "It seems too convenient, but I'm not prepared to take any risks in case everything you've found is exactly as it looks, not just a case of her being in the wrong place at the wrong time."

"What's the plan, then?"

My head was pounding, and I found it difficult to focus on what they were discussing, but I caught what I thought were the Cliffs Notes. Montoya was going to speak with

Sharon about her colleague, and then the nurse in charge. I was to be secretly moved to another room, because Bane was convinced these guys were going to come after me to finish what they'd started.

Personally, I thought they were blowing everything out of proportion. I had Bane and Montoya in the room with me, and Jordan on the door. My room was better guarded than Fort Knox, but Bane was adamant this was happening and no one could convince him otherwise. Especially after Sharon confirmed that Kirsty was the one who had my bag. The fact no one knew if it was a genuine mistake or not seemed irrelevant. The decision had been made, and that was that.

The three of them spent hours talking through their plan and discussing any variables that could fuck everything up while I drifted in and out of consciousness, making my own plans. When Montoya and Jordan left to get something to eat, finally leaving me alone with Bane, the opportunity I needed finally presented itself.

"Shift change is about to happen, so we'll move you to the other room while everyone is distracted. The only person who will know where you are is—"

"N-no," I ground out. The painkillers I was on were strong and kept knocking me out, but with adrenaline surging through my veins, I felt capable of anything. "I-I'm... n-not...going."

"Excuse me?"

"Y-you...he...h-heard me."

"River, what the hell?"

Bane paced the room, looking strung out and exhausted, but so was I. I'd spent my life fighting, even when I was physically broken and mentally checked out, waiting for death. Now, when I had the chance at a life I could have only dreamed of months ago, I wasn't about to sit back and let others put themselves in the firing line. I was ready to fight for the life he'd promised, and I wasn't about to let him stop me.

Exasperated, I ignored the burning pain in my throat and the ever present searing ache that echoed through my bones and pushed through. "I-I'm the...o-one they...w-want..."

"I know, but I promised you—"

I held up a trembling hand, halting him, rubbing my throat as trepidation slithered across my skin and sunk like lead in my gut. "I-I'm the one t-they... raped... and the o-one t...they w-want...to..."

Tears shone in his hypnotic eyes as he sat on the side of the bed. He pulled his knee up, so it brushed my thigh. That single point of connection rocked through me, grounded me, and finally allowed air into my lungs.

"I promised I'd keep you safe, River." He swallowed, the sound audible in the near silence of my room. "I won't make the same mistake again."

My hand wrapped around his, where it was clenched into a fist on his knee. "I-I know, a-and...y-you're...k-kee...ping it. B-but, I...n-need...to...d-do this." Sweat coated my forehead and the top of my lip. My whole body shook as I waited with bated breath for Bane's response. I could see the war raging inside him. I just hoped he'd remember the promise he made to fight my demons at my side as a partner, an equal.

"You need this?" he asked tentatively. I nodded and stroked my fingers over his knuckles, unable to take the pained look in his eyes anymore. "Jesus fucking Christ." He shook his head. "The things you do to me. I can't say no to you, even when I know I should." Resignation laced his every word. "How much did you hear?"

"M-most of...it?" My breath caught as his shoulders

slumped in defeat, and he brushed a kiss to the end of my nose. Unclenching his fist, he slid his hand into my hair and pulled me close enough for his lips to brush mine.

When he spoke, his words reverberated through me and into my bones. "If I let you stay, you must do exactly what I tell you. I could be wrong about them coming for you, but my gut tells me..."

The smile that lifted my lips felt unnatural, the antithesis of everything I was. I'd spent my life broken and wearing my fear like armor to keep everyone away. I'd made myself an island, because it was safer that way. But now I wanted to be strong, even in the face of death. I didn't want to face the future without fighting for it. "Your g-gut is n-never wrong."

"It's not. I must be mad," he muttered, and kissed me until all I could think about was him. I knew what agreeing had cost him, so I did the only thing I could; I gave him every part of me. I kept nothing back, because this could be the last time I got to kiss him. The last time his taste burst across my tongue. There were no secrets hidden in the shadows. I laid myself bare as his tongue licked into my mouth, and his arms wrapped around me, chest to chest, hearts thundering, each beat perfectly synced with one another. Two bodies, one soul, together locked in a final embrace as we stood at the edge of the battleground to fight for our forever.

"I love you."

"I'M JUST HERE TO TAKE YOUR VITALS," A NURSE I DIDN'T recognize whispered as I stirred awake. She wrapped a blood pressure cuff around my arm with quiet efficiency.

Taking her at her word, I closed my eyes and pretended to drift back to sleep. But then it hit me—this was her. Kirsty.

My mind raced, tension ratcheting higher with every passing second. I hadn't meant to fall asleep, but after Bane had kissed away my ability to think and the painkillers had kicked in, exhaustion had overtaken me.

Streetlights framed the edges of the window, casting a ribbon of light that danced with the shadows in my room. When the door snicked shut, I let out a weighted breath. Fear pricked at my skin, cold and sharp. It felt strange knowing I wasn't really alone. Bane, Montoya, and Jordan were lying in wait nearby, ready. The only company I had at the moment was the steady thudding of my heart in my ears and the waves of nausea rolling through my gut.

The piercing wail of an alarm shattered the stillness, sending my heart rocketing into my throat. Instinctively, I knew this was it. They were here. Bane had warned me they'd likely create a diversion to draw everyone away from this part of the ward. Judging by what sounded like a herd of elephants storming down the corridor, he was right.

Every muscle in my body twitched and coiled tight as adrenaline flooded my veins. I stayed perfectly still, feigning sleep. Playing the part had never been hard for me before; faking it came second nature after years of survival. My chest rose and fell in a steady rhythm, but inside, I was drowning.

Low male voices murmured outside my door, and I knew—this was the moment. Sink or swim. Live or die. One monster was dead, another behind bars. These three were the last ones haunting my life.

The plan was simple: stay still, pretend to be asleep, and don't engage. Easier said than done. When the door clicked open, my mind went blank, every memory of their touch rushing over me like a tsunami. The cold air hit me as they entered, and I caught their reflections in the windowpane. The Mitchells. They wore white coats, and had their heads lowered as they moved silently into the room, surrounding my bed. It was an echo of the last time they came for me.

The one closest to the door pulled a syringe from his pocket, flicking it like in the movies. My breath caught as he grabbed an IV line and injected the liquid. I held back a laugh that threatened to bubble up and give my ruse away. Little did they know, none of the lines were attached directly to me.

I would not die at their hands.

When they finished, they turned as one to watch the heart monitor, waiting for it to flatline. But it wouldn't. It never would. Before suspicion could creep in, chaos erupted.

Bane burst from the bathroom like an avenging angel. Jordan and Montoya swept in from the corridor. Wherever they'd been hidden, they moved fast, precise. Each of my assailants were apprehended in less time than it took to blink.

Bane took down the one nearest me with brutal efficiency, kicking the back of his knees in and driving him to the ground. The violent swiftness of it stirred something in me—something my body had no right feeling right now. His knee pinned the man to the floor as he cuffed him and began reading him his Miranda rights.

Jordan and Montoya hauled the others up and dragged them out, leaving no room for escape.

"Well done, angel. I'll be back in a minute," Bane said, his eyes meeting mine as calm settled back into the room. His lips twitched into a grin that made my heart stop. He was glowing. "I love you."

A true smile lifted my lips as they left. I wasn't sure how I was supposed to feel, but the tears that slid down my cheeks were different this time. They weren't from pain, despair, or fear. They were cleansing, a baptism of hope.

I was finally free, and it was all because of Bane.

My safe place.

My protector.

My home.

My heart.

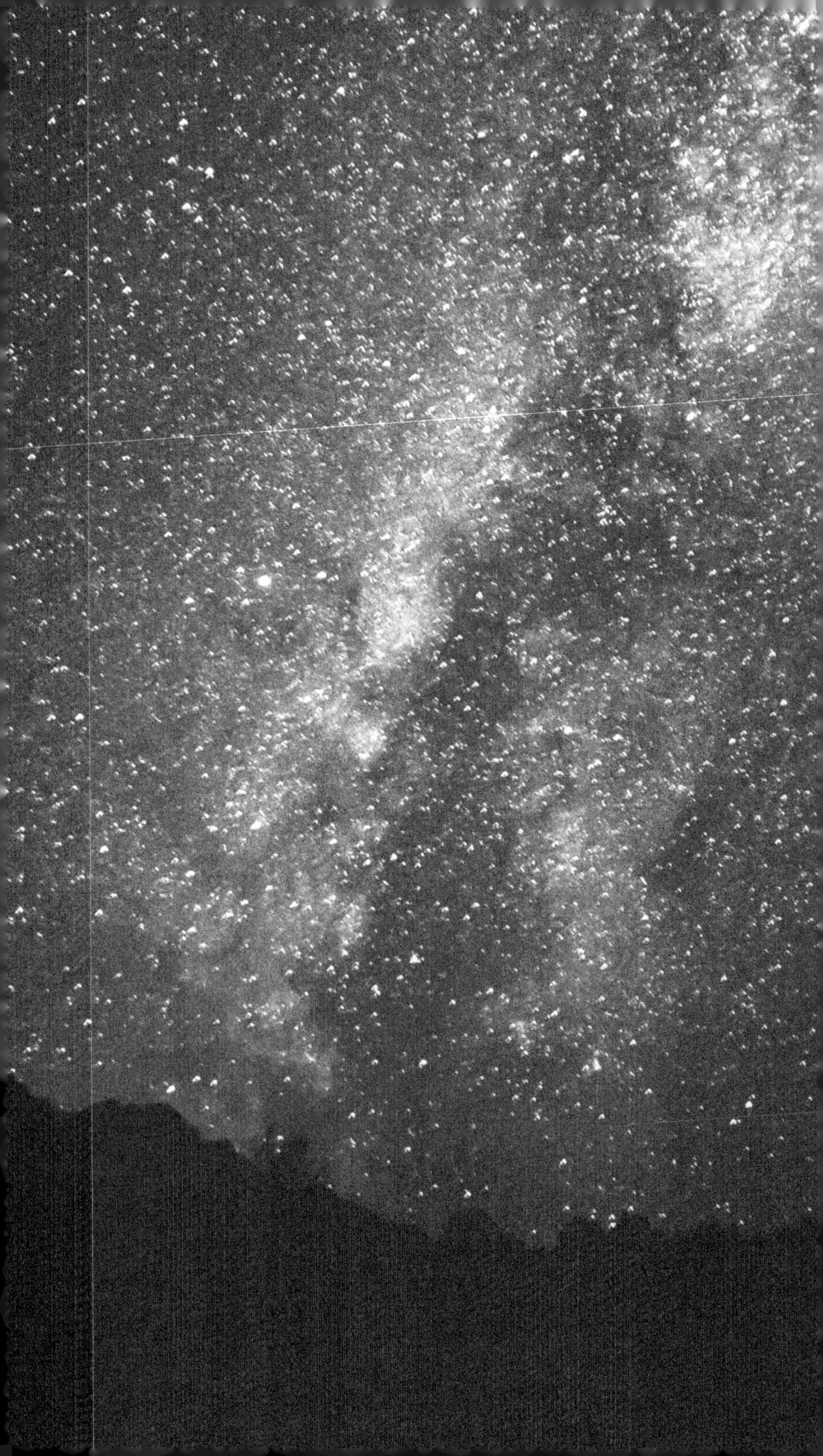

EPILOGUE
River

Two Years Later

"Are you almost ready?" Montoya asked as she swept the box at my feet off the ground. "Jesus, what's in this thing? It weighs a goddamn ton."

I snickered. "Books." Her eye roll was audible. "H-hey," I held my hands up, "Blame Bane." My brow furrowed, and I picked at the rough skin by my thumb nail. "He wanted me t-to have a hobby."

"So you chose books?" she asked incredulously.

"Oh, yeah." A smirk lifted my lips. "T-trust me, you'd love them. It's all boom, boom, bang and the villain gets his dick—"

"Oh my god, you're a smut fan?"

I shrugged and stared out at the yard of the rental, watching as Shadow chased off some birds that had just landed to eat the worms. "What can I-I say? It's like therapy. The really bad guys end up d-dead and the main character ends up in love with s-someone who would burn the world down for them. What's not to love?"

Montoya snorted and adjusted the box in her arms. "Whatever makes you happy, River. If anyone deserves it, it's you."

"Mmmm." I crossed my arms over my chest and stepped up to the sliding doors leading out onto the deck.

The clomping of her boots faded as she headed to the U-Haul we'd hired for the day. It was hard to believe we'd lived here for two years. It passed in the blink of an eye, and yet it seemed like it had taken forever. When I'd been released from the hospital a few days after Bane and the guys caught the Mitchell brothers, Bane had refused to take me back to his house. He'd said after what happened there, it wasn't his home anymore. It was just bricks and mortar, and that his home was wherever I was. I felt that in the marrow of my bones. From that first time I'd found myself in Bane's arms in that interrogation room, it'd felt like coming home.

"Hey angel, how are you doing?" Bane nuzzled into my neck, peppering the sensitive skin with light kisses. I tilted my head to the side, allowing him access, and melted into his embrace as his arms wrapped around my waist.

"I-I'm okay," I said softly, losing myself to his touch. One hand splayed across my abs, fingertips toying with the top of my pants. "It's just..."

"I know." His hot breath puffed against my damp skin, making me shiver and him chuckle as he squeezed me tighter. The low tenor had heat pooling in my gut. "Today is the sentencing hearing, but you have nothing to worry about. None of them will be getting out."

God, how I hoped that was true, that they wouldn't trade any plea bargains in exchange for information. We wanted lifetime convictions for all of them and everyone else associated with Black Dahlia, but it would have been naïve of me to think everyone would serve time. Christine Hamilton, aka the Dahlia I knew, was the head of Black Dahlia. When her true identity came out, her whole family fell under the umbrella of the investigation. When the press revealed the mayor's involvement, it sent shockwaves through Holme Oaks, rocking the town to its core. The scars this atrocity left would be visible for generations to come.

"I hope s-so." I licked my dry lips. "Because if they c-come for me..."

"I'll be waiting, angel. No one is getting their hands on you ever again."

Tears burned the back of my eyes, but I refused to let them fall. I was stronger than that. Ever since that day in the hospital when Bane, Montoya, and Jordan took down the Mitchell brothers, I'd decided I'd be strong and wouldn't let the past hold me back. I had a life I could have only dreamed of, and I was going to fucking live it.

A sob slipped from my lips as I turned in his arms, looked up at him, and gave a watery smile. Bane's eyes glistened, haunted by the memories we shared and the stories I'd told him over the years. There were no words that could describe how much he'd single-handedly altered the course of my life.

My eyes dipped to his full lips, then back to his eyes, which now sparkled as he watched me, a brow arched in question. I didn't need to think about it. I pushed up onto my toes, wrapped my arms around his neck, and pulled him down to seal my mouth to his.

A deep groan rumbled in his chest as our lips met. He was warm and soft and oh so eager as his tongue swiped across the seam of my mouth. It had taken me months to feel comfortable enough to initiate things between us. I was always terrified I was either going to be punished, or he was going to freak on me again like he did with BJgate, but after a few sessions with Joelle, things started to improve. But it took work. We both had to learn how to communicate better and being honest about what we wanted was the first step.

Bane's tongue pushed into my mouth, making my knees weak as it wrapped around mine. His taste exploded across my tongue, and his decadent cedarwood and leather scent drugged me with every inhale. We kissed like it was our last time—all blinding passion and heart-stopping need. He cupped the back of my head, holding me in place as he devoured me and sucked the air from my lungs.

"Fuck, angel," he gasped, his breath coming out in ragged puffs, and rested his forehead against mine. "I want you so much b-but—" He stuttered when my hand toyed with his hard length over his jeans. "You little shit." I laughed and buried my head in the crook of his neck as he lifted me so my legs could wrap around his waist. "What am I going to do with you?"

"Hmm." I rolled my hips. My hard length against his was all I could focus on.

"Stop." Large hands gripped my hips, his fingers dipping into my crease. "I'm going to hate myself for saying this..." Bane's voice was rough and sex drenched. "But we need to get Shadow and get on the road. It's a couple of hours to our house from here. We should get moving."

The front door banged, shaking the walls of the rental, quickly followed by heavy footsteps. "Oh, come on, you two," Montoya grumbled. "Jordan and I have been waiting for you and the dog for fifteen minutes. I want a tour of your house, preferably before it's dark outside, and he's hungry and won't stop whining."

I peeked over Bane's shoulder to find her with a shit-eating grin on her face. My face flushed as I slid down his body and adjusted myself.

"On it." I grabbed Shadow's leash and slipped out through the sliding doors. The cool midmorning air hit me like a slap in the face, but I hoped by the time we made it to our cabin—our new home—the sun would be out so we could sit in the backyard and relax. Bane was looking forward to using his new grill, and I wanted to watch the stars.

Shadow came running to me the second I stepped outside. His black coat glistened in the sun, highlighting the flecks of white that now dappled his coat. He'd become my self-appointed emotional support dog and went everywhere with me, rarely leaving my side. I was hopeful this new beginning would lighten the load he carried on his little shoulders as I left my demons behind in Holme Oaks.

His wet paws landed on my thigh, his tongue hanging out as he panted. "You're such a good boy, aren't you?" I cooed and kneeled down so I could give him some fuss and clip the leash onto his collar. "Are you ready to go on an adventure?" He yipped happily and licked my face as a wave of trepidation washed over me.

I'd tried to keep my emotions on lockdown today, but they occasionally crept up on me when I was least expecting it. Dealing with change was hard. I needed security and the control a routine offered me, and with moving today and everything happening with the Black Dahlia court case, it was throwing me for a loop.

"Come on, Riv," Bane called as he stuck his head out the door. "Let's get going and start our new life."

"Sounds perfect." Bane's fingers slipped through mine as we locked the sliding doors, left our keys on the counter, and shut the front door for the final time.

The drive to Copper Hills passed in the blink of an eye. I'd fallen asleep as we'd left Holme Oaks. In my defense, I had hardly slept the night before. I couldn't tell if it was nerves or excitement that kept me awake, but I'd seen the moon travel across the sky and dawn break and chase away the darkness. It felt like a metaphor for my life as I'd sat on the deck with a cup of cocoa in one hand and my Kindle in another, watching the first rays of sunshine appear on the horizon.

Our new home slowly came into view as Bane maneuvered the U-Haul up the winding track that would become our driveway. We'd spent the last six months fixing the cabin up, turning it from a crumbling ruin of rotten wood to a gorgeous home that encompassed both of our tastes.

The cabin was a decent size, according to Bane, though to me it felt more like a hidden wooden mansion tucked away in the woods, safe from prying eyes. It featured three bedrooms on the first floor, along with a spacious, open-plan living area that seamlessly blended a lounge, dining space, and kitchen. The design was a charming mix of rustic wood and brick contrasted with sleek, modern touches. Floor-to-ceiling windows flooded the space with natural light, and the kitchen looked like something straight out of a magazine.

Bane had been like a kid in a candy store when he first saw it, and it warmed my heart to see him so excited. I was perfectly happy to give him free rein to decorate the space however he wanted. After all, I wasn't planning on spending much time in the kitchen. My culinary experience had officially ended after a failed attempt at making him a grilled cheese nearly burned down our rental. Honestly, I didn't mind. My man could create magic in the kitchen, so it was really a win-win.

The second floor, though, was mine, and I'd poured my

heart into it. Our bedroom was my pride and joy. A custom-made bed stood proudly in the center of the wall opposite the expansive windows, which offered a stunning view of the surrounding woods. I couldn't wait to wake up in the mornings, lying in bed and watching the world come alive outside. Having never spent much time in nature, I was eager to explore our new surroundings, and maybe, if I was brave enough, take a dip in the river running down the mountainside.

But first, I had a plan. After unpacking the essentials for our room, I was going to sink into the Jacuzzi tub we'd had installed. It was big enough for me to sprawl out like a starfish if Bane wasn't with me, though I hoped he would join more often than not.

BANE

I WAS GRATEFUL WHEN RIVER FELL ASLEEP ON THE WAY TO THE cabin. He hadn't slept much over the past week, whether he was nervous over the move or stressed about the Black Dahlia case, I didn't know, but the bruises blossoming under his eyes told me everything he didn't. He was struggling, and I hated it. While we had both come a long way in communicating—River especially—there were still times when it felt like I was banging my head against a wall because I didn't know how to get him to open up.

He woke up just as we hit the track up to the cabin, blinking awake as he jostled from side to side. He looked at me from under his lashes, and my heart skipped a beat. I'd never know what I did to deserve his love, but I was grateful every day for it. Seeing the biggest smile I'd ever seen on him take over his face as we pulled up to our new home was everything I needed to settle the frantic worry coiling inside me.

"Surprise," I said, as tears glistened in his forest-green eyes. They darted around, taking in the little finishing touches Montoya and I had done over the last week. We'd stained the cabin with creosote, turning the large logs black, so they blended effortlessly with the forest that surrounded it. Montoya planted some window boxes and placed large planters at the edges of the steps leading up to the front porch. The addition of a handcrafted swing finished it off.

"Welcome home, angel." I leaned over the console, pulled him into me, and slotted my lips over his. He kissed me back with an enthusiasm that continued to gain traction every time our lips met. The wet heat of his tongue sliding against mine had me opening immediately, desperate to have him closer. As he licked into my mouth, his tongue wrapping around mine, I forgot about everything bar the beautiful boy in my arms.

When we eventually pulled apart, panting hard, trying to regulate our breathing, we caught sight of Montoya and Jordan sitting on the porch swing, laughing. It turned out they were taking bets on how long it would take us to get unpacked once they'd left. I felt sorry for Jordan, because Montoya had an unfair advantage. He had no idea what I had planned. Our first night in our new home and new life would be one to remember. I just hoped everything went to plan, but the outcome rested solely on River's shoulders, even though he didn't know it.

"This place isn't half bad, Benson," Jordan said as he took our cabin in for the first time.

"Yeah, it's something special, that's for sure." I smiled, but my eyes weren't on my new home—they were on River. Jordan laughed when he followed my line of sight and slapped me on the back before heading down to help River open up the truck while I unlocked the door.

"You going to be happy here?" Montoya asked as she set a box down in the kitchen while I plugged the kettle in to make us all a drink.

"More than." This was everything I'd never thought possible—a home with a family of my own. "Now, if I could only find some mugs."

"Here," Montoya said, opening the box she'd just brought in and handed me a couple of mugs. "Would you look at that. Looks like someone knew I'd be in serious need of caffeine to get through this torture."

"You love it, really. You've gone all soft since you met Boston." Deep burgundy stained her cheeks, and she shook her head, looking more bashful than I'd ever seen.

"Is that him now?" I asked when her phone buzzed. She pulled her dark brown eyes off the screen to glare at me. "Ha! It is."

She huffed a laugh. "Nothing, umm, personal." I waggled my eyebrows, and she stuck her tongue out at me. "He went to watch the sentencing because we were here today."

"Yeah, I told him I was trying to keep River's mind off it because he'd been struggling recently. So, good news?"

I waited with bated breath for her to finish reading. My heart was thundering in my chest because we needed this conviction to stick. Otherwise, we'd spend the rest of our lives looking over our shoulders. And for all River's strength, I didn't think he'd survive living another twenty years like that. He was the strongest of us all, but everyone had a breaking point. I just hoped he'd never find his.

Montoya cleared her throat and lowered her voice, impersonating the authority of Jude Mikelson. "Christine Hamilton, known as Dahlia, the head of the Black Dahlia organization, has been sentenced to one thousand years in prison. She was convicted on a hundred counts, eighty involving trafficking."

"Holy fuck." My knees gave out, and I collapsed to the floor, clutching my chest as I struggled to breathe. I could hardly believe it—it was over. It was finally, finally over. Montoya's arms wrapped around my shoulders, steadying me. Without her unwavering strength and determination, I wasn't sure we would've made it through to the end.

This case had shaken the very foundation of our lives, bringing changes we never could have foreseen. But most importantly, it had saved countless lives—more than we could ever measure.

By the time Montoya and Jordan left, the sky had turned a dusky blue, and the surrounding forest had come alive. River sat in one of the Adirondack chairs, hands outstretched toward the fire pit, and Shadow curled up at his feet. He seemed at ease for the first time today, as I walked down from the deck, drinks in hand.

"Here you go, angel," I said, passing him a hot cocoa. Shadows from the flickering flames danced across his face as he took his cup.

"Aww, marshmallow and cream, too." His breath hitched as he pinned the full weight of his gaze on me. "T-thank you." He rolled his bottom lip through his teeth. "Today has been..."

"A lot." I finished for him, and he nodded. We sat in relative silence surrounded by nature, and for the first time since we'd reconnected, it felt like a weight had been lifted off our collective shoulders.

"It has. B-but, totally worth it."

"I'd do anything for you, angel."

He let loose a breath and finished his drink. "You have given me the world." He blinked back the glassiness in his eyes. "You have given me more than I ever thought possible." A tear glides down his cheek, sparkling like a diamond in the firelight. "I never knew it was possible t-to feel this..."

"Happy?" I hedged.

"N-no. Complete."

I felt ten feet tall at his quiet confession, and confidence suffused my veins. It was time to bring an extra dash of magic to the day. "Why don't you go up and have a soak in the tub? I know you're dying to." River snorted, the sound so carefree I had to tuck my hands under my thighs, because they'd started to shake. "Come and find me when you're done."

River eyed me curiously, and it took every last bit of control I had not to blurt out my plan. I had to have patience, because he deserved perfection. He deserved to feel like the center of my universe, because that's exactly what he was, and I'd spend a lifetime showing him.

"Alright. Wait for me here?"

"Of course."

He pushed up from his seat, Shadow at his heels, handed me his cup, and brushed a sweet kiss to my lips before sauntering back into the house.

"You've got this," I coached myself as I quickly rinsed the dishes before loading them in the dishwasher. I crept up the stairs and heard the water running along with River's voice through the open doors as he chatted to Shadow.

River loved to wallow like a miniature hippopotamus, so I figured I had a good forty or so minutes to get everything into place. Our backyard was vast, stretching farther than the eye could see. The areas that had been reclaimed from the forest and laid to lawn followed a gentle slope down to the river, and was the perfect spot to sit and watch the stars glittering in the sky at night. With no light pollution, the view would be spectacular but wouldn't hold a candle to the man who owned my heart.

"What's going on?" River asked when he came downstairs. I shut Shadow in the house and took his hand.

"I thought you might like to sit and watch the stars?"

"Y-yes."

We walked hand in hand down to the river, the sound of the water rushing over the rocks doing little to mask the pounding of my heart in my ears. I was thankful for the warm night and the glowing fireflies illuminating our way.

"Oh my god." River gasped and stopped at the top of the bank, his eyes transfixed by the blanket bed and pillows I'd laid out for us. It was surrounded by large citronella candles to keep the mosquitos away, and if you looked hard enough, you could make out the champagne bottle sticking out of an ice bucket and a small wicker basket filled with all the sweet treats River loved. It really was the perfect night to wish on a star. It just so happened mine wasn't in the sky. "Y-you did all of this?" I nodded, feeling my face flame as he watched me with a wondrous look on his face. "W-when?"

"While you were wallowing in the tub for the last hour." River chuckled and tucked himself under my arm, his hand cinching tight around my waist, pulling me closer. "Admit it, how many times did you top up the hot water?"

I helped him down the bank and onto the shore. "Umm, maybe a couple?" His cheeks pinked, and his eyes glimmered in the darkness like they were lit from within.

"So what you're saying is we have no hot water left?" I chuckled at his gasp and pulled him down in between my legs as we settled on the blankets. His back vibrated against me, giving away his silent chuckle.

"You could say t-that."

I kissed the top of his head and felt the tension leave his body as my hands worked the muscle fibers in his shoulders and down his arms until my fingers laced through his. I brought each hand up to my mouth, brushing a kiss on each knuckle.

Night in Copper Hills was a whole other level of sensory experience compared to the suburbs of Holme Oak. The forest felt alive as it lived each moment with us. The sky was a velvet black backdrop to the millions of glimmering stars and planets above us. River was enraptured by the sight, unable to drag his eyes away as I fed him little bites of chocolate cheesecake and strawberries. He sucked my fingers clean of the juice with a singular focus that had my dick responding, wishing his full lips were wrapped around it instead.

Hours passed, and the candles burned low. The stars grew brighter, and my nerves grew brittle. A full moon hung in the sky, illuminating everything like it was silvered daylight. River turned and straddled my lap, heat burning in the depths of his eyes. His soft lips kissed a path up my neck until his face was tucked in against my throat, each stuttering breath tickling across my skin.

"B-Bane?"

"Yes, angel?" I inhaled his sweet cinnamon and orange scent. A needy groan caught in the back of my throat, and I felt his lips curve into a smile. My hands traveled down his back and settled on his hips, my fingers sinking into his ass so I could pull him closer.

River's hands came up and cupped my face, his thumbs tracing the shape of my cheekbones while his lips peppered tender kisses all over my face. I felt treasured, seen, and wanted. His hot breath smelled of sweet strawberries and indulgent chocolate as it heated my lips, the only place he hadn't kissed. I was a desperate man as lips sat a hair's breadth away from mine.

The warm evening air was charged with electricity that zapped across my skin in pulsing waves. The stars shone brighter, growing in intensity as I lost myself in the fevered heat in his glistening eyes. My heart was pounding against my chest, tattooing my love for him on my bones. I could feel the echo of his through the layers that separated us. River's body trembled, and the color in his cheeks flushed in waves, building like it did when he was lost in the throes of ecstasy.

His tongue darted out and wet his lips, feeling its slow glide against mine. That simple touch rocked me to my core. My cock was thick, aching and throbbing with every roll of his hips. I'd never seen River so incandescent and bright. His light put the moon to shame.

"I-I..." River huffed a breath in exasperation. His brows furrowed before he steeled his shoulders and increased the pressure of his hold on my face, so I couldn't look anywhere but him. Not that I wanted to. Ever. "I...I." He cleared his throat, words sticking on his tongue like they did when his nerves consumed him.

"You can tell me anything, angel," I said, pulling him so close there wasn't even air between us.

"I want to keep you forever." Heat radiated off him, but I wasn't scared of being burned. I'd walk through fire if he asked me to. "I might not know what love is to you o-or... even if what I feel is...l-love or o...obsession. B-but... I want it until all I see is the stars of heaven."

"You mean?" River nodded, tears shimmering on his cheeks like shattered diamonds, the fractals of light dancing amongst the shadows. "Mmm."

"Will you marry me, River Lane?" His wet lips trembled

against mine as I searched my pocket for the ring I'd been carrying around for the last week.

"W-was it ever a q-question? Yes, a thousand times, yes."

I shook my head because I knew he was quoting something he'd read to me or we'd watched together. Not that I could remember it, because every part of me was consumed with this moment. It was my turn to tremble, and I prayed to god I didn't drop it before I got it on his finger. I gently peeled his left hand from my face, and he sat back on his feet, his inquisitive eyes watching my hand intently.

His eyes widened when he saw me pull the ring I'd had specially made for him—a single band of platinum engraved with endless waves to signify my endless love—from the black velvet pouch and held out his left hand. It slid onto his finger and it looked like it had always been there.

"I-I." I cleared the tightness from my throat. River beamed like he was floating in the sky above us with the stars. "I had this whole speech planned, but you got there before me—"

He snorted and licked his tears from his lips. "Sorry, not sorry."

My lips brushed his, chasing away his breathy laugh until he melted into me and breathed my love into him. "I love all of you, angel, even the parts you think are not worthy of love. I love them twice as much."

AFTERWORD

Thank you for reading River & Bane's book. I hope you enjoyed it and have fallen in love with them just like I did.

The Lies We Believe is the hardest book I've written to date. I wanted to give both River and Bane's story the integrity and respect it deserved, and I hope I did them justice. In some ways, these two are polar opposites, while in others, they are two halves of the same whole.

Each one has a complicated and emotional back story that pulled at my heart in different ways. Their trauma manifests through their individual character traits but at the heart of it all, they are two broken boys who desperately want to be loved but fear being abandoned.

Thank you for being here to hear their words and watch their love grow.

ACKNOWLEDGMENTS

Thank you to my amazingly supportive alpha team: Jenna, Jordan, Jenn and Louise. Your comments and feedback were invaluable.

Michaella, thank you for holding my hand and telling me it's not sh!t every time I hit a wall.

ABOUT THE AUTHOR

Skyla Raines is obsessed with romance and broken boys. She's an avid reader and a sucker for hard-fought happily ever afters. When she's not bringing to life the characters in her head, she's watching her family grow and cherishes every moment with them.

You can follow her here:
https://linktr.ee/authorskylaraines

ALSO BY SKYLA RAINES

Without Limits Series

The Lies We Tell Ourselves

The Lies We Believe

The Lies Of Omission (2025)

The Lies Of Temptation (2025)

The Darkness Within Us Series

The Beautiful Dead (2025)

CONTENT NOTE

Please note this book has dark elements and contains themes which some may find difficult to read. Triggers are personal to each individual, but I have listed the main ones below. I have tried to handle these topics with care.

Child abuse
(Mental, psychological, physical, sexual)
Abuse
Mental health rep
Panic attacks
Suicidal ideation
Loss of loved ones
Sex work/trafficking
Drug use
Sexual assault/rape
Stalking
Physical assault
Attempted murder
Murder
Manipulation

Graphic sex
Mentions of homophobia

Printed in Great Britain
by Amazon